y Williams can...
...s as a teenager, ...
...emains an avid ...
...ng romantic sto...
...very book is a new adventure. Cathy lives in
...on. Her three daughters—Charlotte, Olivia and
...a—have always been, and continue to be, the
...est inspirations in her life.

e Connelly was raised in small-town Australia
...g a family of avid readers. She spent much
...r childhood up a tree, Mills & Boon book in
h... . Clare is married to her own real-life hero,
a...hey live in a bungalow near the sea with their
t... hildren. She is frequently found staring into
s...—a surefire sign that she's in the world of
h...naracters. She has a penchant for French food
a...e-cold champagne, and Mills & Boon novels
c...nue to be her favourite ever books. Writing for
M...rn is a long-held dream. Clare can be contacted
v...lareconnelly.com or at her Facebook page.

D0714392

000003046593

Also by Cathy Williams

Contracted for the Spaniard's Heir
Marriage Bargain with His Innocent
Shock Marriage for the Powerful Spaniard
The Italian's Christmas Proposition

Also by Clare Connelly

Spaniard's Baby of Revenge
Shock Heir for the King
Redemption of the Untamed Italian

Crazy Rich Greek Weddings miniseries

The Greek's Billion-Dollar Baby
Bride Behind the Billion-Dollar Veil

Discover more at millsandboon.co.uk.

HIS SECRETARY'S NINE-MONTH NOTICE

CATHY WILLIAMS

THE SECRET KEPT FROM THE KING

CLARE CONNELLY

MILLS & BOON

All rights reserved including the right of reproduction
in whole or in part in any form. This edition is published
by arrangement with Harlequin Books S.A.

This is a work of fiction. Names, characters, places, locations
and incidents are purely fictional and bear no relationship to
any real life individuals, living or dead, or to any actual places,
business establishments, locations, events or incidents.
Any resemblance is entirely coincidental.

This book is sold subject to the condition that it shall not,
by way of trade or otherwise, be lent, resold, hired out
or otherwise circulated without the prior consent of the publisher
in any form of binding or cover other than that in which it is published
and without a similar condition including this condition
being imposed on the subsequent purchaser.

® and TM are trademarks owned and used by the trademark owner
and/or its licensee. Trademarks marked with ® are registered with the
United Kingdom Patent Office and/or the Office for Harmonisation
in the Internal Market and in other countries.

First Published in Great Britain 2020
by Mills & Boon, an imprint of HarperCollins*Publishers*
1 London Bridge Street, London, SE1 9GF

His Secretary's Nine-Month Notice © 2020 by Cathy Williams

The Secret Kept from the King © 2020 by Clare Connelly

ISBN: 978-0-263-27813-2

MIX
Paper from
responsible sources
FSC™ C007454

This book is produced from independently certified FSC™ paper
to ensure responsible forest management.
For more information visit www.harpercollins.co.uk/green.

Printed and bound in Spain
by CPI, Barcelona

HIS SECRETARY'S NINE-MONTH NOTICE

CATHY WILLIAMS

DUDLEY LIBRARIES	
000003046593	
Askews & Holts	27-Jul-2020
AF ROM	£6.99
2ST	

To my three wonderful daughters,
Charlotte, Olivia and Emma.

CHAPTER ONE

VIOLET'S FINGER HOVERED over the send button on her work email. She could already feel the emptiness of loss sinking its teeth into her and she breathed in deeply, banking down the rising panic at the thought of the unknown opening up at her feet like a gaping, bottomless hole. She wasn't a kid any more. She was a twenty-six-year-old adult. And being afraid of what lay around the corner was no longer appropriate. She could deal with this.

She clicked the button, closed her eyes and blanked out all the background noises of life happening outside her little mews house at seven thirty on a lovely summer Sunday evening in London.

She knew exactly how her boss was going to react to the email that would pop up on his laptop.

For starters—thank God—he wouldn't actually read it until the following morning, when he would breeze into the office at the usual ridiculously early time of six thirty. He would make himself a cup of strong black coffee, sit at his desk—which was always littered with papers, notes scribbled on sticky notes, reports and an impressive array of stationery, most of which he never used—and then he would start his day.

Top of the list would be reading his emails, and hers

would be there, and he would open it, and he would… *hit the roof.*

She stood up and stretched, easing her aching joints. There was only so much she could focus on at any one point, she decided, and focusing on her boss and how he was going to react to her resignation would have to be put on hold. She would be facing him soon enough when she went into work the following day, later than usual at the far safer hour of nine thirty, when the place would be buzzing with people and there might just be less chance of him erupting in front of interested spectators.

Not that Matt Falconer ever seemed to give a hoot about what other people thought. He was a law unto himself. In the two-and-a-half years that she had worked for him, she had seen him storm out of high-level meetings because a lawyer, a CEO or a director had rubbed him the wrong way or, more often than not, failed to follow his outspoken and always brilliant logic. She had restrained him from slamming down incorrectly typed reports on the desk of whichever poor employee had submitted them. She had worked alongside him into the early hours of the morning to complete a deal because *it just can't wait.* She had tactfully made herself scarce when he had gone into a funk, staring at the four walls of his office, feet on his desk, hands folded behind his head, because inspiration had temporarily deserted him.

She had prepared herself a salad earlier, but her heart wasn't in it as she dug her fork into lettuce leaves, beetroot and all the other good stuff that invariably tasted like sawdust after five seconds.

Her head was too full.

In the space of just a week, her life had been turned on its head, and she was still reeling.

Violet didn't like change. She didn't care for surprises. She liked order, stability and...*routine*. She loved all the things other girls her age generally despised.

She didn't want adventure. She certainly would never have contemplated jacking in her job although, deep down, she knew that she would have had to sooner or later, because...over time, her feelings for her brilliant, temperamental, utterly unpredictable boss had become just a little too uncomfortable. But to be forced into giving it up...!

She pushed away her plate and stared around her, taking in her surroundings. She felt as though she was seeing them for the first time, but of course that made no sense, because she had been living here, in this beautiful little town house, since she had turned twenty. However, the prospect of renting it to a perfect stranger made her take stock of what she had. Years of perfectly positioned memorabilia...the bookcase heavy with the weight of her tomes of musical works, the manuscripts with so many notations made over the years, the pictures and ornaments and posters...

Tears threatened. Again.

She swallowed them back and turned her attention to tidying up the kitchen while the radio played in the background. Classical music, of course. Her favourite.

She only became aware of someone at the door by the banging, relentless and unnecessary, because whoever it was hadn't even had the common decency to give her time to get to the door.

She hurried out to pull it open before the neighbours started complaining...and there he was.

Matt Falconer. Her boss and the last person she'd expected to see standing on her doorstep. How on earth did the man even know where she lived?

She'd certainly never told him! She'd turned reticence about her private life into an art form.

Violet felt a guilty wash of colour flood her face. Caught on the back foot like this, without any time at all to brace herself for the impact he had on her, she could only stare at him, drinking in the stunningly beautiful lines of his lean face.

Two-and-a-half years and he still never failed to have this effect on her. He was so tall, so beautifully built, with wide shoulders, a tapered waist and long, muscular legs. His hair was just a little too long and his navy-blue eyes were fringed with the darkest, lushest of lashes. And, of course, there was his exotically bronze colouring; there had been Spanish blood on his mother's side somewhere along the line. Alongside him, other mere mortals always ended up looking wan, anaemic and pasty.

'What…? Er, s-sir, what are you doing here?' Violet stammered, tucking some straight, mousy-brown strands of hair behind her ear.

'Sir? *Sir?* Since when have I been knighted? Stand back. I want to come in!'

He straightened, and she automatically fell back, but her hand remained on the doorknob. The door was open a crack. One gentle push and she wouldn't stand a chance of keeping him out. And, from the thunderous look on his face, he wasn't going to think too hard about forcing an entry.

'It's Sunday,' Violet said, using her calm voice, the voice she saved for work, and specifically for her wildly temperamental boss. 'I expect you've come about my… er…letter… Well, email…'

'Letter? *Letter?*' Matt roared. 'A *letter* somehow implies that the contents are going to be *polite*!'

'You're going to disturb the neighbours,' Violet snapped.

'Then let me bloody come in and they won't be disturbed!'

'It was a very polite letter of resignation.'

'Want to have this conversation out here, Violet? I'm happy to knock on all the doors of your well-heeled neighbours and invite them outside to have a good old time earwigging. Everyone likes being outdoors in sunny weather, after all, and all the better if there's a cabaret going on.'

'You're impossible, Matt.'

'Well, at least we've dropped the *sir*. That's a start. Let me in. I need something strong to drink.'

He rested the flat of his hand on the door. Violet sighed and opened it, and then she stood to one side so that he could brush past her into the small but exquisite hall, with its black-and-white flagstones and rich colours.

For a few seconds, he said nothing. He just turned a full circle and stared, taking his time, looking at everything while she remained where she was, already predicting the questions he would ask and resenting the answers she would be forced to give.

When his gaze finally settled on her, there was lively curiosity alongside the raging anger that had brought him to her door.

'How did you get my address?' she asked.

'Going into the personnel files is hardly beyond the wit of man. Nice place, Violet. Who would have guessed?'

Violet reddened and glared at him. The infuriating man met her glare with a slow, curling smile, the smile of a shark that has suddenly and happily found itself sharing space with a tasty little morsel.

She spun round on her heels and headed straight for the kitchen.

The town house wasn't big, but neither was it small. Off the hall, a highly polished staircase led up to the bedroom floor. Several doors opened out downstairs into a generous sitting room, a small snug that she used as her office and music room, a cloakroom lovingly displaying wallpaper and paint from its Victorian ancestry. And, of course, the kitchen, that was spacious enough to house a six-seater kitchen table on which were reams of papers that she hurriedly swept up into a bundle and dumped on the dresser. Then she turned to him, face still flaming red, leant against the counter and folded her arms.

Violet could not have felt more out of her comfort zone. Her neat work suits protected her from him, established all the necessary divisions between boss and secretary.

Here, in her house, dressed in a pair of jeans and an old tee shirt handed down from her dad's bad old days, she felt…exposed and horribly vulnerable.

But she wasn't going to let that show on her face.

'You never told me that you lived in an exquisite little jewel like this,' he mused, settling into one of the kitchen chairs, for all the world as though he was in it for the long haul.

'I don't believe I ever told you anything about where I lived,' Violet returned, and he tilted his head to one side and nodded slowly.

'My point exactly. Why would you hide this sort of thing from me? Most people keep quiet about their homes because they're embarrassed.'

'I have coffee,' Violet offered. 'Or tea. Which would you like?'

'Does that mean that there's no whisky lurking in any of the cupboards? No? Well, coffee it is, in that case. You know how I take it, Violet, because you know everything there is to know about me...'

He sank lower into the chair, his long body dwarfing it, his legs stretched out in front of him, his body language that of someone in no rush whatsoever. He folded his hands behind his head and looked at her with undisguised curiosity.

In terms of nightmares coming true, this was pretty much up there with the best of them.

Matt Falconer, billionaire legend of the IT and telecommunications world, the man adored by the press and women alike, in her house, nose twitching, because nothing would please him more than to ferret out information about her, information she had always made a point of keeping very firmly to herself.

From the very moment she had walked into his office, nestled high up in one of London's most iconic buildings, she had sensed that her boss wasn't going to be like the other two guys for whom she had worked. He wasn't going to be affable or fatherly like George Hill, with whom she had worked for two years before having been made redundant. Nor was he going to be anything like Simon Beesdale, her last boss, who had been a proud new daddy with photos of his family spread along his desk, keen to integrate her into his 'other family', as he called his team of fifteen people, always smiling, always encouraging.

No, Matt Falconer had kicked off proceedings by turning up late on day one, leaving her kicking her heels in his office, and from thereon in she had been tossed into the deep end and left to fend for herself. She'd had to rise to the challenge and learn fast on the spot. And she'd enjoyed every second of it. She'd loved the early mornings and the late nights, the buzz of activity and the frenetic, fast pace. She'd enjoyed the informality of the working environment, even though, orderly as she was, she knew she really shouldn't. And she'd kept up, earning his respect and seeing her salary rise several times in the space of two years.

But Matt's brilliant intellect and demanding work ethic were twined with staggering self-assurance of the kind she found vaguely disconcerting, an abundance of charm that brought out every cautious instinct in her and an inquisitive, questioning personality that was programmed to ignore all boundaries and every single do-not-trespass sign.

She had stood firm against the barrage of questions that had greeted her on a daily basis when she'd first joined his company. She had sidestepped the idle prying into her private life and had failed to rise to the bait when, in week three, he had told her with a certain amount of tetchiness in his voice that women tended to respond when he showed interest in their private lives.

'I'm afraid that won't be me,' she had murmured, with a blatant lack of sincere apology in her voice. 'I believe in keeping my private life strictly separate from my working life.'

And she had not regretted her decision because, as time had moved on, as she had with deep reluctance fallen further and further under the spell of her charismatic boss, she could only thank the Lord that common sense had prevailed from the outset.

So his presence here now, in her charming mews house, was sending her body into panicked overdrive.

'For instance,' he was drawling now, 'I'm guessing that you know me well enough to have realised that I should have been out with Clarissa at the ballet this evening…and so wouldn't have read your email until tomorrow morning. Presumably, you intended to waltz in at some ungodly, late hour in the hope that I might have digested the bare bone message that you're walking out on the best paid job you could hope to find. Not to mention the most invigorating.'

Violet wiped her perspiring hands on her jeans and busied herself making his cup of coffee, just the way he liked it. Black, no sugar. With her back to him, she was spared the piercing intensity of those deep-blue eyes, but she could still feel them boring into her.

Like her, he was in casual clothes. Black jeans and a faded polo shirt and loafers. She'd seen him dressed down many times before. However, the fact that she was similarly dressed down was making her self-conscious and uncomfortable.

'That's not true,' she said, eyes downcast as she pushed a cup of coffee towards him and then took up position on the chair at the farthest end of the kitchen table.

She knew him well enough to know that his curiosity about her personal circumstances had not conveniently vanished into the ether. There just happened to be the more pressing matter of her resignation for him to contend with first, then he would return to the subject of where she lived.

She quailed with apprehension, but her smile remained composed, her expression polite and tolerant, if a little puzzled.

Just the sort of professional image she wanted to convey.

'So you *didn't* remember that I was supposed to be at the ballet…'

'Does it matter?'

'I'm disappointed in you, Violet. I thought we were friends and yet, here you are, too scared to tell me to my face that you're bailing on me.'

'I work for you, Matt, that's all,' she countered and he shook his head sadly.

'So do two hundred other employees who occupy the four storeys of that glass house, but none of them knows me as well as you do. Although…' He paused. 'If you'd known me well enough, you would have known that Clarissa and I were on the verge of breaking up. Going to the ballet with her was just one step too far.'

'You've broken up with her?' Violet felt a twinge of sympathy for the voluptuous, blond-haired, blue-eyed woman who might not be the sharpest knife in the block, but was bubbly, friendly and hardly deserving of the obligatory bunch of goodbye flowers that Violet would no doubt be asked to send in the next few days. If he didn't react to her resignation by showing her the door with immediate effect.

'Don't look so shocked,' Matt said drily. 'You know my life is too busy for committed long-term relationships. Anyway, we're going off-piste here. I came about that resignation email and I want to know why you've suddenly decided, out of the blue, that you're fed up working for me. Is it the money? If it is, then you could simply have approached me and made your case for a pay rise.'

Violet was momentarily distracted by her boss's sweeping assumption that any relationship longer than five seconds qualified as *committed* and *long-term*.

She blinked and focused on him. Her heart sped up

and her pulse raced as their eyes tangled, deep-blue meeting guarded brown. She knew that she was blushing and she hated herself for not having the wherewithal to maintain an air of indifference and neutrality. At work, in her neat suit—grey jacket, white shirt, grey skirt, sensible black pumps—she was well protected from the lethal impact of his charm, but she wasn't in her neat suit here.

Nor was her brain playing ball. She should have remembered that someone like Matt, who was God's gift to the opposite sex, went for a certain type of woman. Leggy, big-breasted, very, very blonde and with a line in conversation that always included the phrases 'of course', 'sure' and 'whatever you want'. He definitely didn't go for little five-foot-three sparrows with straight brown bobs, unremarkable features and slender, flat-chested bodies who stood their ground whatever the provocation.

Why on earth had he descended on her like this? What gave him the right? It was unfair that he should be sitting in her kitchen, lounging back in one of her chairs and getting under her skin when she already had so much on her plate!

'Of course it's not the money,' she said, swallowing some of her coffee and wincing because it was so hot. 'And, yes, if I was unsatisfied with my pay then I wouldn't resign, Matt. I would approach you to discuss it.'

'So, if not the money, what then?' he demanded forcefully. 'You can't say that the job lacks challenge. Hell, Violet, you've got more responsibility than any of the women who have ever worked for me in the past.'

'That's because none of them have stayed very long.'

'Rubbish.' He waved aside that riposte with a casual,

dismissive gesture, keeping his eyes very firmly fixed on her face. 'Admittedly, a number of them were short-lived, but none of them had what it took to cope with anything but the lightest of workloads.'

Violet lowered her eyes and said nothing. When she'd joined, the personnel manager had been tearing his hair out.

'It's a difficult situation.' He had all but groaned with frustration. 'Matt is very…er…demanding… Lots of past candidates have found him impossible to work for. They've also mentioned that he makes them nervous. They're perfectly capable when they enter the building, and they've all passed the series of interviews with flying colours, but ten minutes with him and their nerves are shredded…'

She'd understood exactly what he'd meant the minute she'd spent five minutes in his company. Matt Falconer was brutally clever, horribly intolerant if you couldn't keep up and so spectacularly good-looking that it was a wonder *anyone* had been able to work for him for longer than a day without having their brains scrambled.

Thankfully, she was made of sterner stuff. Life had prepared her for just about anything, and she had dealt with her boss the way she had dealt with all the larger-than-life, crazily impulsive and wildly unpredictable people who had entered and left her life, thanks to her father. With equanimity, keeping to herself and protecting herself behind a wall of impenetrable calm.

'If you want more responsibility,' he growled, 'then say so. I can give you a title…more work…varied projects. You name it.'

'It's not the work.'

'Then what the hell is it?' He narrowed his eyes and sat forward, resting his elbows on his thighs and staring at her until she wanted to squirm with discomfort. 'Has someone been making life difficult for you?'

'What are you talking about?' Violet looked at him with genuine bewilderment.

'Some of those guys who work with me can be a little overboisterous. Comes with the territory, I'm afraid. Working on computer apps and dealing with innovative start-up companies requires a different kind of personality to the stuffy sort who work in banks and insurance companies. There's a chance you might be finding one of them impossible to deal with. Is that it? Give me a name and they get the sack. Instantly. Wait.'

He paused and Violet was too confused by this sudden tangent to say anything. 'Clients have been coming and going for the past few weeks with that new takeover. You know the one I mean… Food-app developer I'm in the process of buying out… Has one of them been pestering you? Is that it? I've noticed that that Draper boy has been lurking by your desk…'

'Matt, I know how to take care of myself!' Two bright patches of colour stained her cheeks.

How pathetic did he think she was? So pathetic that she would resign from a job she loved because someone decided to chat her up?

Suddenly, she was so angry that she wanted to slap him, so she balled her small hands into fists and counted to ten.

She could feel the tension of the past few days simmering, boiling up, spilling over, and she had to bite down on the temptation to shout at him. She wasn't the shouting sort. For a second, she wondered how he would react if his perennially unflappable PA decided to let rip.

'Do you?' he was asking quietly. 'You're quiet, Violet. Refined. Not the sort to give as good as she gets.'

'I wish you could hear yourself, Matt Falconer,' Violet responded, heading fast towards a flashpoint and only holding off by sheer willpower. 'I'm not a complete idiot.'

He had the grace to flush. 'I never said that you were.'

'The implication was there,' Violet retorted scornfully, and she noted the startled expression on his face, because this was a side to her he hadn't seen. 'You think I'm such a weak fool that if someone says "boo", then I'm going to go crying and running away because I just can't handle it!'

'Not at all,' he muttered uncomfortably.

'I'll have you know that I have a great deal more backbone than you probably think!'

'I'm sure you have.'

'Then stop patronising me!'

'Jesus, Violet. Where is this coming from? I only came here to find out what was going on!' He raked his fingers through his hair and Violet gathered herself, but with difficulty.

'I've handed in my notice, Matt, because something has cropped up, something unexpected, and I haven't had a choice.' She took a deep breath. 'I know that my email was a bit...er...brief, but going into details would have been complicated. I had no idea you would pursue the matter.'

'You thought that I would just sit back and let you walk out on me?' Matt demanded incredulously, and Violet blushed, because the phrasing of those words was so unintentionally intimate.

Good job you're leaving! She mentally berated

herself for all her negative thoughts involving voids opening up at the prospect of never going into that fast-paced, adrenaline-charged office ever again. *Just remember how dangerous it is, having a stupid crush on your boss!*

'I'll make sure I find a suitable replacement before I leave,' she responded coolly. 'I won't leave you in the lurch.'

'What if I decide that you're irreplaceable?'

Violet shrugged. She wished he would tailor his remarks, which were just making her even more addled and flustered, but naturally he wouldn't because Matt Falconer never saw fit to tailor his words or his actions to suit anyone. He was a law unto himself. That was just how he liked it and, annoyingly, he got away with it because he was so over-the-top talented at what he did.

'No one's irreplaceable.'

'You say that you didn't have a choice,' he thought aloud, his expression clearing. He sat forward so abruptly that she blinked in sudden confusion. 'You're pregnant, aren't you? I'm very progressive when it comes to things like that, but is he a dinosaur? Is that it? Someone with a value system that's still buried in the Middle Ages? It would be a travesty for some guy to think that a pregnant woman equates to a stay-at-home partner.'

Deep-blue eyes darted down to her stomach and, horrified, Violet instinctively rested her hand on her tummy. 'Who is he, Violet, and how is it that I don't know a thing about him? Isn't that taking secrecy to the very limit?' He shot her an accusatory look from under thick, sooty lashes. 'And tell me that you're enough of a feminist to know that you don't jack a great job in because some guy with antiquated expectations suggests that you do.'

Suddenly restless, he vaulted upright and walked in jerky movements to the kitchen window, staring out for a few seconds before spinning round to glare at her, clearly offended.

'We no longer live in the Dark Ages,' he carried on, leaving her speechless at his wild conclusions. 'And you should know that I am more than considerate when it comes to taking care of my staff, including the ones who have babies. Is there or is there not a crèche available, expertly manned by fully trained staff, on the eighth floor?'

'Yes, but…'

'We've long left behind those bad old days of gender inequality.'

'There's nothing wrong with being a stay-at-home mum!' Violet was distracted enough to retort.

Frankly, she could think of nothing more wonderful, but she wasn't going to become diverted by this non-issue. How on earth could someone with such an incredibly sharp brain be so…*dense*?

'You're not wearing a ring,' he commented sharply. 'Baby out of wedlock, Violet? Not what I would have expected, but then it's very obvious that you've been keeping all sorts of things from me. I'm beginning to wonder whether I knew you at all! Naturally, you never gave anything away, but I thought I knew the kind of person you were. Hasn't the man had the decency to propose to you, or has he done a runner?'

He shook his head in disgust while Violet did her best to keep up, even though her brain was lagging several light years behind. 'Or maybe he's married. Is that it? Did you get yourself embroiled in some kind of sordid situation that's ended up leading to this? You should have come to me for advice, Violet. I would have been there for you.'

Violet stared at him with undisguised incredulity. She was so astounded that she could barely think straight.

'A married man? A sordid affair? And, Matt Falconer, not that it has ever been necessary, but why on earth would I ever contemplate coming to you for advice?'

Matt frowned. 'Because I'm a man of the world,' he said in a voice that implied that he was doing nothing more than stating the obvious.

'You're also a man who has never had a relationship that's lasted longer than three months!' she was riled into retorting, betraying her code of never losing her cool with her boss. Naturally, instead of being annoyed with her outburst, he stared at her with the expression of a man suddenly intrigued.

She had half risen from her chair through sheer frustration, and now he slowly strolled towards her.

Mesmerised against her will, Violet could only stare right back at him as he drew closer until he was standing right in front of her, at which point she sank back into the chair, trembling all over and angry with herself for letting the situation get so completely out of hand.

'This is ridiculous!' she exclaimed, watching warily as he dragged a chair across so that he was sitting far too close to her for comfort's sake.

'I know. It is. So why don't you just take back your resignation and we'll pretend none of this ever happened?' He looked at her narrowly and suddenly, inexplicably, found his imagination start to wander because there was something oddly fetching about her flushed face, parted lips and angry eyes. He frowned and blinked away that sudden drag on his senses.

'I haven't resigned because I want a pay rise.' She tabulated each point carefully and slowly. 'Nor is it because I want more responsibility. If you had read what I said in my email, you'd have noted that I was extremely complimentary about my experience of working for your company—'

'You sound like a cheap brochure when you say that,' Matt interrupted.

Violet bristled. Not only had he interrupted, but he was so damned close that his knees were touching hers and it was hellishly impossible to focus properly.

'Nor,' she continued through gritted teeth, 'has anyone been pestering me on the work front, and if John Draper happened to ask me out on a date, then that is none of your business!'

'I knew that guy was lurking round your desk for no good reason.' Matt scowled and Violet wanted to hit him.

'And more to the point, Matt Falconer, I have *not* been having an affair with anyone! I am *not* pregnant and I certainly could never be attracted to anyone who thought that it might be okay to lay down ground rules about a woman's place. That is not why I have had to tender my resignation!'

'That's good.' He was visibly relieved by that assertion and Violet glared at him. He was just so selfish, she thought waspishly. All he cared about was whether he could get a saint who would be able to cope with his unpredictable, demanding personality! She couldn't believe that she had actually been idiotic enough to have fallen for the guy! Thank God she was savvy enough to know how to contain her inappropriate reaction. Thank

God lusting from afar was a curable sickness, and cured she would be as soon as she left his employ.

'So, tell me what this nonsense is all about.' He relaxed back and gazed at her, and she just couldn't help drinking in his insane good looks, at least for a second, until she blinked herself back to reality.

She sighed and surrendered.

CHAPTER TWO

'IT'S MY FATHER,' she said quietly, and he stared at her as though she had suddenly started speaking in tongues.

'You have a father?'

'Yes, Matt. I have a father. People do. These things happen.'

He grinned and shifted, angling his chair so that he could stretch his legs out in front of him. 'I would say that I would miss your sarcasm, but I won't, because if this is a simple case of parental problems then I'm sure we'll be able to work around it.'

'I'm not sarcastic,' Violet told him politely, and his eyebrows shot up.

'You've made more sarcastic remarks about the women I date than I've had hot dinners.'

Had she? She'd always thought that she was scrupulously non-committal when it came to the blondes who entered and left his life through an ever-revolving door.

'Remember asking me if I'd ever thought of dating women who didn't get worked up about going on spa breaks? Or the time you said that it wasn't true that blondes had more fun? And let's not forget some of your unnecessary asides about my tokens of affection when a relationship has, sadly, run its course...'

'Tokens of affection?' Violet retorted. 'I honestly

don't think that expensive bouquets of flowers from the same expensive flower shop in Knightsbridge could be called "tokens of affection."'

'I've given far more than flowers in the past.'

'When it comes to a break-up, there's no such thing as a token of affection.'

'Which, anyway, is just my arrogant way of appeasing my conscience.'

'You said it,' Violet muttered. 'I didn't.'

'Actually, you did,' Matt returned without batting an eyelid. 'More than once although, admittedly, in various guises. Same message, however. Most people think twice when it comes to letting their opinions go into free fall when they're with me, but you have never been reticent when it comes to saying what you think about my personal life. In your own quiet way, of course. So what's the problem with your father?'

Violet could feel her skin burning. Had she really been that obvious? Or had the man noticed and retained every small, passing, barely audible remark she had made about some of his life choices? She thought she'd always been so careful, but clearly she hadn't been nearly as careful as that.

'I… My father…isn't well…'

'I'm sorry to hear that, Violet. Serious? How old is he?'

There was genuine sympathy in his voice, and something inside her weakened. She wasn't accustomed to sharing, but right now she wanted nothing more than to spill her heart out to the man sitting opposite her with his head tilted to one side, his deep-blue eyes speculative and thoughtful.

'How old is he?' she repeated briskly. 'Young. Not yet sixty.'

'What's wrong with him?'

'It's not really relevant, Matt.' Violet shrugged, ignoring the temptation to say more than she knew she should. Her privacy was so important to her, so much an ingrained trait, that it was almost impossible to shed even when she wanted to.

It was a habit born from circumstance. Life on the move had put paid to friendships. How easy was it ever to formulate firm bonds with people you met in passing? Especially when you were young, too young to think ahead to the bigger picture. And of course, by the time life had become more settled, that habit had taken root, and those roots ran very deep indeed.

'Of course it's relevant,' he said quietly. 'You're upset.'

'And you're imagining things.'

'You don't have to put on a brave front all the time,' was his response, and she bristled, not liking the way he seemed to be circling her, making her feel lost and vulnerable. 'Talk to me. You've handed in your notice. I think it's fair to say that I deserve more of an explanation than "thank you for the opportunity to work for you. I've enjoyed my experience at your company, however, I feel that it's time to move on…"'

Of course he did. Violet realised that somewhere, deep down, she would have been disappointed if he had accepted her letter of resignation with a philosophical shrug of those broad shoulders, no questions asked.

She'd worked for him and alongside him for two-and-a-half years and, yes, she had gradually come to see she knew him in ways far deeper than any of the women he went out with. She knew his idiosyncrasies, his quirks. And he, it would appear, knew her far better than she had ever imagined. It was unsettling, to say the least.

Besides, nothing he could say would change her decision, so where was the harm in a little confiding? She would leave his company and leave him behind and, if he had glimpsed that private side to her, then it wasn't as if afterwards she would be facing him day after day, having to deal with his renewed curiosity in some awful *Groundhog Day* loop.

'My father lives on the other side of the world,' she began, frowning, getting her thoughts in order. 'Australia, to be precise.'

'How long as he been there? Where in Australia?'

'Melbourne. He's been there for…nearly six years. He went after… Well, he remarried. My mother died when I was young.' She chewed her lip and looked away and Matt didn't say anything. He hated crying women. Just something else she knew about him—and she did her utmost to make sure she didn't give in to the wave of maudlin despondency threatening to ambush all her good intentions.

'Take your time. I'm in no hurry.'

'Sure you want this kind of conversation?' Violet lightened her tone, but when their eyes met there was no responding teasing in his. He looked deadly serious.

'Why wouldn't I?'

'Because you don't do long, intense conversations with women. I think that's something you've shared with me in the past.'

'How well you know me,' Matt murmured, with a certain amount of amusement. 'You're not one of my women, though, are you? So it's fair to say that normal rules of engagement don't apply.'

Not one of his women…

Violet felt a sharp pang somewhere deep inside her, a sharp and utterly inappropriate pang. Thank goodness she *wasn't* 'one of his women,' she told herself. Knowing him as well as she did, that would have been a recipe for heartbreak, because he represented everything she didn't want in a guy and would never want.

She might have been a sucker for those sinful, dark looks—who wouldn't be?—but she was way too sensible to go any further down that dangerous road of attraction.

She shrugged, expression veiled. To kill time and get her thoughts in order, she offered him a top up on the coffee and, when he politely declined, she reluctantly suggested a glass of wine, which he accepted with alacrity.

'So, you were telling me about your father...the one you've avoided mentioning for the past two-and-a-half years...who lives in Melbourne, a place I know well.'

'He's had problems with his liver, which he's coped with well enough, but my stepmother died six months ago, and ever since then he's been getting more and more depressed,' Violet said abruptly. She needed a bit of wine as well, and she poured herself a glass before sitting back down. 'He visited for two weeks a couple of months ago and he tried to put a brave face on things, but I could see through that.'

'Liver problems... Drinker?'

Violet reddened. Of course, he would ask questions.

'He used to be, but as you know, drink is always the devil waiting in the wings when it comes to ex...ex...'

'Alcoholics?'

She nodded brusquely and looked away. 'Depression is his enemy and I'm very much afraid that, left to his own devices, he may find that devil on his shoulder just a little bit too tempting.'

'He's still in Melbourne?'

'Yes.'

'Why doesn't he move back over here?' Matt looked around the bijou mews house and Violet could see what he was thinking without him having to spell it out.

The house might not be a mansion, but it was big enough for two. It was certainly worth a lot of money and could easily be sold and something bigger purchased in a less flashy postcode.

'Money issues?'

'If there were money issues I wouldn't be living in a place like this.'

'Which brings me to the question I've been meaning to ask since I walked through your front door...' He paused for a heartbeat, then continued with more urgency in his voice. 'I don't give a damn how you're managing to afford the rent on a place like this. Maybe you have a thing for small, expensive houses and would rather sacrifice your monthly pay cheque renting one of them than throwing your hard-earned cash away on holidays, fast cars and designer clothes. Your business. Bottom line is, if you can't afford to support your father if he returns here, then say the word.'

'Holidays, fast cars and designer clothes?' Violet parroted faintly, wondering if he was actually talking about *her*.

'You know where I'm going with this. If it's money you're after, then I'm prepared to throw as much as you need your way. We can call it a loan with zero interest rate.' He raked his fingers through his hair and stared at her. 'I never thought I'd beg for any woman.' He shot her a crooked smile that did all the wrong things to her nervous system. 'But I'm big enough to concede that there's always a first time for everything.' This time his expression was serious. 'No one has ever worked so well with me before. You understand how I think and you don't go into a tailspin if I get too close to you.'

Violet knew that there was a huge compliment in there somewhere, but all she could think about was *you don't go into a tailspin if I get too close to you.* He could say that with certainty because the unspoken rider was that they both knew he could never find her attractive, so why would she be affected by him the way other, more suitably blonde and busty women might be?

Gossip over the years had informed her that the only PA who had ever stuck it out with him—and she had stuck it out for a lifetime—had been a sixty-year-old married grandmother who had taken early retirement, leaving him in the lurch three years previously. Before Violet had come along, the vacant spot had been filled by an unsatisfactory procession of attractive potentials because, one of the girls in Accounts had confided after a couple of after-work drinks, he'd decided he liked a bit of eye candy.

'Not very PC,' Violet had responded, and Amelia had burst out laughing.

'Oh, Matt wouldn't even be aware of it! No, that's just the conclusion we all reached after a while. Problem is, he's a hunk, and girls go into a tizzy when he's around. Even bigger problem is that he really doesn't get it. Which is why he's kept making the same mistake over and over.'

Until me, Violet had thought.

'I'm very flattered,' she said now, banking down all negative thoughts about her appearance. 'But it's nothing to do with the money.'

Violet sighed and resigned herself to the fact that he would be shocked at a past she had always kept to herself. She stood up, opened one of the drawers and pulled out a photo album, which she handed to him, because in this case, pictures would speak so much more clearly than words.

He opened it. Flicked through the pages. Sat up just a little bit straighter and flicked through the pages again, more slowly, inspecting each and every one. Then he looked at her with astonishment.

'Your father is *Mickey Dunn*?'

'Real name Victor. I'm surprised you've heard of him.'

'Who hasn't? Burnt out young. Drink and drugs.'

'Stop looking at me like that,' Violet said irritably. She drained her glass and felt the buzz of alcohol race to her head. She barely drank. A legacy from being around people who did very little *but*.

'I would never have guessed that you were the daughter of a hellraiser like Mickey Dunn,' Matt murmured, unashamedly curious. He glanced round the kitchen as though seeing it for the first time. 'That explains this place,' he said slowly. 'And all the while, I thought you were saving hard to buy somewhere, being careful with what you earned, avoiding holidays like the plague because a mortgage was more important. And then I figured you were renting. Presumably, you own the place lock, stock and smoking barrels?'

'I never lied to you,' Violet said defensively, and he just looked at her with the sort of shuttered expression that made her feel as though she had, somehow, deliberately deceived him, which of course she *hadn't*.

'You're right,' he said, in a voice as smooth as silk. There was a coldness there that went to the very core of her, making her realise how used to his teasing she had become, to the warmth of those fabulous deep-blue eyes, to the respect that was always there whenever he addressed her.

Things she had taken for granted and, although it hardly mattered now what he thought of her, it was just too painful not to try to justify herself, to set the record straight, even though there was no need.

'My father bought this place for me before he left for Australia. He didn't like to think that I might be staying anywhere…dangerous. I always made it clear that I didn't want any money from him but he dug his heels in.' She smiled. 'You'd think he would have been a lot more relaxed about stuff like that, considering his misspent youth, but he wasn't.'

She took a deep breath and looked him straight in the eyes. 'My mum died when I was eight. In a motorcycle accident. My dad was driving and he never really recovered from the fact that she was pillion, even though he hadn't been drinking. Just skidded. Wet night… Took a corner too fast.'

'Where were you at the time?'

'At home. Home was a hotel room in… I can't even remember which country. Abroad. Paid babysitter. They partied hard but, when mum was alive, weirdly not as often as you'd think. Sometimes they took me but usually they were good at making sure that someone responsible was looking after me. I remember I woke up in the morning and nothing was the same after that. Anyway, to cut a long story short, the life of a rock star made him go off the rails completely. He lost himself in drink and drugs, even though he carried on doing his best for me. It was just that sometimes his best was a little…erratic.' She felt the tears welling up but she didn't dare make eye contact with her boss, just in case.

'He played music, and had his adoring fans, and we

travelled the world, but I saw him when he was on his own. I saw the sadness. Eventually, of course, the band stopped touring, and for a while my dad wrote music for other people. By then, he was in and out of rehab and I had long become his carer. Of sorts.'

'His carer...'

'These things happen.' She shrugged. Thankfully, that moment of wanting to burst into tears had gone, and she was back in control now. The past was the past and she had come to terms with it a long time ago. She might not have had a normal childhood, but it had been colourful, and whatever the distractions, her dad had always been there for her. In his own way.

'So...' She began the process of winding up the conversation. She had said far more than she had anticipated and was thinking that it was just as well that their time together was numbered. Matt Falconer recognised no boundaries when it came to digging deep, and her story would have stoked his curiosity, no doubt about that. His spade would be at the ready, and she quailed at the thought of what her life would have been like if she'd carried on working for him indefinitely.

'My plan is to rent this place out and go to Australia for a while to be with my dad. He doesn't want to return to London to live. He enjoys Melbourne and he's made friends over there. He likes the weather and the laid-back lifestyle. But I need to make sure that he's okay while he goes through this temporary blip.'

She waited for him to say something, but he was worryingly silent.

'It would have been different if Caroline, my stepmother, was still around.'

Silence.

'He's on the waiting list for a liver transplant, if you must know.'

Way too much confiding, Violet thought, angry with herself.

'He met her when he was in rehab. She was a member of staff there.'

She clicked her tongue impatiently and wondered whether she would just keep babbling into the silence until every thought she had and every feeling she'd ever felt had been laid bare. This wasn't like her at all. This wasn't the cool, private, detached Violet Dunn he was accustomed to.

'Are you just going to sit there, Matt?' she found herself compelled to snap.

'You were his carer…' Matt repeated, still pensive and still staring at her in the sort of intense, focused way that made the hairs at the back of her neck stand on end. 'Something must have been sacrificed.'

'What do you mean?'

'The way it usually works,' he said slowly, as if piecing together a complex problem that could only be solved through a series of careful stages, 'is the carer gives something up. Am I right? I'm guessing your education would have been erratic, to say the least, which incidentally says a lot about the fact that you still managed to attain so many qualifications. You must have burnt the midnight oil as a teenager.'

Violet's mouth tightened. If only he knew the extent of the role reversal that had characterised her life! She had not really given it a second thought, growing up, but she had often looked back over the years and gazed at the adolescent who had stayed at home, head in a book, while her dad had been out getting drunk, doing drugs and staggering back in to flop in a heap on the sofa. She had been the one admonishing him about late nights and preaching about the dangers of drugs. She had made sure he took his vitamins and had his five a day whenever possible. By the time the touring had come to an end and the rehab visits had started, she had been very much used to running the household.

So had she given things up?

Had she ever! And top of the list was the carefree, reckless joy of adolescence.

'I enjoyed studying,' she said vaguely. 'It's time you left. You asked me to explain why I had to resign and I have.'

'I'm not ready to go.'

'What do you mean, you're *not ready to go*?'

'I've spent two-and-a-half years wondering what made my überefficient secretary tick...' He leant back in the chair and looked at her from under lowered lashes. 'You'll have to excuse my curiosity. Also, I'm still in the game of trying to get you to change your mind. Likewise, you'll have to excuse my persistence.'

'Can we talk about this in the morning?' she asked wearily.

'You mean when you're in your prim little suit, sitting behind your desk with your professional hat firmly flattened on your head? I think I prefer this slightly less formal Violet Dunn.'

'I don't care what you prefer!'

'I've just taken on two start-up software companies and one of them happens to be in Melbourne. Small start-up in the city. Did you know Melbourne is right up there when it comes to density of small businesses? Getting a foothold there is a coup for me. Lots of promise there and I'm going to nurture this baby. I feel this goose might lay a few golden eggs with the right backing, expertise and encouragement.'

'What does this have to do with me?' Violet queried, standing up and hovering when he didn't automatically follow suit. She dimly recalled those two companies, because the very young directors in search of investment had been brought over to discuss details, and they had been full of it.

She walked to the kitchen door and rested her hand lightly on the doorknob.

'You need routine,' Matt said in a soothing voice that made her grit her teeth together in exasperation. How was it that he could manage to make something as laudable as needing routine sound like a dismal admission of failure?

'I think my life will carry on without it for a while,' Violet responded tartly. 'Get up. It's time to go. I'm exhausted.'

'So I take it that you're not planning on settling down on the other side of the world?'

Violet clicked her tongue and refused to give him the satisfaction of sitting back down, even though he was making less than zero effort to take the hint and leave.

'No,' she conceded after a while. She sighed and sat back down. This wasn't a victory for him, she reasoned, but plain old common sense from her because if he wanted to carry on talking for ten more minutes, then he wasn't going to budge, and her legs were feeling distinctly wobbly—probably because she had had her personal space invaded. 'I couldn't live over there. It would be a lot easier for Dad to move back here, and that's going to be part of my job when I go over. To convince him to return to London.'

'If he's still got ties here, he might think that they

could lead him astray,' Matt suggested shrewdly, and Violet's eyes widened.

'I never thought of that,' she admitted slowly. 'You could be right. He's still pals with the members in his band, and of course they still go to the pub and drink, which would be tough for him. I could persuade him to move closer to the coast. Far enough from London for temptation not to be right there on his doorstep...' She looked at Matt and realised that this was just another of his talents—an ability to see through the clutter and chaos and get right to the heart of the problem in record time.

She had absorbed that trait, just as she had absorbed all those others, and now she wondered whether, subconsciously, they had all bonded together to turn professional respect for him into something altogether more dangerous.

'But back to this little start-up of mine,' Matt drawled, and Violet blinked and focused on him, her mind still playing with the disturbing realisation that he had managed to crawl under her skin a lot more than she had ever suspected.

'The reason I mention it,' he continued with a gesture that smacked ever so slightly of a certain smug satisfaction, 'is because I could use a safe pair of hands over there—steering the newly acquired ship, so to speak. On every single front, it would work for both of us.'

'What do you mean?'

'I mean, Violet, that you plan on disappearing for months—and having nothing to do on the other side of the world except rally your father's spirits is going to get very frustrating for you after a very, very short while. You have a good brain and you need to use it. How are you going to do that in Melbourne? Maybe find some casual work behind a bar somewhere? Or else you could take up a hobby. Something you could make use of within the confines of the four walls of your father's house so that you can keep a watchful eye on him.'

'Stop being so negative.' Violet looked at him steadily and calmly. There had been enough departures from common sense for the evening, thank you very much. 'I'm sure I'll be able to occupy myself when I'm out there.'

'Yes, there'll be adequate cash-in-hand casual labour jobs, although you obviously don't need the money, which will make any not-much-of-anything temp job all the more frustrating. And, of course, anything more challenging might prove a problem, as you're not a national. I've always got the impression that you enjoy a challenge.

'So, joining the dots here, you're going to be bored rigid...and I could use someone I trust implicitly in the initial stages of getting my new company in order. It'll be a sizeable promotion for you. In charge of one of my fledging companies from ground zero. New title, new set of responsibilities and, of course, new pay cheque to reflect both those things. Don't worry about work permits and all that tedious stuff. Consider it sorted.'

He allowed a few seconds to elapse so that she could digest all the considerable advantages to what he was offering.

And, Violet was forced to concede, they were indeed sizeable.

Boredom would weigh heavily on her hands. Yes, of course, her time would be devoted to her father, to raising his spirits and going with him for the medical check-ups that she'd recently discovered he had been ignoring. Lord only knew what else would be unearthed once she got over there. But how well this man knew her. How well he knew that doing nothing would get to her very quickly. However, there was one missing link not even Matt Falconer could factor in, and Violet had no intention of enlightening him.

'I could even set you up in a little apartment of your own, so that you and your father could maintain that very vital independence you've probably both grown accustomed to over the years, if you feel the need to bang the drum for financial independence. You could call it a perk that comes with the job.'

'That's a very generous offer, Matt…'

'So shall we call it a deal? Shake on it?' He dealt her one of those smiles that could knock a person for six. 'Of course, there would be one or two contingents you would have to take into consideration…'

'Of course there would be,' Violet said drily. 'There's no such thing as a free lunch. Isn't that written somewhere in your company manual?'

Matt burst out laughing and his eyes darkened with appreciation at the way she never had any qualms when it came to telling it like it was. Jesus, he would miss that!

'You would have to sign up to returning to my employ in London after a predetermined length of time, and I'd say that six months would be a pretty generous timescale. You might also have to put up with me descending on you intermittently, just to make sure that everything is ticking over nicely.'

'I'm very grateful for the offer, Matt.' Violet pictured him meeting her father and finding a foothold in her life in Melbourne and she suppressed a shudder. He had enough of an effect on her, and that was without him knowing a thing about her. 'But I'm going to have to say no.'

Matt carried on smiling for a few seconds, then he frowned as her words sank in. 'You don't mean that.'

'This situation has all been very sudden,' she said truthfully, 'but it's going to provide me with a break to explore other avenues aside from working behind a desk in an office.'

'What other avenues?'

'I know it's in my contract to work out my full six-week notice period, but if I find a replacement before then, would you consider freeing me of that obligation earlier? Naturally, I wouldn't be paid for any time I didn't work. Maybe you could sleep on that and we can discuss it when I come in tomorrow morning?'

'I can't believe I'm hearing this!'

She'd gone to the door and now he joined her, scowling.

'You don't always get what you want,' Violet told him gently.

'If you want to leave that desperately, then far be it from me to chain you to your desk and force you to work out your notice period!'

'You mean that? Because, the sooner I can be with my dad, the better.' He was going to release her from her contract, she thought. He'd done what for him was the equivalent of begging, and now he intended to throw the towel in the ring with his usual flamboyance. All or nothing. That was his nature.

It was terrifying.

But she kept smiling as he stared down at her, glowering. Then, quite unexpectedly, he rested his hand on the door to the sitting room, which was ajar, and half stumbled as it flew open. And there he was, in the sanctuary of her sitting room.

For a few seconds, he was lost for words as he stared at the baby grand piano positioned by the bay window. Violet followed his gaze. Without thinking, she walked towards the piano and gently smoothed her hand over the rich chestnut lid, then along the ivory-and-black keys, hardly aware of the picture she was painting, just doing something that was purely instinctive.

'You play?' Matt was mesmerised by just how slender and elegant a figure she cut, standing there, half-turned away from him, ethereal and wistful, exerting some weird magnetism over him.

He was right behind her. Violet could feel his warmth radiating outwards, swirling around her, but she didn't feel uncomfortable or self-conscious because this was her comfort zone. She absently played a few keys and a soft, melodious tune took shape under her moving fingers, then she stopped and turned to him, embarrassed now.

'I play,' she murmured. 'I must have inherited some of my father's musical talent.'

He was staring down at her with a veiled, oddly disturbing expression and she smiled, eager to lighten the moment and bring things back down to earth.

'Don't look so surprised, Matt. So what if I'm more than just the efficient, invisible secretary you've spent the past two-and-a-half years taking for granted?'

'Take you for granted? Never,' Matt murmured. His eyes drifted away from hers, down to the surprisingly full and perfectly shaped mouth. A *sexy* mouth, he realised, a mouth fashioned for kissing. 'Invisible? Hardly.'

The atmosphere had changed. Violet felt the shift and backed away, bumping into the piano and instantly straightening so that she didn't sit on the keys. He was so close to her and he was no longer her boss. They were man and woman, eyes locked, breathing laboured, suffused in an electric charge that was suddenly so potent that she wanted to pass out.

'You should go now,' she said huskily. For a few seconds he didn't move, and she wondered what she would do if the unthinkable happened—if that cool, firm, sensuous mouth covered hers.

He backed off, and when there was some safe distance between them he said, gruffly, 'One week. After that, Violet, you're free to go.' He spun round on his heels and headed for the door.

He was already opening the front door by the time she caught up with him. Her body was still burning, as though she'd stepped too close to a conflagration that had suddenly changed direction and begun soaring towards her at speed.

'What about me finding a replacement for you?' she asked, and he looked at her coolly.

'I'll manage.' He paused then said, cutting her to the quick, 'I thought I knew you, Violet. Turns out I couldn't be further from the truth.'

CHAPTER THREE

VIOLET WENT TO work the following morning, at the safe time of nine on the dot, to find the usually buzzing office almost completely empty.

'Hush-hush, top-secret meeting.' Lisa, one of the junior computer software analysts, approached her from behind and Violet spun round with a frown.

'Top-secret meeting? I didn't know that there were any meetings booked for today.' She peered in the direction of the conference room, but the door was open and there was no one inside.

'They've disappeared to one of the hotels. All the CEOs and the head of Accounts and a handful of the tech guys.' She began heading towards her desk and threw over her shoulder, 'Hey, you should be glad you've been spared that ordeal. You know how long they can go on for! Anyway, I'm holding the fort until they decide to start drifting back. Probably lunchtime. Knowing that lot from the tech team, they won't be passing up the subsidised meal in the office cafeteria.'

Bemused, Violet headed towards her office.

By the time she got there, it had sunk in that Matt had delivered what could only be called a body blow.

She had never been left out of anything. She had always been his right-hand woman, had sat in on all meetings. Very soon after she'd joined, he'd told her to scrap the boring business of taking minutes.

'I don't need you to remember on my behalf,' he had drawled in that self-assured way of his. 'I have an excellent memory. And so have you. Between the pair of us, we can remember what goes on in a two-hour meeting. Just make sure you transcribe as soon as we get back to the office.'

Now, here she was, twiddling her thumbs, ostensibly dumped from whatever high-level conference they had gone to.

Coding on new apps as they came to fruition, and before the process of launching them onto the market began, was often a game of timing and secrecy. Beating the competition was everything, and that rested on no one finding out what was going on within the hallowed walls of Matt's considerable business. Loyalty was of the essence.

Violet told herself that it didn't matter. Indeed, it was perfectly understandable, given the circumstances, but it stung and she found herself staring off into the distance, biding her time until everyone returned.

Which they did.

In dribs and drabs. The office filled out. The noise levels rose. It was a young, enthusiastic and wildly exuberant team.

She didn't know whether Matt had said anything about her resignation, and she kept a low profile, but her eyes kept darting to the bank of lifts, looking out for her boss. When he finally showed up, well after she had had her lunchtime sandwich and bottled water, she had given up on him returning at all and was busy collating information that would be needed for a handover.

She was aware of him by the shadow over her desk,

at which point she looked up, a professional smile pinned to her face.

'Apologies if you got here and found an empty office,' Matt said without preamble, before heading into his office. 'Did you get all those emails sorted and sent? Hope you used your time out productively. Can't have you shirking because you're on your way out.'

'All done.' Violet was her usual crisp and efficient self as she followed him into his office and shut the door behind her.

They usually spent at least an hour a day privately debriefing on updates on any of his many companies scattered across the globe. She flipped open her laptop, ready to start, when he held up one hand.

'No need.'

'I beg your pardon?'

'In fact, I'm going to have to get a number of the more sensitive accounts removed from your remit.'

Violet paled. She stared down at her laptop and felt the prickle of tears gathering behind her eyes.

'Of course.' She cleared her throat and quietly closed the laptop. 'If you make a list of them, I'll make sure they're transferred out of my portfolio.'

Matt relaxed back and lounged into his leather chair, hands draped loosely over its arms. He pushed the chair back and angled it so that he could stretch out his legs. 'In fact, maybe it would be better if you surrender your work computer completely.'

'But why?' She gazed at him in speechless consternation. She barely recognised the drop-dead gorgeous guy looking at her with bland, calm indifference. His hair was swept back, curling at the collar of his faded grey tee shirt. His navy eyes were cool and guarded. He was more of a stranger than the man she had met on the very first day she had walked into his office.

'Why do you think you weren't included in this morning's activities, Violet?'

'I had no idea there was a conference planned at all.'

'It was hurriedly arranged last night. A significant development with one of our smaller takeovers in the Far East sparked the need for a conference. I arranged it myself.'

'Because you no longer trust me,' Violet said dully. She stared at her fingers, long, slender fingers, fingers that had delicately begun playing the piano almost before she could walk. She could feel her heart thudding inside her chest and she wanted to choke.

'It's not about trust, exactly.'

'Oh, but it is, Matt.' Violet looked directly at him, her face calm and pale. 'If I surrender my work computer— and of course, I completely understand, and I'll hand it over to you as soon as I leave this office—how am I supposed to carry on here? Should I go to the stationery office and stock up on paper and pencils so that I can write everything down longhand?'

Just for a second, she saw a flash of *something* in those deep-blue eyes, but it didn't last.

'You can work on non-sensitive issues.'

'Like what?'

'Well,' Matt mused, tilting his head to one side and appearing to give her question a great deal of thought. 'There's always a lot of office rearranging to be done.' He waved a hand in the general direction of the industrial metal cabinet that stretched from floor to ceiling against the grey wall in his office, and which contained a ridiculous number of complex computer and coding manuals that were largely ignored by every single employee in the company. 'There's always that monstrosity. I bet half of those manuals are out of date. Could do with a complete clear-out.'

They stared at one another in silence for a few seconds, then Violet asked, in a low voice, 'Why are you doing this?'

'You work in a sensitive business, Violet. You must know that. I can't allow you to leave taking anything with you. For all I know, you might decide to set up shop over in Australia as a direct competitor.'

'You don't mean that!'

'You're defecting,' Matt told her bluntly. 'I have to take the necessary precautions.' He breathed out deeply. 'It's also naturally troubling that you've refused the job offer I made yesterday. Had you accepted, I would have known that your loyalty remained with me. As it stands...' He shrugged and let unspoken words settle between them.

After two-and-a-half years, he no longer trusted her. He was intensely passionate, intensely volatile and, yes, he would see her refusal of his job offer as a kick in the teeth. But did he really think that she was the sort to go behind his back and draw down on his contacts so that she could set up in competition with him?

That stung.

It was as if the time they had spent together had counted for nothing in the end. She shifted, smoothing one shaking hand over her grey skirt. For once, the uniform that had always kept those lines of distinction between them firmly in place seemed to be giving at the seams.

She felt miserable. She wanted to cry, but she wasn't going to yield to the temptation. For a second, she wondered how he would react. He went out with women who were clones of one another, and the duration of his relationships ran to more or less the same timetable. A handful of months, sometimes mere weeks. And he didn't do any form of histrionics. Violet knew this because on a couple of occasions, a weeping ex had descended at the office and had been dispatched with ruthless efficiency.

They worked brilliantly together because Violet had always made sure to keep her emotions to herself.

Had worked brilliantly together, she amended mentally. No more. Now she was leaving and she had been dispatched with ruthless efficiency, a bit like one of his exes.

She didn't know how she was going to stick it out for the remainder of the week. It wasn't a long time, but it was long enough.

'Of course. When would you like me to start on the clearing out?'

'I'm having a late lunch soon. You can begin once I leave. Oh, and while we're at it, I've come to the conclusion that there's no need for you to work out any of your notice.'

'I thought… What about a replacement? I know a week isn't a long time, but I can already think of a few candidates for the job if we promote from within the company.'

Violet realised she was desperate to see a glimmer of the warmth he had always shown towards her and which she had always taken for granted. But his face was as cold as a slab of icy marble as he stared at her quizzically, before saying in a voice that threatened to turn into a yawn, 'Can you, now? Who are they?'

'I've made a list.'

'Of course you have.'

Violet smiled tentatively because this was a running joke between them, her love of lists. She said they were essential to make sure you kept up to speed on everything. He maintained that they were the sign of an uninspired mind and that life was too short for lists.

He didn't smile back. He just looked at her in a way that made her feel hot and bothered and out of her depth for the first time since she had started working for him.

'Maria Callway from Accounts.' Her voice echoed in the silence. 'She's very diligent and I know she would love the work. Then there's John. He's new but he's efficient. You remember he handled all those problems we had with the tech company in Maidstone a few months ago? Well, there's him. And Agatha Child would also fit the bill, and at fifty-two she's got just the right temperament for the job.'

'Right temperament?'

'I mean she's calm. Level-headed.' Violet filled in the blanks quickly. 'As is Maria.'

'Maria… Maria… Maria… Is she the one who's just returned from maternity leave after her third?'

'Yes. She has a brilliant eye for detail. If you like, I could call up their CVs for you to have a look at? I'm not sure whether we would have to advertise the job in the public forum but, honestly, either of those three would fit the bill and the move would be seamless. They're all already familiar with most of the accounts, and you can…'

Matt held up his hand and Violet fizzled into silence and stared at him. Now that she was leaving, and within hours rather than days, she felt free to appreciate his beauty without lecturing herself on the idiocy of it. The only sport she knew for sure he played was table tennis, and only because there was a table in one of the rooms three floors down. It was always in use and many a complex problem had been sorted in between racket hitting ball.

Yet, to look at him, you would have said that he did nothing but work out. He was six foot two of tightly packed muscle and sinew, made all the more beautiful because of his exotic colouring. No one would have guessed that he was a billionaire several times over because the only expensive item she had ever known him to wear was his watch. She had gazed at that watch surreptitiously so many times, taking in the way the dark silky hairs brushed the dull leather strap.

Occasionally, and under duress, he was known to wear a suit, and his suits were all hand tailored, but usually his dress code for work comprised jeans—usually black—loafers—usually tan—and some kind of tee shirt, usually with a logo of sorts on the front. He liked rock, she caught herself thinking now as she looked from under lowered lashes at today's tee shirt which featured a prominent rock group from the seventies. No big surprise he had heard of her dad.

'No need to trouble yourself over a possible replacement,' he was saying now as he vaulted to his feet, taking her by surprise.

'But...'

'I'll be back in an hour or so. Make sure you haven't decided to leave in my absence.'

'I wouldn't. Of course not.' She clumsily stood up but he was already heading for the door. 'I won't be able to get through much of that cabinet in the space of a few hours.'

He waved his hand dismissively, without bothering to glance back in her direction. 'Do what you can. Just make sure you're here when I get back. Oh, and you can take your work computer down to Hannah in HR.' He turned to look at her. 'Wouldn't want you getting any ideas about nabbing customer details in my absence.'

'Matt,' Violet said huskily. She rested her hand on his arm and just as quickly removed it. It was the first time she had ever knowingly touched him in any capacity and the feel of his flesh was as potent as the punch of a branding iron. 'Tell me you don't honestly think that I would ever do anything to undermine you? Yes, I'm leaving, but I would *never* be disloyal. I would *never* consider poaching any of your accounts. Never.'

'Duly noted.'

'I have no idea what that means.'

'It means that I didn't get where I have by trusting other people. After two-and-a-half years, you walk out with a polite one-paragraph email tendering your resignation, and it was only because I showed up at your house that I now have any idea about the person you are and the life you lead. When you discover you don't know someone at all, it's time to consider trust issues. So tidy up the cabinet, Violet, and don't worry about a replacement. I'll be handling that myself.'

Reeling from what he had just said, knowing that he was justified in saying it, Violet remained frozen by the door as he whistled his way out of the office and towards the bank of lifts.

When she faced the metal cabinet, she was grateful for the tedious monotony of the job he had given her to do, a pointless passing-the-time-of-day exercise because he no longer wanted her near anything that might be considered sensitive.

Because, in his opinion, she'd deceived him. She had a whole life that he didn't know about and her secrecy had caught him on the back foot. He saw her now in a different light and it wasn't a flattering one. Violet hated that, but what he saw as secrecy she accepted as just part and parcel of her personality.

She had been thrust into growing up when her mother had died and her father had gone to pieces. She had mourned in her own private way because she had had the job of making sure her father was all right and coping.

From a young age, there had been a gradual role reversal, and Violet had dealt with the responsibilities that had landed on her shoulders by gritting her teeth and getting on with it. She'd focused, amid chaos, on what needed doing—the practical stuff that had kept her father tethered through his wild drinking and drug-taking days. She'd focused on her studies, wherever in the world they happened to be as he toured, taking advantage of the internet and doing all sorts of exams online so that she kept up. There had been private tutors, but they had come and gone without much consistency. She had had to learn to depend on herself and she had.

And along the way, the simple business of opening up to other people, sharing and having a laugh about the things that happened to her, had gradually disappeared under the weight of her responsibilities. She adored her father, and she wouldn't have dreamt of putting herself first, but there had been consequences. Living surrounded by people coming and going, by the noise of guitars being played, pianos being tuned and drums being banged, Violet had learned the value of quiet. There had been few kids around her age who had hung around, so she had missed the phase of girlish confidences.

How was Matt to know all that, however? All he could see was someone who had been by his side 24/7 for over two years, who had decided to turn her back and walk away, and the only explanation had been forced out of her at gunpoint.

She miserably undertook the task allotted to her while mentally trying to convince herself that it was just great that she would be able to leave immediately. Perhaps, next week, she might return to take some of the team out for a farewell drink, but then she thought of Matt coming along and she quailed.

It was after three when she heard the sound of Matt approaching. Noise usually heralded his entrance. People coming over to tell him about some new development, tech guys trying to persuade him into taking time out so that he could sample some new game or app that was on the brink of fruition. There was always someone who needed his signature somewhere and they tended to get increasingly frustrated when he chose to ignore them.

She looked up as the office door was pushed open. The job she had undertaken was far from complete and she was sitting amidst a pool of manuals, textbooks and pamphlets.

'You can drop all that,' he opened, strolling towards his desk. 'I have another job for you to do before you disappear to the vast blue yonder. Candy, meet Violet. Violet, meet your replacement.'

Violet turned and stared. Framed in the doorway was a five-foot-ten blonde who looked as though she had just stepped off the catwalk. Her hair reached her waist, a heavy fall of pale vanilla. Not much was left to the imagination with the dress code, and long, tanned legs were on show. Her eyes were a rich, bright blue and a crop top, barely skirting generous breasts, skimmed across her flat belly, proudly showing a pierced belly button. The piercing glittered in the rays of the summer sun shafting through semi-transparent blinds that covered the floor-to-ceiling glass windows.

'Ooh…' She did a full circle, admiring the office, while Violet carried on staring, literally lost for words. 'I *love* the office.' Her eyes were bright and enthusiastic and they settled on Violet with lively curiosity. 'You must be Miss Dunn.' She dimpled. 'Matt got hold of me from a friend of a friend of a friend and, as luck would have it, I was in between jobs. When shall we get down to things?'

'No time like the present,' Matt drawled, raising both eyebrows at Violet's startled expression. 'Why don't you show Candy the ropes for the rest of the day, Violet?'

'Of course.' Violet levered herself up, acutely self-conscious as she smoothed down the creased skirt and slipped her stockinged feet back into the neat black pumps. The blonde towered over her, five foot ten to five foot and an optimistic three and a half.

She turned her back on Matt. He had sauntered over to his desk and when she headed towards her office with Candy in tow, about to shut the dividing door between them, he called out for her to leave it open.

Violet glanced behind her. He was sprawled in his chair, feet on his desk, hands folded behind his head. His 'thinking mode', he had once told her. Right now, it was going to be his keeping-an-eye-on-the-potential-traitor mode, and she determined to don her best professional hat and ignore him completely.

The next two hours were painful. Candy, it transpired, was a friend of a friend of a girl Matt had dated four months previously, whom he had clearly met somewhere at some point and had stashed her name in that computer-bank memory of his for future reference.

Probably as a potential date down the line but now, remembering her qualifications, as secretary material.

She was bright enough and enthusiastic enough, but she also asked sufficient questions about Matt for Violet to guess that it wasn't going to be quite the boss-secretary relationship he needed. But, hey, if he'd come to the conclusion that having someone decorative around was worth more than having someone less glamorous but a whole lot more grounded, dedicated and, frankly, *qualified*, then good luck to him.

Candy had very long nails, painted a brazen shade of pink, and Violet idly wondered how they were going to fare on the keyboard of a computer. She wondered whether the frantic clicking of long nails on the keys would irritate her notoriously short-tempered boss and promptly decided that it was none of her business.

'You can scuttle off now,' Matt interrupted them when Violet was just about at the end of her tether. 'And I'm talking to Candy. You, Violet, are to stay a while longer.'

They both waited while Candy rustled her possessions together, talking all the while, breathless, bubbly and very much like the women he dated...

'I'm not sure she's the right one for the job,' was the first thing Violet said as soon as they were alone together back in Matt's office, and the outside door was firmly shut against wagging ears and prying eyes.

'Are you saying that because I've put your nose out of joint by ignoring your words of wisdom and not taking on board the suggestions you so very kindly made?' He swerved round his desk, sat down and then pointed for her to pull up the other chair. 'Maybe I fancy having someone open and honest and... What's the word I'm looking for...?'

'Not really up to anything too complicated?'

'Eye-catching.'

Violet flushed and looked away. That hurt but, damn it, she wasn't going to show it. She breathed deeply, gathered herself and met those navy-blue eyes coolly. 'Maybe you do and you and Candy will have a long and rewarding relationship,' she said. 'But maybe you'll end up having to siphon off loads of accounts to Maria because, quite honestly, Candy isn't going to get to grips with that stuff.'

'Damn it, Violet!' Matt roared, leaping up so suddenly that she started with surprise. 'Maybe...' He skirted round his desk to stand right in front of her, all alpha male and simmering anger. 'Just maybe I gave in to the temptation to have someone bloody straight-forward around for a change!'

'Keep your voice down!' But she was shaken because this was the first time he had ever raised his voice to her. He did it all the time. If someone fell short of his stratospherically high standards, he had no qualms in bellowing his disapproval. If he was frustrated, he was not averse to taking it out on inanimate objects.

But he had never directed his anger at her.

'Or else what? You forget that I own all of this!'

Violet looked down and didn't say anything, which seemed to infuriate him even more, because before she could start getting her thoughts together, before she could begin to make noises about clearing out her desk, he leant forward and gripped the arms of her chair, a suffocating presence that made her breath catch in her throat and sent all her thoughts flying through the window.

Her mind went completely blank. Her mouth went

dry. Her pupils dilated and hot colour rose in a tide in her cheeks.

She could breathe him in and the woody scent of whatever aftershave he used filled her nostrils until she wanted to pass out.

'Do you mind?' she gasped and he glowered at her.

'Yes, I bloody *do* mind! Straightforward Candy is going to be a breath of fresh air after you, and if she takes a while getting there with some of the more complex issues, then I can always call one of your recommendations into play. Either the granny or the happily married mother of three. Or maybe the guy who has a boyfriend safely tucked away on the home front! Maybe I'm looking forward to having someone around who doesn't think that it's a gross invasion of her privacy to spend five minutes telling me how her weekend has been! Or that she might have a famous father who used to tour the world!'

Violet felt faint before the full force of his accusing blue stare. She wanted to shrug off his anger, which was understandable, given his temperament, but instead she just felt as though she'd somehow let him down in ways that were unforgiveable.

After today, she wouldn't be seeing this man again. He had dominated her life for over two years, had given her focus. He had trusted her completely and promoted her way beyond her pay grade. He had treated her with respect and admiration and suddenly she didn't want to quit his employ under a black cloud.

She didn't want to leave him thinking the worst of her, thinking that she had it in her to betray the trust he had placed in her by doing a bunk with his client base.

But she had turned down the best job offer he could

have made, and to him that would have signified betrayal.

'You don't understand,' she protested, but without vigour.

'What don't I understand?'

'My life,' she said quietly. 'You don't understand my life. You have no idea what it was like to grow up with a rock-and-roll dad. You couldn't begin to comprehend how that made me the person I am today.' She was mortified at how personal the conversation had become, but she ploughed on anyway, knowing that it was her last day, her last hour probably, before she disappeared to the other side of the world.

Her head was lowered, but she could feel the force of his stare on her and it was hard to think. When she raised her eyes, they collided with his with shattering impact. His face was so close to hers that she could see the streaks of black against navy, the thick, lush fall of his lashes, the curve of his sensual mouth.

She was appalled by a sudden urge to reach out and stroke that lean, sinfully handsome face.

She balled her hands into fists and tried not to cower.

'I didn't accept your job offer because I want to make something of my music,' she continued in a barely audible whisper, nothing at all like her usual calm, composed, assured voice. 'I love playing the piano. I do it all the time. The piano was my constant in a life that was full of upheaval. Dad always felt guilty that it was a talent I never had the chance to develop, and he suggested that I try my hand at getting back into it when I'm over there. He knows people. I could give lessons. I'd enjoy that.' She took a deep breath and exhaled slowly. 'So there you have it, Matt.'

He drew back and stood up and, when he showed

no signs of returning to his chair, she pushed hers back and stood as well, her dainty, slender frame a striking contrast to his overpowering, in-your-face masculinity.

'I'll go and clear my desk.' She cleared her throat and shot him a glance from under her lashes before edging away towards the door dividing their work spaces.

'You do that,' he muttered, flushing and looking away.

He'd wanted to touch…and touching wasn't allowed. Even he knew that. But, by God, that urge had been suffocating just for a second.

'And, Matt…' She waited until he was looking at her. 'I'll miss…' *You. I'll miss you.* 'I'll miss working here more than I can ever say.'

CHAPTER FOUR

WOULD HE VISIT HER...?

Melbourne beckoned because, as he should have expected, there was no such thing as smooth sailing. At the eleventh hour, one of his little baby start-ups, nurtured tenderly for months, had come down with a potentially life-threatening condition and Matt had to go and pay a visit because no one else would be able to handle the situation.

But would he visit her?

She had been gone for six weeks and he'd kept in touch because, after all, they'd worked together as a team long enough for him to recognise that they had formed a bond, and besides, what if she returned to London? It would be tempting to rehire her because only now that she had disappeared he could see just how invaluable an asset she had been. More so than he could ever have expected. It was as though she had taken up permanent residence in some corner of his mind and had hunkered down to stay. So, hey, he could drop in...

After all, Never Kill Your Options had always been his motto.

She had replied to his emails as politely and remotely as if she had been sitting across from him in his office, fending off those personal questions she had always disliked being asked.

Yes, things were fine. Yes, her father was doing as well as could be expected. No, she had not reconsidered his job offer even though, yes, it would have been convenient as it was a mere half hour away from where she lived. The weather was good. The food was good. The people were friendly. The scenery was pleasing.

It piqued him to think that she hadn't glanced back to the life she'd left behind and, were it not for his attempts to keep in touch, she would have galloped merrily into the distance in a cloud of dust.

He would look her up. Aside from anything else, it would be interesting to meet her father. Who didn't enjoy meeting childhood idols?

Just out of curiosity, he'd put a few questions out there, asked around.

He'd been a fan of her father. The guy was well known. Even though he'd binned the touring a while back, people still knew who he was, and Matt had almost struck jackpot on question one.

Scott Dixon, one of the owners of his newly acquired start-up company, had waxed lyrical about Mickey Dunn, who was a familiar name in the music industry. He had recently set up his own small school for underprivileged, talented, budding musicians.

He was reportedly doing his first gig in six years at a hip, cool place in the heart of the city…with his daughter in attendance. As luck would have it, the gig coincided with when Matt would be there, sorting out his eleventh-hour road block. What were the chances?

He'd had a sudden image of Violet behind the scenes, always the carer, making sure her father didn't go wild. She would be dressed in her formal business attire and would probably be directing traffic with all the road-ies and fellow band members. He'd grinned fondly at the thought.

He'd debated whether to warn her of his arrival, and decided that he wouldn't, because who knew whether work would allow him time out to see her at all? Or even whether he *would* drop by. It could prove an awkward visit, best avoided. Rosy memories of his efficient secretary with the mystery background might be better left. After all, it wasn't as though theirs had been a social relationship.

Armed with a shed-load of preconceived notions of what he might find, Matt had not catered for what he would actually be faced with. He'd imagined a queue of polite golden oldies filtering into a venue that, despite what he'd been told, wouldn't be so much hip and cool as cultured and refined, befitting an ageing rocker who now ran a school for budding musicians.

Except, here he was now, and this wasn't what he'd expected. Standing at a distance with the balmy night enfolding him, Matt surveyed the throng of people queuing and entering the exclusive venue. There was some rather stunning graffiti on the brick wall of the nightclub and two bouncers at the door, as though at any moment some disreputable troublemaker might attempt to barge the queue without a ticket.

He joined it. He knew from his research it was the second day of a two-day gig and he had only managed to get hold of a ticket by the skin of his teeth. Who knew that there would be so many old rockers lining up for a taste of the past? But then, it seemed that Mickey Dunn was quite the local celebrity.

He would surprise Violet after the concert. He imagined her anxiously sitting backstage, perhaps from a vantage point where she could keep a watchful eye on her father, making sure a bottle of beer wasn't slipped to him by some well-intentioned groupie.

Matt was the last in. The club was exquisite, lots of exposed brick, long, oversized mirrors and some more graffiti. There were tables on either side of the room, raised on podiums, where dining happened. In the middle, it was standing room only. On the stage was a piano, the usual drums and a couple of guys with beards warming up. Not original band members but, from the tuning going on, Matt could tell that they were going to be pretty good.

His thoughts rambled. He felt invigorated, which surprised him, because until the very last minute he hadn't been entirely convinced he would pay his ex-secretary a visit. Even more surprisingly, he recalled that weird feeling that had seized him when he'd been about to leave her house, when he'd stared down at her and it had been as though the world had suddenly narrowed right down to just the two of them, and something strong and urgent had been calling out to him to touch her. The urge to cover her mouth with his had been overwhelming.

He'd resisted, but with extreme difficulty.

Touching her, kissing her, thinking about making love to her... That was the stuff of madness, and he'd had the sense to steer clear.

But the power of temptation had left him shaken. Why had that memory leapt out at him from nowhere?

He almost missed what was going on because his thoughts had taken off at such a delightfully taboo tangent.

He almost missed Mickey Dunn coming onto the stage to rapturous applause. And Jesus...

He straightened. He couldn't believe his eyes. He stared and his mouth fell open. From the back of the room—and even though at six foot two he towered over most of the audience there, so that his view was uninterrupted—he had to blink to process the sight of his prim and proper secretary dressed like a rocker.

He thought he might actually have made a choking sound under his breath. Surprise didn't begin to cover his reaction. Gone were the prissy outfits he was accustomed to seeing her in. Not even jeans were in evidence. She was wearing a pair of micro denim shorts, black tights, biker boots and a cropped top, and her shoulder-length hair was braided into two stunted pigtails. She looked incredibly sexy, and he wasn't the only guy captivated by the image, judging by the wolf whistles that greeted her appearance on stage.

Her father sat on a high stool with his guitar, with two band members in the background. She took up her position at the piano and…magic happened.

The world fell away as he listened to old ballads, the words of which he knew, and cover versions of a handful of well-known numbers. He couldn't peel his eyes away from Violet, so absorbed in that piano, oblivious to everything around her. They ended on a couple of the band's best-loved fast numbers, old rock hits that had the crowd chanting and singing along. Violet was into it, standing as she hit the notes on the piano, and every so often smiling across at her dad who grinned back at her.

Lots of perspiration, lots of noise, the roar of approval from the crowd, then it was over and the lights were going down, and Matt legged it to where he thought the dressing rooms would be.

If he'd had any doubts in his mind about showing up

here on the other side of the world, and making time to seek her out, then those doubts had been erased.

He'd never felt more alive.

He wondered what she would say. His mind was filled with the image of her, so stupendously sexy. Some small voice was telling him that that was something he'd always known, deep down.

She was sexy underneath the prim suits, the glossy bob and the calm, unflappable exterior. Some part of him had always recognised an inherent tug on his senses, although it had only made itself felt when he had looked down at her in her house and his head had begun to swim.

They almost collided.

He was heading at speed through the carpeted corridors at the back of the club and she was bolting in his direction. She screeched to a halt and her eyes widened with a mixture of shock and disbelief.

'Matt!'

'Surprise, surprise.' He shot her a crooked smile. He'd forgotten how weirdly deep and melodic her voice was and how slight she was compared to him. An ache spread through him that silenced him for a few seconds, then normal service resumed.

'I've had to fly over here on business. Damned start-up has run into a few thorny problems. I don't have to tell you how temperamental three untethered men in a small boat can be when a big liner shows up to bring them to shore. All sorts of sudden doubts. While I was here, thought I'd drop by and see how you were doing.' He paused. Her cheeks were flushed, her eyes bright. He wanted to touch those pigtails, see whether they were real, because it was so out of keeping.

Violet flung herself into his arms.

The move was so unexpected that Matt temporarily froze. Just like that, he was acutely aware of every small curve, the delicacy of her slender body and her small breasts pushing against him. He gingerly put his arms around her in a stilted gesture that was part comforting caress and part bewildered *what's going on here?* hug.

Bad move, a little voice was saying at the back of Violet's head. *Very bad move.*

She could feel the way he had suddenly turned to wood, and she guessed that he was probably horrified at this crazy display of emotion from his otherwise buttoned-up ex-secretary, but she was just so relieved to see him that she could have burst into tears.

She broke free and began dragging him back to the dressing room.

'I'm so glad you're here, Matt.'

'Violet, stop. What's going on?'

'It's Dad.'

'What about him?'

'He's collapsed.'

She was half running and at those words he began striding more purposefully towards the rooms at the back of the club. People had gathered outside one of the cubicles and he forged a way through them.

'Anyone call an ambulance?' he shouted, looking around and clicking his tongue impatiently because they all looked confused and blank-faced, like a herd of terrified sheep in search of a shepherd.

'I did,' a timid voice piped up.

Matt nodded. Mickey had been propped up against a cushion. He was grey, wheezing and perspiring.

In that moment, Matt did what he did best—he took charge, and Violet watched.

She watched with blessed relief as he single-handedly

cleared the room, having ascertained that no one with any medical know-how was available. He confiscated several phones from gawpers trying to capture the chaos on camera and, surprisingly, the phones were surrendered without protest. Such was the power of his personality.

She was shaking like a leaf as she knelt next to her father, stroking his hair away from his face. He wore a ponytail. She'd told him often enough that he was way too old for that style, but he'd steadfastly ignored her, and now seeing that ponytail in disarray was somehow heart-rending.

The ambulance arrived with paramedics and everything became a blur of activity.

'Want me in the ambulance with you?' Matt asked, cupping the nape of her neck and looking at her, and she nodded mutely. 'Good. But first…' He removed his jacket, laid it over her shoulders and shot her a crooked smile. 'Your outfit is great on stage, but you might be a bit self-conscious wearing it in a hospital setting.'

It was a gesture so touching that she couldn't speak for a few seconds, then off they hurried, out to the waiting ambulance that wailed its way towards the hospital.

'I feel so helpless,' she whispered once her father had been whisked away and they were left standing in a room on their own like a couple of spare parts deprived of purpose.

She clutched at the jacket and dabbed her eyes with her knuckles. She hadn't even asked what he was doing here! He'd appeared as if by magic, and it just felt right that he was standing here now in all his magnificence, a rock in a sudden storm.

He was dressed as he always was, in dark jeans, a dark long-sleeved tee shirt and loafers. Casual and effortlessly elegant.

God, how had she managed to forget just how stupendously good-looking he was? How tall? How achingly sexy? She'd replied to his emails as briefly and as politely as she could, firmly believing that the faster she broke off contact with him, the faster her head would stop filling up with images that made her think she was losing her mind with missing him.

He was staring at her with concern and she chewed on her lip.

'Tell me what happened,' Matt urged.

'I wish I knew. He looked a bit peaky this morning, and I told him that if he didn't feel right we should call the gig off, but he insisted, and when my dad gets something in his mind he's an unstoppable force. But I knew he wasn't feeling well. I could tell every time he looked at me that he wasn't right.' Her eyes welled up. 'I know my dad so well. We should have called it quits long before the end. I should have insisted. Now… *What if he dies?*'

'He won't.'

'How do you know?'

'Because I have a hotline to the big guy up there.' He smiled and Violet reluctantly smiled back and began to relax a little.

It was amazing just how calm his presence made her feel.

'I'm being feeble,' she ventured shakily. 'What a coincidence that you're here. I hope the stuff with the start-up gets sorted.'

'Forget that. Let's focus on what matters. Your father. You go and sit down over there and I'll get you a cup of coffee, even though a good shot of whisky would probably be more helpful. And then I'll hunt down a doctor or a nurse or a consultant and find out what's going on.'

He was guiding her gently towards one of the chairs lined up against the wall like soldiers in formation. She obediently sat down. This, she knew, was a side to her he would never have seen. The side that wasn't efficient, professional or calm under stress. The side that was currently wearing next to nothing under the jacket that thankfully he had given her.

She was vulnerable and tearful. She just wanted to lean on him and let him take over because she felt scared and fragile.

He appeared with a coffee, and then disappeared almost as quickly, and when he next returned he knelt in front of her and tilted her chin so that their eyes met. Deep blue tangled with sherry brown.

'First of all, he's going to be fine.'

Violet closed her eyes briefly to control the emotion that single sentence had evoked. 'Did...did the doctor say that?'

Matt smiled. 'One doctor, a consultant and the chart which I insisted on inspecting. He's got, of all things, pneumonia. They're going to have to keep him in for at least a week and monitor all his vitals, but the general consensus is that he's going to be fine.'

'Stress.' The words were wrenched out of her. 'It's all been building up. I should have paid more attention, but my dad has always been good at hiding what he doesn't want anyone to see. He's been busy with a music school he started and then all the underlying worries about his health. He looked a bit peaky, and I know he seemed to be resting quite a bit, but...'

'No point in looking back over what you could or couldn't have done. Bottom line is that there's nothing you can do here right now. He's sedated at the moment. I'm going to take you back to your house.'

'No, it's not necessary. I'm perfectly capable of—'

'You're not and I am returning you safe and in one piece back to your house. You can don the secretarial hat another time. Right now, I'm in charge.'

Those words were like manna from heaven. She allowed herself to be gently led out of the hospital, as gently as if she were the patient and not her father. She was allowed to look in on him, make sure that he was okay, but that was about it, even though she would have set up camp next to his bed if she could.

She and Matt had arrived in an ambulance and now they headed back to her father's house in a taxi. The house sat on a magnificent plot of well-manicured lawn, a two-storeyed concrete-and-glass building with both indoor and outdoor swimming pools and a dedicated recording studio where her father spent a great deal of his time tinkering on his guitar, composing.

'Nice,' was the only comment Matt made. The drive had been silent but the silence had been companionable and now, as the taxi swerved into the drive and pulled up in front of the house, Violet suddenly felt a swell of panic.

'Don't worry,' Matt murmured, pushing open the car door but turning to look at her gravely for a few seconds. 'I'm not going to leave you until I know that you're all right—and don't tell me that you're all right. You're not.'

They entered a house that was a tasteful palette of creams and greys, interspersed with abstract art on the walls and colourful silk rugs on the marble floor. She could feel his presence alongside her and, whilst she didn't want him to go, not really, neither did she want him to stay.

She turned and their eyes collided, and her breath suddenly hitched in her throat.

'I feel so tired,' she murmured, fidgety all of a sudden. She couldn't peel her eyes from him. She was still wearing his jacket and she politely reached to hand it over to him. 'And you're wrong. I'm fine. Just exhausted. You don't need to stay here and babysit me.'

'Maybe I want to,' Matt murmured, his midnight-blue eyes guarded. 'I saw a different Violet Dunn before you left.' His voice roughened. 'I'm seeing an even more different one now.'

'I apologise,' Violet said stiffly. Her eyes skittered away from his face, but nothing could hide the rapid beating of her heart.

'For being human?'

The amused wryness of his voice would have been bad enough, but even more dangerously seductive was the touch of his hand against her cheek.

She curved her head, and it was such a simple, instinctive gesture, but it opened up the lid of that box she had kept so very firmly shut for over two years.

He lowered his head as she raised hers and the kiss was somehow inevitable.

The feel of his mouth over hers was electrifying. She'd been plugged into a live socket and every racing nerve in her body was suddenly and wonderfully sensitised in ways that were unimaginable.

She drew back, but reluctantly. Her body wanted more, but common sense recognised the need to slam shut the door that had been unexpectedly opened.

She couldn't meet his eyes and she stared down at the biker boots.

'What's going on?' she whispered. When she looked

up at him, her brown eyes were filled with dismay and apprehension.

Matt raked his fingers through his hair. 'I'm asking myself the same thing,' he said gruffly.

'You should go.'

'Should I?'

Violet stared up at him. She wanted those lips on hers again so badly that it was a physical ache, spreading from her toes to her scalp and sending a wave of forbidden lust coursing through her.

It was the situation, all that pent-up tension desperate to find release, and Matt standing here was temptation beyond endurance. But, if ever a mistake were staring her in the face, then this was surely it.

She might not be his secretary over here, but she would be foolish to think that that made no difference.

Yet those lips… Firm and cool and so, so wonderfully sensual. And the way her body responded… It was as though she had discovered a network of nerves and tingling sensations she had never known she possessed.

'Matt…' Her voice was helpless and fizzled out into a strangled choke as he traced the outline of her mouth with one lazy finger. She caught his finger with her hand but the slight tremor was a giveaway that control wasn't completely within her grasp. 'This isn't what we're about.'

'You no longer work for me, Violet. You're shaken. I get that. If you want me to leave, then say the word and I'm gone. Want that?'

'Of course I do,' she said weakly.

'I want to kiss you. You have the most tempting lips I've ever seen.'

'Funny, you've never said anything like that before,' she muttered, her skin burning.

'Would you have wanted me to?' Matt mused.

'Of course not!'

'You were like a cat on a hot tin roof the minute anything remotely personal left my lips.' He caught her hand in his and lowered his head to trail his tongue over her mouth. 'I would never have put you in the uncomfortable position of dealing with any advances from me. I was your boss and I have a lot of respect for what that entails. I'm not your boss here.'

No, she thought, he wasn't. And that opened all sorts of doors, all of which should remain very firmly shut.

The guy didn't do relationships and, when it came to guys, she needed the sort who did. She needed stability. In all areas of her life. She needed roots that could be put down and a guy who was willing to put those roots down with her. She wasn't frivolous or flighty and, whether he said that he was attracted to her or not, he didn't do serious. She should know. She'd seen his approach to relationships first-hand.

But her heart was beating very fast and her lips were tingling, along with everywhere else in her treacherous body.

'I'm all shaken up,' she muttered. She determined to listen to common sense because common sense was always right. 'Thank you for dropping me back and for... for coming with me in the ambulance.'

Matt shifted back and looked down at her with brooding intensity, his fabulous eyes veiled.

'I bet you didn't think that you would end up being flung around in the back of an ambulance when you decided to pay me a visit this evening.' This was more like it, she thought as self-control began to reassert itself and those unsettling, frightening feelings of helplessness started to recede. She couldn't quite meet his eyes but her voice was normal and habits of a lifetime were settling back into place.

So she'd kissed him!

What of it? Everyone was entitled to a moment of madness and she never, not once in her entire life, had had a moment of madness.

'Would you like a…a coffee?' She nodded in the direction of the kitchen and began walking towards it—half hoping that he would say a polite goodbye and head off, disturbing kiss firmly forgotten, half hoping that he would follow her into the kitchen, because this tingling, scary as it was, was also so wonderfully, tantalisingly exciting.

'That would be very nice.' Matt followed her into a high-tech kitchen where the only signs of occupation were the plates and cups draining on a metal draining board by the sink.

'Again. Thank you for being there for me this evening.' His eyes were on her. She could feel it. She tried not to focus on the fact that she was wearing an outfit best suited for a raunchy fancy-dress party. He wasn't her boss here and she certainly wasn't his secretary, and common sense only very thinly managed to plaster over that fact.

'There's no need to thank me, Violet,' Matt said drily. 'I'm very happy that I was there for you, although I'm sure you would have had your pick of volunteers for the role of shoulder to cry on.'

'What do you mean?' She glanced round at him, startled, and then handed him his mug of coffee, strong and black just as he liked it, and settled into the chair, facing him with relief.

'I mean you had a very appreciative audience. I'm guessing you heard the roars of approval when you walked in.'

'My father has a lot of fans still left.' She blushed furiously and sipped some of her own piping-hot coffee.

'I'll let that one go, but you know exactly what I mean. You looked the part. How are you doing over here? Your emails back to the home front are stunningly lacking in detail.'

Violet reddened further. Of course, he wouldn't know the effect he had always had on her, so would never guess that the paucity of her responses had all been tied in with her just trying to forget about him, which was the healthy way forward.

'I'm doing very well, Matt. Very busy.'

'With your father's school?'

'How did you know about that?'

'I have friends in high places.' His dark eyes were watchful as he sipped the coffee and he stole a look at her from under his lashes. 'I asked around, just out of curiosity. Your father has quite the reputation over here. Seems the bad boy of yesterday has become a pillar of the community.'

Violet smiled, relaxing, because this was the Matt she was so familiar with—a guy of such abundant, lazy charm that it had never been any source of wonder for her that he could attract women without having to lift a finger or make an effort.

'I'm not sure he would be comfortable with the *pillar of the community* moniker. He still likes to think that he's got a wild side left in him.'

'He's certainly still got the talent,' Matt observed. 'You played well together.'

'Were you surprised?'

'It's fair to say that pretty much everything about you surprises me,' he murmured.

She shifted and harked back to how he had reacted when he had seen where she lived, discovered a past he had never suspected—that fleeting look of betrayal on his face.

She wondered whether the fact that she had surprised him accounted for that kiss. She wasn't the woman he had categorised as his predictable secretary with no personal life to speak of. She'd broken out of the convenient mould and exposed a side to her that had taken him by surprise—and surprise, for a man like Matt Falconer, might prove a very enticing proposition. And then tonight, vulnerable and in her hour of need, she had revealed yet more about herself, as he had pointed out.

Could she, suddenly and unexpectedly, have provided an element of novelty that had roused the interest of a man drawn to the same type of woman?

Violet knew that she would be better off not giving house room to seditious thoughts. The more she tried to analyse the situation, and the raging fire that had ignited between them with such shocking speed, the more her thoughts kept returning to the feel of his mouth on hers and the responses it had generated.

Dangerous.

'You should go.' She dumped the cup on the table and abruptly rose to her feet. 'I probably won't see you again before you leave and I...er... I hope your trip over here proves successful.'

'Is this the bit where we shake hands and pretend we're strangers?' But there was amusement in his voice and, when he rose to his feet, he moved just a little too close to her for comfort. 'I've got a few days left here, Violet, and I wouldn't dream of leaving you to manage by yourself while your father remains in hospital. You can count on me. It's what any good ex-boss would do...'

CHAPTER FIVE

TRUE TO HIS word about not leaving her to manage for herself—a sweeping statement that had filled her with dread—Matt turned up at eight the following morning. Violet had already been up for an hour and was pointlessly pottering around the house, waiting for the hours to slip by before she could go to the hospital and visit her father.

'He's out of the woods,' she had been told when she had telephoned for information at six that morning. 'But he's heavily sedated and won't be able to respond to visitors for at least a couple of days. The body can take only so much stress and I suspect your father has been ignoring warning signs for a number of weeks now.'

She would go and sit by her heavily sedated father, she decided, even if he was sleeping and out of it.

She couldn't bear the thought of twiddling her thumbs. All the caring instincts that had been her faithful companions for so many years had risen to the surface. She almost felt guilty that her father had collapsed in such a dramatic fashion. Surely, she should have been able to see the signs of something more serious than him looking a little peaky? She should never have been swayed by his hearty reassurances that the concert should go ahead, even if he was a bit under the weather.

All this was in her head when she pulled open the door to find Matt standing outside, lounging against the door frame, his blue eyes keenly observant as she gaped at him.

'What are you doing here?' Instinctively, she touched her mouth with her fingers, an unconscious gesture as she remembered the power of that kiss they had shared. She dropped her hand and gathered herself but her skin was prickling all over and her face was red. She had been very grateful for his presence the day before, when everything had been in turmoil and her nerves had been shattered, but in the cold light of day, alarm bells were ringing in her head.

They had kissed.

They had broken a barrier that had been firmly in place for years. Now, out here, it was all a muddle and his presence on her doorstep was the last thing she felt she could deal with.

'I've brought you breakfast.' Like a magician, he whipped a bag out from behind him and dangled it in front of her. 'Thought you might not have eaten.'

'Matt...' she dithered, self-conscious in her cut-off jeans and small, faded tee shirt. She recalled the outfit of the evening before and shuddered. 'There was no need for you to come and check up on me. I'm very grateful that you were around yesterday, but Dad's settled, and I'll be fine.'

Matt looked at her with brooding interest.

Point taken, if he were being honest. There was no need for him to be here, standing on her doorstep with a bag of bread in his hand. He was no one's knight in shining armour, and he didn't do rescuing of damsels in distress, but yesterday...

Yesterday had been a revelation.

He'd gone to that concert as a token nod to the boss-secretary relationship they had successfully shared for over two years. Admittedly, he had been curious to see how she was faring. First and foremost, he was here on business, but she had departed British shores a slightly different person from the one he had boxed, labelled and filed away. And, yes, he had been curious to see how Violet Dunn Mark Two was doing on the other side of the world. That was the story he had spun to himself and he was sticking to it.

When she'd walked out onto that podium and sat at the piano, he'd stopped breathing. The crowded room had melted away and he had only had eyes for a woman who had shed the chrysalis and emerged a butterfly.

And then, to compound the impression, he had seen her without her customary veneer of efficiency and self-control. He'd seen her vulnerable and dependent and the combination had kick-started something inside him that had...brought him right here to her door. With a bag of bread.

'Are you going to ask me in?' He lightly rested his hand on the door. Violet sighed and stepped aside as he brushed past her into the house, heading directly to the kitchen like a man with a purpose.

'Tell me how your father is doing,' he threw over his shoulder as he dumped the bag of bread on the table and spun round to look at her.

Violet watched, noting the way he automatically took charge, the way he dominated and owned the space around him, the way he took her breath away—especially now, when she could no longer depend on the natural divide of him being her employer. They were standing here in this kitchen as equals and it was disconcerting.

To lessen the tension building inside her, she picked up the bread and began busying herself with plates and some mugs for coffee, directing him to a chair so that he could sit down and not tower above her in a way that made her nerves jangle.

'He's resting.' She wasn't looking at him but she was very conscious of the waves of intense masculinity he was exuding. She marvelled that she had been able successfully to withstand his physical impact for all the time she had worked for him, but then again a starched suit and patent pumps had been excellent deterrents for the devastating effects of her volatile boss. Jeans and a tight tee shirt were proving a flimsy barrier, and the memory of that kiss was the icing on the cake.

She produced a plate with some of the crusty bread on it, dumped some preserves and a mug of coffee in front of him and stood back, her body language polite but unwelcoming. And he knew it. She could see that in his shrewd, amused eyes as he briefly looked at her before diving into the bread, lathering it with some of the wild lime marmalade she loved.

'Understandable,' Matt commented neutrally.

'I'm going to visit him…' she glanced at her watch '…very soon.'

'I'm guessing he's going to be out of it for a while.'

Violet narrowed her eyes and wondered whether he had somehow managed to prise information about her father's condition out of the hospital.

'I'm surprised,' she said, hurriedly changing the subject, 'that you're not at work. I know you've always liked an early start.'

'So much you know about me,' Matt drawled, voice lazy, amused, intimate. 'Your successor, capable though he is, lacks your intuitive feel for my movements.'

'It's something that comes with time,' she said briskly.

'But, of course, you make a valid point. I do enjoy an early start. My early starts, however, appear to have hit a brick wall with the guys here. Their preferred day starts at ten.'

'Tough.' Violet tried to hide a sudden smile because he had always been impatient with anyone who didn't view rising with the larks as a golden opportunity to brainstorm or catch up on emails.

'Isn't it? Although,' he said pensively, 'it did mean that I could drop by here with this bread. Excellent bread, by the way, and I like the jam.' He turned the bottle in his hands and inspected the label before dumping it back on the table. 'Also means that I could take you to the hospital to see your father, and I've had some thoughts on the rest of the day.'

Violet's mouth dropped open and she looked at him in consternation.

'You're going to tell me that there's no need.' He waved his hand dismissively. 'But it's not an issue. I'm more than happy to be of help in this hour of need for you. You've spent many an overnighter with me, burning the midnight oil and ploughing through reams of legal paperwork that needed to meet a deadline. Never a complaint. So don't even think for one moment that this will be putting me out.'

Since Violet had not been thinking any such thing, she could only continue to gape at him in silence, temporarily lost for words.

As was his way, he had brought his own picnic to the

party and was happy barrelling ahead with his game plan. Which was… What, exactly? What thoughts did he have for the rest of the day?

She quailed.

'Here's my plan,' Matt told her crisply, the consummate professional now, which should have been reassuring but somehow wasn't. He pushed his plate to one side and tilted his head to look at her appraisingly. 'We go to the hospital so that we can find out how your father is doing.'

'We? *We?*' Violet parroted faintly.

'You were in meltdown yesterday,' Matt pointed out. 'And there's nothing wrong with that, Violet. There's nothing wrong with having to lean on someone else now and again.'

Violet wondered whether she was now occupying a parallel universe. Since when had Matt Falconer ever prided himself on being a man that a woman in a meltdown could lean on? She opened her mouth tactfully to point that out, but he was gathering momentum, leaning forward so that he could direct the full blast of his concentration on her as he finished what he had to say.

'You probably won't want to admit it, but you will have woken up this morning just as anxious as you would have been when your head hit that pillow last night.'

'Don't be ridiculous.' She had, but she was sticking to the brief, because if she strayed too far from it—and kissing him the night before in a moment of weakness definitely qualified for that—then who knew what might happen? She felt faint when her brain started travelling down that road and she very firmly put the brake on it.

'I don't need you to hold my hand, Matt. I'm perfectly capable of dealing with this situation on my own.'

'Are you? Or are you just saying that because that's the persona you've always cultivated?'

'Don't try to psychoanalyse me,' Violet said sharply.

'Why?' He looked at her narrowly. 'So the boot, for once, is on the other foot. Why don't you relax and enjoy it?'

'I'm not your responsibility.' She bristled and shot him a fulminating glance from under her lashes. 'And,' she posed tartly, 'since when have you ever seen psychoanalysing any woman as something to put on your list of good deeds for the day?'

Matt grinned. 'I miss that. The way you can make me laugh. Most men would be cut down at the knees by that sharp tongue of yours, but it's always done wonders for my frame of mind. Moving on, though. We go to the hospital, where it would be pointless for you to sit around watching your dad while he rests. So my plan is to take you to the company, and you can dive in and help me wade through these last-minute stumbling blocks.'

'You want me to *work* with you?'

'Do you have other plans for the day?'

'Yes. No. I might.'

'Mixed messages going on here, so I'll interpret it myself and say that you have no plans except visiting your father and getting yourself knotted up, wondering if you could have done something to prevent it.'

He slapped his thighs and rose to his feet. 'Some healthy distraction would work wonders for you and, as a bonus, you'd be doing me a favour. I hadn't planned on coming over here, at least not at this point in time, and there's more ego stroking, fine-tuning of detail and soothing than I'd banked on. The guys who run this show are like kids, and their paperwork, now that it's all been excavated for inspection, is in total chaos.' He looked at her seriously. 'It would help having you there, Violet. We've always worked well together. No reason why you can't take some time out to help me out now. And it would get your mind off things.'

'I will need to go to the hospital. My dad will need me as soon as he's out. I can't just drop these responsibilities to help you out.'

'At least a week,' Matt told her without preamble and she blinked and looked at him, confused. 'To clarify, I took the liberty of phoning his consultant. I thought I would come here the bearer of glad tidings. In times of stress, sometimes it takes a third party to look at things through independent eyes. You can count on me to be those independent eyes on your behalf.'

'You took the liberty of phoning the consultant?'

'Your father will be recuperating in hospital for at least a week, possibly a bit longer. He's in a private ward with the best possible care, but his overall health has been compromised over the years, so recovery will take slightly longer than might have been the case for someone younger and stronger.'

'You phoned and asked for an update on my dad?'

'No need to thank me. I thought you might be nervous doing it yourself. Bottom line, he's drugged up to the eyeballs at the moment and on a drip. He won't really be conscious of you being there at his side, at least not for the time being. He certainly won't be up for lengthy visiting and I doubt the hospital would encourage it. They want their patient to build his strength up, and he's sure to feel guilty about what happened if you're there 24/7 holding his hand and peering anxiously into his face.'

Speechless, Violet stared at him. 'You can't just appear on my doorstep and start micromanaging my life, Matt!'

'No, but I can provide healthy distraction.' He paused. 'Unless you have more pressing options, then I'm at a loss as to why you won't take me up on this offer. In a week, I'll be gone and you can carry on with your life here and your father should be back at home. You can devote all your attention to him then. In the meantime, where's the harm in burying your very justifiable worries into something productive and challenging?'

Where indeed? was what Violet thought ten days later. He had said that he would be in Melbourne for a week. His dulcet tones, and tantalising offer to take her mind off the horror of her father being rushed into hospital and all the attendant worry that went with that, had seduced her into doing as he'd asked.

Besides, she missed her job. She missed the adrenaline rush and the frantic pace of life. She missed being kept intellectually stretched. She loved her music, and enjoyed the freedom of being able to devote time to it—to help with the foundation her father had set up to give help, tuition and lessons to gifted kids—but she still missed the intellectual rush she had always felt working for Matt.

She'd agreed to work with him, safe in the knowledge that his time in the country would be limited. One week and he'd be off. That had been three days ago and counting.

Admittedly, there was a lot to do. They got stuck in. The very brainy, gifted but juvenile owners of the start-up had to be yanked down to earth at frequent intervals.

Their lawyers were all university friends and conversation went off-piste at an alarming rate. Violet, attuned to Matt's personality, was adept at guessing when he was being pushed to the limits, and she liked being able to step in and defuse potentially awkward situations.

In between all the captivating, time-consuming and thorny issues that had to be untangled, Violet went to see her father. Sometimes Matt came with her and she was ashamed to find that she enjoyed those visits. Her father came alive in Matt's presence, opening up to his charm and his obvious enthusiasm for the rock history that defined him.

And they'd gone sightseeing. A little, here and there. Perfectly normal—except she was uneasily aware that they weren't a 'normal' couple, taking in the sights.

'I'm pretty happy to do my own thing,' he'd shrugged on the first night. 'I'm staying at one of the Hyatt hotels. There's a bar. Food will be available. I'm perfectly capable of lending a helping hand to people when it comes to getting them to talk to me.'

Violet could believe that. The man could charm anyone.

She was working with him, quite out of the blue, and that was one thing. It was quite another thing to start socialising with him, but the lines between them were now so blurred. And she was enjoying his company. She had forgotten how witty he could be. She'd not really made any friends out here and it was nice having an escort. One dinner became two, and two merged into three, and she began blanking out the issue of his departure, not wanting to think about it.

It felt good to talk about her dad. When she talked about him, surprisingly she found herself talking about her past, lulled into confidences that would never have happened when she had been working for Matt in London.

'I like the new Violet Dunn,' he had murmured the night before when he had seen her to her front door and had been about to take his polite leave, as he always did. 'Long may she live.' His eyes had rested on her, hooded and lingering, sending a shiver of racing excitement skittering through her.

She hadn't forgotten that kiss. It was never mentioned. But it had lodged there in her head like a burr, escalating feelings inside her that made her feel as though she were on a rollercoaster ride, soaring up and swooping down so that her stomach was constantly flipping over.

Now at six thirty in the evening, with business finally reaching a satisfactory conclusion and signatures all on paper, they were relaxing in one of the coolest bars in Melbourne. The curved walls were simply bottles of alcohol upon bottles of alcohol on glass shelves, and the lighting was mellow and subdued. They were sitting in two turquoise chairs, facing one another, and as yet the place was uncrowded.

'You've been invaluable.'

Violet blushed. She guiltily thought of all the other non-business entertainment they had enjoyed. At first, it had been hard to overcome her ingrained reticence, but it had been stupidly easy to move on from that place and to start enjoying his company. Way too easy.

'Thank you,' she replied huskily, then added tentatively, 'You were right. It's done me good. Taken my mind off…everything. And with Dad coming back home tomorrow and in such a good place, thanks to your bracing chats and positive encouragement, well, all told it was a good idea. And I've enjoyed getting back into the swing of working to a deadline.'

'The offer still stands,' Matt drawled. 'There's still work to be done now that the takeover has been completed. It wouldn't have to be a permanent situation. A few weeks, no more.'

Violet thought of having a link remain between them—exchanging emails, hearing his voice down the end of a line, even if the conversation was work-related.

'It's fine.' She smiled politely and bid a mental farewell to her momentary weakness. She remembered why she had known that walking away would be for the best. She remembered those stirrings of attraction she had felt, the way he had consumed her thoughts.

'In which case, this...' he raised his whisky glass in salute '...will be our last drink shared. I leave tomorrow. Been here slightly longer than anticipated, but needs must.'

She kept on smiling, but suddenly the bottom of the world had dropped from beneath her. She hated it. Hated the surge of fear that swept over her in a tidal wave. Fear of the void he was going to be leaving behind.

'Of course. I'm surprised no one's sent a jet over to ferry you back.'

Matt looked at her steadily, slightly twirling his glass between his fingers.

'I wouldn't have taken the ride back,' he murmured softly.

'Too much work to get through?'

'All Work and No Play has always been my motto. The play here has been too enjoyable for me to have accepted an early ferry back to base camp.'

'What do you mean?'

'You, Violet. I mean you.'

There was a potent, masculine charm he always reserved for women. She had never been in the firing line of that charm. She was now, and she licked her lips, nerves stretched to breaking point. There was no point asking him what he meant because she knew what he meant. She'd known it for a while, had sensed the frisson of electricity between them, had enjoyed it.

'This is my last night here and I'm going to put all my cards on the table. I want you. I want to go to bed with you.' He relaxed back in the chair, watching her over the rim of his glass as he sipped the amber liquid. They could have been casually talking about the weather.

'I…'

'One night,' he murmured. 'And then I'm gone. I don't want for ever. I don't even want tomorrow. But tonight… That I do want.'

Violet could hear her heart beating hard like a drum and the blood pounding in her ears.

One night. It was such a tantalising thought.

'Just tonight,' she whispered, barely able to meet his eyes.

'You know I don't do for ever.' He paused. 'I don't speak that language and I never will. No permanence, no cosy family life, no pitter-patter of tiny feet.' He had a rare moment of introspection, thinking of his own dysfunctional family life, of his parents, uniting two wealthy families, a complicated union involving assets and holdings. His father's grand country estate had needed his mother's lavish wealth. He had brought class to the table and she had brought hard cash. A perfect union on paper, but in practice, as he had grown from boy to man, what he had seen was the reality of a loveless marriage, and how a loveless marriage made for an unloved child.

'He'll never take over the estate,' his father had once said. Standing outside the formal living room, the fourteen-year-old Matt had paused and listened, every muscle in his body tensing at the dismissive tone of his father's voice. He had heard the clinking of glasses as they had drunk the sherry they always drank at exactly the same time very evening, brought to them by the butler.

'The boy doesn't want to have anything to do with the land. Might just as well not have had the little blighter for all the good he will do when it comes to perpetuating this legacy. Bloody disappointment.'

He'd wondered then whether his cold, silent parents would have stayed together had they never had him. Would they have gone their separate ways and searched for more than life had dished out for them? He hadn't stayed to hear his mother's response but something inside, already toughened over the years, had crystallised into ice.

If his parents were what marriage was all about, then he would always be better off without it. Sure, he knew that there were families out there who interacted and looked out for one another, but he'd never had that. Not only had he come to the conclusion that that sort of emotion was beyond his remit, but it was something he had no intention of seeking out. He'd stopped looking for parental approval, even though the search had pretty much ended long before then, and had devoted his life to doing what he loved and what he was good at. The land and the estate could go to any one of his useless cousins. He didn't give a damn.

Hell, where had *that* come from? Frowning, he slammed the door shut on memories he had little time for. He'd moved on from there.

'Sex, Violet,' he said roughly. 'One night. I want to make your body sing.'

She wasn't aware of nodding. This wasn't romance. What it was, was irresistible. Fantasy could become reality, a few hours of stolen bliss. How could she refuse? The prospect of playing with fire had never felt so good. She was barely aware of finishing her drink and making her way back with him to the house. She was a different person and everything around her was different. Somehow altered.

Everything changed when they were standing outside her front door. Outside, night was a black velvet throw covering the world, capturing them in a bubble of heightened intimacy.

The trip back to the house had been a silent one, charged with anticipation. They had held hands in the taxi and Violet had felt sick with excitement. Now there was a thrilling urgency as he nudged open the front door with his foot and, before they could step inside the house and into a bedroom, he swept her into his arms and kissed her. A long, hungry, demanding crush of mouth on mouth.

She reached up and curved her hands around his neck. He was forbidden territory... She shouldn't be doing this, but then hard on the heels of that thought came another—she no longer worked for him—and, just like that, freed from the captivity of being his employee, and suffused with release from the tension that had gripped her ever since her father had been rushed to hospital, she freely gave herself to the thrill of the unknown.

He swept her up in his arms and began searching for a bedroom, heading up the stairs and pausing only to peer briefly into the rooms he walked past until he landed on hers.

He didn't bother switching on any lights, but the curtains were pulled back and the moon was sending slivers of silver into the bedroom.

'I can't believe we're doing this,' Violet thought out loud. She looked around at the familiarity of the room she had made her own since moving to Melbourne. She had brought over her most treasured score sheets and recordings of her favourite classical tracks, some by obscure but brilliant pianists. Aside from a handful of personal touches, the room was anodyne—pale-grey walls, a mirrored dressing table and cool, high-gloss fitted furniture.

'No? I thought it was pretty obvious over the past few days where I stood on the subject of wanting you...'

He had lowered her and now they stood, facing one another in the darkened room.

'It feels like we're breaking all the rules. I'm hardly your type. You shouldn't be wanting this.' She thought of the blondes who cluttered his life and she thought of herself, so serious, so adamant that there was no room in her life for a guy like Matt Falconer.

'Here's what I don't want,' Matt responded gruffly, 'I don't want you to think that I'm trying to take advantage of you because you're in a vulnerable place right now. That's what I don't want.'

'That didn't even cross my mind.'

'Good. And don't think that I don't fancy you. Trust me, I've never wanted someone more.' He guided her hand to his erection and Violet nearly passed out from the surge of terrifying, overwhelming craving that rolled through her like a tsunami, inexorably obliterating every single shred of doubt in its path.

He was so hard beneath the jeans and she was wet between her legs, hot, wet and aching for him.

And scared as well.

Scared because she had never done this before…and her inexperience was like a weight on her shoulders, stifling her desire.

She placed flat hands against his chest and breathed in deeply. She was shaking as she found herself propelled back towards the bed and, when her knees hit the side of the mattress, she sank down with relief and he sat next to her.

'God, Violet. Maybe you're right.' His voice was terse and he raked his fingers through his hair. 'Maybe this is madness. Tell me if this madness is something you can deal with.'

Don't look for involvement. That was what she heard in that statement. *Make sure you can deal with me walking away.*

'Don't go.' She circled his wrist with her fingers and thrilled at the latent strength there. She wanted to strip off her clothes. She wanted him to touch her so much that her whole body ached with it. 'It's just that…'

'You don't know which way to turn? Understandable.' Because she was what she was, he thought, and that was what made this so exciting.

'I'm a virgin,' she said in a rush before a lengthy guessing game could begin. 'I know you're going to be shocked. It's shocking. You want to know why. Well, it's because sex was never something that seemed to crop up. You once said that something got sacrificed when I became a carer. Well, for me that was normality. A life on the road and then being responsible for dad when I was young… Well, there you go. You should know.'

She looked away, but slowly, by his finger under her chin, she was made to look at him.

'You're a virgin.'

Her smile and calm voice belied the tumult of emotions coursing through her. 'We do exist. In fact, I like to think we're pretty special.'

'Will you let me be the first?' And, when she smiled and inclined her head to one side, he began removing his clothes, taking his time, completely unashamed, watching her as he undressed.

Violet propped herself up and stared. He was so beautiful. The fact that the forbidden was turning into reality was such a turn-on. She wanted to touch herself and balled her hands into fists. This felt right. There was a tenderness between them that made her want to give herself over to this man without inhibition, with complete trust and in defiance of the fact that she had never thought she would have her first experience of sex with any man who wasn't in it for the long term.

And this wasn't about her feeling fragile because of circumstances, either. This was something she had been craving for a very long time, something that had brushed like a feather through her mind every time they'd been together in his office late at night... Every time he had come close to her, had leant over from behind to see something on her computer... Every time his lazy glance had settled on her...

His nakedness, oh, so slowly revealed, staggered her. His beauty. His strength. The width of his shoulders, the breadth of his chest tapering to a narrow waist and lean hips. Her eyes followed the spiral of dark hair and her heart sped up at the sight of his erect, gently throbbing penis. He took it absently in one hand and played with himself while keeping his eyes focused on her.

He was so uninhibited.

She was eager and ready as he approached her. Fear of the unknown still lingered, but excitement to explore it was greater, and her body went up in flames as he undressed her, stilling her fluttering hands, very gently easing her to a place where she didn't feel self-conscious at being observed.

He made her look at him and he talked as he removed her clothing with practised ease, his hands gentle.

When she covered her small breasts with her hands, he tugged them away and lay down next to her, idly toying with her body, smoothing his big hand along her stomach, her thigh, brushing his knuckles against her wet crotch until she wanted to spread her legs wide so that he could do more.

'I'm going to take my time,' he murmured.

'Matt...'

'Shh. Just relax and enjoy, Violet.' He flattened her hands on either side and levered himself into position so that he could pay attention to her small breasts. He licked her nipples. Her nipples were big in proportion to her breasts, and for some reason those perfectly shaped rosy discs turned him on like nothing imaginable.

He said he'd take his time and he did, licking and nipping, then suckling on them one at a time until she was moaning with pleasure. She pressed his head down farther and wriggled under him. Her mind went blank. Pure sensation replaced thoughts. His hands shifted to her rib cage and he journeyed with a leisurely lack of haste down her body, trailing his tongue along her stomach, circling her belly button...

And then lower he went, and she inhaled sharply as he settled between her legs and began to lick along her wet crease. This was so unbearably intimate. She wanted to snap her legs together in prim rejection of his ministrations, but she couldn't, because the thrill of how her body was responding was too powerful. He gently nuzzled, his tongue easily finding her clitoris and stroking it until her soft moans turned into frantic groans and whimpers, and she writhed under him, plunging her hands into his hair and drawing her knees up, instinctively angling her body so that every sensation was heightened.

He didn't stop licking and, as he licked, he stroked the soft flesh of her inner thighs, driving her to a place from which there was no hope of return. She started to spasm against his questing mouth, coming with an urgency that seemed to carry on for ever until she could scarcely breathe from the power of it.

Spent, she drew him up alongside her, eyes wide and dismayed, because how could *he* be satisfied?

'You'd be surprised,' he said with a slow smile when she voiced her concern. He circled her nipple with his finger and, bit by bit, Violet felt her rag-doll body begin to stir right back into life.

This time, he guided her, and it was an erotic journey, touching him just so, holding his penis in just the right way, circling the throbbing head until he was groaning. He covered her hand with his. Her stroking was long and slow and then, when he could no longer take the mounting excitement, he pushed apart her legs and gently inserted his bigness, nudging his entry gradually.

She was so wet.

For a few seconds she knew that she was tensing but it was, oh, so pleasurable, feeling his shaft ease inside her.

A deep, urgent thrill bloomed inside her and spread

out. When his thrusting became harder and faster, she was ready and tuned in. She dug her fingers into his back and arched up, eyes closed, feet wrapping round his lean waist, and her whole body splintered with wild pleasure as he came into her on one final thrust.

He sagged, lay completely still for a few seconds, then rolled off her to one side and shielded his eyes with one hand. When eventually he turned to face her, Violet was convinced that he would start on a litany of regret. She braced herself to assume a light-hearted response, the response of the controlled woman he had always assumed her to be.

She'd done the unthinkable, and was feeling the slow burn of delayed mortification, but when he spoke it was to say quietly, 'That is the first time I have ever made love to any woman without using protection.'

Violet didn't have to be a genius to detect the horror and alarm behind that statement.

'You don't have to worry, Matt. I've been using contraception ever since I got here to regulate my menstrual cycle.' Her face was beetroot-red because this seemed such a prosaic note on which to end what had been the most wonderful experience of her life. She turned to get off the bed, so that she could shower and give him permission to leave without a load of apologies and embarrassed excuses, but he drew her back down against him.

'Where are you going?' he asked in a lazy drawl. 'The night isn't over yet…is it?'

No, it wasn't. That was what Violet thought a month later. The night hadn't ended and it was never going to end. He had stayed another three weeks, then had left without looking back, and her heart had broken in two, but broken hearts mended and hers would mend. He wouldn't be around. He would never again be around.

How could she have known that there would be a price to pay for those stolen moments?

How could she ever have guessed that she would end up pregnant...?

CHAPTER SIX

'MISS DUNN IS HERE.'

He'd been expecting her. She had emailed him from Melbourne. A brief email which had made no mention of the time they had spent together. She'd politely asked how things were progressing with the start-up company they had worked on and then, as an afterthought, had informed him that she would be coming to London and wondered whether he would be available to meet. There was something she felt she had to discuss with him face-to-face.

For Matt, that could have covered any number of topics. Was she after the job he had offered her, after all? It made sense, because she'd enjoyed the adrenaline rush of working under pressure out there, but then wasn't that an easy enough topic to broach via email?

Maybe she was planning to return to London. Her father was back on track. Babysitting duties on the other side of the world could be winding up and it was possible that she might be after her old job. Trouble loomed on that front, if that were the case, because they'd slept together. Returning to their old relationship was not going to be possible. He hoped that she would have sufficient knowledge of how he operated to figure that out on her own.

Or maybe...

He relaxed back into his chair and thought, not for the first time since he had received her email, that she was interested in picking up where they had prematurely left off in Melbourne.

Regrettably, that too would be off the cards, because he knew that a casual relationship wasn't her thing, even though they had been lovers for a while and she had made no mention of taking it any further.

Sex with his prim and proper ex-secretary had been mind-blowing. He'd never known anything like it in his life before. The taste of forbidden fruit had been scintillating, had appealed to his jaded soul on a lot of fronts, but he was realistic enough to recognise the dangers of prolonging that brief liaison, even though he had been sorely tempted. He wasn't in the market for love and happy-ever-afters, but she was.

He would see where the conversation went, but there were few avenues he could think of that would be free of annoying complications.

'Shall I show her up?'

He nodded at his PA who, contravening all rules and regulations of a company that promoted an informal dress code, was attired in a natty pinstriped suit and a bow tie. His dress code was a daily source of amusement for Matt. He thought of Violet, and the neat and prissy suits she had been so fond of wearing to work, and he felt a sharp pang of nostalgia. He breathed in sharply and gathered himself.

'Give it five minutes, John. I have a brief phone call to get out of the way first.' He didn't, but for some reason, he felt unsettled and that wasn't going to do.

John nodded briskly and scuttled off, shutting the

door behind him, and Matt relaxed back, fingers steepled, frowning because for once, his well-behaved mind was refusing to play ball. He realised that she'd been in his head, vaguely but persistently *there* ever since he had returned from Melbourne. It was an acknowledgement he found a little disturbing, because he had never been one to overthink the end of any of his relationships. What they had enjoyed, intense though it had been, was a moment in time, a brief meeting of ways which had always been very clearly defined as having an ending in sight. It certainly hadn't been a relationship, as such.

Even though they had got along extremely well. As they would, all things taken into consideration.

He found himself wondering what she might be wearing. In Melbourne, she had sported a far more casual wardrobe. Tight jeans, small tops, cute flat sandals...

The PA had been nowhere in evidence. He had a very pleasing memory of her playing the piano for him in next to nothing, and then forcing him to do a rendition of 'Chopsticks' so that she could have a laugh at his expense. He hadn't objected. They'd made passionate love afterwards.

He shifted, fighting down a sudden erection. He had no intention of picking up where they had left off, however much his body was tempted by the possibility, so why was he suddenly being bombarded with all sorts of inappropriate memories?

He opened up a file on his computer, a boring list of facts, figures and numbers, the sort of file guaranteed to numb a racing imagination, and waited for her to be ushered in.

* * *

Several storeys down, Violet was nervously reacquainting herself with the towering glass building that had been her home away from home for over two years.

She'd promised her father that she would be back as soon as she could, as soon as some urgent business had been dealt with, and he had been weirdly accepting. He'd said he was toying with the idea that a return to Blighty might be a good idea, now that he was as fit as a fiddle. No more drink, of course—he was over all that—but he could appoint someone to run the music school and keep the house on so that they could visit whenever they wanted. And wouldn't it be great to catch up with old friends back home...?

Violet had no idea what was going on. She had thought that Melbourne would give her clarity and cure her of her ridiculous infatuation.

Yet here she was and everything was an almighty mess.

When she had emailed Matt to tell him that she was coming to London and wanted to see him, she had opted for meeting him at the office on the assumption that it would provide her with just the right sort of businesslike state of mind she would need to deal with a difficult and personal conversation. Now that she was here, memories were dragging her down. Everything was so familiar. The memory of the simmering excitement she used to feel every time she click-clacked her way to that shiny mirrored lift was like a punch in the stomach.

She wondered what had happened to Candy but, honestly, she didn't really care. She could barely think straight and her nerves were all over the place as she and John were whooshed up in the lift and, after some halting progress through those familiar plush offices— because so many people wanted to stop and chat and fill her in on gossip—ended up outside Matt's sprawling quarters.

'I'll leave you here, Vi,' John said, and she thought, in a panic, *Must you?*

She knocked and pushed open that all-too-familiar door that led into the outer office where she had worked like a busy little bee for such a long time. Matt's adjoining door was firmly shut and she took a deep breath as she walked towards it.

'Come!'

Violet pushed open the door and did her utmost to look calm and composed.

'Violet.' He smiled, but his eyes were guarded and watchful. 'You're here. An unexpected pleasure.'

He'd been sprawled in his waiting-for-inspiration-to-strike pose, but now he sat up, smiling and indicating the chair in front of his desk. Ex-boss politely welcoming ex-secretary. He was uncomfortable, because he didn't know why she was here in his office, and she felt a pang of misery, because not so long ago he had been her lover, touching her in places she had never been touched and turning her into a woman she had barely recognised.

'I guess you're surprised to see me,' she opened, not quite meeting his eyes but not looking away, either. Just sort of looking through him and past him with a fixed smile that more or less mirrored his own.

'You have a house here. Should I be? Perfectly natural for you to return for a break. Brought your father with you? How is he, by the way?'

Violet, trying desperately to gather her thoughts,

took her time sitting down. She'd put a great deal of thought into her clothes and was wearing a pair of black trousers, a casual baggy tee shirt tucked into the waistband and some sensible shoes.

'Dad's in Melbourne and, yes, he's fine. If it weren't for you, I might never have got to the bottom of his anxieties over his liver, so I must thank you for that. He must have spent months blowing everything out of proportion until he convinced himself that he was on the way out unless he had a liver transplant. A few words from the consultant taken the wrong way, and he could have been spared an awful lot of anxiety. But all's well that ends well. On that front.'

If they were any more polite with one another, she reflected, he would ask her to send him a memo as to the reasons why she had demanded an audience. As far as he was concerned, they'd had a bit of fun and that was the end of that. He was, after all, the guy who considered anything longer lasting than a nanosecond a commitment from which he was compelled to escape.

'Good to hear.' He paused. 'So, tell me why you're here—not that it isn't good to see you, Violet. Problems to sort out with your house?'

'I wanted to talk to you and I wanted the talk to be done face-to-face,' she told him flatly.

'Please don't tell me that you've returned for your old job.' Matt shifted, uncomfortable with the direction of the conversation but knowing that he had to be blunt. 'As you can see, the delectable Candy didn't work out, but John—one of your recommendations—is doing very nicely in the post. Would be very reluctant to put his nose out of joint by sending him back down to the bowels of Accounts...'

'I haven't come here to talk about getting my job

back.' Violet surreptitiously wiped her hands on her trousers and licked her lips.

'No?' Matt tilted his head to one side and looked at her narrowly. 'What, then? I'm consumed with curiosity.'

'Matt… This is difficult for me to say…' She sighed. Her hair had grown just a little and she combed her fingers through it, eyes skittered away from him.

'Shall I help you out?' Matt asked heavily, suddenly restless, and she darted a look of astonishment at him.

'You know why I've come here?'

'If not for your job, then there's only one other reason I can think of.'

'I'm sorry.' She rushed into speech. He knew! And he seemed to be processing the situation with a surprising lack of drama, which came as such a relief, because it meant that they could have a sensible, unemotional discussion and then she could get on with her life. 'I wasn't lying when I told you that I was on the pill— even though you probably didn't believe me, because you made sure you used protection every single time after…after that first time. I *was* on the pill, but I was so sick after with Dad and everything… Well, I never thought that I would get pregnant, but I was wrong.'

He'd guessed. At least, that was what he had said, but if he'd meant it, then why on earth did he look as though the bottom had suddenly decided to drop out of his world? His jaw had sagged. His expression was the expression of a man who had just been sucker punched. His face had gone a deathly shade of grey.

'You didn't think that was what I was going to say, did you?' Violet managed into the ever-lengthening silence.

Matt managed to shake his head, but his vocal cords were still missing in action.

Violet wondered why she had been stupid enough to leap to all the wrong conclusions when he'd said that he knew why she'd turned up at his office from halfway across the world. 'You thought that I'd come all the way to London because I wanted to carry on what we had in Melbourne. Is that it? Was that why you looked so nervous when I walked in?'

She felt anger surge through her. She thought back to that expression on his face when she had walked in. Wary, cautious. She thought back to his demeanour. Ultrapolite and just the right side of amicable. 'You were braced to gently let me down, weren't you?' That dark flush said it all. 'Of all the egotistic…arrogant…!'

She shook her head and banked down the fury waiting to blow like a volcano. 'Don't you think I know better than to ever go there, Matt? We were two ships that passed in the night! Did you think that I would be stupid enough to imagine that there could ever be more to it than that?' She clenched her fists and tried not to succumb to the hurt of knowing that he'd walked away and had truly been alarmed at the suspicion that she might have wanted to tug him back, that she might have put him in the uncomfortable position of having to gently dislodge her like a stubborn thorn that refused to be pulled out.

'Pregnant?' Matt finally managed to croak.

'Yes, Matt. Pregnant.' His obvious horror had the effect of making her suddenly very calm. 'I'm afraid the pill isn't one hundred percent accurate. I had that stomach upset, if you remember, and as luck would have it I fell pregnant in that window when it stopped working. It wasn't your fault, but neither was it mine.'

'Are you sure?' His voice was cracked and barely audible.

'Yes.' One word. There was no point letting him think that there might be some mistake.

He looked as though the sky had fallen down, right on top of his sexy, unsuspecting head. He was clearly horrified, and she bit down the temptation to cry. Her hormones had been all over the place, but she wasn't going to break down here in his office because she felt sorry for herself. Because the dreams she'd had of having a baby had never involved the father of the baby looking at her as though she'd single-handedly made all his worst nightmares take shape.

He stood up and began to prowl the office, his movements jerky. Violet twisted in the chair and followed him. He was raking his fingers through his hair, staring down at the ground, then moving to peer unseeingly through the floor-to-ceiling window that offered such splendid views of the streets of London and all the stick-insect figures scurrying below.

He spun round and his eyes arrowed down to her stomach, which was almost as flat as it always had been.

Violet instinctively and defensively placed her hand on her stomach and cleared her throat.

'I have stuff to do over here, Matt.' She gathered her wayward emotions. 'I just came to break the news, and now it might be a good idea to leave so that you can process the information.'

'Leave? You want to drop a bombshell and then *leave*?' His voice was incredulous but she held his stare without flinching.

'I haven't come here looking for anything,' she told him, voice glacial, because she was still reeling from the humiliation of knowing just how badly he wanted to escape what was unfolding in front of his horrified eyes. 'In fact, I debated whether I should come at all. I know this is the last thing you would ask for but, in the end, I felt that it was only right that you should know.' Her voice tapered off into silence. If he had looked ashen-faced and shocked before, he was now beginning to look thunderously angry.

'Well, Violet,' he said in a restrained voice. 'How very magnanimous of you.'

'There's no need for sarcasm.'

'No? When you sit there telling me that you're pregnant with my baby and yet you're only here breaking the news because of a sense of duty, having manfully fought the temptation to just say nothing at all and… what? Bring the baby up on your own on the other side of the world? Spin a few lies when he or she got older and started asking questions? Maybe consign me to a premature grave so that the questions didn't start getting too uncomfortable? Is that how it would have played out, Violet?'

He was going to be a father.

Not for a second did he not believe her. He was going to be a father. And all of a sudden, the thought of any child of his looking back on his past the way he looked back on his horrified him. Yet she sat there, calmly informing him that she'd actually considered keeping this to herself.

'Don't be ridiculous. You didn't want me here when you thought I might have come to try to seduce you back into bed, so please don't sit there and start lecturing me about my decision-making process.' Her voice was strained, close to tears.

'No, Violet.' Matt purposefully walked towards her and then leant over her, caging her in, hands on either side of the chair. 'Ridiculous is the thought that you actually entertained the idea of keeping this from me, and whatever I might have thought when I saw you has nothing to do with anything.'

'Oh, really?' She tilted her chin at a defensive angle and stared right back at him. He was so good at making people cower, so good at using the sheer force of his personality and his physicality to intimidate. Didn't he know that she was clued up on all those tactics and had long since learned how to deal with them? Although, this wasn't exactly a work-related situation, was it?

'I'll stop lecturing,' he said tersely, 'when you start explaining how you could have thought that this was something you could keep from me!'

'You're towering over me and it's making me nervous.'

'God, woman! You could try the patience of a saint!'

'Which is one thing you're not,' Violet returned swiftly.

He made an inarticulate sound under his breath and drew back, then he dragged his chair around his desk and positioned it right next to hers. He was no longer towering over her, but neither was he a safe distance away.

'Have you *ever* thought about having a family, Matt?'

He frowned and glowered. 'What does that have to do with anything?'

'You asked me how I could have the temerity to even consider, for five seconds, not telling you that I was pregnant. Here's how. You don't do commitment. You don't really do relationships, at least not significant relationships. And you certainly don't do having kids and playing happy families. What you do are three-month flings that all end in bouquets of flowers from a flower shop in Knightsbridge.'

And, she wanted to tack on, *let's not forget that you are the guy who made it patently clear that there would be no follow-up to our fling because what you were after was a passing liaison. Don't you go forgetting that!*

He flushed darkly and sat back, his long legs sprawled apart. He folded his arms and glared.

Violet summoned all her willpower and returned his glower with cool, calm eyes. The power of his looks was always enough to make her heart skip a beat, and it was no different now, but she had to focus.

She had to erase memories of that blissful bubble they had occupied in Melbourne when they had been lovers, holding hands and doing all the stuff that loved-up couples do. For a while back then, she had managed to forget that they weren't a normal loved-up couple. For a while, she had managed to forget that Matt Falconer hadn't been with her because he loved her, but because he had been intrigued at the new and very different side to her he had seen for the first time in his life. He had been with her because of her novelty value and that novelty value had kicked in the minute he had sussed that she was actually a three-dimensional woman and not the cardboard cut-out who had spent two-and-a-half years at his beck and call.

'Well, this isn't going to be one of those, is it?' he muttered darkly.

'Like I said, I didn't come here for anything, and I'm not expecting anything. I came because I felt you had to know that you were going to be a father. I'm not about to pressure you into doing anything.'

'This isn't the place to discuss the situation. I can't

have this conversation in my office. It's not a business transaction.'

Violet wanted to tell him that it pretty much was, considering emotions weren't involved, at least not on his part.

On her part...

All sorts of emotions were involved. On her part, emotions had been involved for some time when it came to her charismatic boss and three weeks spent in his company, three weeks of making love and pretending that reality was something that could be put on hold for ever, had deepened the swirl of feelings inside her that she had always had for him.

She was in a dangerous place and she was brave enough to acknowledge that that was part of the reason why she had actually considered keeping the pregnancy to herself.

She thought back now, not for the first time, to that very moment when it had dawned on her that her period hadn't come. She'd been merrily continuing with her contraception but, when something should have happened, nothing had. Even so, she had bought that pregnancy-testing kit without thinking that it would actually deliver that positive line.

Of course, it was something that had had to be ruled out, but as she'd waited those few minutes for a result she hadn't really been nervous at all.

And then everything had changed. In a heartbeat, her whole life had been turned on its head. Her blood had run hot, then cold, and in her fancy en-suite bathroom she had suddenly felt as though someone had taken a bat and swiped her behind her knees. She'd wanted to collapse. The unexpected had happened and nothing in her life had prepared her for it, even though she had lived a life full of the unexpected.

But she'd had time to take stock. He hadn't. No wonder he could barely compute what she'd dropped in his lap.

She'd never witnessed him grappling with anything. He was always so dynamic, so in control, whatever happened to be dished up.

Before she could say anything, he was heading for his door and pulling it open, leaving her no option but to follow him.

'Where are we going?'

'My place.'

'I don't want to go there.'

'Tough, Violet. I didn't wake up this morning wanting to discover that I'm going to be a daddy.'

Tears threatened. Of course, he was only speaking his mind, but still it hurt.

She'd never been to his house. Never. The thought of seeing him in his personal space was disturbing even though she had quickly grown accustomed to him seeing her in her personal space in Melbourne.

He summoned his driver, who appeared outside to meet them in a black, low-slung BMW, and she allowed him the silence of his thoughts as the car manoeuvred through the crowded roads, heading out of the city towards the calmer suburbs of west London.

She'd expected a house. Something substantial. But he lived in an apartment. It was a massive apartment and very minimalist. Lots of white and a feeling of something begun but not quite completed. There was minimalist and then there were walls in search of paintings.

It was completely open plan, and as he headed for

the kitchen, where he briefly seemed to contemplate the restorative qualities of alcohol before settling on coffee, she took time to look around her. He offered her coffee but she went for water.

As befitting an IT guru, there were lots of gadgets. She spotted a couple of computers, an elaborate games console and a mound of games. The television on the wall was ridiculously large. There were papers randomly strewn on a glass table and on the silk rug by the white leather sofa, as though he had lain down to read through some work, got bored and decided to shove everything on the ground next to him. The place was so essentially *him* that she felt her heart constrict.

'Of course, it's pointless telling me that you didn't show up to ask for anything. You realise that, don't you?' This as he moved towards the leather sofa and sat down, pushing a couple of files to one side and then tugging what looked like a priceless, one-off glass-and-beaten-metal table towards him with his foot. 'And please, Violet, sit down. We have to talk, so there's no point standing there like a sergeant major about to break ranks.'

Violet shuffled over to a chair and uncomfortably sat down facing him. 'You didn't ask for this situation.' She could feel a wave of nausea roll over her. Morning sickness, but hers lasted most of the day, and dealing with it was a daily challenge.

'You're right. I didn't. But here we are. *Fait accompli*, so to speak, so what do you think we should do about it? I know. You tell me what you think should happen next in this scenario and we'll see whether your prediction coincides with mine.'

'This isn't a game, Matt.'

'Trust me. I'm being deadly serious. So? You came

here, fuelled with a sense of obligation, and you must have had thoughts as to what would happen once you'd dropped the grenade.'

Violet bit down on an explosive response to that statement because every single word of it got on her nerves. But exploding wasn't going to solve anything, so she inhaled deeply and kept her voice well modulated.

'I suppose I thought you might be relieved to be released from having to engage…if that's the right word. Naturally, if you wanted, say, to contribute financially, then that would be up to you, but it wouldn't be necessary at all as I'm quite solvent. I don't think a baby would exactly fit snugly into your lifestyle, but of course, you would be more than welcome to arrange… er…to visit whenever you wanted. I thought the discussion might go a bit like that.'

Why was he looking at her as though she'd just insulted him?

'Interesting… You basically tell me that I can walk away, throw me a couple of options—just in case, on the off-chance I don't go for the abandonment option—and I thank you and see you to the door so that I can have a few weeks to think things over…?'

'No, of course not.'

'Because that's how it's sounding to me. I'm a commitment-phobe who wouldn't want anything to do with a baby I hadn't planned on having. Ergo, I would abnegate all responsibility. God, Violet, I thought you might know me a little better than that.'

He sat forward so suddenly that she started back and stared at him. There was simmering outrage on his face. Gone was the lazy, teasing guy and gone was the urbane, clever raconteur. Gone was the sexy man who could enthral her with his conversation and his wit. This man with the harsh, flat eyes was deadly serious, and she returned his flinty stare uneasily.

'I won't be stuffing some money into an account now and again to ease a guilty conscience. Nor will I be haggling over when I get to see my child. No, Violet, that's not how it's going to work at all. Here's the thing—I may not have bargained on being a father but, now that it's staring me in the face, then I intend to accept responsibility fully and without compromise. Full-time fatherhood. One hundred percent involvement. I won't be conveniently disappearing, leaving you to carry on and do your own thing. I happen to place a great deal of worth on the importance of being an engaged parent!'

Violet knew that her mouth was hanging open. She'd never heard him talk like this before, not in this tone, not with this urgency or searing honesty. His eyes were blazing and angry. Although, she really had no idea what, exactly, he was trying to say. Did he want to sort out visiting rights here and now? Maybe get her to sign something? Or worse…

'I'm not going to hand my baby over to you, Matt…' She blanched, sick at the thought that this might end up as a fight through the courts with an innocent baby as the end prize.

'Did you hear me ask you to?'

'Then I don't understand what you're trying to say.'

'Marriage, Violet. A ring on your finger and a walk up the aisle. That's where I'm going with this.'

'Don't be ridiculous.' Her head was swimming. He'd asked her how she'd thought this conversation would go. The answer was…*not like this*. In what world had she ever seen him as the sort of guy who might want a hands-on relationship with a child he hadn't asked for? There was commitment, and then there was *commitment*, and this definitely belonged to category number two. The sort of bone-deep commitment you took on board for life—no goodbye flowers, no divorce, no *it's been nice knowing you*. How the hell was she supposed to have assumed that he would want to dive head first into waters he had never been called upon to sample?

'And sooner rather than later. In fact, as soon as possible would work for me. Where does your father stand on this? Have you told him that you're pregnant?'

'Yes, just before I left, but…'

'He'll have to move over here. At least, if he wants to be with you.'

'Matt, you're not listening to what I'm trying to say!'

'Oh, I know exactly what you're trying to say, Violet. I'm just choosing to ignore it because we're both in the same position. Neither of us asked for this, but it's happened, and both of us are going to step up to the plate and accept responsibility—because to let a child pay the price of starting life in a tug of war between two parents would be unconscionable.'

'I have no intention of marrying someone for the sake of a baby! That's not how it's done these days, Matt!' Of course, in an ideal world, two parents were always going to be better than one but two *loving* parents, voluntarily sharing the responsibility for the child they had created. She'd benefitted from having two parents, if only for a brief moment in time. Her dad had adored her mother. She assumed, although she didn't know for sure, that Matt likewise was the product of a happily married couple as volatile, charismatic and energised as he was. Which was why he would place so much store on them staying together for the sake of the baby she was carrying.

But, she thought, what about her? And was that the sort of forced relationship that would benefit a child, anyway?

'In all the times I thought about marriage,' she said, 'it was never with a reluctant partner who was dragged into it, kicking and screaming, because I'd accidentally ended up pregnant. And you, Matt—you must surely feel the same as I do? You must have wanted something more than to find yourself having to propose marriage to a woman you would never normally be with...' She lowered her eyes and balled her small hands into fists.

'Don't underestimate the power of your sex appeal,' he muttered roughly. 'And, just for the record, I never pictured myself being married at all, so, no. No romantic fantasies swirling in my head that are now being put to rest because of this situation.'

He vaulted upright and restlessly paced the room, as though in the grip of a power surge he couldn't resist. He paused eventually but remained standing over her. 'It must have been a shock for you,' he said gruffly. He thought of her realising that she was pregnant, alone and doubtless afraid, and he was swamped by a feeling of confusing tenderness that had nothing to do with the baby.

Violet looked up at him. This was what he did so well. Alongside that forceful, driving personality was an ability to empathise that reminded you just how complex and three-dimensional a man he was.

'Of course,' she muttered. 'I never expected anything like this. I'm not like you. I *did* picture myself being married one day, having kids. I just never...'

'Imagined that it would be with someone like me, Violet?'

Violet looked away. Her heart was beating inside her like a drum. Someone like him? If only he knew! She might have idly dreamt of being with Mr Ordinary, who would have been such an antidote to the nomadic life she had endured growing up, but reality had decided to take her down a somewhat different route.

He wanted to marry her, and for a moment she took time out to think about what a life with that might look like. Lazy Sunday mornings lying in bed, laughing at those silly jokes of his... Cooking together... Making love whenever and wherever... And then, when the baby came, parenthood with all its ups and downs, but parenthood as a couple...

It was seductive, but Violet knew that it was the stuff of fantasy. The reality was that she would be hitching her wagon to a guy who had never planned marriage and basically found it impossible to sustain a relationship with any woman for longer than five seconds. He couldn't do that with women he was genuinely attracted to, so what were *her* chances? How long would it take for him to get bored of her, baby or no baby? And then what? Would he fool around behind her back? Or would he become a long-suffering partner, eventually resentful and bitter for having been forced into a marriage he hadn't banked on? Both prospects appalled her because to become dependent on someone only for them to let you down... There could be nothing worse. Her father had let her down. Yes, she had coped, because she adored him, but he had let her down. She wasn't going to be let down again.

'Yes.' She took the plunge, killing rosy dreams of what would never be. 'You can say what you like, Matt, but it wouldn't be fair on a child for us to be harnessed together, always thinking that we could have been happier with other partners if I hadn't fallen pregnant.'

'Oh, but, Violet…' His voice thickened and she shivered as their eyes tangled. 'You make a union between us sound like such a catastrophe in the making, but we both know that it wouldn't be all bad…'

CHAPTER SEVEN

HE CAME CLOSE. He touched her. Just a light, fleeting touch, the brush of his finger on her cheek, but it was enough to make her breath hitch in her throat. Her eyelids fluttered and she inhaled on a sigh, quite unable to control her response.

'See what I mean?' he murmured persuasively. 'One minute you're giving rousing speeches about our unsuitability, and the next minute you're quivering for me.'

'I am *not* quivering for you!' She was alarmed at the undercurrent of weakness she could detect in that protest.

'I still want you, Violet.'

'No.' She shook her head. 'That's not the point.'

'We get married and no one is going to say that the sex isn't going to sizzle.'

'Sizzling sex vanishes after a while. You know that.' She clicked her tongue but her skin was burning from where he had touched her, and her head was awash with hot memories of their brief, intense time together in Melbourne. 'Look at what happens when the sizzling sex fizzles out like a burnt-out firecracker, Matt. It's *bye-bye, it's been good knowing you* time. That's fine when it's just another five-minute relationship, but when two people are tied together by marriage, when there's a child involved, well, the burnt-out firecracker begins to look like a pretty bad idea.'

'None of my girlfriends happened to be pregnant,' he fired back.

'And because I am doesn't mean that marriage is the only solution, however much hands-on time you would want to have with our child. It doesn't mean that you're not going to get bored when the firecracker burns out.'

Matt's jaw tightened with frustration. On the surface, what she said made sense. It was true. Sizzling sex always had a tendency to turn to ashes in the blink of an eye, but this wasn't the same, and he was staggered that she couldn't see that. That a child being involved made all the difference. A child would make staying power the essence, the sizzling sex a bonus.

She wasn't just another woman to him—which was, somehow, what she was trying to say. She was the mother of his child… He frowned as thoughts tried to rearrange themselves in his head. More than that, she was…hell!…more than just someone who had shared his bed. Much more.

His thoughts screeched to a stop before they could gather pace and travel down that unexplored road.

'Marriage is about more than what makes logical sense on a piece of paper. Successful marriages are based on love and a loving background is what a child deserves.' She looked down. She had a fleeting vision of what it might be like if he really loved her. Perfect.

She raised serious brown eyes to him. 'I don't know anything about your background,' she said. 'I've worked with you for over two years, and I know everything about your take on relationships, but I don't know anything about your childhood. It's ironic that I was always the reserved one and yet you now know everything there is to know about me. I saw my dad fetching photos out to show you when he thought my back was turned. Back from hospital, and in the space of a handful of days before you left, he manages to bore you with stories about me and show you pictures of me growing up.'

'Who said I was bored? He's a proud dad. He may have been a wild dad who was fond of going off the rails but, one look at the way the two of you interact, and it's easy to see that you both adore one another. I liked seeing pictures of you as a kid. You looked serious even then. Hair in pigtails, frowning at the camera. All that was missing was a pair of specs. Think that paternal pride counts for nothing?'

'I never said that!'

'Think it's okay to deprive me of that experience because marriage is more than what makes sense on a piece of paper? Do you imagine that I wouldn't want to have the chance to love my child? To be there for him or her?'

'You're twisting my words!'

'You tell me that part-time parenting is acceptable. Would you be applauding that slice of wisdom if you were the one doing the part time parenting?'

'You told me that there was no way you would try and…and…'

'In an ideal world, there would be no lines drawn in the sand between us, given the situation,' Matt told her coldly. 'But the scenario you have in mind has nothing to do with an ideal world.'

'I'm being realistic.'

'You're being selfish.'

'You're not even a family man!' Violet protested heatedly.

No, Matt thought, he wasn't. Never had been. When

you grew up without the warmth of a family unit, when the people you turned to were strangers in an expensive boarding school paid to take the hit, then dreams of cosy sing-songs round the piano with loved ones never even registered on the radar once you reached a certain age.

But here he was, facing the family unit he had never courted. More than anything else, he wanted to make sure that his own flesh and blood didn't *lack* the way he had. He wanted to be the buffer for his child against the slings and arrows of life, which was something he didn't feel he'd had. He wanted to make sure that the past never repeated itself. The remoteness of his wealthy parents had felt like a wall of ice around him, and there was no way he wasn't going to do his damnedest to make sure *he* was there for this child. Being sidelined wasn't going to work. Neither, he thought with mounting frustration, was trying to strong-arm the stubborn, sexy, mulish woman glaring at him.

'Don't push me on this, Violet,' he rasped, but his eyes drifted down her body and he felt an ache in his groin as memories of their passionate lovemaking surfaced.

Violet sensed some infinitesimal shift in atmosphere and her eyes widened. 'Matt, I think it's time I headed back home. I know you mean well, offering to defuse this hand grenade by putting a ring on my finger, but I have no intention of letting you pay such a high price for a situation you didn't see coming.'

'Jesus, Violet!'

Time to go, Violet decided. She stood up, but suddenly the world was doing a giddy twirl and the ground no longer felt quite so steady under her feet. She swayed and in one leap Matt was there by her side. When he spoke, his voice was laced with urgency.

'What's wrong?' This as he lifted her off her feet and began carrying her out of the sitting room and towards a bank of rooms sprouting from either side of the wide, wooden-floored corridor. 'I'm calling a doctor.'

'No!' She didn't bother trying to struggle free. The light-headed feeling was abating, but one look at his face and she could see that he was worried sick.

In an instant, she realised that his marriage proposal wasn't just the gesture of someone resentfully doing something through a sense of obligation because that was how he had been brought up. No. This was his baby, and he genuinely wanted to be there to see things through from beginning to end, and that gave her pause for thought. His concern might not be for *her*, but should she deprive him of the opportunity to be a full-time father because she wanted more from him than he could ever give?

Was she, as he had said, being selfish?

She could see all sorts of complications from a relationship that wasn't grounded in love, but was his black-and-white approach really one she should take? Sometimes a person could become paralysed when they overthought a situation.

Her breathing was shallow as he gently levered her onto the bed. His bed. Giddiness and nausea were not enough to prevent a rush of curiosity.

His room was vast. The bed was the size of a football field. There were no old-fashioned hanging lights, just the twinkle of spotlights on the ceiling. The furniture was grey, built-in, high-gloss. And, as in the sitting room, there were books and papers on surfaces. He was as casual when it came to tidiness here in his house as he was in his office. Clothes had been dumped on a chair by the window and there were two pairs of trainers on the ground, half-submerged beneath a sweatshirt.

His messiness was strangely endearing. It was almost as if he was so intensely clever, his mind so incisive and quick, that the tedious business of tidying up was a hassle he couldn't bother with. He was just too focused on other things.

She assumed he had a long-suffering housekeeper who came in and cleaned up behind him.

He was punching a number into his mobile phone, talking in a low voice, then listening to whatever was being said to him. After a handful of minutes, he disconnected the call and moved to stand by the side of the bed, arms folded.

'A few questions,' he said. 'And honest answers would be helpful.' He rattled off a series of questions and then asked finally, 'Have you eaten anything today?'

About to assure him that of course she had, Violet opened her mouth, frowned and blushed.

'Not as such…' When had she last eaten? The long trip over…the prospect of breaking the news about the pregnancy to Matt…the *stress*... Her appetite had vanished, and now she was having difficulty in remembering just what she had eaten and when.

'Not as such? What does *not as such* mean? Have you eaten anything today or not? It's a straightforward question.'

'I've been busy,' Violet mumbled.

'So when was the last time you ate?'

'Well… I picked at some food on the plane… And of course I've been meaning to pop out and do a shop… but I've been so stressed out. I think I grabbed some—'

'Stop right there, Violet. Even from the depths of my

ignorance I know that you have to have a proper eating routine when you're pregnant!' He shook his head incredulously.

'That's not fair—and it's not just because I may have missed a meal or two. I feel dizzy and nauseous a lot of the time,' she grudgingly admitted.

'We'll talk about what's fair and what's not fair once you've been fed. I'll go and…make something.' He hesitated. 'I could order something in, but I think you need to eat sooner rather than later.'

He was gone a while, during which time Violet tussled with the idea of getting out of his bed and joining him in the kitchen, but when she tried standing up she felt woozy again and had to lie back down. That being the case, the made herself as comfortable as she could. She kicked off her shoes and unbuttoned the trousers that had been a poor choice, but she had not wanted to advertise her rounded stomach any more than was necessary when it had come to confronting him with news of the pregnancy. She hadn't wanted to walk into his office and witness the look of dawning horror on his face because he had taken one look at her and guessed. No, she had wanted to build up to it because it gave her time, but she should have just worn something loose, elasticated and comfortable.

He kicked open the bedroom door and entered with a tray in his hand. 'Juice,' he said, 'and cheese on toast.' There was nothing else he could think of preparing that wouldn't have taken for ever to do.

The snack consisted of two slabs of bread lathered with butter and drowning under layers of thickly cut cheddar.

Suddenly ravenous, Violet tucked into the toast like a starving person at an all-you-can-eat buffet. Meanwhile, Matt pulled a chair to the side of the bed and watched her with narrowed eyes as she ate.

'You were telling me that your nausea wasn't solely the result of your skipping a meal or two…'

'No.'

'Let's flesh that one-syllable answer out a little, Violet. How long has this been going on?'

'From the beginning.' She fidgeted and glanced away from his all-seeing gaze. 'It's not a big deal.'

'It's a big deal. Seen the doctor about that?'

'No, of course not!' Even though she was well aware of all the problems associated with having an unplanned pregnancy—even though she was realistic enough to accept that it had hardly been her dream to have a child without the support of a caring partner by her side—the thought of going to a doctor to be told that something might go wrong filled her with dread. There had never been a moment's doubt in her mind that she very much wanted this baby.

The silence that greeted this was oppressive and forced her into speech.

'I should have eaten.' She plucked at her shirt, mouth downturned. 'I feel much better now. Lots of women suffer from extreme morning sickness. It's not a big deal, like I said. Now, I'll leave you to get on with the day and mull over everything.'

She didn't feel like leaving. She didn't fancy being on her own. She wanted to be with him when the next wave of nausea washed over her, making her want to sit down and put her head in her hands. He made her feel so safe. He was a solid brick wall, a rampart against everything that threatened to overwhelm her, and she just wanted to let him handle everything. It was silly and cowardly, but it was also an irresistible force.

'I don't think so.'

'What do you mean?'

'I mean, this business of your forgetting to eat because you've been busy has shown me that you can't be trusted to look after yourself. Don't get me wrong, I never banked on this happening, but now that it has I intend, like I said to you, to be committed the whole way through. If you can't look after yourself, then you're going to need someone to look after you, and from where I'm standing I'm the only candidate for the job.'

'It won't happen again and, if it does, I'm perfectly capable of handling it.'

'Don't fight me on this.'

Violet looked at him for a long while. She thought about the way he had reacted to news that would turn his orderly life upside down. No complaints, no accusations, no ranting and railing and tearing his hair out. No, he had risen to the occasion and had not hesitated to utter those words which for him would have been the biggest of personal sacrifices. He had proposed marriage. He didn't love her but, as he had said, he wanted to be given the chance of loving his baby on a full-time basis, and who could feel aggrieved at that?

She thought of those dark warnings as well. He was a fair guy, and she didn't think that he would really drag her through the courts to claim his rights as a father, but could she be sure? These were exceptional circumstances, and Matt Falconer was nothing if not unpredictable when it came to handling exceptional circumstances. How ruthless would he be prepared to be, and would she be able to fight him? Would she want to? Would that benefit the baby she was carrying? Her heart sped up because no one rose to the dizzy heights that he had without having his fair streak of ruthlessness.

You sometimes had to fight dirty to win wars and he'd won a lot.

'Are you threatening me?' she asked weakly.

'I seldom threaten,' Matt returned neutrally, his navy eyes never leaving her face. 'I rely on everyone else seeing sense.'

She was tempted to smile at a remark that was so typically *him*. 'I can look after myself, Matt. I've spent a lifetime doing that.'

'But was that something you chose to do, or something that circumstance chose for you?' He allowed that to sink in before continuing. 'All good things come to an end and, while you're waxing lyrical about the joys of single parenting and the nightmare of being harnessed to someone for the sake of a child, I think you should contemplate what it might feel like when you try to explain to our son or daughter down the line that they were denied the stability of two parents because you wanted to be free to find the perfect guy.'

Violet whitened. 'That's below the belt—and whoever said anything about a perfect guy?'

'And I'm very sorry that I have to bring it up, but bring it up I shall—you won't be returning to Melbourne. In your condition, long haul travel can't be a good idea.'

'You can't *kidnap* me, Matt!'

'Kidnap?' He smiled slowly and she felt that familiar warmth spread through her body, felt the tingle between her thighs that was a sharp reminder of how much power this man had over her. 'You have a very colourful image of the sort of man I'm capable of being. I draw the line at many things. Kidnapping is one of them.' He paused and their eyes locked, his stunning navy gaze pinned to her face so that even blinking felt like an effort.

'You act as though doing the right thing is somehow a crime,' Matt told her softly. 'When it comes to children, they should be put first, because they're the ones who end up bearing the scars from selfish, self-serving parents. When your father was showing me those pictures of you in his photo albums, what I saw was a guy who might have gone off the rails when it came to drink and drugs but who, when it came to the things that count, was right there. Am I wrong?'

Violet shifted uncomfortably. 'I get what you're saying, but that doesn't mean that we have to get married, Matt. We can both be here for our child even if we live apart.'

'And have separate relationships?'

'I… I hadn't thought that far ahead.' She stumbled over her words. The picture he was painting was rolling towards her with the inexorability of a tank, crushing all her fine intentions and her conviction that a union born from convenience was beyond the pale. She wanted to marry for love. What was wrong with that?

'I have no intention of letting any man bring up a child of mine,' he said bluntly. 'You can talk as much as you like about sanitised, modern caring, and sharing partnerships where all sorts of extended family members chip in, but that doesn't work for me.'

Violet shook her head in pure amazement at the tangent his thoughts had taken but, then again, Matt Falconer was not averse to dramatic exaggeration if he thought that it suited his purpose, as it did now.

That said…

Her mind drifted. What was good for the goose was good for the gander…

As if he had a direct hotline to her thoughts, he tilted his head back at a proud angle and arrowed searching eyes to her face. 'And tell me how you're going to feel if and when I find myself a doting mother figure for our child.'

'I didn't think you went for the kind of women who doted on little kids,' Violet muttered, for want of anything better to say, and he gave an eloquent shrug of his broad shoulders.

'Needs must,' he stated succinctly. 'I would hardly be interested in continuing my current lifestyle, given the circumstances. As a father, I would want to introduce moral standards that would serve as an example to my child as he or she got older. I hadn't foreseen the necessity for getting serious with any woman but then, face it, I also hadn't foreseen that I would be in this position at this point in time.'

Violet was beginning to get a headache and the nausea was creeping up again. She lay back against the pillows and closed her eyes for a few moments.

'We can carry on this conversation at a later date,' Matt said gruffly. He turned away, and she was only aware of him talking again to the doctor he had previously called when he spun back round to face her and said without preamble, 'You're sick and my guy is coming over right now to examine you.'

'You have *a guy*?' Relief washed over her. It felt treacherously good to have someone take charge. She'd taken charge all her life. For the first time, it was great letting go! She didn't want to have any more uncomfortable conversations. She didn't want to think about that question he had posed, didn't want to project to a time when she might have to look at him with another woman—a woman wearing his ring who would be trying hard to bond with their child. 'You have a random person who drops whatever he's doing to rush over if you get a headache?'

Matt grinned. He relaxed, marvelled at how that quirky sense of humour could break through the clouds like a sudden, unexpected ray of sunshine. She had her eyes closed and her breathing was shallow, and the concern that ripped through him was shocking. Of course, she was having his baby, and he wouldn't have been human if he hadn't been sick with worry—because she was clearly not going to be one of those who blossomed in pregnancy—but he just wanted to reach out and smooth the strands of hair from her face.

'University friend,' he told her. 'I've done him one or two favours in the past. As it happens, this is the first time I've ever had to call upon his professional services.'

'Of course it is.'

'Never get ill. I'm as strong as an ox.'

'I don't need a doctor.'

'What you need...' Matt heard the ping of his phone announcing the arrival of his pal of old '...is to learn to depend on someone else for a change.'

Violet had to admit that it was bliss. The doctor was earnest, serious and treated Matt with the fond affection that came from many years of friendship. He was excellent at what he did, even though he was not an obstetrician but 'a brain guy', as he jokingly called himself.

'He knows everything there is to know when it comes to the human body,' Matt asserted.

'That's either a good thing,' Phillip said as he examined her with quick, efficient hands and asked pertinent questions as he did so, 'because I would clearly be a genius, or a bad thing, because a jack of all trades and master of none isn't great in an operating theatre…'

High blood pressure was the verdict. Not dangerously high, but high enough to be a cause for concern. It wouldn't be a good idea to overdo anything. Likewise, the sickness was more pronounced than usual, but not in the red zone. Combined, the young doctor declared as he headed for the bedroom door, they pointed in the direction of her having to take it easy and get a certain Matt Falconer to start discovering the joys of domesticity.

'So,' Matt drawled once he had shown his friend to the door and returned to the bedroom, 'I guess that settles the immediate question of what happens next in this scenario. It's safe to say that you won't be going anywhere any time soon…'

CHAPTER EIGHT

EVERYTHING MOVED QUICKLY after that satisfied assertion. She had been advised bed rest by a doctor, no less, and it would have been the height of irresponsibility to ignore the advice.

That had been the first arrow shot over the parapet, a warning shot of the series of persuasive arguments that were shamelessly piled on through the course of Violet's bedridden week.

'I don't want you fighting me on this,' Matt told her on more than one occasion. 'You're not interested in giving me a chance because I don't happen to live up to the mental image you have of the sort of guy you'd always dreamt of marrying, but it would be wrong to let our child pay for your scepticism.'

Violet thought back to his track record, but she knew better than to constantly remind him of it because at the back of her mind, like the promise of a storm lurking behind the illusion of clear, blue skies, was always the notion that he might fight her in court.

He'd hinted at it, and she was terrified of taking him to task on the subject because she didn't want to hear him confirm her worst nightmare.

He had also planted a seed of treacherous unease in her head, and not only had it taken root, but it had begun to grow at an alarming rate, like the beanstalk in the fairy story. One minute there had been a harmless bean, and the next minute the bean had sprouted into a rampaging plant inhabited by fearsome creatures.

How would she feel when he began seeing another woman? That was the thought that occupied her as she remained in his sprawling apartment, ordered to stay put, her every need met either by his housekeeper, who came in daily to clean and prepare meals, or by him when he returned from work at stupidly early hours, even though she kept telling him that there was no need.

How would she find the strength to stand back and watch as another woman invested in their child?

She couldn't foresee finding another man. No one could compare to Matt, and she would never have the luxury of moving on, because he would be on her doorstep week after week, relentlessly *present*.

And in the meantime, on doctor's orders, he returned to the apartment with the regularity and perfect timing of a well-oiled Swiss watch, clumsily warming the food his housekeeper had prepared, asking her about her day, coaxing conversation out of her.

Everyone at work was asking after her, he had informed her the evening before. As soon as she was back on her feet—and that should be in the next few weeks, if Phillip was on target with his prognosis—she would have to pay them all a visit. No one could believe that he was going to be a father. She would have to show them her swelling belly to prove it.

Typically, he didn't give a hoot what his employees thought of this development and, when she had vaguely mentioned that her showing up pregnant might be some cause for embarrassment, he had burst out laughing. *Why?* he had asked with genuine curiosity. Who cared?

After a mere ten days of being treated like a china doll, Violet found that she was getting used to having him around. Indeed, she discovered that she actively and guiltily looked forward to hearing the turn of the front door handle as he entered the apartment.

Bit by bit, he was wearing down her defences and making her question the decisions she had made.

He had stopped trying to argue her into submission. Instead, he was doing it by stealth. She wondered whether it was a cunning tactic or just a method of winning that came easily to him.

The nagging thought that he was a man who wasn't made for settling down—a man who would always find temptation lurking round every corner and who would eventually be unable to resist, however dedicated a father he turned out to be—was being replaced by the dawning hope that she could somehow turn him into the guy she wanted him to be. Namely, a guy who could return her love. Given time. It happened, didn't it?

Summer was fading fast into autumn. Outside, the days were getting shorter. She chatted to her father every day on the phone. Somehow, he had cottoned on to the fact that Matt had proposed marriage. She thought she might just come right out and ask him whether he had been having man-to-man conversations with her dad behind her back. She wouldn't put it past him.

Today, bored with languishing on a chair watching telly and reading, Violet dismissed the housekeeper and busied herself making dinner. Ever since she had moved into the apartment, the fridge had been kept in a state of readiness, well stocked with enough food to pander to her appetite whenever she might feel the need to tuck into something nutritious.

It had made her smile because the Matt she remem-

bered when she had worked for him was a guy who
had enjoyed his fast food, and she had never pictured
him with a fridge containing anything but the bare es-
sentials.

Now it was impossible to open the fridge without
being bombarded by a giddying array of healthy options, from salad leaves and tomatoes to yogurt drinks
awash with healthy bacteria.

She prepared a simple pasta dish, having looked up
a recipe on her phone. It looked okay.

She had also done something about dressing in something other than the comfortable, loose cotton bottoms
she had brought with her from Australia, and tired tee
shirts which were wonderfully soft but hardly the height
of glamour.

From the very moment her life had been turned on its
head and she had found herself living in Matt's apartment, Violet had been determined to make sure that she
kept her distance. It was unsettling enough having him
around, knowing that two doors down was his bedroom,
without provoking any unnecessary interest by wearing
clothing that looked as though she cared.

She didn't.

Yes, she was pregnant. Yes, they had had a brief
moment in time together, and so what if she was still
attracted to him and he knew it? That didn't mean her
head had stopped functioning. She had made her mind
up, had decided that she had to detach herself from him
if they were to have any sort of amicable relationship
over time. They would have to learn to be friends and
the way to do that was not to let her body start calling
the shots.

So she had dressed down. If she'd been able to hang
around in her work clothes, she would have been sorely

tempted, but there was no way she could wear anything but loose-fitting clothes. Being comfortable helped the nausea, for a start.

He had gradually bought her stuff, showing up a couple of times with bags that he had casually tossed on the sofa.

'You hadn't banked on being cooped up in this apartment,' he had explained, 'And you probably hadn't banked on staying in the country for this length of time. You need more things to wear, so I got you a few things.' He'd shrugged, headed to the kitchen for a drink and then vanished into his home office to work for a couple of hours, cutting short her protestations with an impatient wave of his hand as he'd disappeared out of sight.

Violet had taken the bags into her bedroom and inspected his offerings with indecent curiosity.

A couple were wearable. Loose silk culottes. Most weren't. They contained the right element of stretch— he'd clearly got advice from a sales assistant who had assured him that his purchases could accommodate a pregnant stomach—but the clothes were sexy, designed to draw attention, which was what she had adamantly decided not to do.

Until tonight.

Tonight, her head would no longer be in charge. The thoughts that had been turning over in her mind had borne fruit and she had come to a decision, one which left her nervous as a kitten as she waited for the sound of the door being opened.

She felt every muscle in her body clench when, at a little after seven, Matt pushed open the door to his apartment. She was waiting in the living room, standing in the doorway with a glass of juice in her hand, more to give herself something to do than because she was thirsty.

He stopped dead in his tracks and she could almost see his jaw drop in slow motion.

Which would have been hilarious if she wasn't busy trying not to feel sick.

'Am I in the right apartment?' he quipped when he had gathered some of his self-control and galvanised his legs into motion.

Eyes still on her, he dumped his leather laptop bag on the ground and shrugged off his faded, black denim jacket, which he dumped on top of the laptop bag. He slowly moved towards her, looking at her with such intensity that she knew her skin was turning bright red. Matching the stretchy dress she had chosen to wear. One of the inappropriate items she had foreseen would hit the back of the wardrobe, never to see the light of day again.

Until she'd decided that it would be tonight's statement piece because a big decision warranted something more dramatic than jogging bottoms and a tee shirt.

'I've cooked.' Violet cleared her throat, eyes skittering away the closer he got, until he was so close that she could smell the woody scent of his aftershave.

'You've cooked,' Matt murmured, his breath a feathery caress against her burning skin. 'What happened to Marita? Did you stuff her in a cupboard somewhere because her soufflé wasn't up to scratch?'

His voice was a warm caress and her skin burned in response. Now that she had come to a decision, she allowed her mind to wander into all sorts of previously forbidden terrain... Lying in bed next to him, his touch, the low, silky murmur of his voice, the strength of his arms wrapped around her. The thought of just being able to drop her guard and laugh at his sense of humour. Only now did she realise how exhausting it had been, keeping up her defences, not allowing herself to fully relax because she'd been so scared that if she took her eye off the ball she would cave in.

All those thoughts he had generated in her head... that beanstalk that had seemingly sprung up over-night... It no longer felt like caving in. It felt like an inevitable outcome and she wasn't sure whether he had deliberately engineered that or not.

'I'm feeling so much better.' She tilted her head to look at him. He was so stupidly good-looking, she thought. All sexy alpha male with a sense of humour that could pull a smile from a block of ice.

'Does that account for the change of outfit as well?' His voice was lazy and curious but his eyes were seri-ous with intent.

'Do you like it?'

Matt stilled. His eyes never left her face. 'I've ei-ther done something wrong or else you're about to tell me something I won't be interested in hearing. Which will it be?'

'I do want to have a talk with you,' Violet admitted, turning away because she could no longer bear the in-tensity of his gaze. 'Maybe we should sit.' She led the way to the low leather sofa and he followed her. She noted that he made sure to keep his distance, sitting on one of the chairs instead of on the sofa next to her.

'Well,' he drawled after a moment's silence, during which Violet tried to get her thoughts into some kind of chronological order, 'are you going to spit it out or will we have a protracted guessing game?'

'I've been thinking,' Violet began, hesitantly. He had proposed marriage once upon what felt like a long time ago, but since then he had taken a back seat, and now she wondered whether he hadn't had a rethink. Had he had time seriously to weigh up the pros and cons of settling down with her? Had close proximity over the past week and a half made him realise that having her around was really too much of an acquired taste?

She thought of all the blondes who had cluttered his life. Had enforced time spent with her made him realise that he missed that type of woman? He'd never had to tailor his work schedule to accommodate any of them and, while it was one thing waxing lyrical about doing the right thing for the sake of the baby she was carrying, it was another thing altogether when he was put to the test and actually had to make sacrifices.

She knew that he was often up when she retired to her bedroom because she was so finely tuned to the pad of his steps on the wooden landing. Two mornings ago, she had woken up to use the bathroom and she had heard him walk past her door, his footsteps barely audible. It had been two thirty in the morning. For a man who had always enjoyed complete freedom of movement, who had become accustomed to dating women who never interfered with whatever routines he had in place, he had now been put to the test, and she did wonder whether it was proving an eye-opener for him.

All those thoughts nearly made her immediately start the process of backtracking, but then she thought of him with another woman sometime in the future… Coming by to collect their child… Zooming off in one of those fast cars of his so that he and whomever he happened to be dating could have a bonding weekend…

'You've been thinking,' Matt prompted. 'Going to share any of those thoughts this side of Christmas? Because I'm all ears.'

'I'll admit that when I found out about the baby...'
she hesitated and frowned, thinking back to what
seemed ages ago '... I wasn't sure what your reaction
was going to be. I know you were furious when I told
you that I'd considered not saying anything at all, but
you have to understand that I know you very well.'

'A little knowledge can be a dangerous thing,' Matt
murmured. 'It can lead to all sorts of misinformed conclusions.'

'Well, yes. But, at any rate, I don't think I would have
withheld the information from you. You had to know,
you had to be given the choice of what you wanted to
do. It helped that I had my own source of income and
you knew that there was no way you could use your
money to control the situation.'

Matt's eyebrows shot up and he stared at her.

'You know what I'm talking about, Matt,' Violet told
him drily, 'so don't even think of playing the innocent
with me. If I'd been broke, you would have used your
wealth to get me to do what you wanted and I wouldn't
have had much choice.'

'That's a terrible accusation.' But there was a ghost
of a smile on his face as he continued to look at her
from under lowered lashes.

'You did make me think when you hinted that you
would consider taking me to court, however.'

The smile dropped from his face instantly. 'It was a
vague threat that I would never have gone through with.'

'And it was a chance I couldn't take.'

'I would like to tell you, right here and right now,
that no decision of yours should be based on any apprehension on your part that I might fight you in a court
of law for custody of this baby. It would never happen.
If I insinuated otherwise, well, you know my nature,

Violet. I'm a man accustomed to fighting the good fight when it comes to getting what I want.'

Violet shrugged. 'Living here with you,' she said slowly, 'has made me realise that you might actually mean it when you say that you would be prepared to do whatever it takes for the sake of this baby. You've gone beyond the call of duty when it came to…to taking care of me. That was something you hadn't banked on and you rose to the occasion.'

'Thank you for the sweeping compliment, Violet, but it's fair to say that Marita did pull her weight. Had you had to rely on my culinary skills, you probably wouldn't be sitting here being quite so effusive in your praise.'

But he was still wary of what she was about to say. Violet could sense that underneath the easy charm and the lazy banter. She knew the way his mind worked. He would be predicting, forecasting, mentally trying to piece together a puzzle that was still missing a few parts. Matt Falconer was a guy who was always a dozen steps ahead of everyone else. It occurred to her that she had turned that routine firmly on its head and she marvelled that he had gone with the flow instead of trying to fight against the current.

'You told me that I was being selfish when I rejected your proposal of marriage. For my part, all I wanted for myself was a conventional marriage with someone who chose to spend his life with me instead of a guy forced into it because of circumstances. So I turned you down…'

'And now?' He tilted his head to one side, giving nothing away.

'And now… Well, this is about more than what I want and what I expected from life. I can't deny this baby the right to both parents and a stable background. So…'

'So…? I book the church and buy the ring?'

If there was one giveaway that this was a marriage of convenience and not something he truly wanted, it was wrapped up in that amused quip. Her heart constricted. Was she doing the right thing? Yes, she thought. She was. Because, if her heart tightened now, then the thought of what the alternative was made it tighten even more painfully.

'Not quite,' she told him quietly. 'There's no need to do either of those things just yet. I suggest…we continue living together. See how things progress. I'm getting stronger by the day. Let's take it a step at a time. We can always reassess further down the road.'

For a few moments there was silence, then he said with just the smallest of shrugs, 'In that case, I think step number one should be meeting the parents…'

It couldn't be avoided. Matt knew that. Whatever the state of play between him and his parents, they had to be in the loop, and who knew? They might have held him at a distance—stiffly, silently and permanently disapproving, disappointed at the direction he had chosen for himself—but maybe, just maybe, what they hadn't been able to show him, they might be able to show their grandchild.

It felt like a terrifyingly huge step. That didn't mean that he could, or even wanted to, shy away from it…

Violet looked at her reflection in the mirror with troubled eyes. She'd foolishly thought that everything would somehow slot into place after that talk but now, three days later, she was still unsure as to what was going on.

He hadn't scooped her into his arms and swept her up to his bedroom, which she had kind of hoped he would.

Instead, they had had a very sensible conversation about what happened next. Yes, the parents. She would have to meet them. Despite the fact that the whole world seemed to know about the baby, he still hadn't broken the news to them, and when she'd shown surprise, he had simply averted his eyes and told her that it was the sort of conversation that had to be had face-to-face and he just hadn't had time to make the trip.

They had discussed the need to move out of London. His apartment was enormous, but it was essentially a bachelor pad. Glass, metal and grey furniture didn't add up to a child-friendly environment.

She had felt uncomfortably out of place in the sexy red dress, because what she had imagined might turn into something a little seductive had actually ended up with the feel of a board meeting. She hadn't really understood what was going on, and she wondered whether his interpretation of her living with him to see how things went, as opposed to marrying him, meant simply a continuation of what they already had. A perfectly civilised relationship in which she inhabited one of the spare rooms, except maybe the spare room would be in a house outside London instead of an apartment in the centre.

She had slept on her own that night, as she had previously, and he had then vanished to New York for an urgent meeting he couldn't afford to skip.

Now, here they were. He would be back from the airport any minute. He'd called and told her that he was en route. That they would then leave immediately for the meet-the-parents visit.

'Don't you want to have a breather after a long-haul flight?' she had asked dubiously, but no, he didn't need a breather, he had told her. Only wimps needed breathers. His parents were expecting him and there was no opt-out clause there.

So here she was, dressed in an outfit that brokered a deal between sensible and a little daring, because she had no real idea what his parents were like. The dress was black, long-sleeved and showed off her now visible bump, but in a way that was still prim and proper even though the dress was reasonably fitted.

She was wearing thick, black tights and her hair was neatly tucked behind her ears. She felt like the PA she had once been.

She was dressed and anxiously waiting when she heard the sound of the front door opening, and she couldn't contain the surge of high-wire tension and excitement that raced through her.

He was in a pair of faded jeans, a black sweater and a beaten leather jacket. And *still* he managed to look effortlessly cool and ridiculously elegant.

Their eyes met and for a few seconds neither said anything, then Matt lowered his eyes and said, huskily, 'You're ready. You look great, Violet.'

He hesitated.

He wanted to move towards her and take her in his arms, but he remained hovering for a few seconds, wondering how it was that she had opened the door between them and yet, more than ever before in his life, he was afflicted with a sense of uncertainty that he didn't quite know how to deal with. She exerted a spell over him. He could feel himself wanting to get closer, wanting to sink into her, and that weakness confused him but still it was there, persistent and ever-present.

He knew that she would have been bewildered at his behaviour. No sooner had she told him that she wanted to try to work things out between them as a couple, as a united team for the sake of their baby, than he had disappeared across the Atlantic, leaving her on her own.

He could barely formulate a coherent explanation to give her, but he knew that he would have to, and soon. Today.

He would have to have that talk with her, tell her that he could never love her, that she should banish any such hopes from her head, if they were indeed there at all.

This would be an arrangement, and a very successful one if she didn't fall into the trap of expecting more than would ever be on offer. There could be no other conversation on the subject. He didn't do love, he didn't know *how* to…and if it sometimes felt as though she might be the one, might occupy a space he had never carved out in his heart, well, he would slam the door on those seditious thoughts.

He hadn't laid a finger on her, and it was driving him nuts, but the speech had to be delivered before any other roads were taken.

He restlessly raked his fingers through his hair and thought that he had never, in his entire life, seen a sight as beautiful as the woman standing uncertainly in front of him, her hand resting lightly on her small bump.

'Would you like something to eat? Drink?' Violet asked hesitantly, and he smiled.

'It's six thirty. Something will be laid on,' he commented drily. 'It's an hour to their house. The sooner we get there, the better.'

'Tell me what I should be expecting,' Violet prodded when they were in the car and powering out of London towards Surrey, leaving the cluttered streets behind.

She couldn't tear her eyes away from his face. She wanted so much to do something simple and intimate—

place her hand on his thigh, feel the ripple of muscle—but the weird distance he had created between them made her cautious.

She so wanted to ask him outright if he had gone off her. Pregnancy, as it progressed, was not that appealing to lots of guys. Was he one of them? One of those men who were ever so vaguely repulsed by the sight of an expanding stomach?

Maybe he had got it into his head that she was off limits because the doctor had advised rest.

Violet had no idea how to broach the thorny issue, but surely they couldn't work as a couple if they still carried on occupying separate bedrooms?

They made amicable conversation as the fast car ate up the miles, speeding to a destination that turned out to be nothing at all like what she had expected.

They had gone from the congested streets of London into open spaces where ribbons of houses were crammed along narrow roads, punctuated with traffic lights, pedestrians and cars. London on a smaller scale. But then that had been left behind, giving way to grander properties enclosed in land and guarded by gates. The car continued to bypass the grander houses until it turned left and they were confronted with the sort of impressive wrought-iron gates that advertised barking guard dogs, CCTV cameras and someone on patrol to keep intruders out.

Violet's mouth dropped open.

'This is where your parents live?'

'Your average mansion.' Matt shrugged and used a beeper on his key ring to open the gates.

'Wow. It's not exactly a four-bedroomed semi on an estate, is it...?' She glanced across at him and frowned, because his body language shrieked tension. His jaw was clenched and his fingers were tightly gripping the steering wheel.

'When was the last time you saw your parents?' she asked, her attention diverted by the tree-shaded drive that wound its way towards… Well, this was beyond a mansion. This was something along the lines of a National Trust estate. She gaped, not because she wasn't used to big houses and over-the-top mansions, many of which she had experienced first-hand over the years with her dad, but because this was just so…unexpected. She tried hard to quench a sickening rush of acute nerves while he briefly informed her that he visited four times a year.

'Exactly four times?' Her mouth felt dry, which was the opposite of the palms of her hands, which were clammy. This felt like a really big deal, a turning point in a relationship that had been pleasantly meandering along, somehow waiting for something to happen.

'Three birthdays and Christmas day.'

'That's very organised.' She looked across at him. 'I didn't think you were that organised a person.'

'When you meet my parents, you'll discover why organisation is important. They're not people who appreciate spontaneous drop-ins.'

The rolling mansion drew closer. It was an impressive but grim edifice of greystone, fronted with a circular courtyard dominated by an amazing fountain. On either side of the house, sprawling, well-manicured lawns rolled off towards the dark shadows of trees.

'Don't worry.' He turned to her wryly when he'd killed the engine. 'It won't be a protracted visit.'

She was struck by a sudden thought. 'Have you told them that I am going to be with you?'

'Like I said, I preferred the face-to-face approach.'

'They're going to be shocked.'

'Maybe they will.'

'Don't you care? You've put me in an awful position!'

'I wouldn't worry about it.' He looked at her for a few seconds, then eased himself out of the car, moving round to open the passenger door for her.

'Of course I'm worried! Most parents love all the excitement of their child announcing that a baby's on the way! They're going to be so disappointed.'

Matt laughed humourlessly. 'Like I said, Violet, don't worry about it. When it comes to disappointment, there are no surprises in store. I've been living with it all of my life.'

CHAPTER NINE

AFTERWARDS, VIOLET THOUGHT that she should have pieced together something of what she would find from that remark.

A man who can indifferently reflect that parental disappointment has been his lot in life would not be a man to enjoy a warm relationship with his parents, and they could not have been less like the fun-loving, outgoing people she had always assumed they would be.

Not that she had ever had any clues to go on because, although he was ridiculously open when it came to the women in his life and the chaotic revolving door of his relationships, he had always been tight-mouthed about his background.

She certainly had not expected them to be made of money, but they were. The front door was opened by a butler—butlers still existed!—and they were shown into a sitting room the size of an airfield.

To look at, Lord and Lady Falconer made an impressively good-looking couple. She was tall and elegant, with luxurious dark hair firmly pulled back. Traces of a Spanish heritage could be seen in her colouring, the slightly olive-toned skin and the dark eyes.

He, likewise, was tall and distinguished, the absolute epitome of an English gentleman, from the way he carried himself to the suit and tie he wore.

Violet had no idea how old they were. Certainly in their midsixties. But their mannerisms, their strained formality, made them seem much older.

Conversation was polite. Violet cringed when his mother's eyes flicked over her stomach but Matt introduced the topic without the slightest hint of embarrassment or apology. Both parents nodded their congratulations and asked precious few questions.

Accustomed as she was to a life filled with exuberant, over-the-top adults, Violet was bewildered and, after an hour of stilted conversation, deeply saddened for Matt and a childhood that had obviously been quite different from her own. Perhaps, had he not been an only child, things might have been a little better. Violet could only shudder at the thought of a young child, packed off to boarding school at the age of seven, spending holidays and free time in a house that had the feel of a mausoleum.

More than ever, she felt *special* to have been introduced to his parents. She was quite sure that he had never allowed any overlap between his parents and his women. Yes, she was pregnant, and that made a big difference, but nothing could take away from the fact that it felt like a significant step.

Dinner was served in the dining room, where they all attempted conversation across a table so vast that megaphones wouldn't have been a bad idea.

The food was delicious. Four courses, with all the appropriate wines, although neither of them had anything to drink. She was pregnant, and Matt was insistent on driving back—even though, as an afterthought, his mother did mention that a room could be prepared for them and the drive undertaken in the morning.

'Work,' Matt informed them with a polite smile, glancing at his watch, which seemed to be an accepted signal as both parents rose without fuss, leaving the dishes to be cleared away by the invisible young girl who had ferried them in.

'Coffee in the snug?' his father asked. 'Or something stronger? I have some excellent port.'

'I have a stack of emails to get through before morning,' Matt informed them both and, whilst neither parent said anything, Violet noticed the fleeting moue of distaste that had crossed his father's face. Then they were at the front door, with coats being brought to them and congratulations repeated on the pregnancy.

'We must lunch,' his mother said politely. 'I visit London every so often and I would be delighted to take you somewhere.'

Violet nodded and wondered how that would go. Lunch with Julietta Falconer? The conversation would not flow, that was for sure.

'I told you it wouldn't be a protracted affair,' was the first thing Matt said once they were in the car and heading away from the country estate.

'Do you normally have such…formal meals with your parents?'

Matt slung her a sideways glance. 'They're not the sort who enjoy casual dining round a kitchen table.'

'I never knew… I wasn't expecting…'

'I prefer not to dwell on my background. I find it muddies the water.'

'Was it always like that?'

He shrugged. 'Boarding school broke it up.' He paused and said neutrally, eyes fixed on the road ahead, making brilliant time in the darkness on the empty country lanes, 'I envy the chaotic life you must have led, Violet, even though you probably might have wished it could have been different when you were growing up.'

'I always felt that there was so much responsibility on my shoulders. Without a mother and with my dad and his carefree lack of self-control—you're right. I used to long for a bit of stability.'

'Which is why you reacted by becoming the very antithesis of your father. Where he was wild, you were grounded. You looked out for him and, in the process, you sacrificed the sort of life most young girls would have led.'

'This is a pretty deep conversation to be having so late in the evening.'

Matt smiled crookedly. 'Sometimes deep conversations are called for. I don't usually do them but, hey, there are exceptions to every rule.'

Violet glanced across at him with uneasy eyes, sensing that he wanted to say something she might not be overjoyed to hear, but really not sure what that something might be.

But that glimpse into his past had made her hungry for more, and curiosity was a greater force than wariness.

'Your parents don't approve of what you do, do they?'

'What makes you say that?' Startled, Matt slid his gaze across to her, eyes narrowed.

'Just a feeling I got.'

'Explain.'

'There was something in your dad's expression when you told him that we had to leave because you had work to do when you got back to London.'

Bitterness crept into Matt's voice when he next

spoke. 'My destiny was to manage that sprawling estate and, for fun, have a career in the city or at the very least at the bar. Something traditional and respectable. Along with marriage to the right girl with the right connections.'

'They told you that?'

'Not in so many words,' Matt said drily. 'But, then again, meaningful conversation has always been thin on the ground. The chosen way has always been to circle around what needed to be said aloud.'

Hence, Violet thought, his remark about being a disappointment. Her heart went out to him. What must he have felt growing up? He was now the biggest success story in the tech industry but, as far as his parents were concerned, he was a let down, pursuing a career they probably didn't fully understand and maybe disapproved of.

'I can hear the sound of you feeling sorry for me,' he continued.

'Of course I do.' She reached out, rested her hand on his arm and felt him stiffen fractionally. In response, she whipped her hand away, cheeks red.

'Matt.' She sighed with exasperation. 'You should tell me what's going on. I thought...' She breathed in deeply and ploughed on, because nothing felt right at the moment. 'I thought that when I agreed to give our relationship a go you might have been a little more enthusiastic, especially considering you were the one to suggest... Well, you asked me to marry you and I turned you down. Now I'm prepared to meet you halfway but I get the feeling that you're not at all overjoyed with the situation. You vanished like a bat out of hell the second I told you that I was prepared to give things a go and now you can barely look me in the face. Meeting your parents…felt like a big step forward, but was it? Or was it just a hurdle that had to be jumped?'

'You deserve to have all those questions answered,' he said roughly.

Violet felt a chill run through her. How had she managed to misjudge the situation so badly? He'd been the perfect partner when he had had no choice but to take care of her, but while he had been fetching and carrying and making sure that her feet were up and she was getting the bed rest the doctor had recommended, he had had time and opportunity to consider his options.

He liked her and she was his responsibility and, whilst that combination had initially propelled him into that rash marriage proposal, things had changed. He had backed away from that drastic suggestion and now saw things the way she had. Standing back at a distance, he had doubtless come to appreciate that they could have a perfectly amicable relationship without him committing to putting a ring on her finger.

Maybe, just maybe, he had even begun casting his net out there. Maybe, just maybe, he had realised that he could have her as a friend and carry on with his Lothario ways. How many men didn't want to have their cake and eat it? Bit by bit, she had thawed and pushed past her inherent fears that he wouldn't turn out to be the dependable guy she needed, that he *couldn't* be that person. Had she made a terrible mistake?

'What are you doing?' she asked, dismayed, as he swung off the main road, heading down a side street signposting a village, a place she had never heard of.

'We need to talk and I don't want to talk in the car. I can't focus on the road and the conversation we have to have.'

'Then let's wait until we're back in London.' Violet was only now appreciating just how much she had come to rely on him and just how far she had taken it for granted that he would be thrilled were she to give ground and do what he had wanted her to do when she had first broken the news of her pregnancy. Mistakes and misjudgements all round, it would seem.

Matt didn't answer. He seemed to know this part of the world well, considering his visits to his parents were confined to four times a year, but then he would have grown up in these parts, maybe wanting to escape the claustrophobia of his ancestral home as soon as he was old enough to do so.

Very quickly, they pulled up to a brightly lit pub. The car park was full but they managed to squeeze into a space and then, without exchanging conversation, they headed inside, where he was greeted by the landlord like an old buddy.

They found a bench seat at the back by one of only the few tables. It was a little after ten but the place was still busy.

Matt went up to the bar and returned with two drinks, something alcoholic for him and a glass of elderflower for her.

'It's late,' he said gruffly. 'There are nice rooms upstairs. I've booked us in for the night.'

'Why?'

'Because I want a drink, and I don't do drinking and driving. Now that you've met my parents, Violet, you can maybe see...why my approach to relationships is somewhat, shall we say, different to yours. You long for stability. You've lived your life pursuing the dream of finding the perfect partner and settling down.' He took one long mouthful of whisky and sat back to look at her. 'I, Violet, have not.'

'No,' Violet said quietly. 'I get that now.'

'Tell me what you get.'

'You never felt loved, at least not loved in the way most people acknowledge it—nothing verbal, nothing tactile,' she ventured tentatively. 'And if someone has never felt loved, then how do they know how to love? You've never done long-term relationships because you've never seen the point of them. In your world, there's no such thing as love, so why would you encourage any woman to look in that direction if you know that you can't deliver. Am I right?'

She thought of his parents, their oppressive lack of emotion. She thought of the hopes she had nurtured of him loving her the way she loved him. Those hopes were slowly evaporating like mist on a hot summer morning. 'You've had time to think things through and you've realised that you can't settle down to any kind of relationship with me, even though you probably wish you could, because like you said, you have dreams of being a full-time father.'

Violet forced herself to smile. It made her face ache. 'Of course, you're right, and I don't know what I was thinking when I said that I was prepared to give things a go. It's all working perfectly well between us as it stands! I'm more or less back on my feet as well, so I should be out of your hair very soon.'

He was frowning and Violet banked down a surge of impatience. Was she being obtuse? She didn't think so!

'What makes you think that I'm no longer interested in marrying you?'

'B-because…!' Violet spluttered. 'Because I can *tell*.'

'Really? How?'

'You act as though I've suddenly become a stranger,'

she muttered under her breath, hating him for directing the conversation down this uncomfortable road.

'How do you want me to act?'

'This is a ridiculous conversation,' Violet said sharply. 'I know the lie of the land, Matt. That's the main thing.'

'I've been distant because I didn't want you to get any unrealistic ideas, should we embark on a full-time relationship.'

'What are you talking about?' Her voice had cooled and her brown eyes were wary and remote.

'Things felt…comfortable, Violet. The way we slipped into a routine.' He lowered his gaze, very much aware that he, too, had become disturbingly accustomed to the routine they had established.

'And you thought that, because there was some kind of routine, I might start pining over what was never going to be on the table.'

'I'm not a man who knows how to love. It's the way I'm built. Can you live with that?'

Violet shrugged but inside something had broken. Could she live with this guy, knowing that he would never love her the way she wanted him to? He was nothing if not honest and he was giving her an opt-out clause. She thought of him moving on and felt faint.

'Like you said at the beginning, Matt, this isn't just about us. This is about a baby who didn't ask to be conceived and about giving this baby of ours the best chance in life. Sacrifices have to be made. What we have is good just the way it is… And if it's not exactly what I had in mind for myself, then that's life. It's all about compromise.'

He was looking at her carefully. 'I've booked us into separate rooms.'

'Have you?'

'I had no idea how this conversation would go.'

'And now?'

'You tell me, Violet.'

'It's stupid to think that we can try to make a go of this without…without…'

Matt smiled, a slow, curling smile that made her pulse race.

'I'll let them know that we'll only need one room, shall I?'

The exhaustion that had wiped her out when she had been at his parents' house faded fast as they finished their drinks and made their way up to a charming, tiny bedroom with old-fashioned chintz curtains and a matching bedspread on the double bed. She felt as nervous as a kitten, and it almost made her laugh when she thought that she was carrying this man's baby, so nerves should have been the last thing she felt as she watched him get undressed, his movements slow and casual, his eyes focused on her the whole time.

'You have no idea how much I've missed this, Violet. Watching you…watching you grow…knowing that I shouldn't touch.'

He stepped towards her, naked and erect, and warmth flooded her. She crept into his arms as easily as if she belonged there and rested her head against his chest.

'I've missed it as well,' she responded gruffly, talking into his chest. He gently held her at arm's length and looked at her.

'Important question. Is this okay for the baby?'

Violet laughed. 'Of course it is!'

'Good. I'd googled, out of curiosity, but who believes what they read on a computer screen?'

'Ninety-nine percent of the population?'

Matt smiled and flushed. 'I've missed more than the

sex, if I'm honest. I've missed your sense of humour.' He swept her off her feet, took her to the bed and then stood to look down at her. Violet couldn't help herself. She reached out and touched him and hot moisture pooled between her legs as his erect manhood pulsed against the slow, feathery brush of her finger.

Very slowly she touched him the way she knew he liked being touched, firm and slow, and he arched back, breathing quickening as lazily she continued to arouse him, then she straddled the side of the bed, her legs apart, and licked the rigid length of his shaft. She let her hands drop to caress the sensitive skin of his inner thighs and he groaned and curled his fingers into her hair, directing her mouth. He finally drew her away with a shudder.

'No way are you going to take me there with your mouth,' he chastised her in a roughened undertone and she grinned back at him.

This felt so good, so right—as though they were meant to be with one another. She locked seditious thoughts away, thoughts of the impossible. He had set her straight on how he felt and, having met his parents, she could see how he had ended up as he had, the key to his heart thrown out like so much useless garbage. But they would be together and, if this was second best, then she would accept that.

She began undressing and desire bloomed even more because he was watching her with that way he had, focused and intense, as though even her slightest movements were a source of fascination for him.

He helped her, in the end. He couldn't resist. Her clothes joined his on the ground and they managed to rid the bed of the chintz spread, laughing as they peeled it back while trying to hold one another at the same time. That, too, ended up in a crumpled bundle on the ground.

She was naked and it felt liberating.

He reverently stroked her swollen stomach.

'Your breasts have grown,' he murmured. 'I'd wondered. Fantasised. Having you share the apartment with me was a test of willpower I never knew I possessed. So don't try to stop me from exploring every inch of your body now.'

'I wouldn't dream of it.'

He curved his hand to cup a breast and held it as though weighing it up for size, then he rolled the pad of his thumb over her nipple and felt it stiffen under his finger.

Her breasts had grown, as had her nipples, which had darkened into big, circular discs.

One touch and Matt knew that he wouldn't be able to steel himself from coming in an undignified premature ejaculation. He closed his eyes and nuzzled the softness of her breasts, eliciting little whimpers of pleasure, then he suckled on her nipple, teasing the stiffened tip with his tongue and simultaneously curving his hand between her thighs so that he could feel the dampness between her legs.

She relaxed against the pressure of his hand there. She arched back in a gesture that was gratifyingly and seductively submissive. Submission wasn't something she did and her unconscious desire to yield to him was a massive turn-on.

The swell of her stomach was a massive turn-on as well.

He nudged into her gently, levering himself in just the perfect position to appreciate her. He moved slowly and firmly, taking his time and gritting his teeth because he wanted to do just the opposite, but, God, he wanted to make this last. It felt as if it had been a long time coming.

Violet succumbed to the surge of indescribable pleasure as one gentle thrust almost took her over the edge. She clung to him and wrapped her legs around his waist. Like this, in the heat of the moment, she could sneak a glance at his face. His eyes were glazed with desire as he pushed into her. He wasn't registering her and, for a few seconds, she could luxuriate in looking at him with absolute love.

Forbidden love. She closed her eyes and inhaled sharply as sensation spiralled, wiping out frustrating thoughts. He was moving faster now, his thrusts deeper and, oh, so satisfying. It had been a long time. It felt like years.

She came with an intensity that shocked her, her body trembling as wave upon wave of pure sensation rocked her with the force of a tsunami.

She clasped his muscled back, her fingers digging into his bronzed skin. She doubted he was aware of anything, though. He was arched up, his eyes closed, nostrils slightly flared as he found his own powerful release, swearing aloud as he orgasmed inside her. She could feel his fluid rush into her body, and for a few seconds she thought of the baby they had created when they had made love that first time without any protection.

The love she felt for him was so strong, her breath caught in her throat. She wanted to pull him close to her but then, almost immediately, she acknowledged the foolishness of her feelings because she, of all the people in the world, should know him for the man that he was. She had dispatched enough farewell bouquets of

flowers on his behalf! Heck, she had the local Knightsbridge florist he used on speed dial!

She'd just never really worked out how how deep his
cynicism ran. Now she knew.

They curved towards one another and he smiled,
hand on her stomach.

'I never thought I'd enjoy saying this to a woman,
but let's make plans.'

'Okay.' She paused. They were a couple and this was
as good as it got with him. There had to be a certain
businesslike approach to the situation or else it would
run away with her and she didn't want that. 'But first,
there's something we should get straight between us.'

'What's that?'

'This has to be a…monogamous relationship. If we're
a couple, then no fooling around.'

Matt propped himself up on one elbow and looked
at her with interest. 'I thought that monogamy was reserved for faithfully married couples,' he murmured.
'Love, cherish, honour, et cetera, et cetera…'

'But we're missing those qualities, aren't we?' Violet
quipped, lowering her eyes to shield the hurt she was
certain he would be able to glimpse, even though it was
dark in the bedroom and he would have needed bionic
vision to read what she was thinking.

'I'm a one-woman man, Violet,' he gently repri-
manded her.

'Even though we're not a faithfully married couple?'

'You could always rectify that.'

Temptation loomed. What was the big difference between living together and being married? Violet knew
that it should have been a case of, in for a penny, in for a
pound, but somehow marriage felt like a huge step. She
would be accepting, without hope of retraction, a situ-

ation that she knew was barely acceptable. She would be signing away her future because a little of this man was better than nothing at all. Except what if, one day, she began to think otherwise? Then what? She couldn't think of the hassle and hopelessness of divorce without her blood running cold.

At least, living together, she could cling to the illusion that there was a way out if things became truly unbearable.

'It's more sensible for us to see how things work out between us.' She dug her heels in and stared at the bronzed, flat planes of his chest. She felt him shrug, then he lay back and stared up at the ceiling.

'Sensible,' he murmured under his breath. 'It's what I've always admired about you. When everyone's losing their heads...'

That stung. Was that still what he thought of her deep down? That she was his practical, sensible secretary who could be relied upon to steer a steady ship when the rest of the world seemed to be going mad? Hadn't he got past that by now? If he hadn't, then it really was for the best that they weren't about to tie any knots any time soon, because the joys of a common-sense wife would wear very thin very fast.

But without a ring on her finger...without the status of *wife*...would his loyalty be something she could ever take for granted?

Violet realised that if she gave house room to all those niggling doubts at the back of her mind, then she would never be free of them, and if she were to stick to her word and really give this relationship a chance, at least to see whether she could actually take the crumbs and forfeit the loaf of bread, then she would have to forge past misgivings.

She rested her hand on his stomach. 'The sensible thing, right now, would be to discuss what happens next. I mean, the nuts and bolts of it. My dad seems to be coming round to the idea of returning here to live. I think he's energised by the thought of having a grandchild. Anyway, he's talking about using the music school he started in Melbourne as a template for doing something similar over here. Not in London. I think he's learned to appreciate a slower lane, living out there.'

'I'm not sure I'm in the mood for talking about sensible things just at the moment,' Matt drawled, flattening his hand over hers and then directing it to where his libido was, once more, making itself felt. 'Let's make up for lost time and throw sensible to the winds…just for tonight.'

Everything, over the next two months, seemed to move at a very slow pace. Matt would not let her do anything he felt might be a set back to her health, even though she had long since been given the all-clear by the obstetrician she had been assigned by the private hospital he'd insisted on. Having rapidly decided that a move out of London was essential, and having discussed in record time where that somewhere might be—ideally allowing a commute into London without sacrificing the country lifestyle they both agreed would be a good choice for a family—it was frustrating that house viewings were confined to when Matt was free, because he flatly refused to let Violet get wrapped up in the stress of house hunting on her own.

She could look at brochures, he told her as they idly lay in bed one Sunday morning, flicking through houses online. Looking at brochures would be good for her blood pressure. She reminded him that her blood pressure was fine, but lying there naked, her leg loosely over his, she had never been happier.

This felt like what being a couple was all about. Time was moving on and, if the whole subject of marriage had gone onto the back burner, then it was because they were both enjoying what they had. So why complicate matters by rocking the boat?

She was luxuriating in all sorts of taboo thoughts about love, happy-ever-afters, and other never-to-be-tabled scenarios, when she heard the buzz of her mobile.

It was a little after six in the evening. Outside, night had fallen and there was a glacial chill to the air that was a reminder that winter was lurking just round the corner. Inside the apartment, Violet was already in her comfy clothes. Bedroom slippers, jogging bottoms and a loose tee shirt, over which she was wearing a hand-me-down cardigan from her father who, as he had grown older, had adopted a curiously traditional sartorial style.

Slouching around was exactly what she would be doing for the next three days because Matt was in New York. As he had been the previous month, although only for two nights. He'd explained the deal to her, but her brain had been fuzzy, and he had burst out laughing when she'd yawned halfway through the details about an app that could do clever things involving personal finance. Not as amusing as the games industry, Matt had said, but anything to keep body and soul together—which was rich, coming from a billionaire.

It took her a few seconds to register the female voice down the end of the line and, even when she did, her first reaction was puzzlement more than anything else.

'Glo?' She parroted the name and then, just for added confirmation, 'Glo Bale from the flower shop?'

'The very same.' Glo laughed.

She was a middle-aged woman with a bubbly personality and an infectious laugh. She and Violet had exchanged many a coded conversation in the past about Matt's predilection for goodbye bouquets without once overstepping the line. It was a telephone relationship that had always been comfortable and amicable.

'I'm sorry to bother you, my darling,' Glo said breathlessly, 'but I've been trying to get through to your lovely boss…'

Ex-boss, Violet thought absently. Clearly, Glo was not in the loop and she wondered what the other woman would think.

'He's away at the moment. New York.'

'Probably busy in meetings,' Glo said. 'But here's the thing. He left a message for me to prepare one of his bouquets. Said he'd get back to me to confirm details, but I haven't heard, and the flowers are going to begin heading for the big botanical garden in the sky if he doesn't get his skates on and fill me in on the details.'

'A—a bouquet?' Violet stammered.

'Over-the-top one, if I'm honest, my darling.'

'Over-the-top…' She cleared her throat. Her stomach was doing weird things, freewheeling, making her feel giddy and sick. 'Thanks for calling, Glo. I'll… I'll tell him to get in touch with you… Thanks.'

She hung up and stared sightlessly at her mobile.

Flowers? A bouquet? Over-the-top?

Who was he saying goodbye to?

CHAPTER TEN

Missed your calls. Sorry. Been busy.

SIX WORDS. BUT the minute Matt read them on his mobile he knew that something was seriously wrong. He just couldn't figure out what that something might be, because up until then life had been going swimmingly, for want of a better word.

He had one more day left. New York was less than its usual invigorating self and he couldn't focus. What was that text message supposed to mean?

The meeting room on the fifty-ninth floor of a skyscraper that had topped the charts for creativity felt stifling. There were dozens of people milling around, almost as though there was no deal to be done, and they had all the time in the world to talk about nothing in particular while guzzling limitless glasses of champagne.

When Matt looked around him, he couldn't see an end to the deal that, yet again, would amass millions in the years to come. The only thing he could see were those cool, impersonal words on his mobile, a response to the unanswered phone calls and text messages.

Been busy. *Doing what?*

Yes, she was back on her feet. Her blood pressure had stabilised. The sickness had gone. Of course, he thought distractedly, she was busy because she was no longer confined to his apartment. She was probably running herself ragged looking at paint colours, furniture or kitchen gadgets! Understandable, because she was not the sort of woman who could sit still.

And yet…

He crooked a finger and the start-up's CEO jumped to attention like a puppet whose strings had been pulled.

He would have to go to Violet. There was no question about it. It took him under a minute to communicate his intentions to his startled sidekick.

'But the signatures still have to hit the paper,' Bob said, frowning. 'Then there's the usual celebrations…'

'Time for you to step up to the plate,' Matt said, looking at his watch and mentally working out how long it would take for him to get to the UK. Private jet or commercial? 'Don't forget the size of the bonus coming your way in a month's time. You can close this deal as efficiently as the next man. Just make sure you keep some of this lot in order and don't let the celebrations run away with you. I expect you back in the UK by the end of the week.'

Commercial, he thought. No time to fuel up and get things in position. He could be back at his apartment in under ten hours and then he would see for himself just what was going on…

Violet stuffed her mobile under the cushion on the sofa. It had been pinging with messages from Matt. He had tried calling five times. Tough. She wasn't going to answer. She would when her brain stopped whizzing round her head like a helicopter rotor. Just as soon as she started thinking in a straight line. But right now, all she could do was picture an over-the-top bunch of flowers being delivered to some poor, dispatched woman who probably didn't have a clue that her charming billionaire escort was actually sleeping with another woman. Another woman who just happened to be pregnant with his child.

How long had it been going on? Weeks? Months? Had he now decided, since they were getting along very well, that it was time to call off his outside affair? Had his conscience been kick-started because the baby was well on its way, no longer something that was going to happen, but something that was imminent?

She was tortured by questions and in no fit state to talk to him on the telephone.

Typically, he wouldn't give up. Of course, she couldn't bury her head in the sand like an ostrich for ever, but just for the moment, she needed time to think.

She wished she had a mum around. Or at least a good friend, someone she had shared the ups and downs of her life with, who could give her a pep talk, make her a cup of tea and tell her that everything was going to be okay.

No such luck.

A good night's sleep, if she could get it, would have to do the trick. He was due back the following evening, and by then she would have to have found a way through the pain, the whirring head, the clammy hands and the sick feeling in the pit of her stomach.

She hit the sack early and fell into a restless sleep. She couldn't stop thinking. She would have to call quits on whatever relationship they had been trying to cultivate. She'd thought they'd been making progress but she'd obviously been mistaken because behind her back he'd been seeing someone. She reminded herself that she'd originally banked on going it alone. It wouldn't be the end of the world. She would just have to power on—and wasn't it great that at least she wasn't financially dependent on him? Not that he would ever fail to contribute his fair share and beyond.

She thought she'd never fall asleep, but she must have nodded off because she didn't hear the sound of the front door opening. She only realised that Matt had returned when a sliver of light penetrated the darkness, and she groggily surfaced in stages to see his shadowy outline framed by the door.

He was so still that he could have been a statue. Heart thumping, Violet propped herself up on her elbows, then clumsily turned to switch on the light by the bed.

Not for one second did she think that the unexpected appearance was anyone but Matt. Certainly, she could not have mistaken his dauntingly impressive frame for anyone else.

'What's going on?' he demanded without preamble, stepping forward.

'Huh?'

'You haven't been answering my calls.'

'What are you doing here?' Violet's brain finally cranked into gear, but her heart was still beating like a drum and her mouth was dry. 'Shouldn't you be sealing the deal on the opposite side of the world?'

'How could I do that when I was worried sick about you?'

'Oh, please…' She was beginning to think straight and the swirling, muddy waters of all the emotions with which she had gone to bed were right back with her, firing her with fury, disappointment and unhappiness.

'What is that supposed to mean?'

'As if you don't know, Matt,' Violet muttered under her breath.

'I don't know.'

The silence stretched to a breaking point between them. She had planned to handle this situation in a very different way. For a start, she had decided that anything but an adult approach wasn't going to do. She had pretty much determined that she wouldn't mention the good-bye flowers at all. She would simply tell him that they had experimented with the concept of living together and she felt that she would not be able to continue it.

She toyed with the idea of telling him that she had feelings for him. That would certainly do the trick when it came to getting him to catapult himself off the starting block at great speed. But then she realised that she would have to live with him feeling sorry for her for ever, even if she moved on to find someone else.

Poor Violet... I warned her not to get emotionally involved but she just couldn't help herself...

'The flowers,' she said quietly, and he frowned in puzzlement.

'I need something to drink, Violet. Water. Then we can continue this conversation.'

He spun round on his heels and no sooner had he left the bedroom than she awkwardly heaved herself out of the bed, slung on her dressing gown, belting it securely round her tummy, and followed him into the kitchen.

She didn't want a conversation in bed. She didn't want him sitting on the edge looking at her or, worse, climbing into bed with her to continue their talk. She was realistic enough to know that a bed plus Matt Falconer was a lethal combination when it came to her defence system.

She padded out to find him gulping down a glass of water, his back to her.

'The flowers, Matt,' she repeated, and he turned round and looked at her, simultaneously dumping the empty glass on the counter. 'And don't pretend that you don't know what I'm talking about. Glo called.'

'Glo? Glo who?'

Of course he wouldn't recognise the name, Violet thought bitterly. He'd always left the nuts and bolts of saying goodbye to her to sort out, while he merrily galloped towards another empty affair.

'Glo from the flower shop in Knightsbridge. You know the one. She called to say that you'd started an order for your *usual* but had failed to complete it so she didn't know what you wanted to do with the flowers. If you tell me who the poor girl is, then I can call her back and arrange for them to be sent to her.'

Violet barely needed to see the expression on his face because the absolute stillness of his body was enough to give the game away. He knew what she was talking about and he wasn't going to try to pretend otherwise.

'The flowers,' he said. 'It never occurred to me that the woman would call you.'

'Why would that be? I've been dealing with her for... for years. Together, we've been taking care of all those broken hearts you've left behind, sending flowers as though a bunch of blooms can patch them up and make them good.'

'There's no need for drama, Violet.'

'This is not what I signed up for.'

'You don't understand.'

'Matt, that must be the most well-worn statement any man can make when he's made a mistake and been caught red handed.' She was managing to keep her voice level, but it came at a cost. Her heart was splintering into a thousand pieces. She looked away and shuffled towards the sofa because her legs felt wobbly.

'Violet...'

His voice was soft right behind her but, when he placed his hand on her arm, she angrily shook it off without looking at him.

'I don't want this for myself, Matt. I don't want *you*.' She sank onto the sofa and didn't look at him as he hovered in front of her, the very essence of a guilt-ridden male, she thought, raking his fingers through his hair, his fabulous eyes not quite able to meet hers... All that was missing was the stammer.

Anger, jealousy, searing hurt all fused inside her and she briefly closed her eyes and breathed in deeply. When she opened them, he was still there, towering over her, arms folded.

'I'm telling you that you don't understand.'

'And I'm telling *you* that I do! I understand because I know you, because I've been down this road before, don't forget! I've arranged the flowers and sent them on your behalf, except this time you were going to send the flowers yourself until you got wrapped up with your deal and forgot.'

'I think I need something a little stronger to drink than water,' he ground out, turning round and heading to the kitchen, to reappear within minutes with a glass of whisky that he downed in one ferocious gulp.

'Please don't try to talk your way out of this, Matt,' she said when he pulled a chair towards her and sat down. 'I deserve the truth and then... Well, we can take things from there, but first and foremost we'll have to agree that this experiment has failed.'

'Please, Violet...'

'Please what? Please try to listen to whatever version of the truth you decide to come out with to placate me? Please accept a situation where I share you with other women? Absolutely not!'

'Do you honestly think that I'm that sort of person?' he demanded, and when she would have turned away he leant forward and tilted her face to his so that she couldn't avoid his searching gaze.

'I didn't,' she said truthfully. 'But, then again, as you once pointed out, we're not married, are we? Some people aren't meant to settle down. They're rolling stones. You're one of those people, Matt, and if I was lulled into thinking otherwise then I'm wide awake now.'

'I can explain...'

Violet looked at him stonily. She had always had her pride, and she had a lot of experience when it came to concealing her emotions from him. She had fancied him from a distance, but he would never have guessed in a million years as she made those phone calls to the flower shop and arranged theatre tickets and opera seats for the women who'd flitted in and out of his life.

She wanted to burst into tears, but there was no way she was going to do that. Every bone in her body hurt from the effort of keeping it together.

'Please don't bother.'

'Okay, I admit that, yes, I ordered the flowers.'

'I told you that I don't want to hear!' The last thing she needed was an agonised confession of infidelity. He would use his words carefully, but the message would remain the same and it was a message she didn't want to hear. There was only so much reality any person could take in one go.

'But then I chickened out from actually having them delivered.'

'Because you couldn't bear to say goodbye to whoever was on the receiving end?' She clenched her hands into tights fists and stared at him with simmering hostility.

How could so much beauty be so lethal? But then,

wasn't nature full of poisonous creatures whose physical appearance could seduce and enchant?

'Because I didn't know how to say hello,' Matt muttered under his breath. She had to strain to catch what he was saying. She was grudgingly riveted because, for the very first time, he was shorn of his usual self-assurance. A dark flush highlighted his cheekbones and he had lowered his eyes. Every muscle in his body shrieked tension.

'What are you talking about?'

'I'm no good at this sort of thing.'

'What sort of thing? Behaving like a decent human being and telling the truth?' An unfair and uncharitable remark. She knew that. He was a decent human being. He'd been decent from the start and it was all her fault if she'd hoped for more.

'Violet...would you listen to me? Please? No interruption?'

Violet shrugged, but the plea in his voice held her still. He was so assertive, so dominant, that that ghost of a plea momentarily derailed her.

'All of this...us...what happened... None of it... I never predicted any of it.'

'That makes the two of us, Matt,' Violet muttered, flicking resentful eyes at him.

'You handed in your notice, Violet, and I didn't think how much I really relied on you until you did that. I read that email and my blood ran cold. Why do you think I raced over to your house? There was no way I could have waited until the following morning.'

'I don't know what that has to do with anything.'

'No interruption. Remember?' He smiled crookedly at her and she felt her treacherous body melt a little. She sternly reminded herself that melting was not an option.

'I've asked myself whether I would have gone to Melbourne if I hadn't had those deals on the go, if I hadn't had an excuse. The more I realised that I would have, the more I realised just how...dependent I had become on you over the years. It wasn't a message I was happy to take on board, so I did the obvious thing and ignored it.'

Violet was listening intently. She didn't know where this was going, but for the moment she had forgotten all about the flowers and was focused instead on whatever road he was leading her down.

He was so intent, his navy eyes so compelling. Part of her wanted to break away but she was held in place against her will. *Dependent how?* she wanted to ask, but that was a dangerous road to follow, so she focused on telling herself that she'd been a brilliant secretary who could handle him and of course he'd unwittingly become dependent on her. There was no point reading beyond that.

'I saw you on that stage, Violet, and something else I never realised hit me like a sledgehammer.'

'What was that?'

'I wanted you. I was attracted to you. Something about you...went beyond physical attraction, and I never registered that because, for me, there had never been anything beyond physical attraction. Physical attraction was something I could understand. Sex was good, but sex was all there was, and as far as I was concerned it was all there ever would be with any woman. A relationship involved feelings I knew I would never have and I was never going to be in the business of pretending otherwise. I grew up in a house where there was never any demonstration of affection between my parents and I guess what you see becomes learned behaviour. I accepted that without really analysing it. But then you left me.'

'Matt, I hardly *left* you.'

'You left me,' he said gruffly. 'That's what it felt like. I should have known that what I felt weren't the usual feelings of a boss who has lost his brilliant PA— and I certainly should have realised that what I felt was something way deeper the very minute we climbed into bed. Nothing had felt so right, Violet. Everything was magnified. Exquisitely intense. I never wanted it to stop. That should have set the alarm bells ringing, but I'd never heard those bells before, and I had no idea what they signified.'

'Please, Matt, don't say things you don't mean.'

'I wouldn't. When I left Melbourne, I thought life would go back to normal, but it didn't. On the surface, everything was as it should be, but below the surface…a crack had opened, and it grew bigger by the day. There was no way I was conditioned to put two and two together but, when you showed up at my office all those weeks later, I was over the moon.'

'You were?'

'You'd come back. And then you told me that you were pregnant and I was shocked at how readily I accepted the situation. I'd never planned on having a family, yet there I was, and I wasn't complaining half as much as I should have been.'

'Matt…' Violet whispered helplessly.

'I wanted to marry you. I couldn't stand the thought of not having you and our baby in my life on a permanent basis. But you weren't having it and, while I understood where you were coming from, I still couldn't stand it.'

'You stopped asking very quickly,' she pointed out, unwillingly drawn into a conversation that was dangerously seductive.

'I didn't want to scare you off, but then you relented, told me that you were willing to meet me halfway.'

'I hated the thought of you finding someone else,' Violet admitted, breaking all her self-imposed rules about revealing as little as possible. 'I hated thinking that I would see you with another woman hanging on your arm whenever you came round to see our child. I hated the thought that you would probably end up marrying one of those women. Like I've said, a single guy pushing a pram is an irresistible temptation. I also knew, whether I wanted to admit it to myself or not, that two parents were always going to be better together than apart when it came to a child's best interests. You were prepared to be unselfish. Why shouldn't I?'

'Violet…' His voice roughened and he looked away, his body language awkward but intensely appealing in its sincerity. 'The flowers…'

'The flowers.'

'For you.'

'I beg your pardon?'

'The flowers were for you. It took me a while, because I was so bloody slow on the uptake, but I finally slotted all the pieces of the jigsaw together and saw what had been staring me in the face from that very first moment we slept together. I love you, Violet. You, your smile, your quick wit, the way you have of standing your ground and not giving an inch. I love the way you stand up to me. I love the way you make me feel.'

'You *love* me?'

'I didn't recognise the symptoms.' He smiled a hesitant smile and reached forward to link her fingers loosely with his. 'Even though I knew I had a virus.'

'Are you really being honest with me?'

'I would never lie about something like this. I always

thought that my heart was firmly locked away, but you managed to get hold of the key…and I think it happened long before we slept together. You have the whole package, Violet, and I was an idiot not to see that sooner.'

Violet's heart was soaring and there was a drumbeat in her ears. 'I love you too, Matt.' It felt a dangerous crossing of lines to utter those words, because she'd spent so long making sure they never left her lips. She almost expected him to pull back, despite everything he had just said, but he didn't. He smiled. She tentatively held her hand against his face and he caught it in his and kissed her palm.

'I was so attracted to you before I left for Melbourne, but I knew that it would never come to anything because we were just so different. The last sort of guy I wanted was someone who played the field, and there was no way you could ever be attracted to me, anyway. I'd seen way too much of the women you went for to ever think that you could go for someone like me.

'Then you came to Melbourne and you were there for me when my father was rushed into hospital. Sleeping with you…felt so incredibly good, but I just looked at it as stolen happiness. It wasn't going to last, but I would hold on to it for as long as I could. When I found out that I was pregnant, I was so confused. I knew I had to tell you, but the thought of seeing you again…scared me. I'm not sure when I realised that I loved you. Maybe I always knew, just as I knew that love was the last thing you would ever want from me.'

She paused. 'Why didn't you send the flowers?'

'I chickened out. I suspected you had feelings for me, but I couldn't be sure. I loved you, but what was that about? How had that happened? I placed the order for forty-eight red roses and then I panicked. Had second thoughts. I told myself that I'd get back to it, make my mind up, take the bull by the horns, but I needed a couple of days to think it through. It never occurred to me that the woman at the flower shop would get in touch with you, but she did, and here we are.

'My darling, darling Violet. We love one another and I have never been happier in my entire life. So, please, will you marry me? Not because we're having a baby, but because we want to share the rest of our lives together.'

'How could I possibly say no to that?'

She smiled at him, then leant forward and pulled him towards her, and the feel of his mouth on hers sent her heart into a crazy tailspin. Oh, how used to that feeling she was—but, oh, how wonderful that this time the feeling was mutual.

They were married less than a month later, plenty of time to have got her father over. Every single employee attended, along with friends from every walk of life, including many of her father's friends, most of whom she remembered well. It was a rowdy and memorable affair. Her father was in his element and, at the end of a brilliant evening, he and some of his former band members formed an impromptu group to play for the newlyweds.

Matt's parents, as stiff-lipped as she had expected, unbent a little by the end of the evening. This time, when his mother politely repeated her invitation to lunch, Violet nodded and conceded that it might not be quite as bad as she had reckoned the first time the invitation had been extended.

Who knew? Maybe a baby would change the dynamics.

They should have had a honeymoon of her choosing,

Matt had said, but with his usual overprotective gene in full flow, he had put his foot down at any destination that involved a plane. She was far too pregnant to travel, he had determined, even if the duration of the flight was ten seconds.

So they had a romantic week in deepest Cornwall, where the weather pretty much did what they wanted it to. They had lovely walks and a roaring fire in the evening.

And then, in the blink of an eye, Matilda was there. Eight pounds six ounces of curly black hair, navy-blue eyes, a rosebud mouth and little chubby hands punching the air.

Now, six months later, Violet could smile at the memory of just how panicked Matt had been when she had gone into labour.

Her cool, collected and self-assured husband had been at his most flustered.

'Just remember to breathe,' she had told him, amused and indulgent in between contractions, 'and you'll be okay.'

She heard the sound of the front door opening, but this time it wasn't the door to his apartment, but the door to the house on Richmond Hill where they now lived. They had finally opted for somewhere close enough for Matt to return home in the evenings in time to see Matilda before she went to bed. Original plans to move farther out had been put on the back burner.

He strode in and was as mesmerising as he always was, walking towards her with that slow smile that still made her toes curl and her skin prickle with love and desire.

'An early Friday,' he drawled, kissing her on the mouth and then kissing her again before pulling back.

'As instructed by my darling wife.' He glanced past her from hallway to open-plan kitchen. 'And I see the table is set for...' He frowned. 'For five people?'

'I thought I'd surprise you,' Violet said, pulling him towards the kitchen. Matilda was sound asleep in her cot and she could sense that he was itching to go in and have a look at his sleeping daughter. 'My dad's coming over for dinner...and your parents.'

'My *parents*?'

'Why not?'

'Why not, indeed?' he murmured. 'What time are they over?'

'We have a couple of hours. They won't be here until seven forty-five.'

'In that case...' He leant down to brush his mouth against her neck and, at the same time, he curved a possessive hand underneath the short-sleeved jumper to find the swell of her naked breasts, because she was braless. On cue, he hardened, and even more so when he pushed up the jumper to tease her nipple between his fingers. 'We have plenty of time for me to look in on Matilda and then have ourselves a little bit of fun... wouldn't you agree?'

Violet smiled. Yes, she would agree. She tiptoed to curl her hands around his neck and pulled him to her so that she could kiss him, a long, lingering kiss, full of love, desire and adoration.

She most certainly would agree.

* * * * *

THE SECRET KEPT
FROM THE KING

CLARE CONNELLY

This book's for you—a romance reader who, just like me, loves to be swept up in a passionate escapist story with a guaranteed happily-ever-after.

CHAPTER ONE

WHEN HE CLOSED his eyes he saw only his father's, so he tried not to close them much at all. Not because he didn't want to see the Exalted Sheikh Kadir Al Antarah again; he did, more than anything. But seeing his eyes as they'd been at the end, so clouded by pain and unconscious of the world that swirled around him, so robbed of the strength and vibrancy that had been hallmarks of his life and rule, made Sariq's chest compress in a way that robbed him of breath and had him gasping for air.

The King was dead. His father was dead. He was now completely alone in this world, and the inescapable reality he had been aware of all his life was wrapping around him like a cable.

He had been crowned. The job of steering the Royal Kingdom of Haleth fell to him. Just as he'd always known it would, just as he'd spent a lifetime preparing for.

'Your Highness? Malik has asked me to remind you of the time.'

Sariq didn't respond at first. He continued to stare out at the glittering vista of Manhattan. From this vantage point, it was easy to pick out the key buildings that were considered the most well-known landmarks of New York. The Empire State building shone like a beacon. The Chrysler with its art deco detailing, and, far in the distance, the spire of One World Trade Centre. And in another direction, not far from this hotel, if he followed a straight line, he'd reach the United Nations, where he'd be expected to make his first official speech since the death of Sheikh Kadir. In the morning, he'd address leaders and delegates from dozens of countries, aiming to assure them that his father's death was not an end to the peace that had, finally, been established between the RKH and the west.

'Emir?'

'Yes.' He spoke more harshly than he'd intended. He closed his eyes—and there was his father. He returned his attention to the view, his features locked in a grim mask. 'Tell Malik I am aware of the hour.'

Still, the servant hovered. 'Can I get you anything else, sir?'

Briefly, Sariq turned to face the servant. He was little more than a boy—sixteen or seventeen perhaps. He wore the same uniform Sariq had donned at that age, black with gold detailing. The insignia indicated he was an ensign. 'What is your name?'

The boy's eyes widened.

'Kaleth.'

Sariq forced a smile to his face. It felt odd, heavy and wooden. 'Thank you for your attention, Kaleth, but you may go now.'

Kaleth paused, as though he wished to say something further.

'Tell Malik it was at my insistence.'

This seemed to appease the young officer because he nodded and bowed low. 'Goodnight, sir.'

He turned back to the view without responding. It was after midnight and his day had been long. Starting with meetings in Washington and then the flight to New York, where he'd had dinner with his ambassador to America—

also installed in this hotel while the major renovations to the embassy were completed. And all day long, he'd pushed his grief aside, knowing he needed to act strong and unaffected by the fact he'd buried his father a little over three weeks ago.

The man had been a behemoth. Strength personified. His absence left a gaping hole—not just for Sariq but for the country. It was one Sariq would endeavour to fill, but there would only ever be one King Kadir.

He moved towards the view, pushing one of the sliding glass doors open so he could step onto the large, private terrace, his eyes continuing to trace the skyline of New York. The background noise of horns beeping, sirens wailing and engines revving was a constant here, and somehow that made it fade into nothing. It was so loud it became a sort of white noise, and yet it made him long for the silence of the desert to the east of his palace, a place where he could erect a tent and be surrounded by silence, and the ancient sands of his kingdom. There was wisdom in those grains of sand: each and every one of them had stood sentinel to the people of his kingdom. Their wars, their famines, their pains, their hopes, their beliefs and, in the last forty years, their peace, their prosperity, their modernisation and acceptance onto the world's stage.

It was his father's legacy and Sariq would do all that he could to preserve it. No, not simply to preserve it: to improve it. To grow it, to strengthen it, to better his country's standing and make peace so unequivocal that the trailing fingers of civil war could no longer touch a single soul of his country.

Sariq was not his father, but he was of him, he was cast from his soul, his bones and strength, and he had spent a lifetime watching, learning, and preparing for this.

In the morning, it would begin. He was ready.

* * *

Daisy stared at the flashing light with a small frown on her cupid's bow lips, then consulted the clock on the wall. It was three in the morning, and the alarm for the Presidential suite was on. She reached for the phone, tucking it under her ear.

'Concierge, how may I help you?'

It had only been a matter of hours since the delegation from the Royal Kingdom of Haleth had been installed in this five-star hotel's most prestigious suite—as well as a whole floor of rooms for servants and security guards—but Daisy had already had multiple dealings with a man named Malik, who seemed to coordinate the life of the Sheikh. As the hotel's VIP concierge, this was her job— she alone was responsible for taking care of every little thing the most prestigious guests wanted. Whether it was organising parties for after their concerts at Madison Square Garden, or, in the case of a Queen from a Scandinavian country, organising a small couture fashion parade in her suite so she could choose what to wear to the Met gala, Daisy prided herself on being able to cope with just about anything that was asked of her.

So when the phone rang, despite the hour, she was calm and prepared. Malik must need something and she would ensure he got it.

What she wasn't prepared for was the timbre of the voice that came down the line, so deep and throaty, accented with spice and an exotic lilt that showed English was his second language. 'I would like some persimmon tea.'

The RKH ambassador had been staying in the hotel for three months while the embassy was being renovated. They now had a permanent supply of delicacies from that country on hand, including persimmon tea.

'Yes, sir. Would you like some *balajari* as well?' she offered, the almond and lemon zest biscuits something the ambassador always took with his tea.

There was a slight pause. 'Fine.' The call was disconnected and Daisy inwardly bristled, though she showed no sign of that. Very few of the guests she'd hosted in the Presidential suite had exhibited particularly good manners. There were a few exceptions: an Australian actor who'd apologised every time he'd 'disturbed' her, a Scottish woman who'd won one of those television singing competitions and seemed unable to comprehend that she'd been jettisoned in the global superstar arena and seemed to want to be treated as normally as possible, and a Japanese artist who had wanted directions to the nearest Whole Foods so she could stock her own fridge.

Daisy called the order through to the kitchen then moved to the service elevator. There was a full-length mirror there—the hotel manager insisted that each staff member check their appearance before going out on the floor, and Daisy did so now, tucking a curl of her blonde hair back into its bun, pinching her cheeks to bring a bit of colour to them, and even though her shirt was tucked in, she pushed it in a little more firmly, straightening her pencil skirt and spinning to have a look over her shoulder at her behind.

Neat, professional, nondescript. Her job wasn't to be noticed, it was to fly beneath the radar. She was a facilitator, and nothing more. A ghost of the hotel, there whenever she was required, but in an unseen kind of way.

By the time she reached the kitchen in the basement, the order was ready. She double-checked the tray herself, inspecting plates for fingerprints, the teapot for heat, then thanked the staff, carrying the tray on one hand as she pressed the call button for the lift.

The Presidential suite was on the top floor and only she and the hotel manager had a staff access card for it. She swiped it as she entered then moved the tray to both hands, holding it in front of her as the lift shot up towards the sky.

When she'd first started working here, two years ago, the elevator had made her tummy ache every time, but she was used to it now and barely batted an eyelid.

The doors pinged open into a small service corridor with a glossy white door on one end. In the presidential apartment, the door was concealed by wall panelling. She knocked discreetly and, despite the absence of a greeting, unlocked the door and pushed into the suite.

The lights were out but several lamps had been turned on, giving the apartment an almost eerie glow.

She loved these rooms, with their sumptuous décor, their stunning views, the promise of luxury and grandeur. Of course, she loved them most of all when they were empty, particularly of the more demanding and disrespectful guests who had a tendency to treat the delicate furniture as though it were cheap, plastic tat.

The coffee table in the middle of the sofas was low-set and a shining timber. She placed the tea tray down on it, then straightened to look around the room. At first, she didn't see him. It took her eyes a moment to adjust to the darkened room. But then, the silhouette of a man stood out, a void against the Manhattan skyline.

The Sheikh.

She'd caught a glimpse of him at a distance, earlier that day, and he was instantly recognisable now. It wasn't just his frame, which was tall and broad, muscled in a way that spoke of fitness and strength. It was his long hair, dark, which he wore in a bun on top of his head. She was used to dealing with powerful, important people and yet that didn't mean she was an automaton. In moments like this, a hint of anxiety always bristled through her. She ignored it, keeping her voice neutral when she addressed him.

'Good evening, sir. I have your tea.' A pause, in which he didn't speak, nor did he turn to face her. 'Would you like me to pour it for you?'

Another pause, a silence that stretched between them for several seconds. She waited with the appearance of impassivity, watching him, so she saw the moment he dipped his head forward in what she took to be a nod.

Her fingertips trembled betrayingly as she reached for the teapot, lifting it silently, pressing down on the lid to avoid any spills, filling the tea to near the top of the cup, then silently replacing the pot on the tray.

She took a step backward then, preparing to leave. Except he still didn't move and something inside her sparked with curiosity. Not just curiosity: duty. He had asked for tea; her job was to provide him with it. She moved back to the coffee table, lifting the teacup and saucer, carrying them across the room towards him.

'Here you are, sir,' she murmured at his side. Now, finally, he did turn to look at her, and she had to grip the teacup and saucer more tightly to stop them from shaking. Her fingers felt as though they'd been filled with jelly. She'd seen him from a distance and she'd seen photographs of him, when she'd been preparing for his visit, but nothing really did justice to his magnificence. In person, he was so much more vital than any still image could convey. His features were harsh, symmetrical and almost jagged. A jaw that was square, cheekbones that appeared to have been slashed into his face at birth, a nose that had a bump halfway down its length, as if it had been broken at some point. His eyes were the darkest black, and his brows were thick and straight. His skin was a swarthy tan, and his chin was covered in stubble. Yes, up close he was quite mesmerising, so she forced herself to look away. Being mesmerised wasn't part of her job description.

'It's supposed to help you sleep.' His voice was unlike anything she'd ever known. If you could find a way to bottle it, you'd be a millionaire.

'I've heard that.' She nodded, crisply, already preparing to fade into the background, to disappear discreetly through the concealed doorway, feeling almost as though her disappearing now was essential to her sanity.

'Have you tried it before?'

'No.' She swallowed; her throat felt quite dry. 'But your ambassador favours it.'

'It is very common in my country.'

His eyes roamed her face in a way that set her pulse firing. Escape was essential. 'Do you need anything else?'

A small frown quirked at his lips. He looked back towards the view. 'Malik would say I need to sleep.'

'And you have the tea for that.'

'Scotch might work better.'

'Would you like me to organise some for you?'

He tilted his head to hers again. 'It's after three.'

His words made little sense.

'It's after three and you're working.'

'Oh, right. Yes. That's my job.'

He lifted a brow. 'To work through the night?'

'To work when you need me,' she said with a lift of her shoulders. Then, with a swift correction, 'Or when any guest of the Presidential suite requires me. I'm assigned to this suite exclusively.'

'And you have to do whatever I ask?' he prompted.

A small smile lifted her lips. 'Well, not quite.' She couldn't suppress the teasing quality from her voice. 'I can't cook and I don't know any jokes, but when it comes to facilitating your requests, then yes, I do whatever is humanly possible to make them happen.'

'And that's your employment.'

'Yes.'

He sipped the tea without taking his dark eyes off her. Ordinarily, she would have taken that opportunity to leave, but there was a contradiction within this man that had her saying, 'I would have thought you'd be used to that degree of service.'

'Why do you say that?'

'Because you travel with an entourage of forty men, all of whom it would appear exist to serve your every whim?'

Another sip of his tea. 'Yes, this is their job. I am King, and in my country serving the royal family is a great honour.'

Something tweaked in the back of her brain. A memory from a news article she'd read a couple of weeks ago. His father had died. Recently.

Compassion moved through her, and empathy, because she could vividly remember the pain of that loss. Five years ago, when her mother had died, she had felt as if she'd never be whole again. In time, day by day, she'd begun to feel more like herself, but it was still a work in progress. She felt her mother's absence every day.

It was that understanding that had her saying something she would normally not have dared. 'I'm sorry, about your father. Losing a parent is…we know it's something we should expect, but I don't think anything really prepares us for what life without them will be like.'

His eyes jolted to hers, widening in his face, so she immediately regretted her familiarity. He was a king, for goodness' sake, and her job was to bring the tea!

Dipping her head forward, she found she couldn't meet his eyes. 'If that's all, sir, goodnight.' She didn't wait for his answer; turning away from him, she strode to the concealed door. Her hand was on it when he spoke.

'Wait.'

She paused, her heart slamming against her ribcage.

She didn't turn around, though.

'Come back here.'

Her pulse was like a torrent in her veins.

She turned to face him. He was watching her. Her heart rate accelerated to the point of, surely, danger.

'Yes, sir?'

A frown etched itself across his face. 'Sit.' He gestured to the sofas. 'Drink tea with me.'

A million reasons to say 'no' came to her. Not once in all the time she'd held this job had she come close to socialising with a guest. For one thing, it was completely forbidden in her contract.

This is a professional establishment. They are not our friends. They are guests at the most exclusive hotel in the world.

But that wasn't the only reason she was resisting his invitation.

He was too much. Too charming, too handsome, too completely masculine, and if her first, epic failure of a marriage had taught her anything, it was that men who were too handsome for their own good were not to be trusted.

'I insist.' His words cut through her hesitations, because, ultimately, he was asking her to join him for tea and surely that was within her job description? What the guests wanted, the guests got—within reason.

'I don't see how that will help you sleep,' she reminded him, gently.

His expression was like a whip cracking. 'Are you refusing?'

Panic had her shaking her head.

Keep the guest happy, at all costs.

'Of course not, sir.' She was already walking through the room, towards the sofas. Only one cup had been on the tray—besides, she didn't feel like persimmon tea. But she took a seat near the tray, her hands clasped neatly in her lap. And she waited for him to speak, her nerves stretching tighter and tighter with every silent beat that passed.

'Good.' His nod showed approval but it was hardly relaxing. The differences in their situations were apparent in every way. He was a king, his country renowned for its natural source of both oil and diamonds, making it hugely prosperous, with a chequered history of power-play as foreign forces sought to control both these natural resources for their own financial gain. Perhaps that explained the natural sense of power that exuded from every pore of his; he was a man born to rule a country that required a strong leader.

'Would you like a tea?'

'I think it would be rude to refuse,' she said quietly, but he heard, if the quirk of his brow was anything to go by.

'I have no interest in force-feeding you drinks native to my country. Would you prefer something else? Room service?'

The idea of anyone else seeing her sitting on the sofa talking to the Sheikh was impossible to contemplate.

'I'm fine.'

'You're sitting there as though you're half afraid I'm going to bite you.'

A small smile lifted Daisy's mouth. 'How should I be sitting, sir?'

He took the seat opposite, his own body language relaxed. His legs, long and muscled, were spread wide, and he lifted one arm along the back of the sofa. He looked so completely at home here, in this world of extreme luxury. That was hardly surprising, given he'd undoubtedly been raised in this kind of environment.

'However you would usually sit,' he prompted.

'I'm sorry,' she said, the words quizzical rather than apologetic. 'It's just this has never happened before.'

'No?'

'My job is to provide for your every need without actually being noticed.'

At that, his eyes flared wider, speculation colouring his irises for a heart-racing moment. 'I'm reasonably certain it would be impossible for you to escape anyone's notice.'

Heat rose in her cheeks, colouring them a pale pink that perfectly offset the golden tan of her complexion. She wasn't sure what to say to that, so she stayed quiet.

'Have you worked here long?'

She compressed her lips then stopped when his eyes followed the gesture, tracing the outline of her mouth in a way that made her tummy flip and flop.

'A few years.' She didn't add how hard that had been for her—to finally accept that her long-held dream of attending the Juilliard was beyond reach, once and for all.

'And always in this capacity?'

'I started in general concierge.' She crossed her legs, relaxing back into the seat a little. 'But about six months later, I was promoted to this position.'

'And you enjoy it?'

Of their own accord, her eyes drifted to the view of New York and her fingers tapped her knee, as if playing across the keys of the beloved piano she'd been forced to sell. 'I'm good at it.' She didn't catch the way his features shifted, respect moving over his face.

'How old are you?'

She turned back to face him, wondering how long he

intended to keep her sitting there, knowing that it was very much within her job description to humour him even when this felt like an utterly bizarre way to spend her time.

'Twenty-four.'

'And you've always lived in America?'

'Yes.' She bit down on her lower lip thoughtfully. 'I've actually never even been overseas.'

His brows lifted. 'That's unusual, isn't it?'

She laughed softly. 'I don't know. You tell me?'

'It is.'

'Then I guess I'm unusual. Guilty as charged.'

'You don't have any interest in travelling?'

'Not having done something doesn't necessarily equate to a lack of interest,' she pointed out.

'So it's a lack of opportunity, then?'

He was rapier sharp, quickly able to read between the lines of anything she said.

'Yes.' Because there was no point in denying it.

'You work too much?'

'I work a lot,' she confirmed, without elaborating. There was no need to tell this man that she had more debt to her name than she'd likely ever be able to clear. Briefly, anger simmered in her veins, the kind of anger she only ever felt when she thought about one person: her waste-of-space ex-husband Max and the trouble he'd got her into.

'I thought you were guaranteed vacation time in the United States?'

Her smile was carefully constructed to dissuade further questioning along these lines, but, for good measure, she turned the tables on him. 'And you, sir? You travel frequently, I presume?'

His eyes narrowed as he studied her, and she had the strangest feeling he was pulling her apart, little by little, until he could see all the pieces that made her whole.

She held her breath, wondering if he was going to let the matter drop, and was relieved when he did.

'I do. Though never for long, and not lately.' His own features showed a tightness that she instinctively understood spoke of a desire not to be pressed on that matter.

But despite that, she heard herself say gently, 'Your father was ill for a while, before he died?'

The man's face paled briefly. He stood up, walking towards the window, his back rigid, his body tense. Daisy swallowed a curse. What was she thinking, asking something so personal? His father had just died—not even a month ago. She had no business inviting him to open that wound—and for a virtual stranger.

'I'm so sorry.' She stood, following him, bitterly regretting her big mouth. 'I had no right to ask you that. I'm sorry.' When he didn't speak, she swallowed, and said quietly, 'I'll leave you in peace now, Your Highness.'

CHAPTER TWO

MANHATTAN WAS A vibrant hive of activity beyond the windows of his limousine. He kept his head back against the leather cushioning of his seat, his eyes focussed on nothing in particular.

'That could not have gone better, Your Highness.'

Malik was right. The speech to the United Nations had been a success. As he was talking, he realised that he wasn't the only one in the room who'd experienced anxiety about the importance of this. There was an air of tension, a fear that perhaps with the death of the great Kadir Al Antarah, they were to be plunged back into the days of war and violence that had marked too much of his country's history.

But Sariq was progressive, and Sariq was persuasive. He spoke of Shajarah, the capital of RKH, that had been born from the sands of the desert, its ancient soul nestled amongst the steel and glass monoliths that spoke of a place of the future, a place of promise. He spoke of his country's educational institutions which were free and world-class, of his belief that education was the best prevention for war and violence, that a literate and informed people were less likely to care for ancient wounds. He highlighted what the people of RKH had in common with the rest of the world and when he was finished, there was widespread applause.

Yes, the speech had been a success, but still there was a kernel of discontent within his gut. A feeling of dissatisfaction he couldn't explain.

'Your father would have been proud of you, sir.'

Malik was right about that too.

'When we return to the hotel, have the concierge come to me,' Sariq told Malik. He didn't know her name. That was an oversight he would remedy.

'Is there something you require?'

'She will see to it.'

If Malik thought the request strange, he didn't say anything. The limousine cut east across Manhattan, snagging in traffic near Bryant Park, so Sariq stared from his window at the happy scene there. The day had been warm and New Yorkers had taken to the park to feel the brief respite from the temperature offered by the lush surrounds. He watched as a child reached into the fountain and scooped some water out, splashing it at his older brother, and his chest panged with a sense of acceptance.

Children were as much a part of his future as ruling was. He was the last heir of the Al Antarah line of Kings, a line that had begun at the turn of the last millennia. When he returned to his kingdom and his people, he would focus more seriously on that. He knew the risks if he didn't, the likelihood of civil war that would result from a dangerous fight for the throne of the country.

Marriage, children, these things would absolve him of that worry and would secure his country's future for generations to come.

'You wanted to see me, Your Highness?' Her heart was in her throat. She'd barely slept since she'd left his apartment the night before, despite the fact she'd been rostered off during the day, while he was engaged on official business. That was how it worked when she had high-profile guests. She knew their schedules intimately so she could form her day around their movements, thus ensuring her availability when they were likely to need her.

He was not alone, and he was not as he'd been the night before—dressed simply in jeans and a shirt. Now, he wore a white robe, flowing and long, with gold embellishments on the sleeve, and on his head there was a traditional *keffiyeh* headdress, white and fastened in place with a gold cord. It was daunting and powerful and she found her mouth was completely dry as she regarded him with what she hoped was an impassive expression. That was hard to manage when her knees seemed to have a desire to knock together.

'Yes. One moment.'

His advisors wore similar outfits, though less embellished. It was clear that his had a distinction of royal rank. She stood where she was as they continued speaking in their own language, the words beautiful and musical, the Sheikh's voice discernible amongst all others. It was ten minutes before they began to disband, moving away from the Sheikh, each with a low bow of respect, which he acknowledged with a small nod sometimes, and other times not at all.

His fingers were long and tanned, and on one finger he wore a gold ring with a small, rounded face, like a Super Bowl ring, she thought out of nowhere and smiled at the idea of this man on the football field. He'd probably take to it like a duck to water, if his physique was anything to go by. Beneath those robes, she knew he had the build of a natural athlete.

Great.

Her mouth was dry all over again but this time he was sweeping towards her, his robes flowing behind her. She had only a few seconds to attempt to calm her racing pulse.

When he was a few feet away from her, he paused, so she was caught up in the masculinity of his fragrance, the exotic addictiveness of it—citrus and pine needles, spice and sunshine.

'You were offended last night.'

His words were the last thing she'd expected. Heat bloomed in her cheeks.

'I was too familiar, sir.' She dropped her eyes to the view, unable to look at him, a thousand and one butterflies rampaging wildly inside her belly.

'I invited you to be familiar,' he reminded her so the butterflies gave way to a roller coaster.

'Still…' she lifted her shoulders, risking a glance at him then wishing she hadn't when she discovered his eyes were piercing her own '… I shouldn't have…'

'He had been sick. It was unpleasant to witness. I wished, more than anything, that I could do something to alleviate his pain.' A muscle jerked in his jaw and his eyes didn't shift from hers. 'I have been raised to believe in the full extent of my power, and yet I was impotent against the ravages of his disease. No doctor anywhere could save him, nor really help him.' He didn't move and yet somehow she felt closer to him, as though she'd swayed forward without realising it.

'Your question last night is difficult for me to answer.'

'I'm sorry.'

'Don't be. You didn't do anything wrong.'

Her body was in overdrive, every single sense pulling through her, and she was aware, in the small part of her brain that was capable of rational thought, that this was a completely foreign territory to be in. He was a guest of the hotel—their boundaries were clearly established.

She had to find a way to get them back onto more familiar territory.

'I work for the hotel,' she said quietly. 'Asking you personal questions isn't within my job description, and it's certainly not appropriate. It won't happen again.'

He didn't react to that. He stayed exactly where he was, completely still, like a sentinel, watching her, his eyes trained on her face in a way that made her pulse stutter.

'I asked you to talk with me,' he reminded her finally.

'But I should have declined.'

'Your job is to facilitate my needs, is it not?'

Her heart began to pound against her ribs. 'Within reason.'

His smile showed a hint of something she couldn't interpret. Cynicism? Mockery? Frustration?

'Are you saying that if I ask you to come and sit with me again tonight, you'll refuse?'

Her body was filled with lava, so hot she could barely breathe.

Her eyes were awash with uncertainty. 'I'm not sure it's appropriate.'

'What are you afraid of?'

'Honestly?'

He was watchful.

'I'm afraid of saying the wrong thing. Of offending you. My job is to silently...'

'Yes, yes, you have told me this. To escape notice. And I told you that's not possible. I have already noticed you, Daisy. And having had the pleasure of speaking with you once, I would like to repeat that—with a less abrupt conclusion this time. Are you saying therefore that you won't sit with me?'

Her chest felt as though it had been cracked open. 'Um, yes, I am, I think.' She dropped her eyes to the shining floor.

Because I enjoyed talking to you, too, she amended inwardly, fully aware that she was moving into a territory that was lined with danger.

'But if you're worried you offended me, let me assure you, I am not easily offended,' he offered, and now he smiled, in a way that was like forcing sunshine into a darkened room. Her breath burned in her lungs.

'Frankly, I'd be surprised if you were.'

'Then you can bring me tea tonight. I have a dinner but Malik will send for you when it's done.'

He had no idea what he was doing. The American woman was beautiful, but it had been a long time since Sariq had considered beauty to be a requirement in a woman he was interested in. Besides, he couldn't be seriously interested in her. His duty was clear: to return to the RKH and marry, so that he could begin the process of shoring up his lineage. There were two women whom it would make sense to marry and he would need to choose one, and promptly.

Enjoying the companionship of his hotel's concierge seemed pointless and futile, and yet he found himself turning his attention to his watch every few minutes throughout the state dinner, willing it to be over so he could call for a tray of tea and the woman with eyes the colour of the sky on a winter's morning.

She had asked the kitchen to prepare tea for two, with no further explanation. And even though they had no way of knowing the Sheikh wasn't entertaining in his suite, she felt a flush of guilt as she took the tray, as though surely everyone must know that she was about to cross an invisible line in the sand and socialise with a guest.

Calm down, she insisted to herself as the elevator sped towards the top of the building. It's just tea and conversation, hardly a hanging offence. He was grieving and despite the fact he was surrounded by an entourage, she could easily imagine how lonely his position must be, how refreshing to meet someone who hadn't been indoctrinated into the ways of worshipping at his feet by virtue of the fact that he ruled the land from which they heralded.

This was no different from the other unusual requests she had been asked to fulfil, it was just a lot harder to delegate. He wanted *her*. To talk to her. She couldn't say why—she wasn't particularly interesting, which filled her with anxiety at the job before her, but, for whatever reason, he had been insistent.

She knocked at the door then pushed it inwards. He was standing almost exactly where he'd been the night before, still wearing the robes he had been in earlier that day, though he'd removed the headpiece, so her heart rate trebled. Because he looked so impossibly handsome, so striking with his tanned skin and strong body encased in the crisp white and gold.

It brought out a hint of blond in his hair that she hadn't noticed at first, just a little at the ends, which spoke of a tendency to spend time outdoors.

He walked towards her so she stood completely still, as though her legs were planted to the floor, and when his hands curved around the edges of the tray, it was impossible for them not to brush hers. A jolt of electricity burst through her, splitting her into a thousand pieces so she had to work hard not to visibly react.

'I'm pleased you came.'

He stood there, watching her, for a beat too long and then took the tray, placing it on the coffee table.

'The first reference to persimmon tea comes from one of our earliest texts. In the year forty-seven AD, a Bedouin tribe brought it as a gift to the people of the west of my country. Their skill with harvesting the fruit late in the season and drying them in such a way as to preserve the flavour made them popular with traders.'

He poured some into a cup and held it in front of him, waiting, a small smile on his lips that did funny things to her tummy.

She forced her legs to carry her across the room, a tight smile of her own crossing her expression as she took the teacup. 'Thank you.'

He was watching her and so she took a small sip, her eyes widening at the flavour. 'It's so sweet. Like honey.'

He made a throaty noise of agreement. 'Picked at the right time, persimmons are sweet. Dried slowly, that intensifies, until you get this.'

She took another sip, her insides warming to the flavour. It was like drinking happiness. Why had she resisted so long?

'Are you going to have some?'

'I don't feel like sleeping tonight.'

Her stomach lurched and she chattered the cup against the saucer a little too loudly, shooting him a look that was half apology, half warning.

She had to keep this professional. It was imperative that she not forget who she was, who he was, and why her job mattered so much to her. She was lucky with this position. She earned a salary that was above and beyond what she could have hoped, by virtue of her untarnished ability to provide exemplary customer service. One wrong move and her reputation would suffer, so too would her job, potentially, and she couldn't jeopardise that.

It helped to imagine her manager in the room, observing their conversation. If she pictured Henry watching, she could keep things professional and light, she could avoid the gravitational pull that seemed to be dragging on her.

'You were at the United Nations today, sir?'

A quirk shifted his lips, but he nodded. 'It was my first official speech as ruler of the RKH.'

'How did it go?'

He gestured towards the sofa, inviting her to sit. She chose one side, crossing her legs primly and placing the cup and saucer on her knee, holding it with both hands.

He took the seat beside her, not opposite, so she was aware of his every movement, the shift of his body dragging on the cushions on the sofa, inadvertently pulling her towards him.

'I was pleased with the reception.'

She sipped her tea, forcing herself to relax. 'I can't imagine having to do that,' she confided with a small smile. After all, he wanted to talk to her—sitting there like a petrified automaton wasn't particularly conversational. 'I'm terrible at public speaking. I hate it. I feel everyone's eyes burning me and just want to curl up in a ball for ever.'

'It's a skill you can learn.'

'Perhaps. But fortunately for me, I don't need to.'

Silence prickled at their sides.

She spoke to fill it. 'I don't feel like you would have needed to do much learning there.'

He frowned. 'I don't understand.'

'Sorry, that wasn't clear.' She shook her head. 'I just mean you were probably born with this innate ability to stand in front of a group of people and enthral them.'

She clamped her mouth shut, wishing she hadn't come so close to admitting that she was a little bit enthralled by him.

He smiled though, in a way that relaxed her and warmed her. 'I was born knowing my destiny. I was born to be Sheikh, ruler of my people, and, as such, never imagined what it would be like to…avoid notice.' His eyes ran over her face speculatively, so even as she was relaxing, she was also vibrating in a way that was energising and demanding.

'I don't think you'd be very good at it.'

'At being Sheikh?'

'At avoiding notice.'

'Nor are you, so this we have in common.'

Heat spread through her veins like wildfire.

'I don't think you see me clearly,' she said after a moment.

'No?'

'I'm very good at not being seen.'

His laugh was husky. 'It's quite charming that you think so.'

She shook her head a little. 'I don't really understand…'

'You are a beautiful young woman with hair the colour of desert sand and eyes like the sky. Even in this boxy uniform, you are very, very noticeable.'

She stared at him for several seconds, pleasure at war with uncertainty. Remember Max, she reminded herself. He'd noticed her. He'd praised her, flattered her, and she'd fallen for it so fast she hadn't stopped to heed any of the warning signs. And look how that had turned out!

'Thank you.' It was stiff, an admonishment.

He laughed. 'You are not good with compliments.'

She bit down on her lip, their situation troubling her, pulling on her. 'I should go.'

He reached a hand out, pressing it to her knee. Her skin glowed where he'd touched her, filling her with a scattering sensation of pins and needles. 'No more compliments,' he promised. 'Tell me about yourself, Daisy Carrington.'

Her eyes flared wide. 'How do you know my surname?'

'I asked my chief of security.'

'How…?'

'All hotel staff are independently vetted by my agencies,' he explained, as though that were no big deal.

Her lips parted. 'Then I suspect you know more about me than I realised.'

'It's not comprehensive,' he clarified. 'Your name, date of birth, any links to criminal activity.' He winked. 'You were clear, by the way.'

Despite herself, she smiled. 'I'm pleased to hear it.'

'May I call you Daisy?'

'So long as you don't expect me to call you anything other than Your Highness,' she quipped.

'Very well. So, Daisy? Before you started working here, what did you do?'

Her stomach clenched. Remembered pain was there, pushing against her. She thought of her marriage, her divorce, her acceptance to the Juilliard, and pushed them all away. 'This and that.' A tight smile, showing more than she realised.

'Which tells me precisely nothing.'

'I worked in hospitality.'

'And it's what you have always wanted to do?'

The question hurt. She didn't talk about her music. It was too full of pain—pain remembering her father, and the way he'd sat beside her, moving her fingers over the keys until they learned the path themselves, the way she'd stopped playing the day he'd left. And then, when her mother was in her low patches, the way Daisy had begun to play again—it was the only thing she had responded to.

'It's what I gravitated to.'

'Another answer that tells me nothing.'

Because she was trying to obfuscate but he was too clever for that. What was the harm in being honest with him? He had reserved this suite for four nights—this was his second. He would be gone soon and she'd never see him again.

'I wanted to be a concert pianist, actually.'

He went very still, his eyes hooked to hers, waiting, watching. And she found the words spilling out of her even when she generally made a habit of not speaking them. After all, what good could come from reliving a fantasy lost?

'My father was a jazz musician. He taught me to play almost from infancy. I would sit beside him and he would arrange my fingers, and when we weren't playing, we would listen to music, so I was filled with its unique language, all the beats that mixed together to make a song, to tell a story and weave a narrative with their melody. I love all types of music, but classical is my favourite. I lose myself in Chopin and Mozart, so that I'm barely conscious of the passage of time.'

He stared at her, his surprise evident, and with little wonder. It was as though the words had burst from her, so full of passion and memory, so alive with her love and regrets.

'Do you play?'

A beat passed, a silence, as he contemplated this. 'No. My mother did, and very well.' Another pause, and, though his expression didn't shift, she had a feeling he was choosing his words with care. 'After she died, my father had all the pianos removed from the palace. He couldn't bear to hear them played. Music was not a big part of my upbringing.'

Her heart twisted in her chest. The pain of losing a mother was one she was familiar with. 'How old were you?'

A tight smile. 'Seven.'

The tightness in her chest increased. 'I'm sorry.'

He nodded. 'As am I. Her death was a grief from which my father never recovered.'

'The flipside to a great love.'

'Speaking from experience?'

Her denial was swift and visceral. 'No.'

Though she'd been married, she could see now that she'd never loved Max. She'd felt grateful to him, glad to have someone in her life after her mother's death.

'My mom died five years ago, and not a day passes when I don't think of her in some small way. At this time of year, when the sunflowers in the street are all in bloom, I ache to take photos for her. She loved that, you know. *"Only in New York would you get sunflowers as street plantings."'* Her smile was wistful.

'How did she…?'

Daisy's throat thickened unexpectedly. 'A car accident.' She didn't elaborate—that her mother had been responsible. That she'd driven into a lamppost after drinking half a bottle of gin.

They sat in silence for several moments, but it was no longer a prickly, uncomfortable silence. On the contrary, Daisy felt an odd sense of peace wrap around her, a comfortable fog that made her want to stay exactly where she was.

It was the warning she needed, and she jolted herself out of her silent reflection, forcing herself to stand.

'I really should go, sir. It's late and I'm sure you have more important things to do than talk to me.'

As with the night before, he didn't try to stop her. She ignored the kernel of disappointment and stalked to the door, pulling it inwards. But before leaving him, she turned back to regard him over her shoulder.

'Goodnight, Your Highness. Sleep well.'

CHAPTER THREE

'HE'S ASKING FOR YOU.'

Daisy had just walked in through the door of the hotel, and she shot a glance at her watch. It was after ten o'clock at night. The Sheikh was supposed to be at a party until midnight. She'd come in early to settle her nerves, and to mentally prepare her excuses in case he called for her to come and talk to him again.

Henry grimaced apologetically. 'He seems more demanding than most.'

'No, he's not really.'

'You sure? You could get Amy to take care of him. She's already been up there a few times today.'

Daisy thought of the woman who'd been recruited to shadow Daisy, taking care of Daisy's clients when Daisy couldn't. Instinctively, she pushed the idea aside.

'He's a very important guest, Henry. It should be me. You should have called.'

'I don't want you getting burned out, love. You can't work around the clock. We can't afford to lose you.'

'I'm fine.' Her heart twisted in her chest. She'd been buzzing with a heady sense of anticipation all day, waiting to see him, wondering if he'd call for her, or if wisdom and sense would have prevailed so that he woke up and wondered why the heck he was bothering to spend so much time talking to a servant.

'When did he call?'

'An hour ago.'

Panic lurched through her. 'Why didn't you page me?'

'He said to tell you to go up when you arrived. I knew you wouldn't be long...'

'Henry,' she wailed, shaking her head. 'What if it was something urgent?'

'Then that Malik man would have made himself known.' Henry exaggerated a shudder. 'He has no problems demanding whatever the hell he wants, when he wants it.'

That was true. Up until recently, all the requests had come from Malik. 'I'll go up now.'

She reached for the buzzer, to order some persimmon tea, but the kitchen informed her the Presidential suite had already requested dinner. 'It should only be another few minutes.'

'I thought he was at a function.'

'Dunno,' came the unhelpful response, so Daisy frowned as she disconnected the call. Double-checking her appearance in the mirror, she wished her cheeks weren't so pink, nor her eyes so shining with obvious pleasure. The truth was, she couldn't wait to see him, and that was dangerous.

Because he was going home soon, and, even if he weren't, he was just a client. A client who was developing a habit of asking for her in the evenings.

She took the service elevator to the top floor, so the doors whooshed inwards and she knocked once. Before she could step inside, the door was pulled inwards and Sariq stood on the other side. He was wearing more familiar clothes this time—a pair of dark jeans and a white tee shirt with a vee at the neck that revealed a hint of curls at his throat.

Damn it, out of nowhere she found herself wondering how far down his hair went, imagining him without his shirt, and that made it almost impossible to keep a veneer of professionalism on her face.

'Thank you for coming.'

'It's my job,' she reminded him.

He didn't move, but his eyes glowed with something that could have been amusement and could have been cynicism. If it was the latter, she didn't have to wonder at why: it was pretty obvious that her being there had very little to do with her professional obligations.

'I thought you had something on tonight.'

'It didn't last as long as the schedule had allowed,' he said simply, drawing the door open without stepping far enough aside, so in order to enter the suite, she had to brush past him, and the second their bodies connected she felt a rush of awareness that was impossible to ignore. Instinctively, her face lifted to his and she saw the raw speculation there; the same interest that flooded her veins was rushing through his. Her knees shuddered and heat pooled between her legs, making thought, speech and movement almost impossible.

He stood so close, their bodies were touching. Just lightly, but enough, and even when Daisy knew she should move, or say something, she couldn't. She could only stare at him. His face was like thunder, but his eyes were all flame. She could feel the war being raged within him, a battle to control his desire, and she didn't want him to. This was madness. It was sheer, uncontrollable madness—and she had a billion reasons to resist. Max was the main one— her experience with him had warned her off tempestuous affairs for life. But she'd married Max, she'd pledged to love him and trust him, to spend the rest of her life with him. That had been her mistake. The Sheikh was only in New York for two more nights, including this one.

But he was a guest in the hotel! A seriously important guest, and she couldn't afford to have anything go wrong. She swallowed, taking a step backwards, except she forgot there was a piece of furniture there and her hip jabbed into it, shunting her sideways, so she might have fallen if he hadn't pushed a hand out, confidently, easily righting her. Her eyes were alarmed as they lifted to his and stuck there like glue, and when he took a step towards her, she couldn't look away.

Her heart was hammering against her ribs so hard and fast that she was surprised he couldn't see its frantic movements against her breasts. If she pushed up onto the tips of her toes, if she lifted her face, oh, God, she wanted to kiss him. The realisation was like fire, even when she knew it should have doused her desire, that it should have dragged her back to reality and put a halt to this foolishness.

But was it so foolish? Daisy had played it safe for so long and, suddenly, she was sick of it. Sick of playing it safe, of being careful with whom she trusted. It was as though she second-guessed her instincts so often that they'd grown blunt.

'Your Highness…' She wasn't sure what she wanted to say, only that they were standing so close, staring at one another, sensual heat heavy in the air around them, and she wanted to act on it. She wanted him.

But he frowned, his eyes darkening, even as he dropped his head closer. 'I asked you here to show you something.'

Neither of them moved.

'What is it?'

He lifted a hand, as though he couldn't resist, pressing his thumb and forefinger to her chin so he could hold her face where it was, lifted towards him. The contact was so personal, it felt as though they'd crossed a line they couldn't uncross. They could no longer pretend this wasn't happening. They were acknowledging the pull that ran between them.

'I wasn't going to do this.'

'Do what?'

With his body in the door frame, he dropped his head by a matter of degrees, so there was ample time for her to move, to say something, to stop this. She didn't. She stayed where she was, her face held in his fingers, her body swaying a little closer to his so her breasts brushed his chest and, through the fine fabric of his shirt and her blouse, she was sure he must feel the hardening of her nipples, the way they strained against her lace bra.

'I swore I wouldn't.' And then, his mouth claimed hers, his kiss fierce, filled with all the passion of having fought this, of having felt desire and resisted it for as long as he was able.

It was a kiss born of need and it surged inside her, his lips pushing hers apart, his tongue driving into her mouth, his other hand lifting and pushing into her hair, his fingers cradling her head, holding her against him so he could plunder her mouth, tasting her, his body so big and broad compared to hers that she felt utterly enveloped by him, swallowed by his strength and power, her senses subsumed completely by this.

It was a kiss of oblivion, so consuming that she didn't hear the dinging of the lift doors. She was lost completely in this moment but he wasn't. He broke the kiss swiftly, his body in the door frame concealing her. 'Go to my room.' His eyes held a warning that she heeded even when nothing made sense and her body could scarcely move. She'd been in the suite enough times to know where the master bedroom was. She ran there, pushing the door shut except for an inch, so she could peer out.

She saw members of the kitchen team walk into the apartment, each pausing to bow for the Sheikh, before moving to the table and setting it. Sariq's eyes chased hers, down the corridor, so she moved away from the door, pressing her back against a wall and closing her eyes, needing her heart to slow down, her breathing to return to normal. She lifted her fingers to her lips; they were sensitive to the touch.

She was grateful beyond belief for his quick thinking. If it had been up to her, she would have stayed where she was, and someone from the staff would have seen her and rumours would have been flying. His quick response had saved her from that embarrassment. What would Henry say? Mortified, she fanned her face and tucked her shirt in more tightly—it had become loose at her waist, and she paced the room as she waited. It didn't take long. A few minutes and then she heard the click of a door, the turning of a lock, and they were alone once more.

She pulled the door to his bedroom open, moving into the lounge area to find him uncorking a bottle of wine and pouring two glasses. His eyes, when they met hers, were loaded with speculation.

'I ordered us dinner.'

Her eyes moved to the table. Surprise usurped whatever she'd been feeling a moment ago. 'You did? Why?'

His smile was without humour. 'Because we have to eat.'

She sighed heavily. 'I don't have to eat with you, though, Your Highness.'

'I can taste your kiss in my mouth,' he murmured. 'Don't you think it's time you called me something else?'

His words were so evocative but she shook her head. 'You're my client. That should never have happened...'

He paced across the room, handing her the wine glass. She took it without taking a drink. He stayed close to her, his body's contact intimate and loaded with promise. 'It shouldn't,' he agreed, after a moment. 'But it did, and I think we both know it will happen again. And again. So let's stop pretending we don't want this.'

Her eyes flared wide. Need punctured sense almost completely—but not quite. 'I can't afford to lose my job.'

She felt his naked speculation. 'Do you think I'm going to jeopardise that?'

'Socialising with clients is strictly forbidden. It's actually in my contract. And what we just did goes way beyond socialising.'

'I have my own reasons for requiring discretion,' he said firmly. 'Whatever happens between us, no one will know.'

Whatever happens between us. The words glowed with promise. Her insides quivered.

'Nothing can happen.'

'Why not?'

'I told you, my job…' but she wasn't even convincing herself.

'And I told you, no one will find out. Do you have a boyfriend?'

'No.' How long had it been since she'd been with a man? That was easy. Max. He was her only lover. He'd been her first, and when they'd divorced three years ago, she thought he'd be her last.

'I think you want me.' His words held a challenge. He took her wine glass from her, sipping from it and then placing it on the table to his left. His eyes glowed with the same challenge as he lifted his fingers to the top button of her blouse.

'I am going to undo these buttons very slowly, giving you plenty of time to ask me to stop. If you say the word, then it's over. You can go away again.' He did as he'd promised, his fingers working deftly to undo the first button, so she felt a brush of air against her skin. Then the next, exposing the top of her lace bra. The next revealed the midsection of the bra and, with the next button, the shirt gaped enough to reveal it completely. At the last button, his fingers slowed.

'You haven't asked me to stop.'

Her eyes were awash with feelings. 'I know that.'

'I want to make love to you.'

'I know that too.'

He turned towards the table. 'Are you hungry?'

She shook her head.

'You don't want anything to eat?'

Another shift of her head to indicate 'no'.

'What do you want, Daisy?'

The final button was separated, so her shirt fell apart completely.

She opened her mouth, but found it hard to frame any words.

'Do you want to know what I want?' he murmured, dropping his head to whisper the words against the sensitive flesh at the base of her throat.

'I think I can guess.' And despite the heavy pulsing of emotion that was filling the room, she smiled, because it was easy to smile in that moment.

He smiled back, but it was dredged from deep within him, so it cut across his face, his lips like a blade.

His grief was palpable. It had been since the first moment they'd met and it was there now, tormenting him, so that this physical act of sensuality took on a new imperative. She understood the power sex held, the power to obliterate grief and pain, even if only for a moment.

Wasn't it her own grief that had made her so vulnerable to Max? He'd promised respite from her sadness and she'd ignored all the warning signs to grab that respite. Was Sariq doing the same thing now?

Should she be putting a halt to this to save him from regret?

His fingers were on the straps of her bra, easing them down her arms so tiny goose bumps danced where his fingertips touched, and his eyes were on her breasts as he pushed aside the scrap of lace, so she felt a burning heat in her chest and a tingling in her nipples, an ache that begged him to touch her, to feel the weight of her breasts in his palms, to touch her nipples, to kiss them.

Her back swayed forward, the invitation silent but imperative, and he understood, lifting his hands to her hips first, bracing her waist as he drew his touch upwards, along her sides until his thumbs swept beneath her breasts and she tipped her head back a little on a plea, biting down on her lip to stop what she knew would be incoherent babbling, the kind of babbling brought on by a form of madness.

'I need you to tell me you want this.' He drew his kiss from her lips to her throat, flicking the pulse point there, dragging his stubbled jaw across her sensitive flesh. She pushed her body forward, her hips moving from side to side, her hands pushing his shirt up so her fingertips could run over his chest. God, his chiselled, firm chest. Her nails drew along the ridges of each muscular bump, running higher so her hands curved over his shoulders, feeling the warmth of his flesh and the beating of his heart against her forearm.

'Daisy?' It was a groan and a plea. His body was tense. He was waiting for her to say that she wanted this and something inside her trembled, because it was such a mark of respect and decency. It wasn't that she hadn't expected it from Sariq, it was that she hadn't known to expect it from anybody. Max had been... She didn't want to think about Max in that moment. He'd already taken so much from her, she wasn't going to give him this moment too. It was hers, hers and Sariq's.

'I want this.' The words blurted out of her. And then, more gently, but the same bone-melting urgency. 'I want *you*.' She couldn't resist adding, with an impish smile: 'Your Highness.'

He lifted a brow, his lips quirking in a smile that was impulsive and so sexy. But he swallowed and the smile disappeared, his expression serious once more. 'I have to go back to the RKH as scheduled. I cannot offer more than this.'

Another sign of respect. Her heart felt all warm and gooey and her voice was husky. 'I know that.' She showed her acceptance by pushing up and kissing him, by wrapping her arms around his waist, holding him close to her body so she could feel the force of his urgent need through their clothing. 'Take me to bed, sir.'

'Take me to bed, sir.'

He didn't need to be asked again. He lifted her up, cradling her against his chest as he carried her through the suite and into the master bedroom. He didn't pause to turn on a light, though he would love to have revelled in her beauty, staring at her as he pleasured her; there'd be time for that. Having abandoned himself to this, he intended to enjoy her all night. He knew this would be the last time he acted on impulses such as this, the last time he allowed himself to be simply a man and not a king. Soon he would announce his engagement and he would be faithful to the bride of his choosing.

Until then though, there was this, and he was going

to enjoy it. He disposed of her clothes quickly, no longer able to pace himself; he needed to feel every inch of her beneath him. Her legs were smooth and slender. He ran his palms over her flesh as he stripped her of the uniform she wore, acknowledging to himself he'd wanted to do exactly that from the first moment he'd seen her. His own clothes followed next so he stood above her naked. The room was dark but he could make out her silhouette against the bed, her blonde hair shimmering gold in the darkness. He brought the full weight of his body down on hers, his arousal pressing between her legs so, for the briefest moment, he fantasised about taking her like that. No protection, no preamble, just white-hot possession.

She arched her back and lifted her legs around his waist, drawing him towards her, as though she wanted that too. He kissed her, hard, his tongue doing to her mouth what his body wished it could do in that moment, and she met his kiss with every stroke, pushing her body up onto her elbows, wanting more of him, needing him in the way he needed her. Her feet at his back were insistent, pushing him towards her, so he let just his tip press to her sex, her hot, wet body welcoming him in a way he knew he had to control. He swore in his own language, pulling away from her with effort, his breathing ragged.

'Wait.' He stood up and her cry was an animalistic sound of disbelief, her need reaching out and wrapping around him. 'One moment,' he reassured her, moving to the adjoining bathroom and pulling a condom out of a travel bag. He didn't make a habit of this—he couldn't remember the last time he'd slept with a woman he'd just met—but he was always prepared, regardless.

Striding back into the room, he pushed the rubber over his length as he went, inviting no further delay to this. Her eyes were difficult to make out in this darkness but he thought he saw a hint of apology in the light thrown from the bathroom.

'I forgot,' she explained, reaching for him.

'I almost did too.'

'Thank you. For remembering.'

He kissed her more gently, reassuringly, parting her thighs with his palm and locking himself against her, as he had been before. She lifted her hips and this time, he didn't hold himself back. He drove his cock into her, his hands digging into her hips to hold her steady as he took control of her body and made her, completely, his.

CHAPTER FOUR

IT WAS A pleasure unlike any she'd ever known. Her breathing was heavy as she lay on his bed, waiting for sanity, normality, reason to intrude. Her orgasm—no, her *orgasms*, because he'd driven her over the edge of pleasure several times in a row—was still dissipating, her body felt heavy and weak at the same time as strong beyond belief, and his body, spent at last, was heavy on hers, his own breathing torn from him with silent torment. She ran her fingernails down his back, his skin warm and smooth, curving over his buttocks, and she smiled like the cat that'd got the cream.

Professionally, this had the potential to be a complete disaster, but in that moment, she didn't care. She pushed up and kissed his shoulder, tasting salt there and moaning softly. He was still inside her and she felt him respond, his beautiful cock jerking at her kiss. A sense of power swelled inside her, because he was as much of a slave to this as she was.

'I…didn't think that would happen when I came here tonight,' she said, when finally her breathing had slowed sufficiently to enable her to speak.

He pushed up on one elbow, so she could make out the features of his face against the darkness of the room. 'Do you regret it?'

'Nope.'

His teeth were white, so she could see them in his

smile. 'Me neither.' He dropped a kiss to one of her temples and then pushed away from her, standing and striding towards the bathroom. When he opened the door, more light flooded the room. She was so familiar with its décor but now she saw it through new eyes—and always would. He would leave soon, and someone else would occupy this suite of rooms, but the rooms would be overlaid with ghosts of her time with the Sheikh of the RKH for ever.

'I've never done this before,' she blurted out, hating the thought of him believing this was a regular occurrence for her. He reappeared, a towel wrapped around his waist, and now he reached for the wall and flicked a light on, so she was stark naked against the crisp white hotel sheets. She reached for the quilt, at the foot of the bed, pulling it up to cover herself.

'Don't.' And he was imperious, a ruler of a country, his command used to being obeyed. She stilled, her eyes lifting to his. 'I want to see you.'

Her mouth went dry, her throat completely thick, as he stood where he was but let his eyes feast upon her body. And she let him, remaining where she was, naked and exposed, her flesh marked with patches of red from where his stubbled jaw had grated against her, or where his mouth had kissed and sucked her flesh until it grew pink. Her cheeks were warm but still she stayed where she was, grateful there was no mirror within eye line that could show her the picture she made, or self-consciousness might have dictated that she ignore him and seek cover.

But she wouldn't have anyway, because the look in his face was so loaded with admiration and pleasure, with need and desire, that she could do nothing but lie there and watch him enjoy her. It was ridiculous, given how completely he'd satisfied her, but desire began to roll through her like an unrelenting wave, so she was full of want for him all over again.

It was so different from how she'd felt about Max. When they'd made love it had been…nice, at best. He hadn't ever driven her to orgasm, and he sure as heck hadn't seemed to care. But the closeness had been welcome, and she'd been too caught up in his lies by then to question whether it was enough for her.

'I didn't know it could be like this,' she whispered, unable to hold his eyes at the admission. She heard him approaching her, then felt his hands reaching for hers, pulling her to a sitting position first then to stand in front of him.

'No?' A gravelled question, his eyes roaming her face. She kept her gaze focussed to the right of his shoulder.

She didn't feel any need to obfuscate the truth with this man, even when the difference in their experience level might have rationally caused her to feel a little immature and embarrassed. 'My ex…my ex-husband…and I weren't exactly…we never…it wasn't like this.' She finished with a frustrated shake of her head. 'Now I get what all the fuss is about.'

He was very still, his Adam's apple jerking in his throat. 'You were married?'

'A long time ago.'

'You're twenty-four years old. It can't have been that long…'

'I left him a week after my twenty-first birthday.' Some present. Finding that her bank accounts had been emptied, and a mortgage taken out on her mother's home. All the security she'd thought she'd had, after her mother's death, had evaporated alongside the marriage she'd believed to be a decent one.

He lifted his hands, cupping her cheeks, and now when she looked at him he was staring at her in that magical way of his, as though he could read her mind when she wasn't speaking.

'Do you want to talk about it?'

'No.' She smiled to soften the blunt refusal. 'He took enough from me. I don't want to let him into this, with you.'

Curiosity flared in his gaze, and anger too, but not directed at her. It was the opposite. She felt his anger directed at Max and it was somehow bonding and reassuring—in that the whole 'enemy of my enemy is my friend' kind of way.

'He was a bastard,' she said, the small elaboration a courtesy, more than anything. 'I'm better off without him.'

His nod was short. 'The food will be cold. Are you hungry?'

'I have no objection to cold food,' she assured him quickly. 'Besides, I'd rather not be interrupted.'

He expelled a slow breath, a sound of relief. 'I'm glad you're not planning on running away again.'

She lifted a brow. 'I think you've given me incentive to stick around. At least for a little while.'

His laugh was husky. He weaved his fingers through hers and drew her towards the door of the bedroom but she stopped walking. 'My clothes.' He was, after all, wearing a towel around his hips.

He paused, turning to face her thoughtfully before dropping her hand and pacing to the pile of fabric on the floor. He liberated her silk underpants, crossing to her and crouching at her feet, holding them for her to step into. She pressed a hand to his shoulder to steady herself, and he eased the underwear up her legs. But at her thighs, he paused, bringing his head forward and pressing a kiss to the top, so she trembled against him and might have lost her balance were it not for the grip on his shoulder. She felt his smile against her flesh.

Another kiss, nearer her womanhood, and then his mouth was there, his tongue pressing against her sex until he found her most sensitive cluster of nerves and tormented it with his ministrations, tasting her, teasing her, sucking her until she exploded in a blinding explosion. She dug her nails into his skin and she cried into the room, pleasure making her incoherent.

He lifted his head, his eyes on hers, his expression impossible to discern, and then he lifted her underpants into place, standing as he did so.

'No more clothes.'

Her heart was racing too fast to permit her to speak.

'I like looking at you.'

The words were delivered with the power that she knew came instinctively to him, and even when there was a part of her that might have felt self-conscious, his obvious admiration drove that away, so she shrugged, incapable of speaking.

'Good.' His approval warmed her. 'Come and eat.'

She was surprisingly hungry, so the feast he'd ordered was a welcome surprise. She hadn't seen it being delivered and unpacked, but it looked as though he'd had a feast of foods prepared, their exotic fragrance making her mouth water.

'Delicacies from the RKH,' he explained. 'Fish with okra and spice.' He pointed to one dish. 'Lamb with olives and couscous, chicken and pomegranate, spinach and raisin flat bread, and aubergine and citrus tagine.'

'Wow.' She stared at the banquet. 'This was just for you?'

'I suspected you'd join me.'

She laughed softly. 'Am I that predictable?'

'I'm that determined,' he corrected softly, running a finger over her arm so she trembled with sensations. 'I wanted you from the moment I saw you.'

'And you always get what you want?'

Darkness coloured his expression for a moment and she could have kicked herself. He was grieving his father's premature death—obviously that wasn't the case.

'Not always, no.'

She nodded, glad he didn't elaborate. 'What should I try first?'

'The lamb is a favourite of mine.' He gestured towards the plate. She moved towards it, inhaling the heady mix of fragrances the table conveyed. Contrary to his prediction, the food was only warm, not cold, which made it easier to taste. She scooped a small heaping of each onto her plate, only remembering she was naked when she sat down and her breasts pressed against the edge of the table. Heat flushed through her and she jerked her gaze to his to find him watching her intently.

She shovelled some food into her mouth to hide the flush of self-consciousness, and sharply forgot to feel anything except admiration for this meal. 'It's delicious,' she murmured, as soon as she'd swallowed.

'I'm glad you think so.'

'I don't know much about your country,' she apologised. 'And I had no idea the food was so good.'

'There are two RKH restaurants in Manhattan,' he said with a lift of one brow.

'Really?'

He nodded. 'One off Wall Street and one in mid-town. This food came from the latter.'

'It wasn't prepared here?'

'No offence to your hotel staff, but RKH cooking is a slow process. Much done in the tagine, which takes hours. There are also a range of spices used that don't tend to be readily available in your kitchens.'

'Still, if we know in advance we can generally arrange anything.'

'RKH food cannot be easily faked.' He winked. 'Better to stick to chefs who prepare it as a matter of course, rather than try to imitate it.'

'You sound incredibly patriotic,' she murmured with a small grin.

'I'm the King—that's my job.'

'Right.' *The King.* A curse filled her brain as the enormity of what she'd done flooded her.

'Don't run away.' He spoke quietly, but with that same tone of command she'd heard from him a few times now. It was instinctive to him—a man who'd been born to rule.

'I'm…not.'

'You were thinking about it.'

She didn't bother denying it. 'It's just…you're a king. I can't…even imagine what your life is like.' She looked around the apartment, a small frown on her face. 'I guess it's like this, but on crack.'

'On crack?'

'You know, to the nth degree.'

He followed her gaze thoughtfully. 'My palace bears little resemblance to this apartment.'

'No?'

'For one thing, there is not a ceiling in the palace that is so low.'

A smile quirked his lips and her heart stammered. He was teasing her. She took another bite of the dinner, this time sampling the fish and okra. He was right. Now that she paid a little more attention, she could taste the difference. The spices were unusual—unlike anything she'd ever known. She doubted even the kitchens in this prestigious hotel could replicate these flavours.

'What is it like?'

'The palace?'

'The palace, the country. I know very little about where you're from,' she confessed. 'Only the basics I researched prior to your arrival.'

'Is this a normal part of your job?'

She nodded. 'I research what I think might be necessary before any guest's arrival. Sometimes that's just their favourite foods or hotel habits, other times it's who they have restraining orders against.' She smiled. 'It depends.'

'And for me?'

Her stomach squeezed as she remembered looking at his photo on the Internet. Even then, she'd desired him. 'The basics,' she said vaguely. 'But nothing that told me of your country or your duties.'

He nodded, apparently satisfied. 'The RKH is one of the most beautiful places you could ever see. Ancient, but in a way that is visible everywhere you look. Our cities are built on the foundations of our past and we honour that. Ruins are left where they stand, surrounded by the modernity that is our life now. High-rise office buildings mingle with stone relics, ancient tapestries hang proudly in these new constructions—a reminder that we are of our past.'

A shiver ran down her spine, his language evocative. 'We are of our land, shaped by the trials of our deserts and the faraway ocean. Our people were nomadic for generations and our desert life is still a large pull, culturally. It is not unusual to take months out of your routine to go into the desert and live nomadically for a time.'

'Do you do this?'

'I cannot,' he admitted. 'Not for months at a time, but yes, Daisy, for days I will escape the palace and move into the wild, untamed desert. There is something energising about pitting myself against its organic tests. Out there, I am just a man; my rank counts for nothing.'

His eyes dropped to her breasts and she felt, very strongly, that he was a man—all man. Desire slicked through her, and her knees trembled beneath the tabletop. She pushed some more food into her mouth, not meeting his eyes.

'Our people were peaceful for centuries, but globalisation and trade brought a new value to resources we took for granted. The RKH stands on one of the greatest oil sources in the world, and there are caves to the west that abound with diamonds and other rare and precious gems. The world's interest in these resources carried a toll, and took a long time to adapt to. We were mired in civil war for a hundred years, and that war led to hostilities with the west.' His face was tense; she felt the weight of his worries, the strength of his concern.

'My father was instrumental in bringing peace to my people. He worked tirelessly to contain our armed forces, to unify our military under his banner, to bring about loyalty from the most powerful families who had historically tilted for the rule of the country. He commanded loyalty.' He paused, sipping his water. 'He was…irreplaceable.'

She considered that. 'But peace has been long-established in the RKH. Surely you don't feel that there's a risk of war now?'

'There is always a risk of war,' he responded quickly, with a quiet edge to his voice. And she felt the weight of responsibility he carried on his shoulders. 'But I was raised to avert it. My whole life has been geared towards a peace-making process, both within the borders of my land and on the world stage.'

'How does one man do that?'

He was reflective and, when he spoke, there was a grim setting to his handsome features. 'In many different ways.' He regarded her thoughtfully. 'Why didn't you become a concert pianist?'

The change of subject was swift but she allowed it. 'Reality intervened.' She said it with a smile, careful to keep the crushing disappointment from her voice—a disappointment that still had the power to rob her of breath.

'Oh?'

She took another bite of her meal—the last on her plate—and waited until she'd finished before answering. 'The Juilliard is expensive. Even on the partial scholarship I was offered, there's New York's cost of living.'

'And you couldn't afford it?'

Before Max, she could have. Easily. Her mother's inheritance had made sure of that. 'No.' A smile that cost her to dredge up. 'It was a pipe dream, in the end.'

He nodded, frowning, then stood. 'I asked you here tonight because I wanted to show you something.'

'Not because you wanted to drag me to bed?' She teased, glad to move the conversation to a more level ground.

'Well, that too.' He held a hand out to her. 'Come.'

It didn't even occur to her not to do as he said. She stood, putting her hand in his, aware of how well they fitted together, moving behind him, her near-nakedness only adding to her awareness of him. The Presidential suite was, as you might expect, enormous. In addition to the main living and dining area, there was a saloon and bar, furnished with the finest alcohol, a wall of classic literature titles, several in German and Japanese to cater to the international guests and now, a baby grand piano in its centre. Her heart began to speed for an entirely different reason now. Anxiety, longing, remorse. She lifted her gaze to him to find that he was watching her.

'That's a Kleshnër.'

He lifted a brow.

'The type of piano.' She moved towards it, as if drawn by an invisible piece of string. 'They're made in Berlin, only forty or so a year. They're considered to be the gold standard.' She ran her finger over the lid, the wood smooth and glossy. Her heart skipped a beat.

'Play something for me.'

She jolted her eyes to his.

'I want to hear you.'

She bit down on her lip, letting her finger touch the keys. How long had it been? Too long. Her insides ached to do as he said, to make music from ivory and ebony, to create sound in this room. But the legacy of her past held her where she was, the pain that was so intrinsic to her piano playing all bound together.

'You are afraid.'

The words inspired a complex response. She shook her head a little. 'Not really. It's just…been a very long time.'

His eyes narrowed speculatively, laced with an unspoken question. 'Play for me.'

She moved around behind the piano, staring first at the keys and then at his face, and it was the speculation she saw there that had her taking a seat behind the piano, her fingers hovering above the keys for several seconds.

'What would you like to hear?'

'Surprise me.'

She nodded again, and then, a small smile curved her mouth. 'This will be a first.'

'Oh?'

'Playing in only my underwear.'

His smile set flames alight inside her body. 'I could get you something, if you're cold, though I should tell you it is likely to decrease my enjoyment of your playing.'

'It's fine.' She winked. 'Just for you.'

He crossed his arms over his chest, waiting. She ran through a catalogue of songs, each of them embedded in her brain like speech and movement. Her fingers found the keys and she closed her eyes for a moment, breathing in deeply, straightening her spine, centring herself to the instrument, and then she began to play. Slowly at first, her interpretation of the Beethoven piece more tempered and gentle than many others. She kept her eyes closed as she played, the strength of the piece building inside her, and as she reached the midpoint and the tempo crescendoed, she tilted her head back, lost completely to the beauty of this form of communication.

The piece was not long—a little over four minutes. She played and when she hit the last notes, both hands pressed to the keys, she opened her eyes to find that the Sheikh had moved closer. He stood right in front of her, his eyes boring through her.

When he spoke, his voice was husky. 'Play something else.'

She lifted a brow, a teasing smile on her lips, but the look was somewhat undermined by the film of tears that had moistened her eyes.

'It's a beautiful instrument.' She ran her fingers over the keys. 'Did you have this brought up today?'

'I wanted to hear you.'

'A keyboard would have done.'

He shook his head. 'Show me something else.'

She did, this time, her favourite Liszt piece, the *étude* one she'd mastered only a week before her father had left home. She vividly recalled because she'd never got a chance to play it for him, and she had been practising so hard, preparing to surprise him with how she'd mastered the difficult finger movements.

'You play as well as you breathe,' he said softly, after she'd finished.

She blinked up at him, her eyes still suspiciously moist. When he pulled her to standing, she went willingly, and when he lifted her against his chest, carrying her back to bed, she felt only intense relief.

CHAPTER FIVE

'YOUR HIGHNESS.'

The voice was coming to Daisy from a long way away. She shifted in bed a little, lifting a hand to run through her hair and connecting with something warm and firm. And it all came flooding back to her, so her eyes burst open and landed on a man she'd only ever seen in a professional capacity. Malik.

Oh, no!

She'd fallen asleep in the Sheikh's bed—she must have—and now it was morning and his suite was teeming with staff. It wasn't a particularly mature thing to do but she dragged the sheet up higher, covering her face, hiding from the servant.

'Privacy, Malik.' Sariq's voice was firm, and, yes, there was irritation there too.

'Yes, sir. Only you have a breakfast meeting with the President. The helicopter is ready to take you to Washington.'

'It will wait for me.'

'Yes, of course.'

A moment later, the door clipped shut.

'You can come out now.' His voice, so stern a moment ago, showed amusement now.

But it wasn't funny. She pushed at the sheet roughly,

and her voice matched it. 'This is so not funny,' she said with a shake of her head, pushing her feet out of the bed and looking for her uniform. 'Oh, God. This is a disaster.'

His frown was way sexier than it should have been. 'Why?'

'Why? Because I told you, no one could know about this, and now that guy, Malik, has seen me *naked* in your bed! Oh, God.' She paced across the room, pulling her shirt on as she went, snagging a nail on one of the buttons and wincing.

'Malik can be trusted,' Sariq assured her.

'Says you, but what if he can't? What if he tells my boss?' She shook her head. 'I can't lose this job, Your Highness.'

At this, he barked a short, sharp laugh into the room. 'Your Highness? Daisy, I have made love to you almost the entire night. Can you call me Sariq now?'

She knew it was absurd, given that she'd already crossed a major professional line, but using his first name felt a thousand kinds of wrong.

'Daisy,' he insisted, moving out of bed, his nakedness glorious and distracting and inducing a panic attack because she'd slept with her client—a lot—and now it was daylight and the magic of the night before had evaporated and she had to face the music. 'Relax. We are two consenting adults who happen to have had sex. This is not something you need to panic about.'

'You don't get it. I'm contractually forbidden from doing this,' she muttered, his amusement only making everything worse. 'It doesn't matter that we're consenting. You're off-limits to me, or should have been.'

'It was one night,' he insisted calmly, coming to fold her in his arms and bring her to his chest. 'Two nights, if you count tonight. And I am counting tonight, Daisy, because I fully expect you to be here with me.'

'What if he tells—?'

He held a hand up imperiously, silencing her with the single gesture. 'If Malik hadn't interrupted us, would you be feeling like this?'

She bit down on her lip, staring at him, and, finally, shook her head.

'Good. Then this problem is easily solved. I will order him to forget he saw you and it will be done.'

She rolled her eyes. 'Nice try, but it's not actually that easy to remove a piece of someone's memory.'

'Malik will do as I say. Put him out of your mind. I have.'

She looked up at him, doubts fading in the face of his confidence. 'I mean it,' she insisted. 'Tomorrow, you go back to your kingdom and nothing changes for you, but I need this job. My life has to go on as it did before, Sariq.' His name—the first time she'd said it—felt like magic. She liked the way it tasted in her mouth, and she especially liked the way he responded, the colour in his eyes deepening in silent recognition.

'And it will.' He dropped his head, his mouth claiming hers, so that thought became, momentarily, impossible. His kiss was heaven and his body weight pushed her backwards until she connected with the wall, so she was trapped between the rock hardness of him, and the wall, and her body was aflame with needs she knew she should resist.

But he lifted her, dispensing with the sheet and pressing her to the wall, his arousal nudging the heat of her sex, so she pushed down, welcoming him deep inside her as though it had been days, not hours, since they'd made love. His possession sent shockwaves of heat flaming through her and he hitched his hips forward and backwards, driving himself into her in a way that had her climaxing within a minute. Her nails scored marks down his back and she almost drew blood from her lip with the effort of not screaming, in case he had other members of staff on the other side of the door.

It was the most sublime feeling, and whatever worries she had seemed far away now. He stilled, holding her, his expression taut, his arousal still hard inside her. She rolled her hips but he dug his hands into her flesh, holding her still.

'What is it?'

'I'm not wearing a condom.' He bit the words out, and she gasped.

'Oh, crap. I didn't even think…'

'Nor did I.' He lifted her from him, easing her to the ground gently, keeping his hands on her waist. 'Shower with me, *habibte*.'

Perhaps she should have declined, but she'd hours ago lost her ability to do what she ought and had abandoned herself, apparently, to doing only what she wanted.

'I suppose it is my job to cater to all your needs,' she purred, earning a small laugh from him. As she stepped into the shower and got the water going, she saw him remove a small foil square from the bathroom drawer and smiled to herself.

Half an hour later, still smiling, she blinked up at him. 'Didn't Malik say the President was waiting?'

Sariq's eyes narrowed. 'He can wait.'

'Your betrothal is all but confirmed.'

Sariq fixed his long-term aide with a cool stare. 'And so?'

'The American—'

'Daisy.' He couldn't help the smile that came to him. Her name was so perfect for her, with her pale blonde hair and ready smile. 'Her name is Daisy.'

'The timing of this could be very bad, if it were to be in the papers in the RKH.'

'It won't be.'

'You are the Emir now, Sariq. More is expected of you than was a month ago. The affairs you once indulged in must become a part of your past.' Malik shook his head. 'Or if you must, allow me to engage suitable women for you, women who are vetted by me, by the palace, who sign confidentiality agreements and are certain not to sell their story to the highest bidder.'

'Daisy won't do that,' he murmured dismissively. 'And the days of palace concubines are long gone. I have no interest in reinvigorating that habit of my forebears.'

'Your father—'

'My father was a lonely man—' Sariq's voice held a warning '—who was determined to mourn my mother until the day he died. How he chose to relieve his bodily impulses is of little interest to me.'

'My point is that these things can be arranged with a maximum of discretion.'

'Daisy is discreet. There are three people who know about this, and it will stay that way.'

'If either of your prospective brides were to find out…'

Sariq tightened one hand into a fist on top of his knee, keeping his gaze carefully focussed on the view beneath him. The White House was just a spec in the distance now, the day's meetings concluded with success.

'They won't.'

'I don't need to tell you how important it is that your marriage settle any potential fallout from your father's death.'

Now, Sariq turned his head slowly, pinning his advisor with a steely gaze. 'No, you don't. So let it go, Malik. This conversation is at an end.'

'He's protective of me, of the kingdom. I've known him since I was a boy.'

Daisy lifted a hand, running the voluminous bubbles between her fingers. The warm bath water lapped at her breasts and, beneath the surface, she brushed an ankle against his nakedness, heat shifting through her. Midnight had come and gone and yet both were wide awake, as though trying to cram everything into this—their last night together.

'He won't say anything?'

'He's more concerned you will,' Sariq said with a shake of his head.

'Me?' Daisy's brows shot up. 'Why in the world…?'

'For money.' Sariq lifted his shoulders.

'Who would pay me for that information?'

His eyes showed amusement. 'Any number of tabloid outlets? Believe it or not, my love life is somewhat newsworthy.'

A shudder of revulsion moved down Daisy's spine. 'You can't be serious?'

'Unfortunately, I am. Malik feels this indiscretion could be disastrous for my country, and, in some ways, there's truth in that.'

'I'll try not to take that personally.'

'You shouldn't. It's not about you so much as it is the women I'm supposed to marry.'

She froze. 'What?'

'I'm not engaged,' he reassured her quietly. 'And I will marry only one. But there are two candidates, both daughters of the powerful families who would have, decades ago, made a claim for the throne. The thinking is that in marrying one of them, I will unify our country further, bonding powerful families, allaying any prospective civil uprising.'

She absorbed that thoughtfully. 'Do you like these women?'

'I've met them a handful of times; it's hard to say.'

'You took me to bed after meeting me only a handful of times,' she pointed out.

'Then I like them considerably less than I like you,' he said, pushing some water towards her so it splashed to her chin.

She smiled back at him, but there was a heaviness inside her. 'What if you're not suited?'

'It's of little importance. The marriage is more about appearances than anything else.'

'You don't think you should care for your bride?'

Something darkened in his features and there was a look of determination there. 'Absolutely not.'

She shook her head. 'Why is that so ridiculous?'

'When it comes to royal marriages, arrangements of convenience make far more sense.'

'It's your life though. Surely you want to live it with someone that you have something in common with?'

'I will have something in common with my wife: she will love our country as I do, enough to marry a stranger to strengthen its peace.'

'And over time, you may come to love her?'

'No, *habibte*. I will never love my wife.' His eyes bore into hers. 'My father loved my mother and it destroyed him. Her death left him bereft and broken. I will never make that mistake.'

She was quiet. 'Do you think he felt it was a mistake to love her?'

'I cannot say. I think at times he wished he hadn't loved

her, yes. He missed her in a way that was truly awful to watch.'

'I'm sorry.'

He shrugged. 'I have always known my own marriage would be nothing like his. If it weren't for the fact that I need a child—and as quickly as possible—then I would never marry.'

Something tightened in her chest—a fierce, primal rejection of that. In order to have children, to beget an heir, he would need to have sex, and, though she had no reason to presume he wouldn't, the idea of him going to bed with anyone else turned parts of her cold in a way she suspected would be permanent.

'Children? So soon?'

'I am the last of my family. It's not an ideal situation. Yes, I need an heir. My marriage will be organised within months.' His eyes assumed a more serious look. 'I have to leave here in the morning. I won't be back.'

Inexplicably, a lump formed in her throat. 'I know that.'

'And you, Daisy? What will your future hold? Will you stay working here, servicing guests of this suite of rooms for the rest of your life?'

Her lips twisted. 'I hope not.'

'The way you play the piano is mesmerising. You have a rare talent. It's wrong of you not to pursue it.'

Her smile was lopsided, his praise pulling at her in a way that was painful and pleasurable all at once. 'Like I said, it was a pipe dream.'

'Why?'

'My circumstances wouldn't allow me to study. Becoming a concert pianist isn't exactly something you click your fingers and do. It's hard and it's competitive and I had to get a job.'

'Why? When you had a scholarship...'

'I couldn't do it.'

He compressed his lips. 'If money was the only issue, then let me do as Malik suggested and offer you a settlement. He wanted me to ensure it was more profitable for you to keep your silence than not...'

She sent him a look of disbelief. 'I'm not going to tell anyone about this, believe me.'

'I know that. But I'd like to help you.'

'No.' She shook her head, tilting her chin defiantly. 'Absolutely not. You might be richer than Croesus but I'm not taking a cent from you, Sariq. I absolutely refuse.'

And while he might have been used to being obeyed, there was more than a hint of respect in his eyes when he met her gaze. 'Very well, Daisy. But if you should ever reconsider, the offer has no expiry date.'

She nodded, knowing she wouldn't. Once Sariq left, she would set about the difficult job of forgetting he ever existed. For her own sanity, she needed to do that, or missing him could very well be the end of her.

It was six weeks after he left that she put two and two together and realised the significance of the dates. A loud gasp escaped her lips.

'What is it?' Henry, beside her, turned to regard her curiously.

She shook her head, but the calendar on the counter wouldn't be silenced. She scanned through the guests she'd hosted in the last month and a half, since Sariq had left, and her pulse quickened.

Yes, she'd definitely missed a cycle. Instinctively, her hand curved over her flat stomach as the reality of this situation hit home.

She couldn't possibly be pregnant, though. They'd used protection. Every time? Yes, every time! Except that once, against the wall, but he hadn't climaxed, he'd been so careful. Surely that wasn't enough…

But there was no other explanation. Her cycle was as regular as clockwork; missing a period had to mean that somehow she'd conceived Sariq's baby.

She groaned, spinning away from Henry, uncertainty making it impossible to know what to say or do. First of all she needed proper confirmation.

'Do you mind if I clock out? I just remembered something.'

'Not at all. Make the most of the quiet days, I say.'

She bit down on her lip, grabbing her handbag. 'Thanks, Henry.'

There was a drugstore just down the block, but she walked past it, taking the subway across town instead. It was safer here, away from the possibility of bumping into anyone from the hotel. She bought three pregnancy tests, each from a different manufacturer, knowing that it was overkill and not caring, and a huge bottle of water, which she drank in one sitting. Once back at her small apartment in the basement of the hotel, she pulled a test from its packaging, taking it into the bathroom and following the instructions to the letter.

It took almost no time for two blue lines to appear on the test patch.

She swore under her breath, staring at the lines, a hardness filling out her heart.

What the heck could she do? Sariq had left America six weeks earlier. She hadn't heard from him and she had no expectation she would. He'd made it very clear that he needed to marry one of the women who would promise a greater hope of lasting peace for his people. He would make a match of duty, of national importance, and he'd need to have a legitimate heir with whomever he chose.

This baby would be a disaster for him, and, by extension, for his people. What if the sheer fact that she was pregnant somehow led to an all-out war in his country?

Nausea rose inside her. She cupped her hands over the toilet bowl, bending forward and losing all the water she'd hastily consumed. Her brow was covered in perspiration. She pressed her head to the ceramic tiles of the wall and counted to ten, telling herself it wasn't that bad, that things would work out. She could raise a child on her own. No one ever needed to know.

Daisy re-read the email for the hundredth time before sending it.

Sariq, I've reconsidered. Tuition for the Juilliard is in the attachment. Anything you can do to help…

There was nothing in there that could possibly give away the truth of her situation. No way would he be able to intuit from the few brief lines that there had been an unexpected consequence of their brief, passionate affair.

And that was what she wanted, wasn't it? To do this on her own? She bit down on her lip, her eyes scanning her phone screen, panic lifting through her. Because in all honesty, she couldn't have said *what* she wanted. Their baby, yes, absolutely. Already, she loved the little human growing inside her.

She'd begun to feel the tiniest movements, like little bubbles popping in her belly, and she'd known it was her son or daughter swimming around, finding their feet and getting stronger every day.

Time was passing too quickly. In only five months she'd have to stop working, and then what? Panic made her act. She needed help and Sariq had willingly offered it. Lying to him wasn't exactly comfortable for Daisy but she had to make her peace with that. Sariq had explained what he needed most—a wife and a legitimate heir to inherit his throne.

He'd be grateful to Daisy for this, in the long run, surely.

She read the email once more, her finger hovering over the 'send' arrow. She'd tried everything else she could think of. Thanks to her ex, her credit rating had tanked. She couldn't get a loan, and, even if she could, what in the world would she pay it back with?

For their child, she would do anything, even offer a tiny white lie, via email, to the man she'd had two passionate nights with months earlier. The end justified the means. The email made a whooshing sound as she finally sent it, but Daisy didn't hear it over the thunderous tsunami of her blood.

He stared at the email with an expression that was impossible to decipher. Three and a half months after leaving New York he had begun to think he would never hear from her again.

He re-read the email and a smile lifted his face. He had prayed she would come to her senses, but instinctively known not to push it. It wasn't his place to run her life. Daisy had to decide what she wanted. He wished he could give her more. He wished he could see her again. But knowing he could give her this small gift was enough.

Except it wasn't.

He awoke the next morning with a yearning deep in his soul and he had every intention of indulging it.

Malik was, naturally, against another trip to America.

'I am going,' Sariq insisted firmly, putting a hand on his advisor's forearm. 'Arrange the jet, call the embassy, notify them I'll be there for the weekend.'

'But, sir...'

'No, Malik. No. I'm doing this.'

He felt a thousand times lighter than he had the day before. It was only a temporary reprieve but, suddenly, seeing Daisy again felt like the right thing to do, and he was going to enjoy this last weekend before he made the official betrothal announcements.

Her email was a gift, and he had no intention of ignoring it.

CHAPTER SIX

To say the building was imposing would be to say the sky was vast. She stared at the RKH embassy, just off Park Avenue, her heart hammering against her ribs.

I'm in Manhattan for the weekend. Come and see me.

A map had been attached to the email with directions to this building, and she'd been staring at it for the last twenty minutes, her central nervous system in overdrive as she tried to brace herself for this.

Keeping the truth of this from Sariq over email had been hard enough! But now? Keeping the secret from him when they were face to face? Daisy suspected it was going to take all the courage she possessed to go through with it.

Every instinct she possessed railed against it. She hated the idea! But what was the alternative? If she told him, then what? He'd be devastated.

She knew what was at stake for him, and why he needed to marry one of the women who would help him keep the peace in his country. The fact she'd fallen pregnant wasn't his fault and he didn't deserve to have to deal with this complication. More importantly, he wouldn't want to deal with it. He'd made that perfectly clear during their time together. It had been a brief passionate affair, nothing more.

He'd gone back to the RKH and moved on with his life—
the last thing he'd be expecting was the news that, actually, they'd made a baby together.

But didn't he have a right to know? This was his child.
When she stripped away the fact he was a powerful sheikh,
he was a man who had the same biological claim on this developing baby as she did. She made a noise of frustration,
so a woman walking past stopped for a moment, shooting
Daisy a quizzical look. She smiled, a terse movement of
her lips, then turned away, drawing in a deep gulp of air.
It tasted cold, or perhaps that was Daisy's blood.

The fact of the matter was, she couldn't strip his title
away from his person. He wasn't just a man, he was a
sheikh, and with his position came obligations she couldn't
even imagine. One day, when he had the wife and heirs
he'd explained to her were necessary, she might feel dif-
ferently. Maybe then this child would be less of a problem
for him. Maybe then he'd even want to know their son or
daughter. But for now, she was better to assume all the responsibilities, to raise their child on her own.

It was the right decision, but she simply hadn't banked
on how hard it would be to keep something of this mag-
nitude a secret when she was going to see him. With
him in the RKH, he was an abstract figure. While she
dreamed of him at night and was startled by memories
of his touch during the day, he was far away, and it was
easy to believe he didn't think of her at all. For the sake
of their child, she had to plan for her future knowing he
wouldn't be a part of it.

Digging her nails into her palm and sucking in a deep
breath for courage, she looked to the right and dipped her
head forward as she crossed the street, approaching the
embassy as though she were calm and relaxed when inside
a wild kaleidoscope of butterflies had taken over her body.

Four guards stood on the steps, each heavily armed and wearing a distinctive army uniform. She swallowed as she approached the closest.

'Madam? What is it?' The guard studied her with an expression that gave nothing away.

'I have an appointment.' Her voice was soft. She cleared her throat. 'His Highness Sariq Al Antarah asked me here.'

The guard's expression showed a hint of scepticism. 'What is your name?'

'Daisy Carrington.'

He spoke into a small receiver on his wrist and a moment later, a crackled voice issued onto the street. The guard nodded, and gestured to the door. 'Go on.'

Go on. So simple. If only her legs would obey. She stared at the shiny black doors, her pulse leaping wildly through her body, and concentrated on pushing one leg forward, then the next, until she was at the doors. On her approach, they swept inwards. More guards stood here but she barely noticed them at first, for the grandeur of this entranceway.

Walls and ceiling were all made of enormous marble blocks, cream with grey rippling through them. The floor was marble too, except gold lines ran along the edges. At several points along the walls there were pillars—marble—and atop them sat enormous arrangements of flowers, but unlike any she'd ever seen, vibrant, fragrant and stunning. She wanted to stop time and stare at them, to learn the names of these blooms she'd never seen before, to breathe each in and commit its unique scent to memory.

'Identification?' The guard's deep voice jolted her back to the present.

She held out her passport—it had been specified as the only suitable form of identification on the directions she'd received. Her passport had no stamps in it, and in fact she probably wouldn't have had a passport at all if it hadn't been necessary for the vetting process at the hotel.

The guard took it, opening it to the photo page and comparing the image to the real thing, then nodded without handing the passport back. 'Go through security.'

'My passport?'

'I need to make a copy.'

She frowned, uneasiness lifting in her belly. But Sariq was here, and so she wasn't afraid. She trusted him, and these were his people.

The security checkpoint was like any in an airport. She pushed her handbag and shoes through the conveyor belt then walked through an arch before collecting her things.

'His Highness is on the third floor,' a man to her right advised. He wasn't a security guard. At least, he wasn't wearing a military uniform. He wore robes that were white, just like Sariq's, but the detailing at his wrist was in cream. 'There is an elevator, or the central stairs.'

She opted for the latter. The opportunity to observe this building was one she wanted to take advantage of. Besides, it would give her longer to steady her nerves and to brace herself for seeing Sariq again.

A hand curved over her stomach instinctively and she dropped it almost immediately. She had to be careful. No gestures that could reveal a hint of her condition.

The stairs were made of marble as well, but at the first floor, the landing gave way on either side to shining timber floors. The walls here were cream, and enormous pieces of art in gold gilt frames lined the hallway. There were more flowers, each arrangement as elaborate as the ones downstairs.

She bit down on her lip and kept moving. The next floor was just the same—polished timber, flowers, art, and high ceilings adorned with chandeliers that cast the early afternoon light through the building, creating shimmering droplets of refraction across the walls.

She held her breath as she climbed the next set of steps. This floor was like the others except there was a noticeable increase in security presence. Two guards at the top of the stairs, and at least ten in either direction, at each door.

'Miss Carrington?' A man in a robe approached her. She thought he looked vaguely familiar, perhaps from Sariq's stay at the hotel. 'This way.'

She fell into step beside him, incapable of speech. Anticipation had made it impossible. She was vividly aware of every system in her body. Lungs that were working overtime to pump air, veins that were taxed with the effort of moving blood, skin that was punctured by goose bumps, lips that were parted, eyes that were sore for looking for him.

At the end of the corridor, two polished timber doors were closed. There was a brass knocker on one. The man hit it twice and then, she heard him.

'Come.'

That one word set every system into rampant overdrive. She felt faint. But she had to do this. She hated having to ask him for money. She hated it with every fibre of her being, but what else could she do? She was already in a financially parlous state, but adding a baby to the mix and her inability to work? Neither of them would cope, and the comfort and survival of her child was more important than anything—even her pride.

The doors swung open and, after a brief pause, she stepped inside, looking around. The room was enormous. Large windows with heavy velvet drapes framed a view towards Bryant Park. She could just make out the tops of the trees from here. The furniture was heavy and wooden, dark leather sofas, and on the walls, the ancient tapestries

Sariq had described. She took a step towards one, and it was then that she saw him.

Her heart almost gave way. She froze, unable to move, to speak, barely able to breathe.

Sariq.

Dressed in the traditional robes of his people, except in a more ornate fashion, this time he had a piece of gold fabric that went across his shoulders and fell down his front. On his head he wore the *keffiyeh*, and she stood there and stared at him dressed like this: every bit the imposing ruler. It was almost impossible to reconcile this man with the man who'd delighted her body, kissing her all over, tasting her, taking her again and again until she couldn't form words or thoughts. He looked so grand, so untouchable.

'Daisy.' Her name on his lips sent arrows through her body. She stayed where she was, drinking him in with her eyes.

'Your Highness.' She forced a smile to her lips, and was ridiculously grateful she'd taken care with her appearance. Her stomach was still flat but she'd chosen to wear all black—a simple pair of jeans and a flowing top, teamed with a brightly coloured necklace to break up the darkness of the outfit. She'd left her hair out and applied the minimum of make-up. His eyes dropped to her feet then lifted slowly over her body, so she felt warmth where he looked, as though he were touching her.

'I feel like I should curtsy or something.'

His look was impossible to decipher. 'That's not necessary.' He stayed where he was, and she did the same, so there was a room between them. The silence crackled.

'Thank you for seeing me,' she said, after a moment. God, this was impossible. She didn't want to ask him for money and, now that she saw him, the idea of having his baby and not telling him was like poison. All the very sensible reasons she'd used to justify that course of action fled from her mind.

He deserved to know. Even if he chose not to acknowledge the child? Even if he turned her away? Even if…the possibilities spun through her, each of them scary and real and alarming.

Her stomach was in knots, indecision eating her alive. She knew only one thing for certain: she had to decide what to do, and quickly. If she was going to tell him, it should be now. Shouldn't it?

She was every bit as beautiful as he remembered. More so. There was something about her today—she was glowing. Her skin was lustrous, her eyes shimmering, her lips, God, her lips. He wanted to pull them between his teeth, to drag her body to his and kiss her hard, to push her against the wall and make love to her as he'd done freely that weekend.

But that had been different somehow. They'd had an agreement. They'd known what they were to each other. Now? He was on the brink of announcing his marriage. Surely he couldn't still be fantasising about another woman?

But he was. He wanted Daisy. Not for one night, not for two. He wanted her for as long as he could have her.

'Sire, you cannot see her again.'

Malik's warning had rung through the embassy.

'You were far from discreet last time. With your engagement due to be announced any day now, if word of this were to get out—'

'It won't. And I'm relying on you to make sure of that.'

But Malik's reaction had been a good barometer. He was worried about Daisy, worried about what the people of the RKH would think if the affair became public, and with good reason. Sariq was no longer free to follow his passions wherever they took him. He was now the ruler. He'd been crowned, and the weight of a country rested on his shoulders.

He needed to remember that, and yet, faced with Daisy, he couldn't. He was not a man to throw caution to the wind. All his life he'd been trained for this, he knew what his responsibilities were, but suddenly he wondered if he could have his cake and eat it too.

His engagement hadn't been announced...yet. He had a little time. And he knew just how he wanted to spend it. He regarded her thoughtfully, something pulling at his gut, given how she was looking at him—as though she was remembering every single moment they'd shared, every kiss, whisper, pleasure.

He could postpone his trip, stay in New York a few more nights. Would she stay with him here, at the embassy? It was hard to read her, hard to know what she'd say if he suggested that. Besides, it wasn't enough. A few nights would satisfy him temporarily, but if the fourteen weeks since he'd last seen Daisy had taught him anything, it was that his need for her was insatiable, and not likely to be easily dispensed with. He wanted longer. As long as she could give him.

There was only one solution, and suddenly Sariq knew that if he didn't reach for it with both hands, he'd regret it for the rest of his life.

'I have a proposition for you. One I think you'll like.'

She stood completely still except for her fingers, which she fidgeted behind her back. 'Oh?'

'Have a seat.' He gestured towards the dark leather sofas and she followed his gaze, but shook her head.

'I'd prefer to stand.'

'Would you like a drink?'

'No, thank you.'

He nodded.

'What is this proposition?'

'When is your admission set for the Juilliard?'

Darn it. She should have researched this. 'Mid-January,' she guessed, glad the words came out with such authority.

'In three months.' He ran a palm over his chin, as though contemplating this.

'Yes.'

'Then here is what I would like to propose. I want you to come to the RKH with me, Daisy.'

Her eyes flew wide and her lips parted. She stared at him, wondering if she'd imagined the words. 'But you're... aren't you getting married?'

He nodded. 'My situation is as it was before. I have chosen my bride, but the wedding date is not set.' Now he moved, closing the distance between them, until he was standing right in front of her. 'I will not marry her until you leave.'

A shiver ran down her spine, and she hated that heat was building low in her abdomen, filling her with a need that was instantly familiar even as revulsion gripped her, making her want to shout and stamp.

'No one could know you were there.' His jaw tightened, as though he were grinding his teeth. 'It would be a disaster if anyone were to find out, so we would have to be very, very careful.' He paused once more, and, for no reason she could fathom, Daisy held her breath. 'Malik would arrange it so that you were installed in an apartment in the capital. He would manage your security, ensure you were not seen by anyone but me. And I would visit you often.' He lifted a finger, tracing a line down her cheek towards her lips. She shivered again. 'It would be just like it was here, in New York. You would have a piano, and you would have me, and anything else you could want. And at the end of it, you would return to study, your tuition paid in full, a house provided for you in New York. Anything you wanted, Daisy.'

She stared at him, her heart dropping to her toes. Pain lashed her. What he was offering was little more than prostitution! Well? What had she expected? She'd come here, cap in hand, after the weekend they'd shared. Could he be blamed for thinking her attention could be bought? Her knees felt weak and her stomach hurt.

'You're asking me to come and be your secret mistress,' she repeated, incredulity ringing through her.

'I'm asking you to be my lover for as long as possible.'

'Before you get married.' She nodded, numb to the core.

He dipped his head in silent agreement.

'And in exchange, you'd give me money.'

Her insides lit up. Nausea crested through her.

'I will give you money anyway,' he assured her, as though just realising how mercenary the proposition sounded. She closed her eyes, wanting to blank him out for a moment, but even then, he was everywhere. His intoxicatingly masculine fragrance filled her. She was drowning in his presence and she desperately needed to think rationally and calmly.

'I cannot offer you more than this,' he said slowly, the words filled with the authority that came naturally to him, so she jerked her eyes open and looked at him once more. 'My duties to my country come first. I could never openly date you. A divorced American? My people wouldn't tolerate it. I know this isn't sensible. In fact, it's the opposite of that. If you were discovered, it would pose a real risk to my rule, but I don't care. Daisy, I want you to come home with me. I want you to be my mistress more than I've ever wanted anything in my life.'

A divorced American. His mistress!

She felt so dirty! As though she was somehow lesser than him, and it brought back so many awful memories of her marriage, when Max had so cleverly undermined her confidence in herself until she saw her only value as being His Wife, rather than a person all her own. A shiver of revulsion ran down her spine, because she wasn't that woman any more.

'I can't believe you'd even suggest this.'

He moved forward, his body pressed to hers so weakness threatened to reduce her anger when she needed it most. 'How is it any different from that weekend?'

'You're getting married.'

'And I was getting married that weekend, too.'

'I had no idea the fact I was divorced and an American were such issues for you.'

He frowned, but it was swallowed quickly, as he dropped his head, his lips brushing hers. 'It isn't.'

'Not for your "mistress", anyway. I dare say someone like me is the perfect candidate for that role.'

His hands found the bottom of her shirt, lifting it so he could hold her bare hips, his lips more determined at hers now so a whimper filled her mouth and she felt herself kissing him back, needing him in a way that infuriated her.

'You are the perfect candidate to be in my bed, yes,' he agreed, but it hurt. God, it hurt. She'd never felt so...cheap.

She lifted her hands, pushing at his chest, putting some vital distance between them. 'Damn you, Sariq, no.' She shouted the words and then lowered her voice, aware that there were dozens of guards on this level. 'No.' A whisper. She wrapped her arms around her chest, moving away from him towards the sofas. Her knees were trembling but still she didn't sit. Her eyes were on him, showing her pain and hurt.

'I cannot offer you more than this,' he said again. 'You know what expectations are upon me. My marriage is a bargaining chip; my bride an important part of my political strategy. I cannot bring you to the palace as my mistress— it would offend my future Emira and it would offend my people. I'm sorry if this hurts you, but it is the truth.'

Her heart looped through her. Offend his bride. Offend his people. 'And what about me, Your Highness? Do you care that I am offended by this offer?'

He had the decency to look—for a brief moment— ashamed. But he rallied quickly, his expression shifting to a mask of determination. 'You shouldn't be. I'm offering us a way to both get what we want.'

She made a scoffing noise.

'Money aside, think about how good this could be. How much fun we'd have...'

She closed her eyes, the temptation of that warming her, because if she weren't so horrendously offended, she could see the appeal of his offer. On one level, he was offering her something she desperately wanted. More of Sariq? But everything about the way he'd made his offer filled her with disgust and loathing. He had somehow managed to cheapen what they'd shared so it felt tawdry and meaningless. And he didn't seem to get that!

'I thought you actually *liked* me,' she said with a small shake of her head. 'I thought you enjoyed spending time with me. That you valued me as a person.' Pain lashed her, because he didn't. He was just like her ex. The realisation was awful and horrifying.

'I do,' he promised immediately, crossing towards her. 'But I'm a realist and I see the limitations of this.'

'Which is sex,' she said crudely, lifting her brows, waiting for him to acknowledge it.

'As it was in New York,' he said firmly.

Her heart dropped. Her stomach ached and tears filled her eyes. It had just been about sex for him? She wracked her brain, trying desperately to remember anything he'd said or done that indicated otherwise, but no. There was nothing. He'd wanted her. He'd made a point of saying that over and over, but that was all.

She'd been a fool to think there was more to it, that they were in some way friends or something.

'I shouldn't have come here. I shouldn't have asked you for money. It was a mistake. Please forget…'

'No.' He held onto her wrist as though he could tell she was about to run from the room. 'Stop.'

Her eyes lifted to his and she jerked on her wrist so she could lift her fingers to her eyes and brush away her tears. Panic was filling her, panic and disbelief at the mess she found herself in.

'How is this upsetting to you?' he asked more gently, pressing his hands to her shoulders, stroking his thumbs over her collarbone. 'We agreed at the hotel that we could only have two nights together, and you were fine with that. I'm offering you three months, on exactly those same terms, and you're acting as though I've asked you to parade naked through the streets of Shajarah.'

'You're ashamed of me,' she said simply. 'In New York we were two people who wanted to be together. What you're proposing turns me into your possession. Worse, it turns me into your prostitute.'

He stared at her, his eyes narrowed. 'The money I will give you is beside the point.'

More tears sparkled on her lashes. 'Not to me it's not.'

'Then don't take the money,' he said urgently. 'Come to the RKH and be my lover because you want to be with me.'

'I can't.' Tears fell freely down her face now. 'I need that money. I need it.'

A muscle jerked in his jaw. 'So have both.'

'No, you don't understand.'

She was a live wire of panic but she had to tell him, so that he understood why his offer was so revolting to her. She pulled away from him, pacing towards the windows, looking out on this city she loved. The trees at Bryant Park whistled in the fall breeze and she watched them for a moment, remembering the first time she'd seen them. She'd been a little girl, five, maybe six, and her dad had been performing at the restaurant on the fringes of the park. She'd worn her Very Best dress, and, despite the heat, she'd worn tights that were so uncomfortable she could vividly remember that feeling now. But the park had been beautiful and her dad's music had, as always, filled her heart with pleasure and joy.

Sariq was behind her now, she felt him, but didn't turn to look at him.

'I'm glad you were so honest with me today.' Her voice was hollow. 'It makes it easier for me, in a way, because I know exactly how you feel, how you see me, and what you want from me.' Her voice was hollow, completely devoid of emotion when she had a thousand throbbing inside her.

He said nothing. He didn't try to deny it. Good. Just as she'd said, it was easier when things were black and white.

'I don't want money so I can attend the Juilliard, Your Highness.' It pleased her to use his title, to use that as a point of difference, to put a line between them that neither of them could cross.

Silence. Heavy, loaded with questions. And finally, 'Then what do you need such a sum for?'

She bit down on her lip, her tummy squeezing tight. 'I'm pregnant. And you're the father.'

CHAPTER SEVEN

WHEN HIS MOTHER had died, Sariq had been speechless. Perhaps his father had expected grief. Tears. Anger. Something rent with emotion. Instead, Sariq had listened to the news.

'She died, Riq. So did the baby.'

He'd stood there, all of seven years old, his face like stone, his body slowing down so that blood barely pumped, heart barely moved, breath hardly formed, and he'd stared out of a window. Then it had been a desert view—the sands of the Alkajar range stretching as far as the eye could see, heat forming a haze in the distance that had always reminded Sariq of some kind of magic.

Now, he stared out at New York, streets that were crammed with taxis and trucks, the ever-present honking of horns filling him with a growing sense of disbelief. There were trees in the distance, blowing in the light autumnal breeze. His heart barely moved. His blood didn't pump. He could scarcely breathe.

Time passed. Minutes? Hours? He couldn't have said. He was conscious of the ticking of the clock—a gift from a long-ago American president to his father, on the signing of the Treaty of Lashar. He was conscious of the colour of her hair, so gold it matched the thread of his robes. The fragrance she brought with her, delicate and floral. He was conscious, somehow, of the beating of her heart. In contrast to his, it was firing frantically. It was beating for two people. Their unborn child was nestled in her belly, growing with every second that passed.

He closed his eyes, needing to block the world out, needing to block Daisy out in particular.

His breathing was ragged as he went back in time, calculating the dates. It had been what?—almost four months?—since his visit to America. When had she found out? And why had she waited until now to tell him?

Except, she hadn't come here to tell him.

His eyes flared open and flew to her with renewed speculation and his heart burst back to life, pushing blood through his body almost too fast for his veins to cope. The torrent was an assault.

'You weren't going to tell me.'

A strangled noise was all the confirmation he needed. He stood perfectly still, but that was no reflection of his temperament or feelings.

'You came here today to collect a cheque. If I hadn't suggested you join me in the RKH, you would have taken the money and left. True?'

She didn't turn to face him and suddenly that was infuriating and insupportable. He gripped her shoulders and spun her around. Tears sparkled on her lashes and his gut rolled, because he hated seeing her like this but his own shock and anger and disbelief made it impossible for him to comfort her.

'This baby is a disaster for you.'

She was right. His eyes swept shut once more as he tried to make sense of the political ramifications of having conceived a child with a divorced American—a woman he spent approximately forty-eight hours of his life with, if that.

'I didn't come here to tell you, because I understand your position. You have to get married and have children with someone who will strengthen your position, not weaken it. This baby was a mistake.' Her face paled. 'No, not a mistake,' she quickly corrected, her hand curving over her stomach so his eyes dropped to the gesture, something different moving through him now. Was that joy? In the midst of this? Surely not.

'A surprise,' he substituted, his voice gravelled by the emotions that were strangling him.

'You could say that.' Her short laugh lacked humour.

'So what was your plan?'

'Plan?' She bit down on her lip. 'I wouldn't say I have a plan.'

'You came to take money from me under false pretences? And then what?' It was unreasonable, and not an accurate representation of how he felt. He wasn't sure why he had chosen to hone in on that. The money was beside the point, but her duplicity wasn't.

She flinched but nodded, as though his accusation had some kind of merit. 'Believe me, I hate that I came here with my hand out. I hate having to ask you for anything. But I can't afford a child, Sariq. I can't afford this.' Tears ran down her cheeks now and his chest compressed almost painfully.

'The hotel doesn't pay you well?'

'My salary's fine.' She dashed at her tears, her eyes showing outrage. Outrage that she was crying. Outrage that she had to explain her situation to him. But he needed to understand...

'I lost a lot of money in my divorce. I have a mountain of debt with interest rates that are truly eye-watering. My salary lets me chip maybe five thousand dollars a year off the total owed. I should be out from under that in about, oh, I don't know, seventy or eighty years?' She shook her head. 'I can't afford to stop working. The hotel provides my accommodation so once I stop working, I'll need to find somewhere to live, which I can't afford. Benefits won't cut it. I hate that I'm asking you for money,' she repeated, and he felt it, every single shred of her hate and fury and fear, too. 'But we're having a baby and I need to do what I can for her or him.'

'Yes.' It was an immediate acquiescence. He turned away from Daisy, stalking towards the door, staring at it for a moment. His mind was spinning at a thousand miles per hour. His marriage was important. Unifying his country further mattered. But so did begetting an heir. His situation as the last in his family's line had troubled him for a long time, but never more so than since losing his father. He was conscious of how much rested on his survival, how vulnerable that made him. And if there was one thing he hated, it was feeling vulnerable.

This child alleviated that.

He had an heir—or he would, in six months' time.

'Look at me, Sariq.' Her voice cut through him, the grief there, the pain. He turned and his heart jolted inside him, because she was clearly terrified. If he stopped for a moment and saw this from her perspective, he could see how unsettling the discovery of her pregnancy must have been. Neither of them had wanted complications from that weekend. It had been a stolen time of passion, short and brief. And definitely over.

But it wasn't.

This baby would bind them for ever.

'I can't afford to do this on my own, and I hate that, but the alternatives don't bear considering.' A shiver moved her slender frame. Her too-slender frame. Had she *lost* weight since he'd seen her last?

A frown pulled at his mouth. 'You're slim.'

She blinked, the statement apparently making no sense.

'You haven't gained weight. In fact, the opposite appears to be true.'

'Oh.' She nodded jerkily. 'Yes. I haven't felt well. The doctor at the free clinic says that will probably pass soon enough.'

His frown deepened. He didn't feel that was it. Was it possible that she hadn't been eating? That she hadn't been eating well enough? Because she was worried about money?

And as for a *free clinic*? She was carrying the sole heir to the throne of the RKH, one of the most prosperous countries in the Middle East—and the world! She should have top-level medical care. He needed to fix this—he needed to find a way to make this work, for everyone.

'The baby's healthy,' she said quietly. 'I'm fine, apart from the all-day nausea and complete lack of appetite.'

He nodded slowly, fixing his eyes to her. There was only one solution, and he needed it to happen immediately. 'I'm glad you came to me today, Daisy. I'm glad you told me.'

She let out a whoosh of breath, her relief apparent. 'You are?'

A simple nod. 'But we must move quickly in order to avoid a major diplomatic incident.'

She blinked. 'Oh, I'm not going to tell anyone about this, Your Highness.'

He laughed then, a deranged sound. 'For God's sake, we've conceived a child together. We're going to be parents. Call me Sariq.'

She bristled, her eyes showing strength and determination. 'We are *not* going to be parents together.' She spoke with a cool authority that was belied by the quivering of her fingers. 'You're going to be in another country, far away. I'm going to raise our child.'

His eyes narrowed imperceptibly. 'You know what this baby means to me.'

She froze.

'You know how imperative it is that I have an heir.'

'But this baby *isn't* your heir,' she mumbled after a moment. 'We're not married. It can't be…'

'We're not married, *yet*.'

Her eyes flared wide in her beautiful face, and her lips dropped to reveal her glossy white teeth. She didn't speak. She couldn't. Good. He needed a moment to organise this. He crossed to his desk, picking up the phone. 'Have Malik call me.'

He disconnected the receiver once more and turned to face her. She was standing where he'd left her, shaking her head.

'Sit down, *habibte*.'

She shook her head harder. 'I'm not marrying you.'

Determination flooded him as he saw the only path before them clearly, and knew he had to guide them down it. 'There is no alternative, Daisy, so I suggest you move past shock to acceptance. The sooner you do so the better, for both of us.'

She stared at him, her insides awash with uncertainty and disbelief. 'You can't be serious?'

'Does it sound like something I'd joke about? This child has more value to my people and me than I can possibly describe. You are carrying my royal heir. There is no option but for us to marry.'

'I beg your pardon,' she spat, crossing her arms over her chest, wishing his eyes didn't drop to her cleavage in that way that reminded her of everything they'd shared that weekend. 'There is one option, and it's the one we're going to take. I'm going to leave here now, with a cheque that will help me cover medical expenses and rent in some kind of home in which to spend the first year of our child's life, until I can go back to work—'

'Go back to work?' His laugh was a caustic sound of derision. 'And who will be raising the crown prince of the RKH?'

'Or princess,' she snapped caustically. 'And I don't know. I'll find a family day care.'

'Family day care?' he repeated, and she nodded, though she could understand his reaction to that. It was a little haphazard and ill-thought-out.

'I don't know, okay? I haven't gotten that far. I just know that I can do this on my own.' She lifted her chin, breathing in deeply in an attempt to calm her nerves. 'I haven't told anyone anything about what happened between us and I don't intend to. I won't say a word about the fact you're this baby's father. Your name won't appear on the birth certificate. It will remain untraceable.'

His jaw clenched. 'You think this will please me? For my own child not to bear my name?' His nostrils flared with the force of his exhalation. 'Honestly, Daisy, your naivety would almost be adorable if it weren't so inappropriate.'

Anger flared inside her. 'I beg your pardon?'

'How hard do you think it would be for someone to piece this together?' He held her gaze with obvious contempt. 'You cannot imagine the scrutiny my life is subject to. You are acting as though I am any other man, as though this child is like any other love child.'

'I'm sorry, it's my first time being pregnant after a one-night stand,' she muttered sarcastically. 'I have no idea how I'm supposed to act.'

'You're supposed to be reasonable,' he responded flatly. 'There is no way I'm having my child raised anywhere besides my palace and I think you knew that when you told me about your pregnancy.'

His words hit her like a mallet. She shook her head again, feeling like one of those bobble-head dolls.

'Listen to me, Daisy.' He began to move closer to her so she braced instinctively. Not out of fear of him so much as fear of her reaction. How, even in that moment, could she be aware of trivial matters such as the breadth of his shoulders and the strength of his arms?

'I need an heir. You know this, and you understand why it's an urgent concern. As the last remaining heir of my family's line, I am in a vulnerable position...'

She jerked her head in an aggressive nod. 'Which is why you're marrying and planning to have a child as soon as—'

'I have a child.' The words cut through the room, loud and insistent. He paused, visibly calming himself. 'We are having a child.' And now, he closed the distance, gripping her hands and lifting them between them, his eyes boring into hers with the force of a thousand suns.

'You're wrong. I didn't come here to tell you about this. I understand your position, which is precisely why I intended to do this on my own. You don't want to marry me. You don't want to raise a child with me. Your people need you to do what's best for them, and that includes marrying a woman who will secure the peace of your kingdom. I can't do that.' She was trembling, she realised belatedly. He squeezed her hands tighter. 'I won't marry you.' Oh, no. Her teeth were chattering. Panic was setting in.

'You must.'

'No.' Fear strangled her words. 'I've already been married, and it was a disaster. I swore I'd never do that again. I can't.' Tears fell from her eyes. How angry they made her! How frustrated with herself she felt. This was not a time to cry!

She ripped her hands free and wiped at her face, hard, turning away from him and grabbing her handbag. She didn't even remember discarding it but she must have placed it on the chair near the door when she'd entered this room, because it sat there, looking at her in a matter that felt accusatory.

'I want you to forget I came here.'

'I can't do that.'

She spoke as though he hadn't. 'I want you to forget I'm pregnant. No, I want you to forget we ever met.'

'You are not leaving here.'

'Oh, yeah?' She pushed the strap of her bag over her shoulder and whirled around to face him. She felt like a wild animal, all emotion, no civility. 'Try and stop me.'

'I do not need to try to stop you.' He was so infuriatingly calm! It only flared her anger further. 'Have you forgotten where you are, *habibte*?'

'I'm in New York City. You might be King of all you survey in the RKH, but here in America we believe in the rule of law, which means no one, regardless of their position or station, has more legal rights than another.'

'I know what the rule of law is.' He crossed his arms over his chest. 'I'm sorry to say it won't help you here.'

It was like being hit with a sledgehammer. Cold, claw-like fingers began to wrap around her as the enormity of her own stupidity hit her like an anvil.

She wasn't in America any more. Not really. She'd willingly stepped into his embassy, buried herself in the thick of dozens of his guards and surrendered her passport.

'Oh, my God.' She stared at him, her face heating to the point of boiling, her eyes showing her comprehension. 'You...bastard.'

His head jerked a little, as though she'd slapped him. 'You tricked me.'

His eyes flashed with impatience. 'I did no such thing. I invited you here because I wanted to see you again—'

'To proposition me,' she corrected witheringly, but her voice shook, panic making it impossible to speak clearly, much less think straight. 'That's why you lured me here to your embassy?'

And despite the tension, he laughed, and it did something to her insides, reminding her of the warmth they'd shared, of his easy affection. Her stomach squeezed and she reached behind her, feeling for the chair that had, until a moment ago, held her handbag.

'Do you think I have to resort to kidnap in order to get a woman into my bed?'

His eyes lanced her and she felt angry, stupid and jealous as all heck, all at once.

He softened his tone. 'And I didn't lure you here. This is where I live when I'm in the States. Up until a month ago, it was being renovated and wasn't fit for habitation, hence I stayed at your hotel. As it's now restored to its usual condition, I'm here. This was not a trap.'

'It sure feels like it.'

He dipped his head forward in silent acceptance of that. 'I'm sorry.' His eyes pinned to hers and she was powerless to look away. He strode across the room, crouching before her, clasping her hands in her lap. 'I am sorry.' His expression showed the truth of his words. 'I'm sorry I didn't prevent you from falling pregnant. I'm sorry that my position makes our marriage a necessity. But I am sorriest of all for the fact that I cannot take the time to slowly convince you this is the right thing for us to do. I cannot risk letting you walk out of here because we *must* marry. It is imperative.' He stroked her hand and her heart ached, because she wasn't sure how she felt and what she wanted but she could see, so clearly, what this meant to him and his people.

But what about her and her needs? Memories of Max had her shaking her head from side to side, needing him to understand. 'I don't want to get married. I can't.'

'I understand that. Put that to one side for the moment and think about our child.' His hand shifted, moving from her wrists to her stomach, pressing against it, and for a moment he appeared to lose his train of thought as he lost himself in the realisation that inside her belly was their own baby.

'Don't you think our child deserves this?'

She bit down on her lip. 'Our child deserves us to love it,' she said quietly. 'To do the best for it, always.'

'And raising him or her together is the best.'

'My mother raised me on her own after my father left,' she insisted, tilting her chin with pride for the job her mother had done even when she'd struggled with her health for years.

'I didn't know that.'

'Why would you? We don't know each other, Sariq. We don't know each other.'

'Don't we?' The question laid her bare and forced her to look inside herself. They might not know one another's biographical details back to front, but she would have said that despite that, after their time together, she *did* know him. But that he was capable of this? Of holding her prisoner in his embassy?

It renewed her anger and disbelief, so she stood a little shakily, moving towards the door. 'You're not going to keep me prisoner here until I agree to marry you.'

'No,' he acquiesced, and relief burst through her. 'We are getting married this evening, Daisy. There is no point fighting over the inevitable.'

* * *

He watched her from the mezzanine, and he felt many things. Desire. Shock. Certainty. Admiration. But most of all, he felt a sense of guilt. Her displeasure with this was understandable. She'd arrived at the embassy with no concept of how he would react, and he'd wielded his power like a sledgehammer.

He hated this.

He hated what he was doing, he hated that he was doing it to Daisy, and yet he knew he had no alternative. Not only was their child incredibly politically powerful, if he didn't marry her and bring her to the RKH there was a very real threat to both of them. Only in his palace, with the royal guards at his disposal, could he adequately protect them.

He hadn't wanted to hit her over the head, metaphorically speaking, with the truth of that. It felt like the last thing you should say to a pregnant woman, and yet undeniably there were some factions within his country who would strike out at his heir. And particularly an illegitimate yet rightful heir who could, at any point, return to the RKH and claim power.

For years, he'd believed his mother had died in childbirth. His father had wanted it that way. But when Sariq was fifteen, he'd learned the truth. She'd been murdered. When she was heavily pregnant, while on a private vacation, someone had killed her. Sariq should have been there. He was part of the plan, too, but at the last moment he'd come down with a virus and his father had insisted he stay home to avoid making his mother sick in her delicate state.

He knew, better than anyone, what some factions were capable of and there was no way he was seeing history repeat itself. He would protect Daisy and their unborn child with his dying breath.

No, he had to do this, even when it left a sour taste in

his mouth. As to her suitability? He had no doubts on that score; she'd be a fish out of water at first. Who wouldn't? She wasn't raised with these pressures; she had no concept of what would be expected of her. She'd never even travelled outside America, for Christ's sake. His advisors would question his judgement, and they'd be right to do so. There would be political ramifications, but he was counting on the spectre of a royal baby on the horizon to quell those.

At the end of the day he had made his decision and there was no one on earth who could shake him from his sense of duty and purpose. She was angry now, but once they arrived in the RKH and she saw the luxury and financial freedom that awaited her, surely that would ease? In time, when she realised that their marriage was really in name only, a legal arrangement, more than anything, to bind them as parents and to right their child's claim to the throne.

And the fact he couldn't look at her without wanting to tear her clothes from her body?

It was irrelevant. He had a duty to marry her, to protect her with his life. Everything else was beside the point.

CHAPTER EIGHT

THE DRESS WAS STUNNING. It was perfect for a princess. A pale cream with beads that she was terrified to discover were actual diamonds, stitched around the neckline, the wrists and at the hem, so that the dress itself was heavy and substantial. It nipped in at her waist to reveal the still-flat stomach. On her feet she wore simple silk slippers, for which she was grateful—the last thing she wanted was to be impeded by high heels.

They'd make it far more difficult to run away.

Except she wasn't going to run away. She caught her reflection in the windows across the room. Evening had fallen, meaning she could see herself more clearly. And more importantly, New York was gone. There were lights, in the distance, and the tooting of cars, but the trees of Bryant Park were no longer visible. She lifted a finger to her throat, toying with the necklace her mother had given her, running the simple silver locket from side to side distractedly.

There were guards everywhere. Escape wasn't an option. But even if it were, Daisy wasn't sure she would take it. She knew there were many, many single parents out there doing an amazing job, and perhaps if Daisy hadn't already been worn down by extreme poverty, hunger, and the fear of living pay cheque to pay cheque, she might have had more faith in her abilities. But the truth was, she knew what it was like to be poor, to be broke, to have enormous debts nipping at her heels, and she wanted so much more for her baby.

It wasn't just the financial concerns though. It was the certainty that if she didn't marry Sariq she would need to go back to work as soon as possible, and already she hated the idea of leaving her baby.

Still, marriage felt extreme.

So why wasn't she fighting? Insisting that she be allowed to call a lawyer?

Was it possible that on some level she actually wanted this? That her body's traitorous need for his was pushing her towards this fate, even when she wanted to rail against it?

She couldn't say. But she knew a thousand and one feelings were rushing through her and not all of them were bad. Which made her some kind of traitor to the sisterhood, surely?

She ground her teeth together, looking around this enormous space idly until her eyes landed on a figure on the mezzanine level and she froze.

'Sariq.' His name escaped her lips without her consent. Then again, it was preposterous to keep calling him by his title. He was watching her like a hawk, his eyes trained on her in a way that made her stomach clench with white-hot need, so fierce it pushed her lips apart and forced a huge breath from her body. She spun away, ashamed of her base reaction. A moment later, he had descended the steps and was behind her, his hands on her shoulders, turning her to face him.

He didn't speak. His eyes held hers, and he studied her for several seconds. 'Are you ready?'

Her heart began to tremble. 'If I said "no", would it make any difference?'

He eyed her for several seconds. 'Yes.'

Her pulse raced. Disappointment was unmistakable and that only made her angrier.

'So you'll let me go?'

'No.' He shook his head. 'But I will delay. We can wait a day or two to let you get used to this. We can talk until you understand. I can prepare you better for what's in store once we arrive in the RKH…'

'But you won't let me leave this embassy?'

Silence prickled between them. 'I cannot.'

'Then I see no point in delay, except to assuage your conscience, which I have no intention of doing.'

He stared at her, surprise obvious on his features. She knew she was lashing out at him out of fear, and that it wasn't fair. He had been as caught off guard by this as she was. He was acting out of duty for his country, and she understood that. But becoming a commodity didn't sit well with her, and her desire for him was making everything else murky and uncertain.

'You're forcing me to marry you, Sariq. I'm not going to let you think otherwise.' His face paled beneath his tanned skin, and she was glad. Hurting him, arousing his conscience, made her feel a hell of a lot better. She struck again: 'You should know that. I'm marrying you because I have to—not because I want to—and I will never forgive you for this. Tonight I'm going to become your wife and I may appear to accept that, I may appear to accept *you*, but I will always hate you for this.' She glared at him with undisguised fury so it was easy for Sariq to believe her. 'I love our child, and, for him or her, I will try to make our marriage amicable, at least on the surface, but don't you ever doubt how I really feel.'

His eyes swept shut for a moment, the only movement

on his stone-like face the furious beating of a muscle in his jaw. 'I wish we had an alternative.'

'You do,' she said quietly.

His eyes glittered with something like fire and he reached into his robes, removing a phone. It was a familiar brand but the back was pure gold. He loaded something up on the screen then handed it to her.

She stared at it, her own photo looking back at her, beside his picture, and beneath a headline that screamed *Secret Royal Wedding!*

She read the article quickly.

> *News broke overnight that the Emir of the Royal Kingdom of Haleth married American Daisy Carrington when he was last in the United States in July.*
>
> *The wedding, conducted in secret, means the unknown woman is now Emira to one of the world's most prosperous nations.*
>
> *Little is known of the woman who stole the famously closed-off ruler's heart, or of how their romance began.*
>
> *More details to follow.*

'We're not married.' She handed the phone back to him, wishing her fingertips weren't trembling.

'Our marriage certificate will be backdated, to remove any doubts as to my paternity.'

Her eyes narrowed. 'This is your child.'

'I know that.' He pocketed his phone once more. 'I have no doubt on that score. It makes things easier, that's all.'

'But...'

'Your name is in the papers, Daisy.' There was urgency in his tone. 'The whole world will know that you are carrying my baby before the morning. And that baby is the heir to my throne. Can you not see how vulnerable that makes you both?'

She stared at him in disbelief, and desire died, just like that. Now, her feels were not unambiguous at all. Anger sparked through her, overtaking everything else.

'You are such a bastard. You did this on purpose, so I'd go through with this?'

'I didn't need to,' he murmured. 'Our marriage is a *fait accompli.*'

'But this is insurance,' she insisted. 'Because if I somehow managed to walk out of here, my life would never be the same again, right?'

He didn't respond. He didn't need to. He'd manoeuvred her into a position that made her agreement essential. She wasn't as naïve as he seemed to think. She knew what this baby would mean for her, she knew that there'd be a stream of paparazzi wanting to capture their child's first everything, following her around mercilessly.

'I need you both in the RKH where I can protect you.' He spoke simply, the words so final they sent a shiver down her spine. 'I'm sorry for the necessity of this, but I am not prepared to take any chances with your life.'

'You're being melodramatic.'

His eyes narrowed. 'My mother was killed by terrorists. She was eight months pregnant. I was supposed to be with her that day.' Each sentence was delivered with a staccato-style finality but that didn't make it any easier to digest. 'I will not let anyone harm you.'

Her heart slowed down. Pity swarmed her and, despite the situation she found herself in, she lifted a hand and pressed it to his chest. 'I'm so sorry, Sariq. I had no idea.'

He angled his face away, his jaw clenched. 'It was kept quiet. My father was determined to maintain the peace process and so news was released that she died in childbirth.' His features were like granite. 'The perpetrators were found and convicted in a court convened for the purpose of conducting the trial away from the media's eyes.'

She sucked in a breath, with no idea what to say. A shiver ran down her spine. She was deeply sorry for him, for the boy he'd been and the man he was now, and yet she had to make him see things were different. 'I'm in America, not the RKH, and if you hadn't released this, no one would even know who I am.'

'You underestimate the power and hatred of these people.' He lifted a hand, touching the back of his fingers to her cheek so lightly that she had to fight an impulse to press into his touch.

'But no one knew me.'

'They would have found you. Both of you. Believe me.'

His hand dropped to her stomach. 'I know we each want what is best for our child, Daisy.'

He was right. On that point, they were in total agreement.

'Tell me what you want from me, when we are married,' he said quietly. 'What will make this easier for you?'

It was an attempt at a concession. She bit down on her lip, with no idea how to answer. The truth was, she really couldn't have said. She had so many questions but they were all jumbling around her head forming a net rather than a rope, so she couldn't easily grasp any single point.

'I just need space,' she said simply. 'Once we're married, I need you to leave me alone and let me get my head around all this. And then, we'll have this conversation.'

He looked as though he wanted to say something but then, after a moment, he nodded. 'Fine. This, I can do.'

Daisy's head was spinning in a way she doubted would ever stop. From the short wedding ceremony at the embassy to a helicopter that had flown them to a private terminal at JFK, to a plane that was the largest she'd ever been on that was fully private. It bore the markings of the RKH and was, inside, like a palace. Just like the embassy, it was fitted with an unparalleled degree of luxury and grandeur. A formal lounge area with large leather seats opened into a corridor on one side of the plane. Sariq had guided Daisy towards it and then gestured to the first room. 'My office, when I fly.' A cursory inspection showed a large desk, two computer screens and a pair of sofas.

'A boardroom, a cinema,' he continued the inventory as they moved down the plane. 'A bathroom.' But not like any plane bathroom she'd ever been on. Then again, they'd been short domestic flights from one state to the next, never anything like this. A full-sized bath, a shower, and all as you'd find in a hotel; nothing about it screamed 'airline'.

'Here.' He'd paused three doors from the end of the plane. 'It's a twelve-hour flight to Shajarah. Rest.'

She'd looked into the room to see a bed—king-size—made up sumptuously with cream bed linen and brightly coloured cushions. She still wore the dress in which she'd said her wedding vows—in English, out of deference to her, but at the end in the language of Haleth. She'd stumbled while repeating the words and her cheeks had grown pink and her heart heavy at the enormity of what was ahead of her. She would need to learn this language, to speak it with fluency, to be able to communicate with her child, who would grow up hearing it and forming it naturally.

'I'm not tired.'

Except she was. Bone tired and overwhelmed.

'There are clothes in there.' He gestured towards a small piece of furniture across the room, but made no effort to leave her. His eyes were locked to hers and her pulse began to fire as feelings were swamped by instinct and she wanted, more than anything, to close her eyes and have things go back to the way they used to be between them. She remembered the feeling of being held by him, his strong arms wrapping around her and making her feel whole and safe. But there was no sense seeking refuge from the man who had turned her life upside down.

'Thank you.' A prim acknowledgement. She stepped into the room, looking around, then finally back to facing him. Just in time to see him pull the door closed—with him on the other side of it.

Alone once more, she still refused to give in to the tears that had been threatening her all day. She blinked furiously, her spine ramrod straight as she walked across the room, pulling open the top drawer of the dressing table and lifting out the first thing she laid her hands on. It was a pair of pants, and, despite the fact they were a comfortable drawstring pair, they were made of the finest silk. Black, they shimmered as she held them, and at their feet there was a fine gold thread, just like the robes he wore. A matching shirt was beneath the pants. With long sleeves and a dip at the neck, it was like wearing water—so comfortable against her skin that she sighed. The engines began to whir as she pulled the blankets back and climbed into bed. She was asleep before the plane took off.

Daisy would have said she was too tired to sleep, but she slept hard, almost the entire way to the RKH. She might have kept sleeping had a perfunctory knock at the door not sounded, wrenching her from dreams that were irritatingly full of Sariq. His smile when they'd talked, his laugh when she'd made a joke. His eyes on her in that way of his, so thoughtful and watchful, intent and possessive, so her blood felt like lava and her abdomen rolled with desire.

And then, the man himself stood framed in the door of

her room and her dreams were so tangible that she almost smiled and held a hand out to him, pulling him towards her. Almost. Thank goodness sanity intervened before she could do anything so stupid.

'Yes?' The word was cold. Crisp. He didn't react.

'In two hours, we will land. There is some preparation you will need to undergo, first.' His eyes dropped lower, to her décolletage, and she was conscious of the way the shirt dipped revealing her flesh there, showing a hint of her cleavage. 'You must be hungry.'

The last words were said in a voice that was throaty.

'I'm not.'

Disapproval flared in his features but for such a brief moment that it was gone again almost immediately, so she thought she'd imagined it. 'Come and join me while I eat, then.'

'A command, Your Highness?'

Silence. Barbed and painful. Her stomach squeezed. 'If that's what it takes.' He looked at her for a moment longer. 'Two minutes, Daisy.'

He pulled the door shut before his frustration could become apparent. But he *was* frustrated. In his entire life, he'd never known someone to be so argumentative just for the sake of it. Sariq was used to being obeyed at all times, yet Daisy seemed to enjoy countermanding his words.

And when they were in the RKH? While the country was famously progressive in the region, there was no getting away from the fact it was still patriarchal and mired in many of the ways of the past. Her flagrant flouting of his wishes would raise questions he'd prefer not to have to answer.

Couldn't she see that their situation required special handling? It was as undesirable to him as it was to her—

but what choice did either of them have? She was carrying his child, the heir to the RKH. This marriage, living together as man and wife, was the only solution to that situation.

He had to make her understand the difficulties inherent to her situation without terrifying her. He pressed his back against the door, closing his eyes for a moment, so that he saw his father again and a darkness filled him. He didn't want to think about what his father might say about this. Sariq was Emir now. The safety and prosperity of the kingdom lay on his shoulders, and his alone.

Alone again, Daisy flopped onto her back and stared at the ceiling, his command wrapping around her, making breathing difficult. She wasn't hungry, but she was thirsty—the thought of coffee was deeply motivating—and yet she stayed where she was, an emptiness inside her. And she knew why.

The Sariq of her dreams had been the man she'd fallen into bed with, the man who had bewitched and made her feel alive for the first time since Max. But he was gone, and there was only this Sheikh in his place. All command and duty. The juxtaposition was inherently painful.

She bit down on her lip, not moving, the emptiness like a black hole, carrying mass of its own, weighing her down, holding her to the bed. She lay there for a long time, certainly past the allotted two minutes, and at some point, she heard the door open.

She didn't realise she'd been crying until he said something, a curse, and crossed to the edge of the bed, sitting down on it heavily and moving his hand to her cheek, gently wiping away the moisture there. His expression was grim, his eyes impossible to read, but his fingertips were soft and determined, moving to remove the physical signs of her emotions.

'I would do anything in the world not to have had to do this,' he finally said, the words dragged from him.

She knew that to be the truth. This marriage wasn't what he wanted either. He was as trapped by their baby as she was. 'I know that.' She pushed up to sitting, dislodging his touch, lifting her own hands to wipe at the rest of her cheeks.

'I'm fine.' She was glad her voice sounded clear. 'I've just been more prone to emotions since I got pregnant. It's out of my control.'

It didn't exonerate him. He continued to look at her as though he were fighting a battle with a superhuman force. He hated this. She was openly expressing her disbelief, he was holding his deep inside him, but there was no doubting that both of their lives had been torn open by this pregnancy.

'What did you want to talk about?'

His jaw clenched. 'Will you eat something?'

His words were so reminiscent of the version of him she'd known in New York that for a moment she let herself slip back through the cracks of time, cracks that yearning had opened wider. 'I'd kill for a coffee.'

'Murder is not necessary,' he responded immediately. 'Though I could understand if you felt a little driven to it.' A joke. A smile teased the corner of her lips but her mouth and heart were too heavy to oblige.

'Come.' He stood and her stomach rolled.

She nodded slowly. 'I'll just be a moment.'

He hesitated.

'I'm coming. Honestly.'

A crisp nod. 'Fine. This preparation is important, Daisy. It's for your sake, so you know what to expect.'

Anxiety shifted through her. 'Okay.'

In the bathroom—smaller than the main one she'd passed—she took a moment to freshen up, brushing her hair and teeth, washing her face and applying a little gloss to lips that felt dry courtesy of the aeroplane's air conditioning. But she worked quickly, aware that time was passing, bringing them closer to the RKH and her future as its queen.

He was in the main living space of the plane, but he wasn't alone. Six men and three women were sitting with him, each dressed in suits, so that in contrast Sariq in his robe looked impossibly regal and forbidding. When she entered, all eyes turned to her, yet she felt only the slow burn of Sariq's.

'Leave us.'

Their response was automatic. Everyone stood, moving past Daisy, pausing briefly to dip their heads in a bow that was deferential and unsettling. When she turned back to Sariq, he was standing, still watching her.

'Some members of my government,' he explained.

'Women?' She moved to the table, deliberately choosing a seat that was several away from him, preferring a little physical separation even though it did little to quell the butterflies that were rampaging through her system.

'This surprises you?'

'I guess so.'

'The RKH is not so out of step with the west. Women hold the same rights as men.'

A woman appeared then, carrying a tray, which she placed in front of Daisy. The aroma of coffee almost brought a fresh wave of tears to her eyes. It was so familiar, so comforting, that she smiled with genuine pleasure at the attendant.

'Thank you.'

'*Ha shalam.*' The attendant smiled back, encouragingly.

'*Ha shalam* means thank you,' Sariq explained.

Daisy repeated it.

'This is Zahrah. She will be your primary aide.'

'I am pleased to meet you, Your Highness.' Zahrah bowed as the others had, but lower, and she lifted Daisy's hand in her own, squeezing it. Her eyes were kind, her smile gentle and friendly. The woman was beautiful, with glossy dark hair, long, elegant fingers, and nails painted a matte black. Daisy's heart swelled. Something like relief flooded her.

'She will help you ease into this,' Sariq continued. 'To learn the language and customs of my people, coordinate your schedule, oversee your needs.'

'I think I'll need a lot of help,' Daisy murmured, lifting her brows, the words directed towards Zahrah.

'You're too modest, Your Highness.'

'Please, call me Daisy,' she insisted.

In response, Zahrah smiled and bowed once more before leaving the cabin.

'She won't do that.'

It took Daisy a moment to understand what he meant.

'Do you remember in New York, how hard you found it to use my name?'

Daisy sipped her coffee without answering.

'And you are a foreigner with very little understanding of royalty and its power. Imagine having been raised to serve the royal family, as Zahrah was. Deference is ingrained in her. Do not let it unsettle you. Being treated like this is something you will have to become accustomed to.'

'I don't know if I can—I'm just a normal person. I can't imagine being treated as anything other than that.'

'In the RKH, you are equal to only one person. Me. To everyone else, you are like a goddess.'

A shiver ran down her spine. 'And this is how you were raised? To see yourself as a god?'

'I don't see myself that way.' His response was swift and there was a heaviness to the words. 'Gods have unlimited power. I do not.'

'I'm glad you realise that.' The words were delivered drily but a smile flicked across his lips, widening the cracks into the past. She gripped onto the present with both hands, refusing to let herself remember what that weekend had been like. It was a lifetime ago, and they were two different people. Then, they'd been together by choice. Now? Circumstances required it, that was all.

'When we land, there will be a small group of photographers, vetted by the palace. You will step out of the aircraft first, onto a platform, where you will stand alone a moment and wave. It will be morning in Haleth, and not too warm yet. I will join you once they have had a moment to take a photograph of you alone. Protocol dictates that we do not touch, publicly.'

She lifted a brow. 'That seems somewhat arcane, given I'm pregnant with your baby.'

'It is as it is.' He lifted his shoulders.

'Fine by me.' She sipped her coffee, closing her eyes for a moment as the flavour reached inside her, comforting her, bringing peace to her fractured soul. 'I'd prefer it that way, anyway.'

His eyes flashed with something she couldn't interpret. Mockery? Frustration? Pain? She blinked away.

'You are afraid.'

'Of you? No.'

'Not of me.' He didn't move, but his words seemed to wrap around her. 'Of yourself.'

'What?' She took a gulp of coffee.

'You are afraid of wanting me, even after what's just happened.'

Her heart began to thud inside her. She couldn't tear her eyes away from him, and there was a silent plea on her features, a look of confusion and uncertainty, and, yes, of want. Of need.

He stood then, bringing himself to the space beside her, propping his bottom on the edge of the table and spinning her chair, so she was facing him. 'We should not have slept together.' His hand lifted to her hair, running over its find gold ends as though he couldn't help himself. 'I knew I wanted you the moment I saw you, and yet you should have been off-limits to me.' His hand dropped to her cheek. 'Just as I should have been to you. And yet we couldn't stop this.'

She swallowed, her throat shifting with the movement. His hand dropped to her shoulder, his thumb padding across the exposed bone there. 'I want to promise you I won't touch you again, but I am afraid too, Daisy.'

The admission surprised her.

'I am terrified of how much I want you, even now. Even when I know you must hate me for bringing you here, for railroading you into this marriage.'

Her mouth was so dry. She could only stare up at him, but his confession was tangling her into a thousand knots.

'I do hate what you did,' was all she could say.

His eyes swept shut, briefly, his lashes thick and dark against his caramel skin. Her stomach hurt. Her heart ached. Her body was alive with fire and flames and yet inside there was a kernel of ice that refused to budge.

'I can conquer this,' he said simply, dropping his hand and standing. 'I had no choice but to marry you, but I will not sleep with you again. You have my word.' His hand formed a fist at his side as though even then he was having to force himself to rail against his instincts and not touch her. 'You do not need to fear this.'

Oh, but she did. She was terrified of how she wanted him. Hearing him be so honest about his own struggles made her acknowledge her own—inwardly at least. Yes, she wanted him. Even as they'd said their vows her insides had been heating up, her body acknowledging that, in him, she had met her perfect match.

But she could barely admit that to herself, let alone to him. 'Thank you. I appreciate that.'

So prim! So formal! Good. Let him think she was grateful for this reprieve instead of desperately wanting to contradict his edict.

If he was disappointed, he didn't show it. 'Let's keep going. There is much you need to know before we land.'

CHAPTER NINE

In New York, he'd made a promise to her. Space. Time. Freedom to think, away from him. And he intended to uphold it even when the knowledge that she was in the palace, only a wall separating them, had him wanting to go to her, to speak to her, to see her, to assure himself she was okay. Yet he had made this promise and it seemed small, in the scheme of all that he was asking of her, and therefore vital that he respect it.

In the three weeks since they'd arrived in the RKH, he'd upheld his promise. Maintaining his distance, receiving his updates from Zahrah to assure himself that Daisy was coping, and that she was well. He'd organised medical appointments to ascertain her physical health, and that of the baby. And he'd managed the politics of their marriage like a bull at a gate. A top PR firm was engaged to sell the message in the media. This was a new age for the country and his marriage to Daisy Carrington symbolised a step forward with the west. Reaction had been, for the most part, positive. Though there were some quarters that publicly questioned his choice and voiced great offence that the Sheikh of the RKH should turn his nose up at the two women who had widely been known to be candidates as his prospective Emira.

As for those women, he'd met with each privately, and to them he'd sold it as a love story.

'I was not prepared for how I would feel to meet her. I wish I had been able to resist, but there were greater forces at play.'

It had been easy to sell that message. It hadn't been love at first sight with Daisy, but it had been infatuation, and that was equally blinding.

There were those who seemed to accept his choice to marry an American, but not Daisy. Stories about her had run in the press. Fewer in the RKH papers, which were generally respectful of the palace and its privacy, but, in the blogs and cheaper tabloids, derisive pieces about her status as a divorced woman had been printed. Someone had found photos of her first wedding, so he'd seen her smiling up at her first husband, and something inside him had fired to life, filling him with darkness and questions. He wanted to know about this man she'd married—by choice. The man she must have loved at some point, even if she didn't now.

And he'd wanted to silence the stories that speculated on all sorts of things in Daisy's life before him, things he knew to be false without having had the conversations. Rumours that she'd travelled across America with a rock band, the inference being that she'd slept with the whole slew of musicians. Suggestions that her role at the hotel had been to appease guests in whatever manner she found suitable. And yes, the inevitable suggestion that this baby wasn't actually his.

He had read them with fury at first and, as the weeks went by, with muted anger and disbelief and, finally, with guilt and regret. She didn't deserve this.

'Has she read them?' he'd asked Zahrah on the fifth morning.

'I believe so, Your Highness.'

A grim line had lodged on his lips and it hadn't lifted since, and after three weeks of feeling as if he wanted to see her, to ensure she was okay, but resisting that impulse because she'd asked it of him, he was close to the breaking point.

So it wasn't precisely Malik's fault that they argued. Sariq had been ready to unleash his fury at anyone who looked at him the wrong way, let alone what Malik said.

'You cannot blame these people, sir. She is not suitable and it will take time for the country to adjust their expectations.'

Fire had filled Sariq's blood. 'In what way is your Emira not suitable?'

Malik hadn't appeared to realise he was on dangerous ground. 'Her nationality. Her marital status. Her pedigree.'

'If I have no issue with these things, how dare you?'

Malik's head jerked back. 'I beg your pardon, sir, I did not mean to offend you. I have spent my life protecting your interests…'

'My interests are now her interests.'

Malik was silent.

'You will organise a ball. Invite the parliament and foreign diplomats. It's time for the people of Haleth to meet my wife.'

Malik dipped his head but it showed scepticism.

'She is pregnant with my child.' Malik scraped his chair back and moved towards the open doors that led to the balcony. A light breeze was lifting off the desert, bringing with it the fragrance of sand and ash, and a hint of relief from the day's warmth. 'I wish, more than anything, that it hadn't been necessary to marry her.' His shoulders were squared as he remembered the way he'd had to bully Daisy into this. Regret perforated his being. 'She is now my wife. That's all there is to it.'

It was another baking-hot day. Daisy stood where she was, on the balcony that wrapped around this segment of the palace, staring out at the shimmering blue sky and desert sands that seemed to glow in the midday sun until a raised voice caught her attention. She turned in that direction right as a door pushed open and Sariq strode out, his frame magnetic to her gaze, his expression like thunder.

She stayed right where she was, frozen to the spot, her eyes feasting on him, her brain telling her to move, her blood insisting that she stay. It had been three weeks since she'd seen him. True to his word, he'd left her in peace, and she knew she should have been gratified that he'd respected her wishes, but deep down she felt so lonely, and so afraid.

Emotions she'd never show him, though. She tilted her chin in defiance. At least he looked as surprised to see her as she felt to see him. His chest moved with the force of his breathing; it was clear he was in a bad temper.

But why?

The raised voices—had one belonged to him?

Her mouth felt dry, and that had nothing to do with the arid desert climate.

He stared at her as though he was trying to frame words and she stared back until the silence became unbearable. What did she have to say to this man, anyway?

His eyes roamed her face in a way that sparked fires in her blood. How she resented his easy ability to do that! She felt her nipples pucker against the lace of her bra and her abdomen clenched hard with unmistakable lust. A biological response that she had no intention of obeying.

A bird flapped overhead, its wingspan enormous, drawing Daisy's gaze. She watched as it circled the desert and then began to drift downwards, its descent controlled and elegant.

It flew beyond her sight and so she looked away, back to Sariq. He was frowning now, but still regarding her with the full force of his attention, as though he could understand her if only he looked for long enough. But she didn't want to be understood.

Swallowing to bring much-needed moisture back to her mouth, she said quietly, 'Excuse me,' before turning and heading into the blessed cool of the tiled sitting room of the palace. Her heart though wouldn't stop hammering. She knew their suites of rooms were in close proximity, but she hadn't realised this balcony was shared by both. It seemed to create a greater intimacy than she was comfortable with. She used this space often, particularly in the evenings when the sting of the day's heat had dropped, and she was able to sit beneath the blanket of jewels dotted through the inky night sky, reading or simply existing, quiet and contemplative.

'Daisy.' His voice held a command. She ignored it. 'Daisy.'

Damn it. He was closer now, his voice right behind her. She stopped walking and turned, but she was unprepared for this—the full force of attraction that would assail her at his proximity. But attraction was beside the point—she wouldn't give in to that again.

'Yes, sir?'

He closed his eyes, his nostrils flaring as he inhaled. 'Sariq.'

'Yes, Sariq?'

He latched his gaze to hers and her pulse throbbed through her. Still, he stared, and for so long that she wondered if he had any intention of speaking. She was about to turn away from him anew when his gaze dropped to her stomach and a hint of guilt peppered her mood. She was pregnant with his child, and he'd spent three weeks away from her. Naturally he was curious.

'I'm fine. The baby's fine, too. We had a scan two weeks ago.'

'I know.'

'You do?'

And then, a smile lifted one corner of his lips, a grudging smile that wasn't exactly born of happiness. 'Did you think I wouldn't involve myself in the medical care of our child?'

Their child. This had nothing to do with her.

'How are you?'

'This wasn't included in your report?'

'Basic health information.' He shrugged with ingrained arrogance. 'Nothing more.'

'What more is there of consequence?'

His brows knitted together. Her tone was unmistakably caustic. 'You're happy?'

She couldn't help the sceptical laugh that burst from her. 'Really?'

'Zahrah says you're settling into your routine well?'

Daisy ignored the prickle of betrayal that shifted inside her. Everyone in this palace reported to Sariq. It shouldn't surprise her that the servant she'd begun to think of as a friend was doing likewise. 'My routine involves being pampered around the clock. I don't imagine many people would struggle with that.'

Frustration, though, weaved through her words.

'But you do,' he insisted. 'You don't like it.'

Her expression was a grimace. 'I'm more comfortable doing the pampering than I am being spoiled. I don't need all this.' She lifted a hand to her head, where her blonde hair had been braided and styled into an elaborate up-do. 'I'm not used to it.'

'You'll become used to it.'

A mutinous expression crossed her face. 'Do I have to?'

'Yes.' And then, more softly, 'You're aware of the media stories?'

Pain sliced inside her being. She wrenched her face away, unable to meet his eyes. Some of the stories—most, in fact—had been absolutely appalling. 'Are you wondering how many are true?'

He said a word in his own language that, going by the tone and inflection, was a bitter curse. 'I am asking how these preposterous stories have affected you. This has nothing to do with me.'

'You don't care that I'm a rock star groupie?'

'I don't care about any of it.' But something in his eyes showed that to be a lie. He wasn't being completely honest to her, and she hated that. She hated that he might have read the headlines and believed them, that he might believe she'd made a habit of sleeping with guests of the hotel. After everything she'd been through with Max, Daisy had made a point of remaining guarded with members of the opposite sex.

The irony of these stories—when she'd been a virgin on her wedding night, and slept with no one since her divorce—filled her with a desire to defend herself. Except Sariq didn't deserve that. What did it matter if he thought her promiscuous? Who cared? As if he hadn't had his share of lovers in the past?

There was only one element of the stories that she cared to contradict. 'You are the father.'

A look of anger slashed his features. 'I know this.'

She bit down on her lip then, staring out at the desert. 'We were together two nights, but it was enough for me to see inside your soul, Daisy Al Antarah.' It was the first time her new name had been spoken aloud to her and it sent a *frisson* of response shuttling down her spine. 'I saw you and I wanted you. I seduced you. There was nothing practised about your responses to me. I am aware that I put you in the position of doing something outside your usual comfort zone.'

Which meant what? That she was bad in bed? Great. It was a silly thing to care about in that moment. A thought not worthy of her, so she relegated it to the back of her mind.

'I should have seen the signs. Perhaps I did, and chose to ignore them.'

'What signs?'

'Your inexperience, your innocence.' He shook his head, as though he were angry at himself. 'I knew you were out of your depth and I ignored that because it suited me, because I wanted you, and now we must both pay the price for that.'

Something like pain clenched her heart, because his regret was heavy in the tone of his words, but, more than that, she could feel it emanating off his frame. 'You don't want me here.'

He shifted his gaze to hers without speaking.

'You wish this hadn't happened, that we weren't married.'

A muscle jerked in his jaw and he regarded her silently. When the air between them was unbearably thick with tension, Daisy took a small step backwards, intending to leave, but his hand on hers stilled her.

She froze, her body screaming at her for something she couldn't fathom. 'Don't *you* wish that, Daisy?'

Wish what? She swept her eyes shut for a moment, gathering thoughts that had been scattered by his simple touch. As she stood there, his thumb began to move slowly over her inner wrist, sending pins and needles scuttling through her veins.

'I…' She darted her tongue out to moisten her lower lip at the same moment she opened her eyes, so she saw the way his attention was drawn to her mouth and the flame of desire began to spark harder.

'This marriage is the last thing either of us wanted.' The words were soft, and yet they cut something deep inside her. 'When we met in New York, I was in a deep state of grief.' Her heart softened. 'I was weak, where you were concerned. I wanted someone to take the pain of loss away, and you did. When you came to my bed, it obliterated everything besides my need for you.'

She stared up at him, her heart thudding in her chest. Her head and her emotions were at war with one another. Everything she knew she felt about men and love and sex demanded that she pull away from him, but instincts and feelings were holding her right where she was, a flash of sympathy making her want to comfort him and reassure him even when she doubted he deserved that.

'I wanted to be with you,' she said quietly, absolving him of the guilt of feeling that he'd overruled her in some way. 'Believe me, if I hadn't, I would have been perfectly capable of shutting down your advances.'

He lifted his other hand, reaching it around behind her head to the pins that kept her style in place. 'You had to do so many times, I suppose.'

Pain shifted inside her. 'The articles aren't true.'

'We've covered that.' Each pin he removed, he dropped to the ground, so there was a quiet tinkling sound before he moved on to the next. 'That doesn't mean you weren't the object of interest from many guests before me.'

A hint of heat coloured her cheeks, because he was

right. 'From time to time. But I've always found it easy to deflect unwanted attention.'

'To fade into the background,' he remembered, moving to the fourth pin, loosening it so a braid began to fall from her crown.

'As my job required of me.' Why did her voice sound so husky, so coarse?

'And you tried to do this with me.' Another pin dropped.

It shouldn't have been biologically possible, but somehow Daisy's heart had moved position, taking up real estate in the column of her throat. 'Not hard enough.'

His eyes narrowed by the smallest amount. Another pin dropped. And another. When he spoke, he was so close his breath warmed her temple. One braid fell completely. His gaze moved to the side as his fingers worked at freeing it completely, so half her hair hung loose about her face. 'Do you think you could have done anything that would have put a stop to what we shared?'

It was hard to speak with her heart in her throat. 'Are you saying you wouldn't have taken "no" for an answer?'

The other braid fell. 'I'm saying you weren't capable of resisting what was happening between us.'

She wanted to defy him, to deny that fiercely, but there was a part of her that knew he spoke the truth. 'You're wrong.' The words were feeble.

He ignored them. 'So step away from me now.' He loosened the braid. She held her breath, staring up at him, fierce needs locking her to the spot when her brain was shouting at her to draw back, to show him that he was wrong about her, that she was very much in control of her responses to him.

But she wasn't and never had been, and she hated that.

Challenge lay between them, sharp like a blade. The air was thick and nothing could ease it. Breathing hurt.

'I told you I wouldn't touch you.' His fingers loosened her hair. A breeze lifted it so some ran across her cheek. 'I intend to honour that promise until you release me from it.'

Her harsh intake of breath sounded between them. That wasn't fair. She couldn't want him—she sure as heck shouldn't—but her knees were trembling and heat was building between her thighs, whispering promises she desperately wanted to obey.

'Sariq.' She didn't know what she wanted to say, but his name seemed like a good place holder, and she liked the way it felt on her lips, as though it were a promise. But of what?

'If I kissed you…' he moved his hand to her lips, padding his thumb over her flesh '…we'd be in bed within minutes. If we even made it that far.'

Her temperature spiked at the vivid imagery.

'Just like in New York.'

Her lips parted.

'You see, your body tells me a story, *habibte*. I see desire in your eyes, with how wide they flare and how dark your pupils are. Your cheeks are pink, your breathing rushed as though you have run a marathon. Your breasts move quickly as you try to fill your lungs, and your nipples…' he dropped his gaze '…have been begging for my attention since I stopped you from leaving this room. If I touched your most intimate places, I would feel your heat and need for me against my palm, just as I did in New York.'

She sucked in a ragged breath.

'It would be easy for me to kiss you and make you forget the path you've chosen, just as I did in America. It would be easy for me to override your instincts and make you mine. But you would hate me for that, wouldn't you?'

Would she? She couldn't say. She was a mess.

'You think forcing me to marry you isn't already sufficient grounds for hate?'

The anger of her statement surprised her, though it shouldn't. She felt backed into a corner—lashing out was a normal response.

'It's ample,' he agreed with a small shift of his head, but his eyes were dark and they bore into hers.

'Why are you doing this?' she whispered quietly. 'You don't want this to be a real marriage. You told me that at the embassy that night.'

He pulled a face. 'I wasn't referring to sex.'

'No?'

His features shifted for a moment. 'I have known, all my life, that I would never love whomever I married. That's what I was referring to that night. So far as I'm concerned, sex is just a biological act. It can be shared without any true danger of intimacy.'

She felt as though her chest were being cleaved in two. She stared up at him, unable to explain the pain that was lashing her, or its source. But on some level, she found his assertion to be repugnant.

'And intimacy is bad?'

'It's not bad. It's simply not part of the equation for me. I accepted a long time ago that my duty to my country would require me to choose this path.'

He brought his body closer, so his broad chest was pressed to her breasts, and her nipples tingled painfully in anticipation. 'But sex? Sex without emotion, without love, can still be amazing.' He lifted a hand to her face, holding her still, and she caught her breath, waiting for him to kiss her, certain he would.

She felt his needs as surely as she did her own, his desire palpable, his body hardening against hers. Nothing moved, even the very air of the desert stood still, waiting, expectant.

'However, I swore I would keep my distance.' He dropped his hand and, with obvious regret, moved away from her. 'And I intend to honour that promise.'

It took several moments for her breathing to achieve anything close to normal.

'I have given you space, since you came to Haleth.'

Still, she couldn't speak.

'But three weeks without a sighting of the new Queen has left a hole for the media to fill. It's time for my people to begin a relationship with you.'

Her heart began to speed for a different reason now and anxiety caused a fine bead of perspiration to break out on her forehead. It took her several moments to remember how to form words. 'Do you mean…like an interview or something?'

'An interview is a good idea.' He nodded, no sign of the conversation they'd just had, which had left her all kinds of shaken up, in his handsome face. 'But initially, there is to be a ball. My parliament and foreign diplomats will attend. The event will be held in your honour.'

Whatever she'd been feeling moments ago was gone completely. 'Is that necessary?'

'Do you intend to stay hidden here for ever?'

She considered that. Did she? These last three weeks had been blessedly quiet but she'd been cognisant of the fact she was dodging her responsibilities, hiding from the world she knew to be out there.

'Do you care? About the rumours?'

He frowned. 'No.'

'So why does it matter?'

'Rumours in foreign papers that speculate on matters I know to be false? This is laughable. But you are the Emira of the RKH and my people must respect you; they must accept our child as their future ruler.'

A prickle of danger shifted through her. 'You're worried they might not? That this baby might not be accepted as your heir?'

'I'm not worried.' Nor did he look it. 'But I do not wish your life, or his, to be harder because of steps we could easily take now to smooth the way of this transition.'

It all made so much sense. She knew she should agree, but agreeing with Sariq stuck in her craw, so she maintained a somewhat dubious silence.

'Malik is organising the ball. I'll have Zahrah notify you of the details in due course.'

He couldn't sleep. Hours after he'd last seen Daisy, and he felt a curdling sense of foreboding, a kernel of worry he couldn't dispel. Telling himself he was being melodramatic, he threw his sheet back and stood, pacing to the small timber piece of furniture against the wall, lifting the ancient pewter jug and pouring himself a glass of water. In the distance, through the open doors of his bedroom, he could hear the familiar call of the *nuusha* bird, the night creature's song a cross between a bell and a whip. It was delicate and resounding, reaching across the desert from their nesting grounds in the cliffs of sand to the west of the palace.

He'd promised her he wouldn't touch her, but, oh, how he'd ached to do exactly that. When he'd seen her that afternoon, her cheeks pink from the heat, her hair so beautifully intricate but in a way he'd needed to loosen, so that he could remember the way it had fallen around her face when they'd made love...

He shouldn't think about that. He couldn't. Those nights

were from a different lifetime, when he was free to act on impulse and she to indulge her desire.

He'd promised he wouldn't touch her and yet he'd come so close that day. He'd ached to kiss her. He very nearly had. And now, memories of her kept him awake, tormenting him, so he had a keening sense to go for a run, or a ride, to leave this gilded cage of a palace, to throw off the expectations incumbent upon him and be his own man. For one night. He strode onto the balcony, his eyes finding the looming shape of the caves, tracing their outline, wondering if he could absent himself from the palace for the four days it would take to make the round trip. There was an oasis there; he'd camped at its edges often.

Her strangled sound of surprise was barely audible at first, swallowed by the gentle breeze and the bird's cries.

It was as though he'd thought of her so hard and so often that she'd miraculously appeared before him. She wore a simple cream shift, barely covering her beautiful body, so he strained to keep his eyes on her face rather than allowing them to dip to the swell of cleavage revealed there. After their contact that day, seeing her like this was the last thing he needed. Knowing he had to be strong didn't alter the fact he wanted, more than anything, to drag her against him and make love to her.

'I...' Her tongue darted out, moistening her lips, just as it had earlier that day. His cock hardened.

'You couldn't sleep,' he murmured, knowing he should stay where he was, even when other forces were pushing him forwards, closing the distance between them.

She shook her head. Her hair was loose now, just as he'd wished it to be, and the breeze caught at the lengths, lifting them so a skein of the moon's light cut through it. Silver against gold. Magic and captivating.

When he'd read the articles, only one had caught his attention, only one had played on his mind as being worthy of examination. 'Tell me about your ex-husband.'

Even in the scarce light thrown by the full moon, he could make out the shift in her features, their arrangement into a mask of surprise, at first, and then hesitation.

'Max? Why do you want to know about him?'

'Did you love him?'

Her smile was cynical. 'I'm not like you, Sariq. Love is the only reason I would have ever married anyone.' And then, quickly, with a look of mortification, 'Present circumstances excluded, obviously.'

'Obviously.'

She turned away from him then, but her profile was all the more alluring for she was hiding herself from him. He had to move closer to see her better. He caught a hint of her delicate fragrance and his body tightened. His fingers ached to reach for her.

'And what happened to this great love, then?'

She angled her face to his, her clear eyes analytical, studying him in a way few had ever dared. It was unusual for Sariq to have an equal. Most people feared his power even when he wielded it so rarely, but Daisy was unflinching in his presence, and always had been.

'We got divorced. End of story.'

'I don't think so.'

'What do you want to know?' Her voice rang with discontent. 'All the gory details?'

'The pertinent ones at least.'

'Why?'

'You don't want to tell me?'

A flicker of a frown. He wanted to smudge his finger over her lips, but didn't. 'Is it relevant?'

'It's...of interest.'

She turned back to the view, her eyes following the

sound of the bird in the distance. For a long time, she was quiet, and it was easy for Sariq to believe she had no intention of speaking. But then, finally, after a long exhalation, as if gearing herself up to discuss the matter: 'We met shortly after my mother died. I inherited. Not a lot— our house and her small investment portfolio. Enough for me not to have to worry about money for a while. It was her dearest wish that I pursue my musical career and I promised her—' Daisy paused, her voice becoming gravelled, her throat moving beneath his gaze as she swallowed fiercely so he felt a surprising urge to comfort her. 'I promised her I would. It was one of the last things I said to her.'

She was going to cry. He held himself rigid, adhering to his promise, but, oh, how that cost him when his arms were heavy with a need to drag her against him, to offer her physical comfort to her emotional wounds.

'After my father left, I stopped playing. I couldn't bear to any more. It was something we shared.' Her smile lacked warmth; it was a grimace of pain masquerading as something else, something brave when he could feel her pain. 'But then Mom got sick—' she frowned '—and it was one of the only things I could do to get through to her, to help her, so I played and I played and when she was well, she'd beg me never to give up. She'd beg me to play so everyone heard.'

Every answer spawned a new question. What had happened to her mother? Where had her father gone? They'd been so open and honest in New York, it had been easy to ask her whatever he wished, and he'd been confident she would answer. But there were barriers between them now, necessary and impenetrable, so he didn't ask. He stayed on topic even when a part of him wanted to digress.

'And your husband?'

'Max loved my playing too.' Her words were scrubbed raw. 'And I loved to play for him.'

Something moved in Sariq, and he wasn't naïve enough to pretend he didn't know what it was. Jealousy. He had listened to Daisy play and wished, on some level, that she were playing just for him.

'Max had a lot of big dreams. But they were... I helped him as much as I could. I trusted him implicitly. He was my husband, why wouldn't I? I wouldn't have married him if I hadn't.' Her eyes lifted to his and the strength of the ghosts there almost knocked the breath from his lungs.

'And?' His word held a command, there was that imperative he was used to employing, but it was born now not of regal title so much as a desperate hunger to comprehend. Something terrible had happened between them, he could feel it, and it was vital that he understand it.

'He lied to me.' The words were filled with bitterness. 'He didn't love me, he loved my inheritance and the implicit trust I had in him. Trust that led me to add him as a signatory to my accounts, that meant I never questioned his transactions. It wasn't until I began to prepare for the Juilliard that I realised he'd taken everything. *Everything.*'

Sariq was completely silent but inside, her explanation was exploding like the shattering of fine glass.

'Not only had he cleared my accounts, he'd taken out a mortgage on Mom's home, which I had owned clear of debt. I had to sell it, but that debt is still there, so I'm chipping away at it as best I can but...'

'It's onerous,' he supplied, after a moment, sympathy expressing itself in his tone.

'You could say that.' A bitter laugh. Then, her hand lifted to her throat, where a delicate line of diamonds ran across the detailing at the neckline of her nightgown. 'I suppose that's not one of my problems now.'

'Of course not.' Relief spread through him, because this was something real and palpable he could do, to relieve at least one of her worries. 'Have Zahrah provide Malik with the details and he shall clear this debt.'

'Have my people call your people?' she murmured, shifting to face him, so their bodies were only two or three inches apart.

'Something like that.'

Her features compressed with exasperation, and then her eyes lifted over his shoulder, so he wanted to reach out and drag her face to his, to look into her soul through their green depths. 'I thought I loved him, but, over the years, I've given it a lot of thought and, honestly, I think I was just so grateful.' The words were laced with self-directed anger.

'Why grateful?'

'When my dad left, it was easy to believe it had been my fault, that I was in some way unlovable. Then Mom died and I was all alone, and it was terrifying and empty and quiet. When Max appeared, he seemed to worship me. He was so full of praise and flattery and couldn't bear to be away from me.' She shook her head. 'It cooled once we were married. Now I see why: he got what he needed from me, but I was so grateful still, and I kept telling myself everything would be okay when my instincts were warning me all along.'

'Were you able to recoup any of the money?'

'He lost it.' She gripped the railing with one hand; the other remained at her side, as if weighted there by the burdensome diamond wedding ring he'd placed on her finger. 'Or hid it so well I didn't have the means to find it.'

'And so you took a job working at a hotel, trying to chip down a massive debt by waiting on demanding guests?'

'They weren't all demanding,' she corrected.

'If the debt is the size you're implying, surely that would have been a fool's errand?'

'What were my other options?' she pushed, a hint of steel touching the words. 'To accept defeat? To let him win?'

Her fierce fire stirred something to life in him.

'Many would have.'

'Not me.'

'No, not you.'

She swayed forward a little, but not enough. He remembered the way she'd felt that afternoon, her soft curves against his hard edges, and he wanted, more than anything, to feel that again. And then what?

The flicker of flames would convert to so much more. They would touch and he would kiss her, and then carry her to his bed where he'd spend the entire night reminding her that, aside from her pregnancy and their marriage, there was something between them that was all their own. But there couldn't be. All his life he'd understood the danger that came from caring for one's spouse. His father had been destroyed by his mother's death. Sariq would never care for anyone enough to feel their loss so keenly. His country deserved such sacrifice—his duty demanded that of him.

And perhaps she intuited the strengthening of his resolve, because she blinked, her huge eyes shifting to his with a look he couldn't comprehend, and then she stepped backwards, wrapping a single arm across her torso. 'It's late and I'm tired. Goodnight, Your Highness.'

She was gone before he could remind her to call him Sariq.

CHAPTER TEN

HE READ THE intelligence report with a frown on his face that gave little of his anger away. But inside, a fury was unravelling that would know no bounds. 'And they were arrested at the border this morning?'

'Two security agents intercepted their vehicle as it crossed into the old town of Rika.'

'Armed?'

'To the teeth.'

Sariq's expression was grim. 'Where are they being held?'

'In the catacombs.'

'Fine.' He scraped his chair back. 'We shall go there now.'

Malik's displeasure was obvious. 'But, sir, the ball begins in an hour...'

'The ball will wait.' The words were louder—harsher—than he'd intended. With an effort, he brought his temper under control. 'These men were intending to kill my wife, were they not?'

'That is the charge, yes, Your Highness.'

'Then before I parade my wife in front of a slew of people, I would like to ascertain, beyond a shadow of a doubt, that they have no links to anyone in attendance this evening.'

'The guards will investigate this.'

Sariq held a hand up to silence his oldest, most loyal advisor. 'That is not sufficient. In this, I will not delegate.' He stalked towards the door. 'Come, Malik.'

Daisy wasn't sure what she'd expected. In the hotel in America, the ballroom was impossibly grand, with tall columns and exceptional art, but even that was nothing to this. A wing of the palace stood vacant of all furniture. The walls were gold, and each was decorated with an ancient piece of art. Flower arrangements were placed on marble pillars at regular intervals, so the air was rent with sweetness. At the end of the enormous room, glass doors had been thrown open to reveal a dance floor made of white marble tiles. While there were fairy lights strung across it, nothing dimmed the beauty of the desert night, the brightness of the stars that shone down on them. The music was traditional, lyre, flute and sitar combining to create an atmospheric and intriguing piece.

Daisy hovered above it all, waiting in the wings, safe from being seen, her anxiety at the role she must play increasing with every moment that passed.

'He won't be much longer,' Zahrah, standing a little way away, murmured soothingly.

Daisy made an effort to relax her expression, even attempting a smile. 'It's fine.'

The music continued and, below her, beautifully dressed guests milled, champagne in some hands, iced tea in others. Some of the women wore western-style ball gowns with enormous diamonds and jewels at their throats. Others wore ornate gowns and robes, the delicate, bright scarves arranged over their hair, adding mystery and intrigue to their appearance.

Daisy had worn what Zahrah had provided her with. 'It was the Emira's,' Zahrah had explained.

'Who?'

'His Highness's mother.'

'Oh.' She'd dressed with a sense of reverence, careful not to break any of the delicate fabric that made up the ceremonial gown. White with gold, just as Sariq often wore, it was heavier than it looked courtesy of the yellow diamonds that were stitched into the neckline and waist. It glittered from every angle. At her throat, she wore a single yellow diamond, easily the size of a milk-bottle cap, and on top of her head, a tiara.

Her hands were covered by white satin gloves that came to her elbows. 'They're hot,' she'd murmured to Zahrah, when she'd pulled them on. 'Perhaps I'll give gloves a miss.'

'You must wear them. It's protocol.'

'Gloves?'

She'd made a noise of agreement. 'No one is allowed to touch your hand but the Sheikh.'

Daisy's brows had lifted.

'You're not serious?'

'It's tradition.'

'So I'm meant to wear gloves my whole life?'

'Well…' Zahrah had smiled kindly '… I think we can relax the traditions behind closed doors, just as much as you'd like to. But when on state business, it will be expected that you do this.'

Daisy had compressed her lips, biting back an observation about the silliness of such a requirement. Haleth was an ancient and proud country. There were many habits and rituals that were new to her, but that didn't mean she could stand in judgement of them.

The guests swirled beneath them, an array of fabulous colour and finery. Twenty minutes later, Daisy looked to Zahrah. 'This is becoming rude.'

Zahrah frowned. 'Madam?'

'Keeping all these people waiting. Where on earth is he?'

'The message I received just referred to urgent business, I'm sorry.'

'I hate the idea of going down there on my own, but surely that's preferable to ignoring the guests?'

Zahrah's alarm was obvious. 'You can't. Not for your first function. His Highness would never approve.'

Daisy's interest was piqued. 'Oh, wouldn't he?' The idea of flaunting his authority was wildly tempting and she couldn't really say why.

'Of what would I not approve?'

Daisy whirled around, her eyes catching those of her husband immediately. He wore another spectacular robe, this one emphasising the strength and virility of his frame, the darkness of his complexion. On the balcony, he was the man she'd met in New York, but like this, he was an untouchable ruler. There was something unusually forbidding in his appearance, a tightness in his frame that had her brows drawing together.

Zahrah bowed low at his entrance and before she could straighten, Sariq had dismissed her. 'Leave us. Allow no one to enter.'

'Yes, sir.'

Alone, Daisy gave her husband the full force of her attention. 'Where have you been? People have been here an hour. *I've* been here an hour.'

He wasn't accustomed to being questioned by anyone, but somehow he'd become so used to that with Daisy that it no longer surprised him. He shouldn't have come here straight from the prison. It would have been far wiser to give his temper time to cool down, but the plans that he'd discovered on the would-be assassins had chilled him to the core. Seeing Daisy now, knowing he was the reason her life had potentially been in danger, filled him with a deep and immovable anger.

'An urgent matter called me away. Are you ready?' His voice was curt. He couldn't help it, though he knew he must. Daisy didn't deserve to feel the brunt of his anger. Even though the threat had been contained—his expert security teams had done just what they were supposed to and perceived a threat before it could come to the fore—the knowledge of what these men had planned sent a shiver down his spine.

'Sure.' Her smile was brave, but he detected her hesitation beneath it. Something pulled at his gut—guilt—a desire to absolve her from this life, to set her free from all of this. But even as he thought that, there was an answering certainty that he never would. That he couldn't. She was the mother of his child and her place was here with him. If this evening's arrests had taught him anything it was that her position as the mother to the heir of the RKH put her at grave risk. He intended to do what he could to protect her from that.

But at the doors that led to the wide, sweeping marble stairs that created the entrance to the room, she stopped. 'Wait.'

'What is it?'

When he angled his face to look at her, he saw that she was pale and alarm filled him. 'You're well?'

'I'm fine. I'm fine. I'm just…' She lifted a hand to her throat, pressing her gloved fingers to the enormous jewel there. 'You said they'd never accept me. A divorced American. Why do you think tonight will be any different?'

Her anxiety was palpable, and of his making. And yet,

he'd been speaking the truth. 'You're my wife now. It *is* different.'

'But it's not. You were talking about why you couldn't marry me, about what was expected of you. No one wants me to be here with you.' She curved a hand over her stomach and his eyes dropped, following the gesture. Something moved inside him then because, without his notice, her stomach had become rounded. Not hugely, but enough. His child was growing inside her. Something locked into place within him, making words difficult to form for a moment.

'No one wants me to be pregnant with your child.'

The threat was contained. There was no danger to Daisy in this crowd. And yet he put a hand on her forearm and turned her to face him. 'Would you rather avoid tonight?'

Her eyes lifted to his, surprise in their depths, but it was squashed by defiance. 'No.' She looked towards the crowds once more. 'This ball has been organised in my honour, like you said. The least I can do is turn up, right?'

Admiration shifted through him. 'We won't stay long.'

Daisy was surprised when she realised she was enjoying herself. She wasn't sure what she'd expected. Hostility? Open dislike? And there had been some people who'd regarded her with obvious scepticism and misgiving, though she was shepherded away from those people by an attentive Sariq, who hadn't left her side all evening. For the most part, though, the crowd had been welcoming and generous. Most of the women she'd spoken to had conversed in English in deference to her. Sariq had translated for people who spoke only the native language.

Yes, she was enjoying herself but, after an hour of making small talk with strangers, her energy was flagging.

As if he could read her thoughts, Sariq leaned towards

her, whispering in her ear so his warm breath filled her soul. 'There is a dance, and then we can leave.'

'A dance?' Of its own accord, her heart began to move faster, beating against her bones as though it were trying to rattle free.

'Just one.' His smile was alarming, because it reminded her so strongly of the way he'd been in New York. Seeing him like this surrounded by his people, she was in awe of not only his charisma, but also his strength and intellect. In every conversation, he was able to demonstrate a complete understanding of matters that affected his people. Whether it was irrigating agricultural areas to the north or challenges facing the country's education system, he was informed, nimble and considered. She listened to him and saw how easy it had been for him to work his way into her being.

It hadn't purely been a physical connection between them. While she found him attractive, it was so much more than that. And suddenly, out of nowhere, she was struck by a desire to be alone with Sariq, to have the full force of his attention on her as it had been in New York, and briefly on the balcony that evening several weeks ago.

'Ready?'

She bit down on her lip and nodded slowly, her heart slowing down to a gentle thud. 'Okay.'

'Don't look so afraid,' he murmured in her ear, so only she could hear. 'We have a deal, remember? This is just for show.'

Her heart turned over in her chest and she pulled back, so she could look in his eyes. Just for show.

This marriage was the last thing he wanted. She needed to remember that. While it was inevitable that they'd get to know one another, she'd be a fool to hope for more.

To hope for more?

Her insides squirmed. What was she thinking? She was the one who'd sworn off marriage. She'd promised herself she'd never again be stupid enough to get so caught up in a fantasy that she lost who she was. No one deserved that, least of all this man, who'd insinuated she was good enough to take to his bed as a mistress but not good enough to marry. The man who'd told her, point blank, that he'd never love his wife. That, for him, sex and intimacy were two separate considerations.

She straightened her spine, thrilled to have remembered such pertinent facts before his body enfolded hers, drawing her close to him. And as if by some silent cue, the music paused and another piece began to play, slow and lilting. With the stars shining overhead, the dance floor cleared so it was only Sariq and Daisy, their bodies moving as if one.

'You dance well.'

She wasn't sure she could take the compliment. He led, she followed—it was effortless and easy. They matched one another's movements as though they'd been designed to do just that. But they were silent and, after a few moments, that began to pull at her nerves.

'This is such an incredible courtyard.' For now, from this vantage point, she could see that the dance floor was surrounded on three sides of the palace. On the fourth, the view opened up to a manicured garden in the foreground and, beyond it, the desert. The wildness of the outlook, juxtaposed with the grandeur of this ancient building, created a striking effect.

'It was one of the first parts of the palace. In the eleventh century, these walls were erected. This courtyard was, then, the court, where the Emir presided over official matters.'

'Really?'

He made a sound of agreement. 'Over there—' he gestured with his hand, so she followed the gesture '—you can see the relics of the throne.'

And indeed, she could. It was made of marble, only a leg remained, but it was cordoned off, as though it were an object of great value. 'The walls provided defence—from enemies and sandstorms that are rife in this region.'

She looked around the courtyard with renewed interest, making a mental note to come back and study it in more detail in daylight.

'Where is your court now?'

'I have an office,' he responded with a smile that was lightly teasing. Her belly flopped. 'Here, at the palace, and one in the city. There are state rooms for conducting the *rukbar*.'

'What's the *rukbar*?' She repeated the foreign-sounding word, imitating his accent.

'Very good.'

His approval warmed her.

'Literally translated, it means "relief". It is a day each month when the palace doors are thrown open and any-one, regardless of their wealth and stature, may come to the palace.'

'What for?'

'To eat and be seen.' His smile deepened, and a kaleido-scope of butterflies launched itself through her belly. 'The tradition began in my great-grandfather's day, when pov-erty and famine were crippling in this country. The palace provided a banquet for any who could make it, and, more than this, he sat in and listened to people's needs from dawn until nightfall, helping where he could.'

Daisy had slowed down without realising it. Sariq shifted, moving her with him. 'You still do this?'

He dipped his head in silent agreement.

'How do you help people?'

'It varies. Sometimes it's a question of a child not being able to get into school, in which case Malik has the education secretary look into matters. Other times, it's a family where the father has died and the mother cannot work, in which case we grant a stipend to help support her.' He lifted his shoulders in a gesture of nonchalance but there was an expression in his face that robbed Daisy of breath. 'In Haleth, you would never have struggled as you have.'

Daisy's feet stopped obeying her altogether. She was moving purely under Sariq's guidance. 'No?'

'No.' He lifted a hand, brushing his fingertips across her cheek as though he couldn't help himself. 'Here in Haleth, you would have come to me and I would have had Max held for questioning before he could "lose" your money.'

'Just like that?'

'Just like that.'

Her smile was lopsided. 'So you're the knight in shining armour for every distressed person in Haleth?'

'It's not possible to help everyone. We have social security agencies in place but the *rukbar* provides a catch-all. An additional layer for the people.' He paused. 'The RKH is a phenomenally wealthy country. Distributing wealth wisely is one of the purviews of my role, and I intend to see the resources of this country benefit the people of the land.'

She felt the strength of his convictions and understood. She knew what his position meant to him. Admiration shifted inside her, and it brought with it a dark sense of foreboding. She didn't want to admire him; she didn't want to like him. But dancing beneath the stars in the arms of the man she'd married, Daisy felt as though a spell were being cast, and there was no antidote to it.

Sariq didn't believe in fate. He didn't believe in destiny. But dancing with his wife in the ancient courtyard, beneath a blanket of stars, he knew one thing: there was perfection in how they fitted together. Not only in the physical sense, but, more than that, in the way they thought.

He liked speaking with her. He liked hearing her thoughts, her answers. She fascinated him and intrigued him, and it was easy to see how he could become addicted to that.

'I'd like to see it.'

He didn't follow.

'The *rukbar*.'

Hearing her use his ancient language was an aphrodisiac. He kept moving, careful not to display the effect she had on him, even as his body was stirring to the beat of an ancient drum.

'It convenes in one week. I will advise Malik you shall join me.'

'Really?'

Her happiness stitched something in his gut. He nodded once. 'But I should warn you, Daisy, it can be harrowing. Some of the people who attend have nothing. Their stories are distressing.'

Her lips twisted in a way that made him want to drop his head and capture them with his own. He might have, to hell with the complications of that, if they hadn't been surrounded by hundreds of dignitaries.

'I can cope.' There was steel in her words, and he wondered at the cause of it. There was so much about her he didn't know, and yet he felt that on some level he understood every cell of her being. That wasn't enough though. The gaps in his knowledge of her seemed insupportable all of a sudden. There was an urgency shifting through him.

'Has anyone told you about the *tawhaj* tower?'

She frowned. 'No?'

He moved his fingers by a matter of degrees, stroking

them lightly over the flesh at her back. He felt her body tremble in response. Desire kicked up a notch.

'No.' Her voice was soft, husky. 'What is it?'

'Look.' He stopped dancing so he could gesture behind her. She shifted her gaze, her neck swanlike as she followed the direction he'd indicated. 'Do you see it?' He couldn't stop looking at her. He had to get a hold of this. They were being watched and the seduction they were enjoying was palpable. Surely everyone would be aware of the heat that was moving between them.

'No?'

'There.' It was an excuse to move closer. His arm brushed her nipples as he pointed more clearly and he felt her response. It was imperative that he remove them from this environment. He no longer wished to be surrounded by a hoard of onlookers. He needed his wife all to himself.

'Oh! Yes, I think so?'

It was, indeed, difficult to make out the tower in the moonlight. The spindly structure, forged from marble and stone many hundreds of years ago, was slender and elegant.

'Would you like to see it?'

She shifted to face him just as the music slowed to a stop. Her eyes held his and it was as though a question was moving from him to her, silent and unspoken, but heard nonetheless. 'Yes, Sariq. I would.'

CHAPTER ELEVEN

HIS HAND IN the small of her back was addictive. They didn't speak as they moved through the ancient corridors of this palace. Floors of marble, walls of stone, tapestries, flowers, gold, jewels. It all passed in a blur. All Daisy was conscious of was the man beside her. His nearness, his touch, his warmth, his strength. She could feel his breathing as though it were her own.

It took several minutes for the noise of the party to fade from earshot completely and then there was silence, save for the sound of their footfalls and the pervasive throb of anticipation.

'In the thirteenth century, Haleth was made up of three separate kingdoms. War was frequent and bloody. The tower was built, initially, as a lookout. It is the highest point of palace land, and has a vantage point that, on a clear day, extends to the sea. It gave the Emir's forces the ability to detect a likely skirmish from a great distance.' He guided her through a pair of enormous timber doors, each carefully carved with scenes she would like to come back and study, another time.

'It meant that most of the approaches to the palace took place during sandstorms, when visibility was poor.'

She shivered. 'Such violence.'

'Yes.' He looked down at her, something unreadable in

his expression. There was a tightening to his features that spoke of words unsaid.

'What is it?'

'Nothing.' He shook his head, as if to clear the thought. 'Here.'

They approached another set of doors. These were gold, and guarded on either side by two members of the RKH military, dressed as the guards in the embassy had been.

Sariq spoke in his own language, a short command. Each bowed low and then the guard on the left pulled a ring of brass keys from his pocket, inserted one into the door. Both guards worked in unison to open them.

Inside, there was a marble staircase, but it wasn't possible to see more than the first two steps. One of the guards moved ahead, and when Daisy and Sariq followed, she saw that the guard was lighting heavy lamps attached to the walls. The staircase smelled of kerosene and damp.

On they went, each tread worn down in the centre by the thousands of steps that had come before theirs, until finally the air grew clear, the stars shone overhead, and they emerged into an open room right at the top of the tower.

The guard was lighting the lamps, giving the space a warm glow, but Daisy barely noticed. She was too busy taking in the details of this spectacular tower. The walls were open, just spindly supports every few metres, to create the impression of windows where there were none. Those same spindles rose like the branches of a tree towards the sky, curving inwards at great height, stopping well before they reached the centre so the roof was open, showcasing the night sky in a way that was breathtaking. The moon was full and it caught the pale marble in such a way that it seemed to shine against the inky black of the heavens.

'Wow.'

The guard was leaving. They were alone.

'These pillars are incredible.' She moved to one, running her hands over the carefully carved shapes. 'They must have been made by talented craftsmen.'

His expression was rueful. 'They were carved by prisoners. I used to come here a lot, as a child.' His features grew serious and, without any elaboration, she understood what he was alluding to.

'After your mother died?'

Surprise flashed in the depths of his dark eyes. 'Yes.'

She nodded slowly. 'Losing a parent at seven must have been incredibly difficult. Were you and she close?'

His jaw clenched, and he stared out from the tower, his body rigid, as though he weren't going to speak.

'She was my mother.'

Daisy considered this. 'That's not an answer.'

His gaze pivoted to hers. 'Isn't it?'

She traced her finger over a line in the marble, following the swirling texture contemplatively. 'I loved my mother, but we weren't close. That didn't stop it from hurting like anything when she died. I think a relationship with your parents can be complex.'

'Why were you not close?'

She was conscious that he was moving their conversation to her, and perhaps it was a technique for deflection, a way of moving the spotlight off him. She allowed that, with every intention of returning to her question in a moment.

'My mother was bipolar.' It was amazing how easy she found that coming from her lips, when for years she'd grappled with discussing the truth of her home life. 'When she was in a manic phase, she was the most incredible fun.' Daisy shook her head, her brow furrowed as she looked up at the stars across the night sky. The view from here showcased the incredible silver of the desert sands, filling her with a desire to lift her wings and fly across its wide expanse.

'But there were times when that wasn't the case?'

'Oh, yes. Many times. As a child, I didn't understand it. I mean, one day she'd be pulling me out of school so we could go to the movies, or feeding me ice cream for breakfast, and then the next she wouldn't get out of bed.' She shook her head. 'Our house was either scrubbed to within an inch of its life, the smell of bleach on every surface, or completely abandoned. Milk cartons left out, dishes not washed, floors filthy.'

Sariq didn't say anything, but she felt the purpose for his silence. He was drawing her out, letting her keep talking, and despite the fact she generally kept her past to herself, she found the words tumbling from her now.

'There were times—when she stayed on her medication—when things were okay. But not really, because the medication just seemed to hollow her out. I don't think she really persisted in finding a good doctor and getting the right prescription. She hated the feeling of being "stable". Without the lows, she couldn't have the highs.'

'And your father?' Sariq prompted after a moment.

Daisy felt her throat thickening, as it often did when she thought of that time in her life. 'Dad couldn't deal with it. He tried to get Mom help but she was beyond that. He left home when I was ten.'

'Without you?'

'He wanted to take me. I refused. I know my mom wouldn't cope.' She frowned. 'I was so angry with him, Sariq. To leave her just because she was sick? He failed her, and he failed me.'

'He did.' The words held a scathing indictment that was somehow buoying.

'Towards the end, Mom's manic phases grew fewer, her

depression deeper. She began to self-medicate. Marijuana at first, then alcohol. Lots of alcohol.' Daisy closed her eyes, trying to blot out the pain. 'She was drunk when she crashed her car. Thankfully without hurting anyone else.'

He was quiet beside her but she felt his closeness and his strength and both were the balms to a soul that would always carry heavy wounds of her past. Silence sat between them, but it was a pleasant silence, wrapping around her, filling her with warmth. She blinked up at him and even though their eyes locked, she didn't look away.

He was staring at her and she felt something pass from him to her. There was magic in this tower, a great, appreciable force that weaved between them.

'When my mother died…' he spoke, finally '…my father sent me away. Partly for my own protection, but mainly, because I reminded him of her. He couldn't bear to spend time with me.'

She frowned. 'I thought…'

'Yes?' He prompted, when her voice trailed off into nothing.

'I just, the way you speak about him, I presumed you thought the world of your father.'

'He was an exceptional ruler. I admired him greatly. I feel his absence every day.' Sariq's gaze moved, returning to the desert beyond them. 'He loved only one person, his whole life. My mother. When she died, he lost a part of himself with her and he learned a valuable lesson.'

'What lesson?'

'That love leads to hurt.'

'Not always.'

'Really?' He lifted one brow, his scepticism obvious. 'You can say this after your own experience? Your father? Your husband?'

She bit down on her lip, wondering at his perspective.

'Dance with me?'

She blinked, looking around them. 'Here?'

'Why not?'

She was about to point out the absence of music, but she didn't. Because her heart was creating a beat in her ears, and it was all she needed. Wordlessly, she nodded, so he brought his arms around her waist, shaping her body to his.

They moved without speaking for several moments, but his revelations were playing through her mind. 'I think,' she murmured softly, 'that you don't know your own heart.'

He didn't respond, but that didn't matter. Deep in her own thoughts, she continued. 'Losing someone you love hurts. Betrayal hurts. But I don't think knowing there's a risk of that inures you to caring for another person. You think your father didn't love you? That you didn't love him? I think that's biologically impossible.'

'Your father didn't love you,' he pointed out after a beat had passed.

'Well, my dad's a somewhat deficient human. And anyway, he did love me. He just loved himself more.' She shook her head. 'Your father pushed you away because he was scared of being hurt again—because he knew that he loved you so much hurt was inevitable, if anything were to happen to you.'

He stroked her back in such a way that made it hard to hold onto a single ribbon of thought.

'Being afraid doesn't mean an absence of affection.'

'You're a romantic.' His words were murmured across her hair, teasing and light, pulling at her.

Was she? Daisy had never considered this to be the case. 'I think I'm more realist than romantic.'

'Not going by what you've just said.'

'Love is a reality of the human condition. You can't deny it's within you. You can't close yourself off to it.

You loved your father and he died. The night we met, you weren't simply mourning a leader. You were grieving for the loss of your dad—something that goes beyond position and title. He was your father—the man who gave you life.'

Sariq stilled for a moment and then began to move, his steps drawing her towards the middle of the marble floor. 'It's different.'

'How? Why?'

He expelled a sigh. 'A royal child isn't… I was his heir. Not only his son. My purpose was always the continuation of the family.'

'You make it sound as though you were property rather than a person.'

'I was required.'

Daisy considered that a moment. 'Just like our child is "required"?'

A slight pause. 'Yes.'

The confirmation knotted her stomach in a way that was unpleasant. 'And so you won't love our child?'

'You are fixated on the notion of love.' The words were said lightly but they did nothing to ease the seriousness of her thoughts.

'I didn't have a father in my life for very long. I don't want my child to know the pain of an absent parent.'

'I was the one who insisted we raise our child together, wasn't I?'

'No.' She stopped dancing and looked up at him, her eyes sparking with emotions she couldn't contain. 'You insisted that I move here so your child would be in the RKH. Your heir. There's a difference.'

'What do you want me to say?'

She bit down on her lip, unable to put that into words. 'I don't want you to keep our child at an emotional distance,' she said, after several moments had passed. But it wasn't all-encompassing. She felt so much more.

I don't want you to keep me at an emotional distance.

'I won't.' The assurance was swiftly given, but it did little to assuage her concerns.

'Because I'd rather take my chances in America, regardless of what you say, than expose our child to the kind of upbringing you've described.'

He froze, his body completely still, his arms locked around her waist. There was such contrast—the strength and warmth of him juxtaposed to the rigid cool of his stance. 'America is not an option.'

Something flashed inside her. Anger! And it was so welcome. In the swirling, raging emotions she felt, anger was one she could grasp. It made sense. She liked it.

'You don't get to command me.'

His nostrils flared as he stared down at her, his attempt to control his temper obvious. 'You're wrong.'

'No, I'm not. You told me I was coming to the RKH as your equal. Well—' she pushed her hands onto her hips, glaring right back at him '—if I want to go to America then there's nothing you can do about it.'

His laugh lacked humour.

'I'm serious.'

'As am I. Deadly serious.' He brought his body closer to hers, but it seemed accidental, as though he were simply moving without conscious thought. 'Do you know why I was late this evening?'

She shook her head.

'I was in the catacombs that run beneath the city. They were converted to prison cells a few decades ago. Two men are detained there, right now, who were planning on hurting you, Daisy.'

She froze, his words slamming into her like bricks.

Out of nowhere, she began to tremble. Her ears rang with a high-pitched squealing sound. 'You're making that up.' She wanted to reject it. It couldn't be true.

'I wish I were.'

The shaking wouldn't stop.

Sariq swore under his breath, then his big, masculine hands were cupping her face, holding her steady for his inspection. 'Here, I can protect you. My guards can protect you. And believe me, Daisy, nothing matters more to me than your safety.' Neither of them moved. 'You and our child will have the full force of my army at your disposal. You must remain in the RKH. Can you see that?'

She nodded quickly. Fear—not for herself so much as for the life of her unborn child—was instinctive and swift. 'But why?'

His lips were a grim slash in his face. 'Because of what you represent. Because of the stability our child will bring.'

'I… Why didn't you tell me?'

'I just did.'

'I mean sooner.'

'I dealt with it.'

A shiver ran down her spine. 'What does that mean?'

'These men will not harm you.'

Her eyes flashed with fear. 'What did you do?'

His laugh was gruff. 'Not what I wished, believe me. They will spend a long time in prison for this though.'

'So if the threat is gone…'

'There are always madmen, Daisy, with political agendas.'

'You can't protect me from everything for ever.'

'No.' A muscle jerked in his jaw. 'But I can try.'

She thought of his mother then, who was murdered by madmen such as those apprehended this evening. His mother who had been pregnant with another child, and whose death had caused the beginning of the end for Sariq's relationship with his father. And a part of Daisy wanted, more than anything, to console Sariq. It was a selfish need though, because she also needed consoling. She needed distracting. She wanted to feel alive and safe, and present in the moment.

Reaching to her face, she pulled his hands away, stepping back from him to give them a little space. Then, slowly, deliberately, she reached for the straps of the dress, guiding them down her arms slowly, her eyes on his the whole time.

'What are you doing?' There was an expression of panic on his features, as though he knew that if she started this, he wouldn't be able to stop it.

'What does it look like?'

His eyes closed for a moment, then pierced her with their intensity. 'Daisy...'

She shook her head then, and the desert breeze lifted some of her fair blonde hair, blowing it across her cheeks.

'I don't want to think right now. I don't want to think about plots to kill me, threats, nothing. I don't want to think about dangers and politics.' The dress dropped to the floor at her feet. She stepped out of it, mindful of the beautiful silk lingerie she wore, grateful Zahrah had presented her with the set that evening.

'I just want to feel.' She stood where she was, her eyes fixed to his, her lips parted a little. 'Will you make me feel, Your Highness?'

Invoking that formal title made his eyes flare wider. He released a low, growling sound, then shook his head, but it was obvious he was holding on by a thread. 'You'll regret this.'

'Perhaps.' She lifted her shoulders. 'But that doesn't mean I don't want it to happen right now.'

He took a step towards her and her breath hissed from

between her teeth, sharp and intense. 'You don't know what you're asking of me.'

She lifted a brow. 'Really? Do you need me to spell it out?'

He didn't react to her attempt at humour.

'Make love to me, Sariq. Please.'

He cursed every word he knew in all the languages he spoke, but nothing helped. His wife—his beautiful, pregnant, desirable wife—was asking him to sleep with her and, despite the promise he'd made on the plane, he felt his resolve weakening.

He wanted her every bit as much as always. There was no absolving himself of this desire even when he knew it was fraught with potential dangers. They were married, true, but not for any reason other than this child. Becoming lovers could complicate that.

He needed to be clear.

He was a man of honour, and he had no intention of misleading his wife. 'Just sex.' He lifted a finger to her lips, pressing there gently. 'And just tonight.'

Her eyes flared wide and he held his breath, needing her to agree to his terms. He couldn't confuse what they were with physical desire. It had no part in this.

'If you say so.' Her eyelids fluttered and then she was pushing towards him, so he caught her in his hands, holding her to his body as he dropped his mouth and did what he'd been craving since the moment she'd walked into his embassy.

He kissed her, hard, hungrily, and it was like coming home.

Her eyes were heavy, her body too. She was warm, safe. Cradled against Sariq's chest, his heart beating beneath her ear. Steps, marble, kerosene. A door. She nuzzled closer. Something warm was wrapped around her, a robe? His robe? She inhaled. Yes, it smelled of him. Another door, footsteps. She closed her eyes. His heartbeat was steady, loud.

Another door. Something soft was beneath her. She forced her eyes open and looked around. Her room. Sariq, beside her bed.

'Don't go.' She lifted a hand, holding it towards him. 'Please.'

If he were a man of honour, he would leave her now. For hours they'd pleasured one another, his body answering the call of hers, instincts driving them together, making it impossible to remember anything except the sense of what they each craved from the other. But in a few short hours the sun would crest over the desert dunes and reality would intrude.

She didn't want this, and nor did he. It was an illusion. A snatch out of time.

Danger lay before him. If he joined her in bed, he'd fall asleep. They'd wake up together, facing a new day as lovers.

His eyes dropped to her belly, rounded with his child, and a paternalistic pride fired in his belly. He owed it to their child not to mess this up. Sleeping with Daisy tonight had been, undeniably, perfect but it was also problematic. He wanted her.

He wanted her in a way that was addictive, that could threaten his legendary self-control if he didn't take care.

'It's late.' The words were crisp and he saw her flinch in response. He was already ruining this. Just as he'd said in the tower, pain brought pleasure and pleasure brought pain. 'Go to sleep.'

He left before she could respond.

CHAPTER TWELVE

HE BARELY SLEPT. Just as the sun lifted above the desert, he pushed the sheet from his body and strode, naked except for a pair of boxer shorts, onto the balcony. Frustration gnawed at his gut. Dissatisfaction too.

He shouldn't have left her without an explanation.

He'd panicked, but she'd deserved better.

Without intending to, he moved along the balcony, towards the doors that led to her apartment. If she was asleep, which she surely would be at this hour, he would leave her. And if she was awake?

He stood on the other side of the glass, looking in at his wife's room, wondering at the thundering inside his chest. The morning was perfect. Clear and cool, none of the day's stinging temperature apparent yet.

Daisy slept. She was so peaceful like this, so beautiful. Memories flashed through his mind. New York. Her smile. Her laugh. The fascination he'd felt with her from the beginning.

Her face when he'd propositioned her to become his mistress.

The obvious shock. Despite the normality of such an arrangement, she'd been offended. Her fire when she'd thrown her pregnancy at him, with no idea what that revelation would mean.

And finally, her words on the night they'd married.

'I'm marrying you because I have to—not because I want to—and I will never forgive you for this. Tonight I'm going to become your wife and I may appear to accept that, I may appear to accept you, but I will always hate you for this. I love our child, and, for him or her, I will try to make our marriage amicable, at least on the surface, but don't you ever doubt how I really feel.'

She'd begged him to make love to her in the tower, the night before. Their physical connection was real and raw. There was no questioning that. But beyond it? She hated him. She despised him, as she had every reason to.

Did she still though? Even after time had passed and they'd grown...what? Closer? Did he really think that? Did he really *want* that?

His heart thumped.

Yes.

He wanted it, and yes, they had. He'd shared more of himself with Daisy in the short course of their marriage than he had any other soul in his entire life. He'd felt painfully lonely when they'd met and now?

He didn't want to examine it because the answer terrified him.

He would never allow himself to love her. No woman, ever, but especially not Daisy. There was far too much risk there. If he ever really let himself care for her, he suspected he'd lose himself completely. When he'd confronted the prisoners in the catacombs the night before, he'd wanted to kill them with his bare hands. The impulse had assailed him from nowhere but it had been strong and desperate. The idea of anyone hurting Daisy had been anathema to him.

He stood up straighter, his breathing forced.

For Daisy, he would give up his kingdom, his crown.

Anything she asked of him. Revulsion flooded him, and a heavy sense of guilt. Being Sheikh of Haleth was his purpose in life. He had been born and raised for this, and desire for a woman wasn't anywhere close to a good enough reason to doubt his duty.

Except it wasn't just desire, a voice niggled inside him. There was a complexity of considerations here, but none of these could permit him to forget what he owed his country.

He cursed under his breath and spun away, stalking back into his own room and dressing quickly. What he needed was to think.

All his life, Sariq's life had followed a path, a plan, and now he was stepping into the unknown. It wouldn't work. He didn't want it. He needed a new plan, one that would work for him, Daisy, and their child.

He needed to think without the knowledge that Daisy was only a wall away.

'Have a horse prepared. I'm going to the desert.'

He would never love her.

Daisy lay on her back, one hand on her stomach, patting the rounded shape there, her eyes chasing the detailing in the ceiling. Her body bore the marks of his lovemaking but it was all a lie. Sex and intimacy were not connected for Sariq.

How many times and in how many ways had he said this? Even at the embassy, when she'd first arrived and he'd asked her to become his mistress.

Why had that hurt so badly?

Her stomach dropped, because an answer was beating through her, demanding her attention. In New York, she'd been drawn to him because she'd never known anyone like him. And at the embassy, she'd been furious with him, but also, she'd felt a thousand and one things—good things.

And now?

She closed her eyes and remembered all of their conversations, shared moments, desire, need, a tangle of wants, impulses that had been pushing her towards him even when she wanted to dislike him so, so badly.

But for him?

Just sex. And just tonight.

Nothing had changed. It was the same parameters he'd established in New York, the same parameters he'd tried to enforce when he'd asked her to come to the RKH as his mistress. And every time he'd reminded her of those limitations, it had twisted inside her, like a snake's writhing. Pain, discontent. Why?

'Oh, crap.' She sat up, her throat thick with emotion. 'No.' She'd thought she loved Max when she'd married him, but she hadn't. She'd had no idea what love felt like—until now. It wasn't something you decided to do. It was all-consuming, a firestorm that ravaged your body. It was lighting her up now, making her feel…feel everything.

She'd fallen in love with her husband and that might ordinarily have been considered a good thing but, for Daisy, she couldn't see any way to make this work. He didn't love her. He never would. That was his one proviso.

Her stomach looped fiercely. Her heart contracted.

And suddenly, this marriage, this palace, the prospect of raising a child with him, felt like cement weighting her down. Living here with him had been scary enough, when he'd insisted on this marriage. She'd thought her fear came from the unknown, the pressure of being the mother to the royal heir. But it was so much more than that now.

She'd fallen in love with him, and he could never know. She couldn't tell him. She wouldn't.

But how could she keep it secret? Flashes of their night together came back to her. It might have been sex for him but every touch, every moment, had been a connection, a moment of love. She communicated her feelings in everything she did.

How could he not know?

And then what? If he realised how she felt?

Mortification curled her toes. He would become the third man in her life she'd offered herself to, the third man she'd loved or purported to love, who'd found it easy to withhold those same feelings. After her father, she'd been wary with men, but Max had found a way under her defences. After Max, she'd been wary to the extreme, but Sariq… It wasn't even that he'd charmed her. He hadn't. He'd been himself but there was something in his manner that had made it impossible for Daisy to forget.

But the idea of having *this* love rejected was anathema to her. It would hurt too much. She knew how he felt—she didn't need him to spell it out to her. No good could come from having this conversation.

Maybe she could make him love her? Her heart began to stammer. But she was being a fantasist. You couldn't make anyone who wasn't so inclined fall in love with you—as her first marriage had taught her.

At no point had Sariq given her even the slightest reason to hope. This feeling was her fault. Her mistake.

She had to conquer it.

He rode for hours, until the heat of the day, so familiar against his back, was almost unbearable. He rode towards the caves, knowing he would not make it there on this occasion. Knowing even as he set out from the palace that cowering from this wasn't worthy of him. He was not a man to run from anything, and he wouldn't run from this.

Last night was a mistake.

He couldn't blur the lines of what he wanted from Daisy.

She was right to insist on boundaries being in place. With every fast-moving step of the steed beneath him, his certainty grew that their marriage would only succeed if he insisted on structure. Formality. He'd been mistaken to let his interest in Daisy as a woman cloud what he needed from her.

Before he met her, he'd been preparing to marry, and his wife, whomever he chose, would have simply been a ceremonial addition to his life. Someone with whom he would have perfunctory sex for the sake of continuing the family line and then leave to her own devices.

He'd had no intention of having his bride installed in the apartment beside his own. That had been for Daisy, because to have her in his palace but any further from him felt wrong. His first instinct—and it had been a failure.

She was beautiful and desirable but how he felt about her personal charms was irrelevant now she was pregnant with his child. He wouldn't make the same mistake his father did. He wouldn't let affection for a woman weaken him.

He rode on, his face a mask of resolve. With every day that passed, he would conquer this.

It was some time around three when Daisy began to feel the exhaustion from the early start. Zahrah had woken her for the *rukbar* before day's break, so she could dress in a special ceremonial robe and be prepared for the procedures of the day.

'You'll sit beside Sariq. You won't need to say anything, though people will no doubt be very excited to see you. Some might ask to touch your belly—it is considered extreme good fortune to do so to any pregnant woman here in Haleth. But you, carrying the royal heir, your stomach would be seen as very fortunate.'

Daisy had found it hard to smile since the morning after she'd slept with Sariq. Having not seen him since then, she found that smile had felt even heavier, but she lifted it now, turning to see Zahrah. 'You haven't asked to touch my stomach.'

'I presumed you wouldn't want me to.'

Daisy lifted her shoulders. 'It's just a tummy.'

Zahrah extended a hand, her fingertips shaking a little, and it was in that moment Daisy understood the momentousness of this child she was carrying. Any child was special and important, but their baby meant so much to the entire country. Sariq had said as much at the embassy in Manhattan but she *could see that for herself* now. For Zahrah and she had become friends, yet the enormity of touching Daisy's pregnant belly was obviously overwhelming for Zahrah.

The sky was still dark when Zahrah led her towards the ancient rooms that bordered the courtyard where they'd had the ball a few nights earlier. Her eyes found the spot where they'd danced and ghosts of his touch lifted goose bumps over her skin.

'Here,' Zahrah murmured. It was only as Daisy approached she saw Sariq locked in serious conversation with Malik. He turned towards her, so she had only a moment to still her heart and calm her features. It was the first time she'd seen him since he'd carried her back to her bed. Since she'd asked him to stay and he'd left.

Just sex. Just tonight.

He'd been true to his word.

'Your Highness.' Malik bowed low.

Sariq said nothing.

Uncertainty squeezed her gut. 'Good morning.'

At that, Sariq nodded, his eyes holding hers for a moment too long before he turned back to Malik and finished his conversation. Daisy felt as though she were on a roller coaster, hurtling over the highest point at great speed.

'I'll be fine,' she assured Zahrah. 'You should go back to bed.'

Zahrah's smile was so normal. Daisy wished it could tether her back to her real self, to the woman she'd been before she realised how she felt. 'I'll be to the side of the room,' Zahrah murmured. 'If there's anything you need, just turn to me and I will come.'

Daisy nodded, but having this kind of attention bestowed on her still felt unusual. 'You're so kind to me.'

Zahrah smiled. 'You're easy to be kind to.' And she reached down and squeezed Daisy's hand. 'You'll be good at this. Have courage.'

It was a relief that Daisy's nervousness could be attributed to the *rukbar* she was about to take part in and not the first sighting of her husband in days.

Sariq spoke in his native tongue, which she was getting very proficient at understanding, if not speaking. 'Leave us now.'

Zahrah and Malik both moved further along, towards the doors that would lead to the room.

Now, Sariq offered a tight smile that was more like a grimace. 'You remembered.'

It was a strange thing to say. She lifted her eyes to his and felt as though she'd been scorched. 'You're still happy for me to be a part of this?'

Something flashed in his eyes and her stomach dropped. He wasn't happy. She didn't know how she knew it but she did. Waves of uncertainty lashed at her sides. 'The people will be gratified by your attendance.' It was so insufficient. The people. Not him.

A noise sounded, like banging against a door. 'That's our signal. Ready?'

And so it began. Once they were seated at two enormous, elaborate thrones made of gold and black metal, she'd heard the din from the external doors of the palace. A sense of fear and awe filled her when the doors were thrown open, but there was no stampede. An orderly queue had formed, and she learned, when they'd taken a small break to eat lunch, that security screening had been implemented, for the first time in the *rukbar*'s history, on the other side of the doors. Because of her?

Undoubtedly.

She'd seen his determination to keep her safe. For a moment that lifted her spirits until she remembered that her value, at this point, had more to do with her child than it did her.

She couldn't dwell on her own fracturing heart though. Not when the room was filling with people who were, so obviously, doing it tough.

Sariq listened patiently to each who came before him, offering a brief summary of each situation to Daisy in English once they'd finished speaking. Each story was hard—some were almost impossible to bear. Parents who'd lost children touched her the deepest of all. There were no medical bills here, the state provided, but there were other concerns. The cost of the funeral, the legacy of caring for other children while too grief-stricken to return to work.

Daisy felt tears filling her eyes on a number of occasions but worked hard not to show how deeply affected she was by these tragedies.

As the afternoon progressed though, she grew tired, her heart heavy, her mind exploding. And through it all, Sariq continued, looking as fresh as he had that morning, his concentration unwavering. She turned towards Zahrah, who immediately appeared at her side.

'Do you need something, Your Highness?'

'Just a little water.'

'Of course.'

Sariq turned to her, from the other side, and Malik paused proceedings. 'Are you okay?'

It was such a ludicrous question that she almost laughed. Okay? Would she ever be okay again? Did she even deserve to lament such a question in the face of so much suffering? 'I'm fine.' A bright smile and then a nod. 'Just thirsty.'

His eyes roamed her face, his expression unconvinced. 'You're pale.'

'I'm American.'

His impatience was obvious. 'Paler than usual.'

'I'm fine.' She couldn't say why she sounded angry at him, because she wasn't. Her anger was all directed at herself and her own stupidity for falling in love with a man who was so completely determined to be unavailable. 'Let's keep going. It sounds like there are still a tonne of people to see.'

And there were. The line continued until the sun set. 'Traditionally, this is when the *rukbar* concludes. Food is served in the adjoining room. I usually join the guests for a short time. You do not have to.'

'Of course I will,' she insisted, despite the fact she was bone weary. Pride wouldn't let her show it. 'But do you have to stop now? There are people out there who've waited all day.'

His eyes clung to hers and then he nodded. 'Ten more.'

As Malik turned to the crowd to announce what the Sheikh had decided, Sariq leaned closer. 'Those that were not seen today will be given tickets for the next *rukbar*, so they're seen first. And any that feel they cannot wait have an email address to use to have their matter dealt with more speedily.'

That appeased her. The whole day had been eye-opening and fascinating. She felt, sitting beside Sariq, as though she was truly getting to know the fabric of this country. There was no hostility towards her—a divorced American. In fact, it was quite the opposite. People had been unstintingly kind, curious, polite.

Another hour stretched and then the *rukbar* was declared closed. Daisy was a little woozy when she stood, swaying slightly so that those in the room gasped and Sariq shot out a hand to steady her.

'I'm fine,' she said through a tight smile. 'Just not used to sitting down for so long.' He didn't relinquish his touch though, and her skin burned at the contact, her body throbbed, that same fire ignited, stealing through her soul. He guided her down the steps, away from the thrones, towards doors that led to another room.

'You should go to your room.'

Her gaze shifted. 'Is that an order?'

She saw the way his jaw tightened, and felt the battle raging within him. 'It's a suggestion.'

'Then I politely decline.'

He didn't like that, it was obvious. It wasn't fair to be angry with him. He'd done nothing wrong, nothing whatsoever. All along he'd been honest with her. Loving him was her fault, her problem. And yet she did feel anger towards him, because it simply wasn't fair. How could her heart be full to bursting and his determinedly empty?

'Daisy—'

'Everyone's waiting,' she said through clenched teeth, shifting away from him a little, just enough to dislodge his hand from her waist. 'Let's do this.'

Daisy was charming and lovely. He watched as she spoke to the assembled guests, moving from group to group and using the native language. He hadn't realised how good she'd become. Her accent was excellent and while she paused from time to time to search for a word, she was able to cover more than the basics. He watched the effect she had on his people and a warm sense of pride lifted him.

She was a natural.

No one, regardless of their lineage or birth, would have been a better Emira than Daisy. He turned back to his own conversation, listening to the rainfall statistics for the last quarter, but always he was aware of her location in the room. From time to time he would hear her laugh, soft but imprinted on him in such a way that meant he could pick it out easily. Would he ever lose this fascination with her? Would he have the ability to inhabit the same space and *not* hone in on her with every cell in his body?

Yes.

Of course.

Because that was what he wanted, and Sariq knew that with determination and focus he could do anything he wished. Daisy was beneath his skin at the moment, but he would dispense with that in time. Once the baby was born, he could even contemplate giving her exactly what she wanted, sending her to live away from him.

His body tightened. Rejection, anger, dismissal. Doubt. Disgust. She wasn't a piece of trash he could simply discard once she'd served her purpose. And yet she was the one who'd suggested going to America.

But her security was of paramount concern. The men held in the prison beneath the city were not part of a wider organisation. They were rogue militants with their own agenda. There was no reason to think she was in any greater risk than she had been before, and yet the idea of any harm befalling her, even the slightest harm, filled him with the sense of burning acid.

His eyes found her once more. She was in conversation but she looked as though she wasn't listening. His eyes narrowed. Her skin was so pale, like milk. She nodded, but then she swayed a little, just as she had before, at the end of the *rukbar*.

His chest clutched.

He cursed inwardly. She was going to faint. 'Malik.' His voice cut through the room and Sariq began to stride quickly, just as Daisy stumbled. Another curse, this one said aloud, and he broke into a run, catching her only a moment before her body crumpled. She would have fallen to the floor if his arms hadn't wrapped around her, lifting her and cradling her against his chest.

The room was silent; he barely noticed. Holding her to him, just as he had when they'd left the tower and she'd been exhausted from the lateness of the hour and the way they'd spent their night, he carried her from the room now, his heart slamming against his ribs in a way that told him all he needed to know.

CHAPTER THIRTEEN

'PLEASE PUT ME DOWN.'

Such stiffness in her voice, cold and hurt, and he winced inwardly because he understood it. He'd disappeared and he'd hurt her. Pleasure turned to pain, always.

'Sariq? I'm okay. It was just hot and I was tired.'

'You should not have stayed so long.'

He wished condemnation didn't ring through his words but, damn it, didn't she see? Protecting her was important.

She didn't say anything and that was wise. He felt worry and a worry that was close to turning to frustration and anger. Panic, too. A team of men stood outside the doors to her room. 'Where is the doctor?'

'Here, Your Highness.'

At this, Daisy scrambled against him, trying to stand, but he held her tight, pushing through the doors. Only when he reached her bed did he loosen his grip, laying her down on the bed, not wanting to remember the last time he'd done that.

'Please.' Her cheeks were pink. 'This is so silly. I'm fine, really.'

'The doctor will confirm that.' Sariq stepped backwards, allowing the doctor room to move.

He could see Daisy wanted to argue so he played the

trump card, which he knew she would listen to. 'Think of the baby, Daisy.'

At that, she stilled and, after a moment, nodded. 'Thank you.' But her gratitude was directed to the doctor. The examination was thorough yet brief. He checked Daisy's blood pressure, heart, temperature, felt the stomach and then listened to the baby's heart using a small handheld device that spilled the noise into the room. And Sariq was frozen to the spot at this small, tangible proof of their child's life. Daisy too lifted her eyes to Sariq's and he saw the emotion in them, the understanding of what they'd done.

Together, they'd made life. It hadn't been planned, and the pregnancy had led to all manner of complications, but it was, nonetheless, a miraculous thing.

'Your blood pressure is a little high, but not alarmingly so. You must rest. Stay hydrated. I'll come back to check on you in an hour.'

'Is that necessary?'

'Yes.' The doctor's smile softened the firmness of his response. 'Absolutely.' He turned to Sariq and bowed, then left.

Sariq stood there for what felt like a very long time, looking at his wife, as the clarity of his situation expanded through his mind. 'Zahrah will sit with you. I'll check on you in the morning.' He stalked towards the door, turned back to look at her as a sinking feeling dropped his stomach to his feet. 'You did well today, Daisy.'

He pulled the door inwards but Daisy was there, moving behind him, grabbing his wrist. 'Don't you dare walk out on me.'

He stared at her, surprise on his features. 'Calm down.'

'No.' And then, she lifted her hands to his chest and pushed him, her expression like fire. 'Damn you, Sariq, stop walking away from me. Can you not even stand to be in the same room with me? Are you worried I'm going to beg you to make love to me again?'

Her anger was so obviously born of hurt. He held her shoulders and lightly guided her from the door, away from the ears of the guards beyond.

'Don't!' She wouldn't be placated.

'I'm not leaving,' he assured her and in that moment he was so desperate to say or do anything that would placate her. 'Just sit down and be calm.'

'I don't want to be calm!'

'For the baby.'

'The baby's fine, you heard the doctor.'

'I heard him say your blood pressure is elevated. Arguing is not going to help that.'

'I don't want to argue with you. I just want you to tell me why you're avoiding me.'

He ground his teeth together, her accusation demanding an answer. But he didn't know what to say—he couldn't frame into words the complexity of his feelings.

'You regret sleeping with me.'

Damn it. He felt caught on the back foot, and it was a new experience, one he didn't like at all. 'It was…unwise.'

'Why?' She thrust her hands onto her hips so even then he was conscious of the jutting of her breasts, the sweetness of her shape, rounded with his baby. What was wrong with him that even in that moment he could want her?

Everything.

That was the problem.

His feelings for Daisy weren't logical. They weren't safe. Nothing about her fitted his usual modus operandi. That was why he had to gain control of this—it was in their mutual interest that he did so.

'I've thought about your request to return to America.' That was true. In the desert, it was all he could focus on.

'That would be unwise and potentially unsafe. I want our child raised here, in Haleth.'

She glowered. 'I'm not asking to go back to America. Not really. I understand why that's not possible.'

He ignored that, continuing with his train of thought as though she hadn't spoken. 'But you do not have to stay here at the palace. There is another palace on the outskirts of the old city. You should move there and live your own life, away from me and the pressures of this royal life.'

She stared at him for several seconds and he had no idea what she was thinking.

'Is that what you want?'

When he thought about what he *wanted*, it was a very dangerous path. So he concentrated instead on what he knew they needed. 'I want our child to be healthy. I want you to be happy. And I want to be able to focus on ruling the RKH, just as I was before.'

'And you can't do that with me here?'

He clenched his jaw, fierce memories burning through him. 'The situation is more complicated than I would like.'

'What does that even mean?'

He expelled a hot sigh. 'You're not like the wife I imagined,' he said, dragging a hand through his hair.

'I'm aware of that.' Her voice was scathing.

Great. He'd offended her once more. 'I mean that we have this history. Even before I knew about your pregnancy, I came to America intending to be with you again. From the moment we met I haven't been able to stop thinking about you. You take up too much space in my brain and I can't have that, Daisy. I can't.'

Her lips parted, her eyes widened, and she was completely still, perhaps replaying his admission.

'You don't want me to leave because you don't like me?'

He frowned. 'Why would you think that?'

'Because you've been ignoring me for a week?'

He was quiet a moment. 'I can't offer you what you need, and it's not fair for me to take what I want from you when I want it—'

'Sex,' she interjected acerbically.

He dipped his head in a silent admission. 'I won't use you like that.'

'So don't use me. Open yourself up to more.'

Her words burst through him, but he was already shaking his head, denying that. 'There's no more. My responsibilities require my full attention.'

'Liar.'

His laugh was a sharp burst. 'I don't think anyone's ever called me that before.'

'Perhaps you've never lied before but you're lying to me now, and to yourself. Why do you think you can't get me out of your head, Sariq? Hmmm?' There was a challenge in her voice, an angry, determined tilt to her chin. 'Why do you think you came to the embassy and propositioned me?'

'Sexual infatuation is one thing,' he said firmly, his tone flat, but she shook her head, dismissing it before he'd even finished.

'If it was sexual infatuation we'd have been sleeping together ever since our marriage. You wanted me, I wanted you. Instead, you've deliberately kept me at arm's length because you're terrified of what this could become. You keep *everyone* at a distance. You have no friends, no family. Malik is the closest person to you and he's a curmudgeonly old man who exists purely to serve you. That's not about your damned duty to Haleth. It's about fear. You don't want to get hurt so you're pushing everyone away. I won't let you do that to me.'

He stared at her, disbelief numbing him. 'You can have

no idea what my life is like,' he said, after a moment. 'So do not stand there and judge me, Daisy.'

'I know what your life *could* be like.' She changed tack, her voice lower, softer, working its way into his bloodstream so he had to work hard to hold his course. 'Do you think this is easy for me? I'm terrified! Terrified of telling you how I feel, of opening myself up to you, of opening myself up to yet another disastrous marriage. And yet I'm standing here, saying that I feel—'

'Don't.' He lifted a hand, silencing her. 'Don't say what you cannot take back. I don't want to hear it. I can't. I can't offer you the same, and it will be easier for both of us if we pretend—'

'Coward!' She stamped her foot, and he shifted backwards a little, shocked by her reaction.

'I'm in love with you. There! I've said it! Now what are you going to do? Are you going to admit you love me too? That we fell in love in New York and it's inconvenient and crazy and unpredictable but that doesn't change the fact we're in love? Or are you going to cling to the notion that your life will be better if you stay closed off, completely your own person? Immune from emotional pain but so lonely with it.'

His heart was like a hammer inside him, relentless and powerful. Another challenge, just as she always hit him with. He stared at her, and shook his head slowly, his mind like putty.

Her words threatened to overrun him with joy, but the rational, sensible approach to life he'd fixed on many years earlier was not easy to shake.

'I have never suggested I would love you.'

'Damn it, that's not an answer.' She pushed his chest again, her frustration understandable. 'Tell me you don't love me. Say you'll never love me.'

Say it! Tell her what she needed to hear, if that was how he could put an end to this conversation.

Except he couldn't say those words. Contrary to what she had accused him of, Sariq was not a liar. In fact he was unstintingly honest. 'No.'

Her eyes flared wide.

'I will not talk about you and me in the context of love. That's not what our marriage is predicated on.'

'Yes, it is! You're a fool if you can't see that we fell in love in New York. It's not a one-sided thing. I know, because I've been in a relationship like that and this feels completely different. I believe you love me. And I think you're trying to send me away because love is a complication you're not prepared to deal with.'

A muscle throbbed in his jaw. He stared at her, the stark truth of her words so simple, so right.

'Can't you see how right this is? We could have everything we both want in life. I'm not going to distract you from your responsibilities. I want to help you with them. I want to be your partner in every way.'

'No.' A harsh denial, when his heart was bursting through him, begging him to agree to what she was proposing. But his attitudes were forged from the coal fire of pain and were immovable.

'No? Is that all you've got?'

He glared at her. Damn her fire and spirit. Couldn't she see this wasn't going to work?

'I'm sorry, Daisy. I'm...flattered that you care for me.' She made a scoffing noise. 'But our marriage will work better if we treat it as a business arrangement.'

He began to move to the door but she stalled him with a fierce cry. 'You stop right there.'

He turned to face her, his expression like thunder, matching the strength of his feelings.

'I will not spend the rest of my life in a marriage like you've just described. I should never have agreed to this.'

'But you did, and you're here, and soon our baby will be born.'

'I don't care. If you're telling me our marriage is going to be so cold, then to hell with it. I want a divorce.'

He stared at her, panic strangling him for a moment, making it difficult to frame a response. 'That's not possible.'

'Oh, don't be so ridiculous. Of course it is. It's not what you *want*, but it's absolutely possible. You'll still have your heir. I'll even raise our child here in the RKH so you can be a part of his or her life. But no way am I going to tie myself to you for the rest of my life knowing you'll never accept that you have feelings for me.'

The ultimatum was like an electrical shock, galvanising him. He stared at her for several moments and then nodded. 'I need to think about that.'

This time, when he left, she didn't try to stop him.

Daisy stared at the closed door with an ache in the region of her heart. She'd done it. She'd laid all her cards on the table and he'd refused to admit he cared for her. She'd been wrong, then. It wasn't love. Not from him, anyway.

And now? He was thinking about granting her a divorce.

God, where had her request come from? Fear? Anger? Had she hoped it would snap him out of his state of denial? That it might wake him up and force him to be brave?

She was trembling all over, the fight knocked out of her by the shock she might get exactly what she'd asked for. Another divorce. Another failed marriage. But this one, so much worse than the first. The idea of not having Sariq in her life in any capacity filled her with a hard lump of pain.

But wasn't it better this way? A lifetime was a long time, and she couldn't see that this would get any easier.

* * *

The next day she played the piano Sariq had had brought to the palace the day after she'd arrived. She played Erik Satie because there was a pervasive sadness moving through her and Satie suited that. She played for almost two hours, and didn't hear the door pushing inwards. Nor was she aware of Sariq standing in the door frame, watching her, his eyes running over her as if committing her to memory.

When she finished playing though, he shifted and she turned, her blood pounding through her veins at the sight of him. He wore trousers and a business shirt. She wasn't prepared for that.

'Well?' It was like waiting for the executioner's axe to fall.

He moved towards her, coming to stand by the piano. 'I refuse to keep you here against your will.' His face was grim. 'I was wrong to pressure you into this marriage. I acted on instincts. I panicked. If you were serious about wanting a divorce, I'll grant it.'

Oh, crap. It wasn't what she wanted. But what she needed, he wouldn't give her, so that meant divorce was her only option. 'Fine.' She couldn't meet his eyes. She wanted this over. Like ripping off a plaster.

'You will need to stay in Haleth, as you offered. Once our child is born, we can come to a custody arrangement.'

Was she imagining the emotion in his voice? She didn't know any more. Perhaps her own feelings were so strong, so urgent, that they simply coloured her perception.

She nodded, still not looking at him.

'I apologise to you, from the bottom of my heart.'

Now, her gaze met his, but it hurt too much to hold. The look of pity there was the worst thing. She didn't want him to pity her. She wanted his love.

'I should never have slept with you in Manhattan. I

have been selfish this whole time. I hope one day you will forgive me.'

'I can forgive you for almost everything,' she said with a small lift of her chin. 'Manhattan. The embassy. Our marriage. Those were decisions you made because you *felt*.' She pressed a finger into his chest, her eyes like little galaxies. 'Agreeing to divorce me is because you refuse to feel. I don't know if I'll ever get past that.'

'Damn it, Daisy.' He dropped his head then, his forehead to hers, his breathing ragged. 'You ask too much of me.'

'I ask nothing of you,' she corrected. 'Except your heart.' But he wasn't going to give it. Daisy could see that. Slowly, she stood, her fingers finding the keys once more, pressing two together. 'It's a beautiful instrument. Don't make the same mistake your father did—don't shut music from your life once I'm gone.'

Her words chased themselves through his mind for days. They whispered to him overnight, waking him before dawn, they spoke to him at the strangest times. When he was running or working, meeting with foreign politicians. Always that strange parting statement settled around him.

'Don't make the same mistake your father did.'

He kept the piano and he went to it often. Every day the sun rose and he went through the motions of his day, just as he had before Daisy. He remained committed to his schedule. He didn't enter her suite of rooms. Nor did he use their adjoining balcony. But the piano he visited. He sat at the stool once, pressed the keys, remembered her fingers in those exact same places, the passion that ran through her.

And he thought about the life she should have been living, and would have been leading had her own plans not been so thoroughly derailed by those who were all too willing to take what they could from her without a second thought for what Daisy needed.

He'd been right to refuse to complicate their marriage. Right to insist he wouldn't use her. How much easier that would have been! To pretend there was hope for them. To sleep with her each night, to fold her into his life only so far as he was willing, but all the while remaining steadfastly committed to his duties as ruler of the RKH.

'Let me help you.'

She didn't understand the pressures he lived with. He hadn't been raised to share that burden. Daisy was gone, and he was glad. Not because he wanted her to be anywhere else but because he hoped whatever she thought she felt for him would pass.

Except it wouldn't.

She wasn't like that.

She loved him and she always would.

His gut clenched. Guilt cut through him. He turned away from the piano and stalked to his apartment. Malik was there but Sariq dismissed him quickly. 'Not now.'

Forty sunrises had passed without Daisy. Forty mornings, forty nights, forty days that each seemed to stretch for weeks. Time practically stopped. Only in sleep, when she filled his dreams, did he relax.

He craved sleep. Each day, he longed for it, and all because of Daisy. But it wasn't enough. Forty days after she left, he felt broken enough by missing her to accept that the solution to their marriage wasn't so simple. He couldn't send her away and forget about her.

He wasn't the same as he'd been before. She'd changed him, and he'd never change back. Everything was different now.

Cursing, he strode from his room. 'Malik? The helicopter. Immediately.'

CHAPTER FOURTEEN

'YOU ARE NOT EATING.'

Daisy regarded Zahrah over her water glass. 'I am.'

'Not like before,' Zahrah chided affectionately. 'When you first came to Haleth you could not get enough of our food.'

Daisy's smile was thin. She had nothing in common with the woman she'd been then. 'I'm eating.'

Zahrah compressed her lips but Daisy was saved from an argument she couldn't be bothered having by the sound of helicopter rotor blades. At the same time, a knock sounded at the door. Zahrah moved to intercept it, and a moment later, returned.

'His Highness is here.'

Daisy's pulse was like a tsunami. She curved a hand over her stomach, her eyes flying wide open, her lips parting in surprise. It had been over a month since she'd left the palace. Their last conversation was painfully formal. He'd spoken to her as though she were a stranger.

Why was he here now? She couldn't bear the idea of another stilted, businesslike interaction.

She stood uneasily, pacing towards the windows where she might get a glimpse of him. But the doors opened and she turned, her flowing turquoise dress blowing in the breeze created by his entrance. And she stood there and stared at him, her face too disobedient to flatten of all expression completely.

Butterflies beat against her and she hated that. She hated how reliably he could stir her to a response when she wanted to feel *nothing* for him.

'What are you doing here?'

There was no point with civility, was there? Perhaps there was, but she couldn't be bothered. She was tired, so tired.

He didn't speak though. He stared at her and with every second that passed, her blood moved faster and harder so that it was almost strangling her with its intensity.

'Your Highness?' It was like waking him from a dream. He straightened, turning to Zahrah, then back to Daisy.

'I'd like to speak to you. Is now a good time?'

She startled. His uncertainty was completely unusual. 'I'm…yes.' She nodded a little uneasily. 'I suppose so. Zahrah?'

'Yes, Your Highness.' Zahrah bowed low. 'Would you like any refreshments, sir?'

'No.' The word was swift. 'Thank you.'

Zahrah left, and still Sariq didn't move. It unsettled Daisy, so she wiped her hands down her front, drawing his gaze to her belly. In the forty days since she'd left the palace, her bump had 'popped'.

She waited for him to speak but he didn't and the silence was agonising. So eventually, she snapped. 'Please tell me why you're here, Sariq.'

He nodded, moving deeper into the room. 'I came—' He shook his head.

'What is it?'

'I came because…'

Nothing. She ground her teeth together. 'What? Is everything okay?'

Emotion, heavy, obvious emotion, moved on his face. 'No.' So simple. 'It's not.'

Daisy's heart rate doubled. 'Why not?'

He stepped towards her, then froze. 'I came because I couldn't not.'

'You're not making any sense.'

'I know.' His throat shifted as he swallowed. 'I came to apologise, because I cannot live with what I said and I did, with how I made you feel. I came because it occurs to me you're living here believing that I don't love you, that I won't love you, when you were right. I do.' Again he pulled at his hair, shaking his head, his eyes heavy with his emotions.

Daisy couldn't move.

'The night of the ball, when those men were apprehended for what they intended to do to you, I went to see them. I wanted to kill them, Daisy. There was nothing measured or calm in my response. Because of how I feel for you I risked undoing all of my father and grandfather's work and dissolving our entire legal system so I could take my revenge. Even my father didn't do this when my mother was murdered.' He swallowed once more.

Daisy was incapable of speech or movement.

'Loving you terrifies me because there is no limit to what I would do for you if you asked it of me. If anyone hurt so much as a finger on your hand, I would have the kingdom turned upside down until they were found and brought to justice. I'm terrified that I cannot be what my country needs of me when I feel this way for you.'

A strangled noise escaped Daisy's throat.

'But if the last forty days have taught me anything, it's that I cannot live without you either. Perhaps it's the smart thing to do, but I cannot be smart if it means losing you. I won't.' He crossed the room, lifting her face in his palms, staring down at her with such obvious amazement that her heart turned over as though it were being stitched into a new position. 'You are so brave. Fearless and strong, courageous, incredible. You faced up to how you felt about me even after what you've been through. After what *I* put you through. You are generous and good and I pushed at you, just like you said, pushing you away, unable to see a middle ground with you. Perhaps there isn't one. Perhaps loving you will mean I cannot rule as I otherwise might have. I don't care.'

But a sob burst through her. 'I care. I won't have you choose a life with me if you believe it weakens you.' She lifted a hand to his chest though, softening her statement with a gentle touch. 'I have too much faith in you for that.' Her fingers moved gently across the flesh that concealed his heart. 'You didn't kill those men. You stayed within the bounds of the law, because you are a good sheikh and an excellent man. You will rule this kingdom with all your goodness, and I will be at your side, making sure of that. I have no intention of being your weakness, Sariq. I want to be your biggest support and your greatest strength. Understood?'

He groaned, shaking his head. 'How can you be so good to forgive me after what I put you through?'

She bit down on her lip. 'I didn't say I'd forgiven you.'

His features tightened. 'No, of course not. I misunderstood. I know it will take time for me to make it right between us, but I want to do that, Daisy.'

Her stomach flipped. 'I believe you.'

'And because you are clearly so much wiser than I in these matters, I ask only that you tell me how. What do I do to make amends?'

His hands dropped to her stomach and he closed his

eyes, inhaling. 'I want you and our child to be in my life. Please, Daisy.'

And she smiled because she knew he meant it, and because she wanted, more than anything, to grab the dream of this future with both hands.

'Well…' She pretended to think about it. 'Perhaps we should put the divorce on hold. At least while I consider my options.'

He was disappointed, and there was a tiny part of her that enjoyed that. But she couldn't string it out any longer—it was too cruel.

'There are some things you could do to help me with that, you know.'

Hope flicked in his eyes. 'Oh?' Then, more seriously, his voice gruff, 'Anything.'

She lifted a finger to his lips, silencing him.

'Love me.' That was it. Nothing more complex than that. 'I do.'

'Good.' Her smile beamed from her. 'Love me with all your heart, for all your life, and don't ever stop.'

He pulled her against his chest, holding her tight, breathing her in. Their hearts beat in unison. Happiness burst through her.

'Not only is that something I can manage, it turns out it's completely non-negotiable.'

His kiss sealed that promise, and she surrendered to it, to him and to the future she knew they'd lead.

A year later, she stared out at the packed auditorium, anxiety a drum in her soul that was lessened only by the presence in the front row of her husband, the powerful Sheikh Sariq Al Antarah. Since returning to the palace, he'd insisted she further her piano studies. Leaving to attend a school like the Juilliard wasn't possible—once their son

Kadir was born, named for his grandfather, she found she
didn't want to go anywhere anyway. But Sariq saw no ob-
stacle to that. He engaged world-famous pianists to come
to the palace and work with her.

And now, all that effort had culminated in this. A per-
formance that had sold out within minutes, the proceeds of
which were going towards the charitable institution she'd
established, helping women with mental health issues.
Nerves were like fireflies in her veins but she closed her
eyes and lifted her hands to the keyboard.

It was a perfect moment with infinite possibilities. She
began to play and felt all the hopes of her childhood, the
aspirations she'd nurtured for so long, bearing fruit. Who
she'd been then, who she was now, unified in one dazzling,
magical moment. She smiled, because she was truly happy,
and suspected she would be for ever after.

* * * * *

COMING SOON!

We really hope you enjoycd reading this book.
If you're looking for more romance, be surc to
head to the shops when new books are
available on

Thursday 14th May

To see which titles are coming soon, please visit
millsandboon.co.uk/nextmonth

MILLS & BOON

MILLS & BOON

Coming next month

BEAUTY AND HER ONE-NIGHT BABY
Dani Collins

Scarlett dropped her phone with a clatter.

She had been trying to call Kiara. Now she was taking in the livid claw marks across Javiero's face, each pocked on either side with the pinpricks of recently removed stitches. His dark brown hair was longer than she'd ever seen it, perhaps gelled back from the widow's peak at some point this morning, but it was mussed and held a jagged part. He wore a black eye patch like a pirate, its narrow band cutting a thin stripe across his temple and into his hair.

Maybe that's why his features looked as though they had been set askew? His mouth was...not right. His upper lip was uneven and the claw marks drew lines through his unkempt stubble all the way down into his neck.

That was dangerously close to his jugular! Dear God, he had nearly been killed.

She grasped at the edge of the sink, trying to stay on her feet while she grew so light-headed at the thought of him dying that she feared she would faint.

The ravages of his attack weren't what made him look so forbidding and grim, though, she computed through her haze of panic and anguish. No. The contemptuous glare in his one eye was for her. For *this*.

He flicked another outraged glance at her middle.

"I thought we were meeting in the boardroom." His voice sounded gravelly. Damaged as well? Or was that simply his true feelings toward her now? Deadly and completely devoid of any of the sensual admiration she'd sometimes heard in his tone.

Not that he'd ever been particularly warm toward her. He'd been aloof, indifferent, irritated, impatient, explosively passionate. Generous in the giving of pleasure. Of compliments. Then cold as she left. Disapproving. Malevolent.

Damningly silent.

And now he was...what? Ignoring that she was as big as a barn?

Her arteries were on fire with straight adrenaline, her heart pounding and her brain spinning with the way she was having to switch gears so fast. Her eyes were hot and her throat tight. Everything in her wanted to scream *Help me*, but she'd been in enough tight spots to know this was all on her. Everything was always on her. She fought to keep her head and get through the next few minutes before she moved on to the next challenge.

Which was just a tiny trial called *childbirth*, but she would worry about that when she got to the hospital.

As the tingle of a fresh contraction began to pang in her lower back, she tightened her grip on the edge of the sink and gritted her teeth, trying to ignore the coming pain and hang on to what dregs of dignity she had left.

"I'm in labor," she said tightly. "It's yours."

Continue reading
BEAUTY AND HER ONE-NIGHT BABY
Dani Collins

Available next month
www.millsandboon.co.uk

Copyright ©2020 by Dani Collins

LET'S TALK
Romance

For exclusive extracts, competitions
and special offers, find us online:

 facebook.com/millsandboon

🐦 @MillsandBoon

📷 @MillsandBoonUK

Get in touch on 01413 063232

For all the latest titles coming soon, visit
millsandboon.co.uk/nextmonth

MILLS & BOON
A ROMANCE FOR EVERY READER

- **FREE** delivery direct to your door

- **EXCLUSIVE** offers every month

- **SAVE** up to 25% on pre-paid subscriptions

SUBSCRIBE AND SAVE

millsandboon.co.uk/Subscribe

WANT EVEN MORE
ROMANCE?
SUBSCRIBE AND SAVE TODAY!

'Mills & Boon books, the perfect way to escape for an hour or so.'

MISS W. DYER

'Excellent service, promptly delivered and very good subscription choices.'

MISS A. PEARSON

'You get fantastic special offers and the chance to get books before they hit the shops.'

MRS V. HALL

Visit millsandboon.co.uk/Subscribe and save on brand new books.

MILLS & BOON

THE HEART OF ROMANCE

A ROMANCE FOR EVERY KIND OF READER

MODERN

Prepare to be swept off your feet by sophisticated, sexy and seductive heroes, in some of the world's most glamourous and romantic locations, where power and passion collide.
8 stories per month.

HISTORICAL

Escape with historical heroes from time gone by. Whether your passion is for wicked Regency Rakes, muscled Vikings or rugged Highlanders, awaken the romance of the past.
6 stories per month.

MEDICAL

Set your pulse racing with dedicated, delectable doctors in the high-pressure world of medicine, where emotions run high and passion, comfort and love are the best medicine.
6 stories per month.

Celebrate true love with tender stories of heartfelt romance, from the rush of falling in love to the joy a new baby can bring, and a focus on the emotional heart of a relationship.
8 stories per month.

Indulge in secrets and scandal, intense drama and plenty of sizzling hot action with powerful and passionate heroes who have it all: wealth, status, good looks…everything but the right woman.
6 stories per month.

HEROES

Experience all the excitement of a gripping thriller, with an intense romance at its heart. Resourceful, true-to-life women and strong, fearless men face danger and desire - a killer combination!
8 stories per month.

DARE

Sensual love stories featuring smart, sassy heroines you'd want as a best friend, and compelling intense heroes who are worthy of them.
4 stories per month.

To see which titles are coming soon, please visit

millsandboon.co.uk/nextmonth

JOIN US ON SOCIAL MEDIA!

Stay up to date with our latest releases, author news and gossip, special offers and discounts, and all the behind-the-scenes action from Mills & Boon...

 millsandboon

 millsandboonuk

 millsandboon

It might just be true love...

MILLS & BOON
DARE

Sexy. Passionate. Bold.

Sensual love stories featuring smart, sassy heroines you'd want as a best friend, and compelling intense heroes who are worthy of them.

our DARE stories published every month, find them all at:

millsandboon.co.uk/DARE

MILLS & BOON

HEROES

At Your Service

Experience all the excitement of a
gripping thriller, with an intense romance
at its heart. Resourceful, true-to-life
women and strong, fearless men face
danger and desire - a killer combination!

Eight Heroes stories published every month, find them all a

millsandboon.co.uk/Heroes

JOIN THE
MILLS & BOON
BOOKCLUB

* **FREE** delivery direct to your door

* **EXCLUSIVE** offers every month

* **EXCITING** rewards programme

50% OFF
YOUR FIRST
PARCEL

Join today at
Millsandboon.co.uk/Bookclub

GET YOUR ROMANCE FIX!

MILLS & BOON
— *blog* —

Get the latest romance news, exclusive author interviews, story extracts and much more!

blog.millsandboon.co.uk